THE Lucky

WESTERN LITERATURE SERIES

THE Lucky

H. LEE BARNES

UNIVERSITY OF NEVADA PRESS / RENO & LAS VEGAS

Western Literature Series

University of Nevada Press, Reno, Nevada 89557 USA

Copyright © 2003 by H. Lee Barnes

Manufactured in the United States of America

Library of Congress Cataloging-in-Publication Data

Barnes, H. Lee, 1944–

The lucky / H. Lee Barnes.

p. cm. — (Western literature series)

ISBN 0-87417-539-9 (pbk. : alk. paper)

1. Boys—Fiction. 2. Casinos—Fiction. 3. Single mothers—Fiction.

4. Father figures—Fiction. 5. Single-parent families—Fiction.

I. Title. II. Series.

PS3552.A673854L83 2003

813'.54—dc21   2003007999

The paper used in this book meets the requirements of
American National Standard for Information Sciences
—Permanence of Paper for Printed Library Materials,
ANSI Z39.48-1984.
Binding materials were selected for
strength and durability.

First Printing

12 11 10 09 08 07 06 05 04 03

5 4 3 2 1

Dedicated to my sister Jenny,
my childhood coconspirator and oldest friend.
When I was two, she hit me over the head with
a Coke bottle, which, when you think about it,
may be the only inspiration a writer really ever needs.

ACKNOWLEDGMENTS

It's hard to think a book this size would find print without the help of others, and in the case of this one some very gracious people contributed to the final result. First, I must thank Trudy McMurrin, the acquisitions editor who recognized its value and confirmed that more than eight years of effort produced something worthy. Second, I want to express my appreciation to Bill Branon for his interest in this project, his time and effort at getting to the guts of the book, his occasional praise, and especially his generous friendship. Thank you, T. M. NcNally; you're a fine reader. I cannot say enough for the selfless encouragement that came unexpectedly from Les Standiford, who went out on a limb, taking time away from his own work to write a screenplay treatment based on a lengthy manuscript he read by an obscure writer he'd never met. Also included in my list of helpers is Ron Carlson, who stood on the sidelines and helped call some of the plays. Last, this book wouldn't be what it is without the keen eye and sensibilities of Deke Castleman, who spent hard hours fine-tuning it. I thank you all, and so do Peter, Willy, and the gang.

THE Lucky

1

The weekend I met Willy Bobbins, my sister, Miriam, forgot to bring a book, an oversight she rarely committed. She and I sat in the back of the Ford convertible and watched popcorn clouds float toward the San Gabriels while Mother's best friend, Lana, box camera swinging between her breasts, paced back and forth on the sidewalk. Inside the California bungalow, Mother stood before the bathroom mirror putting final touches on her eyelashes. It was sometimes hard to pry her away from the mirror, and Lana, short on patience, grimaced as she paced.

Finally Lana went up to the two-bedroom bungalow we shared with an old woman named Hortensia, flung open the door, and shouted, "Elizabeth! The damned ball won't happen if we never arrive!" Her fists moved furiously up and down as she hollered at Mother to hurry, hurry.

When the screen door opened, Mother posed in the sunlight. She wore a yellow cotton sundress with spaghetti straps, matching patent pumps, and around her throat a collar of cultured pearls with a silver clasp. She walked casually down the sidewalk, paused halfway, smiled, and pirouetted so sharply that the hem of her skirt rose like a parasol.

"Whatta you think, Lana?" she asked.

"Gorgeous. A gal who can knock 'em dead," Lana said, caught Mother in the lens, and snapped the shutter. "Now, let's get."

Mother skipped to the car and tossed her purse on the seat. On the surface, she looked girlish and smart, and pleased with the world, but she was restless. Anticipation sizzled beneath the skin. It was time to fall in love again. The strain of waiting was getting to her, evidenced by the frown that appeared when she set the rearview mirror and studied her reflection.

Mother was a stunning auburn-haired woman with crystalline green eyes. Her beauty was the start of her downfall. She was attracted to a certain type of man, and that *was* her downfall. Between periods of loneliness she experienced brief moments of joy and extended intervals of despair. She fell in love easily and often, and each episode took a piece of her smile.

That spring of 1956 she'd shed herself of a man named Samuel. He had dark, curly hair, a white-toothed smile, and a penchant for rapping me with the second knuckle of his index finger. I was not unhappy to see him gone. In fact, I wished him dead. Nothing unusual—I wished death on all her men, for they had smiles like clear skies but eyes like dark storms and a meanness about them that defied understanding.

As we drove off, Miriam shouted, "Stop! I forgot a book."

Mother turned just enough to catch her daughter's eye and said, "There's things in life besides books."

"Like what?" Miriam asked.

"Oh, you'll find out," Lana said.

Mother and she looked at one another secretively and giggled, and the Ford didn't stop.

After crossing Cajon Pass we drove under a cloud-masked sky. To the north an occasional ribbon of lightning flickered, and the sky was pitch-black near Yermo and the Calico Mountains. Lana said it looked like a storm for certain, but Mother said that wasn't possible, that luck would intervene. She believed strongly in luck, a belief based mostly on her experience with its bad side.

Except for an occasional bout with motion sickness, I loved to ride in the car. About the only time we were a family was while driving somewhere. On those rides Mother was our hostage. We didn't have to share her or wait for some small crumb of attention. Occasionally, especially following a breakup with a boyfriend, she'd be overcome by remorse and make an effort to turn us into a normal family. And she was sincere, but sincerity didn't necessarily translate to competence. Not in our family. Not with our mother.

But she was always sincere.

In Barstow we pulled over at a roadside diner for coffee. Lana volunteered to buy, which meant milk shakes for my sister and me. We put up the top "just in case" and found an open booth by the window. Mother and Lana sat across from us and laughed about nothing that made sense to Miriam or me. But they were happy. They propped their elbows on the table and chatted and smoked Lucky Strikes as they watched us sip on our chocolate milk shakes. Someone played "Glow Worm" on the jukebox. Mother and Lana sang along.

Outside they repeated the chorus of "Glow Worm" over and over as they skipped lightly across the gravel parking lot. Miriam put on her hall-monitor face to show disapproval. On the road they sang whatever song played on the radio until the lights of Vegas bloomed against the clouded sky like a daub of rouge on a soft cheek. A hush fell over the car as Mother put a stern eye to the road.

Just as the sky broke loose, we pulled into Empy's Desert Villa next to the Flamingo. Mother took a small room with twin beds. After bringing hamburgers from the Flamingo coffee shop for Miriam and me, Mother and Lana took turns changing in the bathroom, where they hung their wet clothes on the shower curtain rod. When both were dressed, Mother used a hand mirror to examine her red evening gown from every possible angle. Satisfied, she sat on the bed and patted the mattress for us to sit beside her. She put her arms around our shoulders, kissed us on the cheek, and asked us to wish her luck.

Miriam shook her head. "It's not a good idea for you to go out in the rain," she said.

"Listen to her," Lana said. "You hafta wonder who's the mother."

"I know you don't want to be left alone, Missy, but isn't this better than staying with your aunt?"

Miriam and I exchanged looks.

"C'mon now, wish me luck," Mother said.

Sad-faced, Miriam looked up at her and muttered, "Luck."

Mother opened the door and let Lana go out. "Lock it behind me," she said, pointing to the night latch.

"Mother, your dress is caught in your girdle," Miriam said.

Mother reached behind and grabbed a handful of material. A smile spread over her cheeks. "Got me," she said, nodded twice, and the door snapped shut.

Miriam took one of the beds. The other would be shared by Mother and Lana. Wrapped in a blanket, I lay on the floor and went to sleep to the sounds of rain pelting the roof and car tires splashing water in the parking lot.

The next afternoon the sky was clear, and when we pulled to the curbside at the Lucky, Mother flung open the door and swung her feet out onto the curb, the hem of her dress ruffling in a slight breeze. She opened her purse and handed Miriam a fistful of change. "We'll be gone a while," she said. "Feed the parking meter when it gets low. And don't fight. Behave yourselves. And if someone bothers you, tell him to kiss off." She planted a peck on Miriam's cheek, then mine, and told us to kiss Lana.

"C'm 'ere, handsome," Lana said and grabbed my cheeks. I didn't want to kiss her. Her mouth smelled of peppermint gum and cigarettes, and her face was orange with makeup, and her lipstick was purple, and it made me think of death. I kissed the air near her lips, which wasn't enough for Lana, who said I was just being shy. She held my face firmly and smacked my lips squarely, then told me not to fall in love while they were gone.

Mother cranked the first hour on the parking meter and waved. "Be good," she said, blew us a kiss, and turned up Fremont Street, where she disappeared around the corner of the Lucky.

Miriam pulled out Mother's crossword puzzle book, folded the page over, and began to study, her face screwed up in concentration. She would look up from the page now and then and once in a while ask what a word might be for something or other. I said I wasn't even nine and wasn't supposed to know and asked why she cared. She told me to watch the meter.

"I wanna play cards," I said.

"No, one of us has to watch the meter, and Mother left me in charge, so I'm telling you to watch. It's called delegating responsibility."

Miriam, three and a half years my senior, liked being in charge, especially since turning twelve the month before and getting her first brassiere. She affected maturity beyond her age and used grandiloquent language, like being "resolutely aware of sexual matters," or "examining the nature of something's aspect," or "not condescending to dignify this or that." But she condescended all the time without adding much dignity to anything.

"At least I don't stand in front of a mirror looking at myself in my bra," I said.

"I'll tell Mother you've been spying on me."

I shrugged and watched a stray terrier as it wandered through the legs of pedestrians crossing Fremont Street and daydreamed, as I usually did, looking in my fantasy for the man I would become, for I had to become that man that my father wasn't, the father who'd left us. A boy has no control, but a man might. I believed this. And I would be calm in a crisis and sure of myself and never angry with children. I imagined myself an adventurous type, tall, certainly that, a paladin, the kind of man who has virtue backing his action.

My very idea of virtue was romantic; a lean, angular notion with no real shape. But I was sure that as a man I wouldn't do as Mother's men friends did—slouching on the couch watching *All Star Wrestling* and *I Love Lucy* while grumbling about kids who make noise. This discourse, all too familiar, led to one truth: The men Mother loved were cruel.

In the course of my daydreaming the time on the meter ran out, and I was too deep in thought to notice the motorcycle cop pull up. He wore a powder-blue uniform, white helmet, and dark glasses, a pretty ordinary traffic cop until you took into consideration that he was the tallest man I'd ever seen. He looked at the meter, then at us, and shook his head.

"You kids by yourselves?"

I looked at Miriam, who whispered, "You forgot! Now we're in for it."

It was true. I'd forgotten to watch the meter. Though Mother loved us, she didn't care to be disobeyed. I wasn't about to compound my felonies. I looked up at my grotesque reflection in the cop's darkened sunglasses and said, "Kiss off."

He nodded a few times, removed his sunglasses slowly, and squinted as if examining a speck of dust between my eyes. "What'd you say?"

I looked at Miriam, who buried her face in her arms. I figured no matter what I said I was in trouble. "I guess I mean, kiss off, sir," I said.

He nodded again, three times, slowly, as if reeling in a thought. He rubbed his eyes and stepped up to the seat, and in one swift motion yanked me over the side of the car. He stood me before him, where my view was limited to his silver belt buckle, the weave pattern of his shiny black belt, and his holster, which held a revolver with checkered walnut stocks. He held my arm and asked Miriam where our parents were.

Miriam sat tall and met his eyes with a smirk. I guess he expected her to wilt under his gaze, but even if made of wax, she wouldn't have melted in a raging fire. "I can't be certain at the moment, Officer, but I believe we can settle this dispute without involving her, as in her absence I'm in charge."

The cop shook his head. "Are you for real?"

"Yes, Officer. You see, Mother explicitly informed us that if a stranger approached, we were to respond as my brother did. Peter isn't smart enough to use discretion. You're a stranger."

Though uncertain as to what "discretion" meant, I glared at her and said, "I am too."

The cop told me to keep my mouth shut and addressed Miriam. "How old are you?"

She lifted her chin and took his eyes straight on. "Nineteen, sir. I happen to look quite young for my age, which Mother says will be a blessing as I mature."

Now the cop looked down at me. "Is she always like this?"

"Always." I shrugged and pointed to his motorcycle. "That's a seventy-four-cubic-inch twin beater," I said. "How fast you been on it?"

I admired nothing more than a loud motorcycle and could have rattled off a string of facts about the cop's bike that I'd learned from Uncle Harve's friend, a man named Buck, who rode a Harley-Davidson. While bent over the motorcycle engine, Buck had tutored me in the fine points of leaky pan heads, worn chains, and compression loss. He also taught me to how cuss under my breath and apologize for using French. For a long while I believed, because of Buck, that French was a language of four-letter words uttered semi-intelligibly in anger.

Without answering, the cop raised an eyebrow and turned to Miriam. "Okay, Miss Nineteen-year-old, here's what we're going to do. I'm calling a car to take you two to juvey, then I'm impounding this one. When your mother decides it's time to go, she can call us."

Undaunted, Miriam said, "You'll be making a tragic mistake, Officer. Mother is not without influence. Very important people, I might add." She folded her arms and smiled.

The cop grimaced, opened the door, and said, "Step out on the sidewalk."

Miriam released a sigh, pursed her lips as if sipping unsweetened lemonade, and slid across the seat. She stood on the edge of the sidewalk, hands on her hips, and said, "You'll probably end up feeling very foolish."

She never gave up.

The cop ordered us to stay beside the car and swaggered over to his motorcycle. We'd drawn a small crowd who were muttering among themselves. Miriam whispered that Mother was going to get in trouble and it was my fault. She said she would take none of the blame.

"Who asked you to?"

A uniformed guard from the Lucky looked out to check on the commotion, then vanished.

As the officer lifted the microphone to his mouth, a man wearing a dark-brown double-breasted suit and a Stetson turned the corner and eased into the crowd, excusing himself as he slipped through. He stood at the front of the spectators, a toothpick clamped between his teeth, his cordovan boots shined up to magnify light. He flicked the toothpick into the gutter and touched the brim of his white hat, which he tilted back until his high forehead showed.

"Andy," he said. "Nice to see you."

The cop lowered the microphone. "Hello, Willy."

"Got a couple of hard cases here?"

The cop grinned and nodded. "Smart-mouth kids."

Willy studied us momentarily. His blue eyes sparkled with amusement. "Killers or just bank robbers?"

The cop looked our way. "Probably both."

"Fixin to take 'em in, I see," Willy said and winked at me. "Tell you what, Andy. You'll be doin me a favor if you don't call the station. These here desperadoes belong to a frienda mine an I promised to take care a them. Got delayed. Bidness, you understand."

"What's your friend's name?" the cop asked.

Miriam, quick as ever, shouted, "Elizabeth Elkins!"

Willy didn't miss a beat. "'At's her, awright." He fingered his string tie as he looked at the license plate. "From California. Hollywood. A lady. I'd sure 'preciate you doin this little favor."

"Boy told me to kiss off."

Willy's blue-eyed gaze laid on me like the tip of a sword. "You do that, boy?"

I lowered my head.

"We'll tend to that later," he said.

"There's the matter of the meter, Willy. It ran out," the cop said.

Willy told him to write the ticket and hand it over, that he'd take responsibility for us. He scooped a handful of change from his pocket and fed a quarter into the slot. The cop finished marking the ticket. Willy took it with a smile and thanked him. That was it, except, of course, for Miriam telling the cop she'd told him so as he mounted his motorcycle. Taking one last look at her, he kicked the starter.

"Well, come on, now," Willy said in his Texas drawl.

He marched us through the casino to a restaurant, set us at a booth, and told the waitress to feed us anything we wanted, and if it wasn't on the menu, have it made. "It's my table. Don't no one sit here lessen they's a relative or friend."

Unwilling to surrender authority without a struggle, Miriam said, "Sir, we earn our own way. At the moment we're shy of funds, and our mother has instructed us not to take charity." It was an utter lie; Miriam had, on occasion when Mother forgot to buy groceries, borrowed food from many a put-upon neighbor.

Willy furrowed his brow, and his blue eyes appeared impish. "She a'ways like this?" he asked as he nudged us into his booth.

I nodded. "She reads all the time and never forgets anything. Ask her the capital of any place in the whole world."

"Why would I wanna know?" he asked and slid in next to me. He offered his hand to both of us. "Name's Willy, Willy Bobbins," he said.

"Amsterdam's the capital of Holland, which is technically the Netherlands," Miriam said.

Willy nodded. "Happy to hear that."

I told him I was Pete and my sister's name was Miriam. She informed him my name was actually Peter. He smiled and called me Pete, then said, "I'll give some advice. Don't go angerin the po-lice. They's better off bein friends. You kids stay here an don't worry about that car. Got me a guard gonna feed that meter when it gets low. Now, I got bidness to attend to."

He tilted his hat to my sister and left shaking his head.

That was how I met Willy Bobbins—gambler, cowboy, killer, the man alleged to have caused Sam the Slav to vanish without a trace from the face of the earth, the man who ran the underworld in Dallas during the Depression. Willy Bobbins, target of countless investigations conducted by police and federal agencies, seemed anything but a gangster that day. He was certainly a gentleman, perhaps even a savior.

Later that day Willy, along with a huge black man I would later know as Croaker, escorted Mother and Lana to the restaurant and pointed to the booth where Miriam and I were drinking our third milk shakes. He whispered something, winked at us, and left. How could I know then the extraordinary role Willy would play in my life or that among the many things he would do would be to reveal my father's identity? We expected her to be angry, but she greeted us with kisses on the forehead. Years later I would discover that her restraint was due in part to the fact that Willy had told her she should behave more like a mother. The other reason would make itself evident later that night, but Miriam and I already suspected the truth—Mother had fallen in love again.

2

The telephone calls began the week after we met Willy. Mother ran the extension cord into her room and shut the door—a bad sign. Her words breathed intrigue—another bad sign. Miriam and I knew right away what had happened. We recognized the early symptoms of our mother's malady. The question was who. We waited.

Any doubts or hopes we held evaporated two weekends later when Mother piled Miriam and me into the back of her car and drove us across town to Uncle Harve and Aunt Viv's. She walked us to the door, apologizing because she couldn't take us with her.

"Who is he, Mother?" Miriam asked as Mother knocked on the door.

"He who? Who said anything about a he?"

"Mother, you've been talking to someone long distance. We can barely afford the rent."

"We can afford more than you can imagine, Maid Miriam," she said. She called my sister Maid Miriam when Miriam happened to sink her teeth into the fruit of truth.

Aunt Vivian opened the door and immediately the smell of lilac and mint and soap rushed out. In the doorway stood my mother's brother's wife, pudgy and pretty with her poreless little nose and squinting brown eyes that glittered as she smiled. No sooner had Aunt Vivian said hello to Mother than she began to fuss over us. What a pretty dress Miriam has on. Do we have toothbrushes? Are you staying the whole weekend? That sort of thing.

While Lana waited in the car with the top down, smearing lipstick on her cheeks and rubbing it in, Mother explained to our aunt that come Sunday night, she'd be back for us even if it was after dark.

Aunt Vivian lifted her chin to look Mother in the eye. She was barely five feet tall, while Mother stood seven inches taller. She cleared her throat to make her words carry more weight. "I read that it's not good to wake children up in the middle of their sleep, Elizabeth. Harve will make sure they get to school on Monday and you can pick them up there."

"I'll be back," Mother said.

"Well, just in case. You know how things go."

"I said, I'll be here."

Mother tended to be short with Aunt Vivian, whom she thought slow, meaning stupid. Though Mother wouldn't come out and say so directly, she would offhandedly mention that Aunt Vivian's mind had turned to oatmeal from watching mush on TV, or she'd laugh as she explained how our aunt caught jokes after a fourth explanation. Aunt Vivian, too good-natured to let Mother get her goat, merely repeated, "Just in case, Harve will take care of it."

Mother kissed my cheek and used a tissue to rub the lipstick mark away. She tried to kiss Miriam, but my sister stepped back.

"Who is he?" Miriam demanded.

"Since when is it a child's place to ask personal things of a parent?" She took a ten-dollar bill out of her purse and stuffed it in the pocket of Miriam's plaid dress. "In case you need anything." She stepped down from the landing and waved.

"Drive carefully, Elizabeth," Aunt Vivian called.

"I wish you'd take something for baby-sitting," Mother called back to Aunt Vivian, who answered with something that sounded like "posh" and flagged Mother off with her hand.

As she dashed to the car, Mother promised to bring us each something special. She always promised surprises at partings, but invariably, by the time we were reunited, the surprise was forgotten and never again mentioned. "Does she really mean it this time?" I asked.

Miriam pushed me inside the door and said, "Of course she means it." And when Mother was in the car driving away, Miriam assured me that Mother meant what she said every time she promised something—"She just forgets." We both saw through the ritual, though Miriam pretended not to.

I spread the curtains and watched her Ford turn the corner. My ribs seemed to shrink as the car drove away. I had the terrible feeling that one day or another she would choose someone else again and leave me behind, as she had when she left us at the orphanage in Teako. Miriam tugged at my sleeve and told me to come along, but I pulled my arm away. Mother might have forgotten something. She might, I hoped, change her mind, just . . . this . . . once.

Miriam spread the curtains open as proof that Mother was gone. The street was empty. I asked what if Mother didn't come back.

"She always has."

"Remember the orphanage? What if she doesn't?"

"It was a Catholic school."

"An orphanage. You know it was. She wanted to get rid of us."

I wanted to hurt someone, so I mentioned the one thing sure to bring on tears, the secret that Mother said we should never tell anyone. Miriam wiped her eyes with the backs of her hands and said, "Don't say it or it might happen. Don't ever say it."

Aunt Vivian crossed the room and told us not to let our mother's leaving upset us, that we shouldn't fight and should realize there are people in the world with some serious problems, so we shouldn't focus on our little discomforts. Miriam wiped her eyes again and whispered that I better not mention the orphanage or else. When our aunt noticed Miriam had been crying, she put an arm over my sister's shoulder and invited us to the table for doughnuts and milk, her cure for everything from depression to cancer.

As Aunt Vivian filled us in on details of the latest crisis on *Days of Our Lives,* Miriam nibbled at a doughnut and listened with the expression of a tired judge.

"You shouldn't worry. Your mother drives very carefully," Aunt Vivian said when she noticed Miriam paying no attention.

But Miriam heard every word. "Mother drives like a maniac," she said.

"Well, fast but not that bad," Aunt Vivian countered.

"Peter, how does Mother drive?" Miriam asked.

I swallowed my milk so fast I had to pause. Miriam glared at me. "Like a maniac," I said.

"See," Miriam said triumphantly.

I felt like a traitor to my aunt, who was too good-hearted and, honestly, too slow to match wits with Miriam. For the time being they called a truce. Aunt Vivian went back to talking about soap operas and finished three doughnuts in that time. Miriam barely touched hers. Aunt Vivian asked if she wanted it. Miriam shook her head. Our aunt forked the doughnut onto her own plate, and it vanished almost immediately. Smiling now, she rested her chin on her hand and said to Miriam, "You should never wallow in self-pity. I heard that on one of the shows just yesterday. Doesn't that say everything? I mean, everything?"

Miriam gave me a look that said I should keep my mouth shut. "Aunt Vivian, those aren't real people," she said.

"I know that, Miriam, but that doesn't mean their situations aren't real."

"That's exactly what it means. It's made up."

Sometimes, based on what came out of her mouth, I couldn't believe my sister was only twelve years old, or that she was my sister. Neither could Aunt Vivian, who was searching for a way to rescue herself. Her jaw dropped, her mouth hung open, her face went white. Finally she said, "You're right, Miriam. I'm a lonely woman who has no children. I should know better."

No one loved us more than the woman who'd married our mother's brother. She'd been overly kind, and her house was always open to us. Miriam, seeing how she'd wounded Aunt Vivian, ran around the table and threw her arms around her. "You're right, Aunt Vivian. You mean they represent the real world in a metaphorical setting."

"No, I mean, other than your uncle, I don't have anyone to care for."

Miriam patted our aunt and kept assuring her that we loved her until a smile appeared on Aunt Vivian's pale lips and color returned to her cheeks. Her breathing again normal, Aunt Vivian squeezed Miriam around the waist and stood. "I tell your mother all the time what a smart daughter she has. A genius."

She hugged Miriam again and asked if she wanted to watch a soap opera. Miriam hesitated. She despised TV as much as she loved books, but she smiled and said, "Sure, I'd like that."

My aunt asked me to join them on the couch. I did, but only because I had nothing else to do.

After the soap opera finished, Aunt Vivian went to the kitchen to make sandwiches. As she was fixing the bologna and Swiss cheese with mayonnaise, she asked if we wanted to hear an idea she and Uncle Harve were going to approach Mother with. Miriam didn't want to injure any more feelings that day, except maybe mine if she got a chance, so she said fine. Aunt Vivian set the platter of sandwiches down on the coffee table. The sandwiches were typical fare for Aunt Vivian, about as moist as talcum powder and only slightly tastier. Miriam winced. I rolled my eyes.

Aunt Vivian scooted between us, patted our knees, and smiled the kind of smile a wife offers when her husband has just been elected to office. "Your Uncle Harve and I have been thinking about asking your mother if you two could stay with us when she moves to Las Vegas. You know, just live here at first until you decide whether you'd want us as parents."

Miriam and I looked at one another. Move! we both thought.

"Willy," I said, my voice filled with hope.

"Not her type," Miriam said. "Not at all her type. Too nice."

Aunt Vivian couldn't follow our conversation. A bit peeved, she asked, "Well, what do you think?"

Miriam thought a moment before answering. "It's very considerate, Aunt Vivian, and we know you're thinking of our best interest, but Mother will be needing us. You know her."

Aunt Vivian held her disappointment in and nodded. She gathered us under each of her fleshy arms and told us the offer was always there, adding that she would miss us and hoped we'd come from time to time for a visit. That's how we found out for certain that Mother was in love again and that we were moving to Las Vegas.

When Uncle Harve came home from the office—he'd started a one-man tax accounting business the year before in a small shopping center in Bellflower—he sat down on the couch and declared he wasn't moving, that Aunt Vivian could fix us TV dinners and "we would sit and watch the box." Miriam snuggled in next to him and circled his arm with her small hands. She said she'd be happy to fix dinner for everyone.

"You're a good girl," Uncle Harve said. "That's not necessary. Is it, Viv?"

"No. I'm well stocked on TV dinners, especially beef tips."

Miriam's head sank like a defendant's upon hearing a guilty verdict. Then she stood between Uncle Harve and the television. He said it was time for the news and asked her to sit down so he could watch. She clasped her hands behind her back and swayed back and forth. I knew something was up when she started acting her age. She never acted her age.

"Uncle Harve, Aunt Vivian, I've got the best idea." She pulled out the ten-dollar bill that had been folded up in her pocket and snapped it open with her thumbs and index fingers. She held it up for them to see. "Mother gave us this money. Why don't the four of us go out for dinner? Like a family. We'll be so happy."

Uncle Harve smiled and looked over at Aunt Vivian, who was gathering up TV trays. "Viv, what do you think?"

"It's your Friday night, Harve. You decide."

"Please, oh pu-leeeze," Miriam said.

She'd done it again.

As Uncle Harve and Aunt Vivian dressed to go, the telephone rang. It was Mother calling from a pay phone in Baker, California. She asked for Miriam. Always Miriam, never me. I tried to eavesdrop. Miriam stood next to the phone stand, the receiver to her ear, and turned away whenever I asked to talk. She nodded several times, said she'd tell me, then hung up.

"Mother was in a hurry. She says the man's name is Julie D'Rittio, and that she'll be here early Sunday evening and that we should be ready to go. She says he really likes children and can't wait to meet us."

"Julie? That's a girl's name," I said.

"Don't be stupid, Peter. His real name is Julius, you know, Julius Caesar, killed in the Roman Senate by assassins for being ambitious, March 15, 44 B.C."

"How do you know?"

"I know. That's all."

It was true: Miriam *did* know everything, even how to get out of eating TV dinners.

Mother lied again. She didn't arrive to pick us up until past two in the morning, and Julie, as events in time would prove, cared nothing for children. No matter, she was in love and we were soon to move to Las Vegas. As I blinked my eyes open several hours before dawn to Mother's soft but urgent voice, how could I imagine that my destiny was linked to Willy Bobbins or fathom in any way what that would eventually mean? All I knew when the light hit my eyes was that I wanted to curl up and go back to sleep.

3

When we moved to Las Vegas, Mother had a job waiting as a cocktail waitress at the Stardust. We rented an apartment in the Meadows area called Naked City. When Mother unlocked the door for the first time, she threw off her shoes and skipped down the hall on the shag carpet, smiling and twirling about so that the pleats of her white skirt opened like petals. She swept us into her arms and said this was our home and everything was going to be wonderful.

"But, Mother, the carpet is orange," Miriam said.

Mother laughed. "It's rust, Miriam. Very stylish."

I didn't care if the carpet was pink and purple and ran halfway up the walls. At last I had my own room and a real bed.

We resided in a half-mile stretch of one- and two-story stucco apartments northwest of Sahara Avenue and the Strip, where newcomers settled until moving on to a real neighborhood, something more permanent. The flats spoke of turbulent lives tossed together, of drifting, of futures stuck in the starting blocks, of outcasts looking for a place where every house was made of glass and no one tossed stones. Miriam once described Las Vegas as the one city in the world where it was possible to experience interstellar travel merely by talking to a few residents. Our narrow four-walled community bore out her axiom.

Two cops who howled at the sky when they went on all-night binges lived upstairs, over the apartment of a former silent-film actress who'd played Jane in a Tarzan movie. She was the apartment manager, the "acting manager," as Miriam called her. Our neighbors also included a one-legged musician who played banjo and sang in lounges downtown and a homosexual comedian who practiced golf swings on the lapping surface of the pool and suffered bouts of depression.

A couple lived next door—Evangeline, a cocktail waitress, and Jasper, whom we all called "Goddamn Bartender" because that was what Evangeline called him when hurling insults and various household items in his direction. This went on every Wednesday and Thursday night, their nights off, until one or the other slammed the door and left, only to return within the hour and make up with the offended party. They opened their windows, so that their arguing and lovemaking, their pain and their pleasure, heard late into the hours of darkness, became public events. Miriam said they were disgusting, but I didn't think so. I would lie awake listening to them groan and labor on the mattress.

The faces have receded into the caves of my memory, where they hang suspended like bats, and when I do see them it is as flurried shadows—all of them, that is, except the comedian, who would play a pivotal role in my life, not once but twice. His name was Ernie and he lived on the second floor. He often sat at the pool by himself, a glass of Chardonnay in hand, as he took occasional one-armed swings at the ripples with a putting iron. It was hard to figure him making people laugh, but he was an opening act. His material came from anguish, his and others.' Like other tenants, I poked fun at him, said cruel things, and passed around gossip at his expense because he was homosexual. I was not a good boy.

The neighbor who captured Miriam's eye was a French unicyclist who worked in the Lido d' Paris. He was thin and narrow-faced with deep-set blue eyes and wavy brown hair that flowed like a mane years before long hair on men became fashionable. He looked both wild and sophisticated, and like Miriam, Ernie adored him, but Richard, pronounced "Ri'shar," seemingly adored himself too much to notice that others also did.

He performed a daily regimen of five hundred push-ups and five hundred sit-ups on the pool deck, counting each repetition out in French. On weekends Miriam spread the curtain, sat with a schoolbook propped under her chin, and watched Richard doing his exercises. She'd been instantly infatuated with him, said he was divine as a mythological god and nicknamed him Hermes, which I said sounded like a name for a weirdo. She claimed I was just jealous because he was so Continental. How could I be jealous if I didn't know what "Continental" meant?

"I'm not jealous."

"Do your homework, Peter, or I'll tell Mother."

"You never tell her anything," I said, which was the truth, for we covered for one another, telling Mother what we figured she wanted to hear—that everything was fine.

Julie D'Rittio, Mother's new beau, proved to be the type we'd come to expect Mother to find, a pretty generic kind of crotch-scratcher with a toothy, sensuous smile and a quick, disdainful scowl. Miriam and I had beheld the campaign before, a process that seemed like a tactical offensive by a ruthless enemy against a defenseless target.

The ritual was similar every time. First came the marvels of falling in love. Julie showed up—fastidious dresser that he was—in summer-white pants, shoes, and shirt—the last unbuttoned to the second hole. The white in contrast to his rich, dark tan. Miriam held the door for him, as Mother thought it in bad taste to open the door herself. She didn't want to appear anxious or pushy. He extended a bouquet when the door opened.

"Don't you ever bring candy?" Miriam asked.

Mother strolled out of her room, saying something about having thought she heard the door ring. "Flowers!" Mother said, as if they were a surprise.

"He always brings flowers," Miriam said.

"Hello, beautiful," Julie said to Mother, who buried her nose in the flowers as if she'd never smelled a rose before.

"How are the kids today?" Julie asked.

"Peter's been vomiting all day," Miriam said. "I think he's got cholera. We should be quarantined, Mother."

"If I vomited, it's because of you," I said to Miriam.

"What a kidder," Julie said.

"You two get along," Mother said.

We hated to leave her alone with him. We would rather have left her alone in the garden with a batch of vipers. Julie, a natural tactician, was attentive, full of phrases that flattered. He bought roses, lilies, and carnations in glass vases, took her to dinner twice a week and dancing several times at the Top of the Strip at the Dunes. They saw lounge acts at the Sahara or the Sands' Copa Room. Mother wasn't like the other women he'd known, he claimed. She wasn't yet "soiled by her experiences," a phrase Mother repeated to impress Lana when she came up for a visit. It seemed obvious that Lana's gut response had been the same as Miriam's and mine, but she'd pretended empathy, stroked the back of Mother's hand, and said she was happy for her.

"Let's have a drink first," Mother said and placed the flowers on the tabletop. As she mixed martinis, he sat at the table and watched.

"How much vermouth?" she asked.

He gave his standard answer. "Show it the bottle cap."

They laughed. She carried the martinis to the table, where she sat opposite him. As they sipped cocktails, they stared into each other's eyes, his casting a spell. His were heavily lidded—bedroom eyes, Mother called them—charmer's eyes, the eyes of the serpent. Eat this apple, they said.

They lit cigarettes and held them shoulder high, angling them at the ceiling and using them like pointers as they talked in circular fashion about things only hinted at, suggestive things, secret things, adult things. He told her that her chin was pretty and her eyes pulled things out of his soul. Miriam faked a gag at hearing that one.

He said he wished his mother was alive to meet her. He wished he'd met someone like her before he'd made such a mess of his life. He said things that made him seem vulnerable but were intended to exploit her vulnerability. He didn't want sympathy; he wanted her to eat the apple.

This was more than I could take.

"Miriam said that Julie's very Continental," I said.

"Why, that's a nice thing to say," Mother said.

Julie smiled and brushed his fingers over a tuft of black chest hair that showed out of his open shirtfront. "She appreciates class," he said.

"Peter made it up," Miriam said.

I grabbed my arithmetic book. "Excuse me. I have to study."

To demonstrate his sincere interest in children, Julie showed up one night with a half-gallon of ice cream and a bag of cookies, which he plopped down on the kitchen table, obvious bribes for Miriam and me. Miriam broke a cookie in half and sniffed it. "Stale," she declared. As for the ice cream, he'd brought vanilla, and Miriam preferred chocolate, though had he brought chocolate, she would have preferred strawberry.

Several nights later he brought Neapolitan, thinking he'd found a solution.

Miriam said, "No one eats Neapolitan."

He asked if we liked school or if we'd gone to football games or had ever been camping. "Does sleeping in the car in the woods count?" Miriam asked. "We did that once when Mother skipped out on the rent." Mother said that was a lie, that we were just too tired to drive to our new home that night.

Miriam was even more skeptical than I, especially when she asked Julie why he'd never had children if he liked them so much.

"That's a personal question," Mother said.

Julie said he didn't mind answering. "'Cause I never been lucky that way."

"Isn't that lovely?" Mother said.

Pick the cliché—Mom was gone, buried, well done, ready for the fork, smitten, ruined, staked down, up the creek. He'd disarmed her entirely, but we were another matter. From whatever angle he looked at Miriam or me, he saw sedition. Miriam blinked, feigning innocence, and forced a smile. "Lovely, Mother. It's poetry, in fact. Isn't that right, Peter?"

"Yes, poetry," I agreed. "Wonderful stuff."

"Ignore them," Mother said.

And he tried to, but it's hard to ignore the enemy, especially if you're an invader. The line was drawn. No amount of ice cream or cookies was going to bring us to the peace table.

This singular attention to Mother lasted for about two months, during which she gradually traded autonomy for flowers and dancing and candle-light dinners. She provided him his own key to the apartment, his own side of the closet, his own seat at the table, a towel in the bathroom, a spot in front of the TV, a place beside her in bed. These allowances he won one and two at a time, and when finally he prevailed, he ruled her with callousness and absolute authority.

Inevitably, Julie established himself and soon enough forgot cookies and ice cream for us and flowers for her. If he wanted Mother and we were there, he told her to get rid of us. And she did. She'd give us two or three dollars and tell us to go to Foxy's for a banana split or a sundae. The rest of the time she worked or waited for him to show up. She was allowed to do nothing without him except earn money that he borrowed to squander at the dice table or sports book without repaying her. He fancied himself a gambler.

Miriam had had more experience at witnessing Mother's affairs than I. Julie, she was sure, would go in time. Why should he be any different? Always the pragmatist, Miriam summed it up: "Does a man want a woman with two kids? We just have to wait."

Miriam became caretaker. She calculated the budget and each day forced Mother to set money aside, money Julie couldn't get his hands on. She shopped for groceries, walking to the Mayfair Market at the corner of Sahara and the Strip. Every evening she cooked dinner and every morning, breakfast. She vacuumed the carpet, orange and hated though it was, and washed the laundry and separated Mother's dry cleaning. She taped notes at strategic spots, to doors, refrigerator handles, or makeup mirrors, instructions to Mother to set money aside for shopping or the power bill or the dry cleaning.

Miriam ran the house with the systematic efficiency of the commandant of a stockade. She insisted that "our first true home" be kept neat and clean. She made me iron my shirts and even my jeans. She checked to make sure the creases were to her liking. If I left a sock out, I'd find it tied to my door-knob. When I forgot to make my bed, the sheets would be waiting for me pinned to my door. She wrote schedules for everything, for chores I was to perform, how long I was to shower, the time I could spend watching TV. Under her eye, I constructed sandwiches for school lunch, and after school I took out the garbage and cleaned the commode, my job exclusively since Miriam refused to "deal with men's disgusting urine splashes."

Protesting under my breath, I cleaned, washed, dried, and dusted. She treated objections with the patience and kindness one might get from a dungeon master. "Shut up, Peter, and do it or fix your own meals," she'd say, which I tried once, only to find cooperation to my advantage. She inspected every detail, holding glasses and dishes up to the light. Miriam hated water spots.

After my duties were done, she ordered me to the table and watched me do homework, then hovered by the sink to make certain I brushed my teeth up and down, ten times on each tooth. "We can't afford cavities," she would say. Once a week she sat me down on the steps outside with a newspaper to polish my loafers. Hard money had paid for them, and she intended them to last. Every other Sunday she walked me a mile and a half to the Episcopal church at St. Louis and Maryland Parkway and waited outside. It seemed silly for her to force me to attend, as she'd proclaimed herself an atheist the year we moved to California. I reminded her of this. She said, "Shut up, Peter. It's not for me. It's for you. You may still have a soul, though you certainly display no signs of it." I said that at least I wasn't an atheist.

"I'm not an atheist. I'm an ag-nostic," she said, emphasizing the first-syllable stop on the roof of her mouth as if she were the archbishop of Canterbury himself. I guess she liked the sound of "agnostic" better than "atheist."

If I mentioned to Mother that Miriam was bossing me around, Mother would tell me to be thankful I had a sister so responsible. I said I was thankful . . . that she didn't have a whip.

Every two days or so the sound of Julie's key would grind into the keyhole and the knob would twist open. It was like having a fog settle over a picnic. There he'd stand, dark, slightly slouched at the shoulders, usually a two-day stubble on his face, his lower lip protruding.

"Whatchu up to?" he'd ask, without variation.

We might be playing Monopoly or Clue or reading or studying; no matter, he would ask anyhow. And Miriam would say, "We're building a bridge," or "We're excavating corpses to find your twin." He'd sneer and call her Miss Know-It-All or Genius-in-the-Bottle, and tell her she wasn't funny, not one bit.

While Miriam was confrontational, I was not. I rarely spoke to him, just watched while never looking him in the eye. My gaze followed his shoes as he crossed the room. I watched each step as if he were Abner Snopes scraping manure on the carpet. He ignored me.

I was learning the manly art of profanity, as it was one way of establishing my position in the school hierarchy. One morning as Julie walked to Mother's room, I said just loud enough for him to hear, "What a turd! Acts like he owns the place."

He wheeled about and walked back to the front room. "You wanna repeat that?" he said.

I was scared and looked away, but Miriam took him head-on. "No, he doesn't," she said. "And don't bully him."

She gave me the courage to look up. He walked away. Miriam and I sat looking at one another until he shut the door to Mother's bedroom.

"Don't cuss, Peter," Miriam said just above a whisper. "I'll tell Mother. Besides, it's undignified, and the situation could be worse."

"How?" I looked at her as if her brain had just oozed out of her ear.

She grinned. "At least the turd doesn't beat her—or us," she said with utmost dignity. We simultaneously broke out in laughter.

As depraved as it seems, we were thankful he hadn't beaten Mother, hadn't raised a hand in anger toward her or us, even though we intentionally provoked him. If nothing else, for those first few months we lived without the threat of physical harm. That seemed enough.

One Saturday afternoon we heard Julie's white Lincoln drive up, and shortly the doorknob turned and he came in without a knock. Mother was still asleep in the bedroom, exhausted from a double-back she'd worked at the Desert Inn. She was on the extra board, serving drinks in the keno lounge, at the mercy of a ruthless schedule. Miriam and I were playing Monopoly on the coffee table. He looked at her and said, "Get lost. Both of you."

"We're playing," she said.

Julie, on a three-day binge, had gambled away Mother's money and was obviously in a foul mood. When we hesitated, he snarled, "Get. I mean right now."

Miriam jumped up. Though deliberately slow, I got up just the same and as I passed by him I pointed to his crotch. "Your fly's undone," I said.

Reflexively he looked down.

"What a jerk," I said.

He grabbed my collar and yanked me around. Though he smelled strongly of tobacco and gin, he was on the sobering-up side of his tear and knew exactly what he was doing. Miriam told him to let me go, but he didn't. He cocked his arm and doubled his fist, deliberation in his eyes. But before he could hit, Miriam said, "I'll tell Willy Bobbins."

Everybody knew the name. It even circulated at school. And Mother had told Julie how nicely Willy had treated Miriam and me—milk shakes in his private booth—and hinted that they were familiar, and offered proof—what, I didn't know. Though two years had passed since the incident, I'd not forgotten how he'd handled the cop. I couldn't yet distinguish between fame and notoriety, but Miriam could, and she counted on the weight of Willy's reputation to affect Julie.

Miriam said, "You'd be putting yourself in jeopardy by hitting Peter. Willy Bobbins has a particular fondness for the two of us."

"Listen to Miss Priss," Julie said, but you could see his eyes going *ka-thunk, ka-thunk, ka-thunk* like blanks lining up on a slot machine. He released me. Miriam was satisfied, but I wasn't.

"Willy asks me about Mother all the time. He likes to keep up on how she's doing," I said.

"So what?"

I smiled and backed away. Mother came out of her room and rounded the corner. She looked at me, then at Miriam, then at Julie. "What's going on?"

"Nothing," Julie said. "The kids were just leaving."

He was looking me right in the eyes and I was looking back. "I'm going to call him," I said. Miriam said we had enough money to split a sundae at Foxy's and grabbed my arm to pull me away. I kept looking at him as I backed away, mouthing the warning again for emphasis.

Mother didn't ignore us entirely. When things went smoothly between Julie and her, or he'd made a score at the tables, she would shower us with attention, take us shopping for games and clothes and out to eat, treat us to a movie, and lavish us with praise, saying how fortunate she was to have two such well-behaved children. My sister reminded her that the money we were spending was needed elsewhere, but Mother seemed to enjoy those moments, so Miriam ceased nagging. For my part, I resented that Mother's love for us depended on the tides of her romance with a craps-dealing degenerate from Newark, New Jersey.

Then one night Mother refused to give him money, money she didn't have anyhow. We listened to the argument spiral as he accused her of holding out on him, but the only money in the house was hidden in Miriam's room, and that had to go for the rent. We'd heard arguments before; he would give up and leave or Mother would convince him to lie down and sleep it off. But this time he didn't leave, and Mother failed in her efforts to get him to lie down.

There came a sudden burst of sound, his hands striking her, the dull, frightening sounds of knuckles on bone and flesh, and her moaning. She told him to stop, begged him, but he didn't. Tears in her eyes, Miriam pounded on the door and said she was going to call the police, but Mother said, "No, no." No to the cops? No to him? Miriam ran to the kitchen and snatched up the receiver. The bedroom door came open as she was dialing. Julie shoved past me and grabbed the receiver from her.

"No fuckin' cops, Miss Priss, Miss Fuckin'-Know-Everything," he said and dropped the phone into its cradle.

"I'm telling Willy," I said. "You know what that means, don't you?"

Julie swung about. His head cocked at an angle, he stared at me menacingly. I was scared, but to preserve my pride, I stared back.

"Don't fuck with me, kid."

"If you go, I won't call the police," Miriam said.

"Did you hear me, kid? I'm talking to you."

All I said was, "Willy Bobbins."

Miriam shouted, "Don't hit him," and ran to her room. She came out with a handful of bills and shoved them at Julie. He stormed down the hallway into Mother's room. This time there was no noise. A few minutes later he stepped out of the room. After tossing a few insults at Mother, he walked out of the apartment. Miriam shut the door behind him, ran back to Mother's room, and opened the door. Mother said, "Don't come in. Please, don't come in."

The air seemed compressed, stifling. Miriam closed the door quietly, pressed her back against the wall, and slumped slowly to the carpet, where she buried her head in her arms. I stood silently, counting labored breaths and watching the front door. When the occasional muted sob came from Mother's room, Miriam jerked.

Eventually the light went out in Mother's room, and a welcome calm settled over the apartment. When it seemed Mother was sleeping, I offered Miriam a hand up, which she shook off. She pulled herself up from the floor.

"Someday," I said, "I'll be big enough. Someday."

"Someday," she said.

"Yeah. And I'll kill him."

"Don't, Peter. Don't even think that."

In time we turned away and drifted to the living-room couch, where we sat in front of the television, which we pretended to watch until the National Anthem blared and the screen turned to fuzz. Only then did we give up our station.

Two hours later Mother's door opened. It must have been past three in the morning. She felt her way down the hallway to the bathroom and ran the water for several minutes. Then without looking in on us, she quietly returned to her room. Miriam and I emerged from our rooms as Mother's door shut. We entered the bathroom and switched on the light. Miriam shook her head and gathered up the towels, three of them, and carried them to the kitchen sink to soak out the blood. I sat on the couch and waited for her, staring at my feet, hoping he was gone but knowing the door could open at any second.

Within the month, inevitably, Julie came back, flowers in hand. He spent a couple of days playing at humility to get back in Mother's good graces. Miriam was particularly subdued. I alone looked at him as he deserved and made it a point to mention the name of Willy Bobbins now and then to get a reaction. He would look for an instant, then pretend he'd heard nothing. I wanted him to know I hated him. I wanted to see fear in his face, but all that was evidenced in his expression was arrogance. He'd won.

One morning before school, when Mother was finally sleeping and Julie hadn't yet returned from a night of rounding, Miriam motioned for me to sit at the table. Light shone through the curtains, illuminating specks of dust. She stirred a whirlwind as she sat down and the specks danced on the currents beside her head. A corona of yellow light outlined her face. Her eyes were red from crying or not sleeping, or both.

"Peter, if you get him mad, he'll hurt her again."

I folded my arms and leaned back. "I'll kill him if he does."

"Don't be so stupid."

"I will. I'll wait till he's asleep and cut his throat."

"You're barely eleven. That's crazy." She ran her fingers through her hair and the dust sparkled like sequins. She nodded slowly. "You won't kill anyone. Please, all I'm asking is just be quiet when he's here and don't ever threaten him with Willy Bobbins again."

"Okay, maybe I wouldn't, but Willy Bobbins would kill him for us or get the cops here."

She shook her head. "Willy Bobbins doesn't know we're alive. It was one day a long time ago. That's all. Promise me you won't antagonize him."

"That turd?"

"That turd."

This time we shared no laughter. She stood at the window peeking out the curtains like a fugitive awaiting the cops, her profile tense and solemn. She seemed wise and far older than she had been the month before. She was becoming a woman, and I wondered what that meant to us. Our world was changing fast enough.

"Okay, I won't mention Willy," I said.

Miriam reached over and ruffled my hair. "Thanks, Pete." She seemed pleased, but remote. She returned to the window and looked out.

"But if he beats her again. I'm going to the Lucky."

"Lucky," she muttered. She looked over her shoulder. "Do you ever wonder why we're so unlucky? Why Mother is?"

"We're not unlucky," I said.

Even while at the orphanage, we'd persevered together. Once I'd refused to eat cinnamon apple pie, so a nun made me sit at the table for three hours while the other children played and attended evening services. Despite the nun's imprecations of eternal damnation for pride and selfishness, I stared at the far wall and refused to touch the pie. Miriam had told her this was no way to treat a young boy and joined in, crossed her arms and stared at the wall. Surely Miriam and I could make it through this.

I left and walked to Sahara Avenue, where I sat at the bus stop and watched cars roll by.

4

Miriam, bent over the table with an open textbook, wanted to know what had kept me after school. I told her it was none of her business. She said I was making things tougher by behaving badly. I didn't care and told her so.

Timmy knocked on the door in his usual manner, *bap, bap-a-bab-bap—bap, bap*. Miriam looked up from her book and said, "It's the worm," her name for Timmy Pendergast. I opened the door. He winked and stepped in.

"The Mafia lord around?" he asked, meaning Julie.

"No, he's at work."

"Let's go," Timmy said.

Miriam set her book aside. She had to get ready for her job as a carhop at the Blue Onion in a few minutes anyhow, so she closed it and stood up. "He's not supposed to go anywhere," she said. "And your presence isn't mandated, which should indicate that it's never been welcomed."

Timmy pulled two quarters out of his pocket and held them up. "These are yours. All you have to do is let me see your underpants."

"You're so sophisticated, Blow Worm. How does your mother justify not allowing the psychiatrists to perform a lobotomy on you?"

"She doesn't justify anything. She gave me the quarters." He raised his eyebrow and grinned.

"Someday science will discover you, Worm, and probe all those twisted little paths in your brain with a few hundred volts of electricity. I've got to go now." She headed for her bedroom.

"I'll give you three quarters if you let me watch you dress," he said.

"Sick, undeniably sick," Miriam said and slammed her door shut.

"Let's go," Timmy said. "I've got something you'll wanna see."

"You should back off of my sister. I mean, saying the things you say."

"Ah, she loves it."

"No, she doesn't. You don't know her."

"C'mon," he said and opened the door.

Five years after moving to Las Vegas, five years during which not much had changed except that I had become a tall, ungainly teenager with outsized, clumsy hands and feet, we still lived in the same apartment. Other than kids I hung around with during school, I'd gone without playmates all those years. Then one year before, Timmy Pendergast, the only other kid in the complex, moved into an apartment at the far end of the community pool. Six months older than I, he was a sneak, a liar, and a know-it-all, and merely because we were cast together, he was the one person I could call friend. He played the big shot and talked like a hustler, smooth, fast, and unsettling, always seeking angles. He taught me not to trust anyone who talked faster than I could think. His nickname, Blow Worm, came from Miriam calling him a worm and telling him to blow.

Timmy quickly found his way around, located all the soft drink dispensers and washing machines and dryers, anything with a coin return. He had a regular route he followed, jamming coin return drops with gum so that he could later collect the change. Though it burned holes inside my guts, I would stand watch while he made his rounds. That was where his quarters came from, and he always had a pocketful.

We passed near Ernie, who sat half tipsy by the pool with his wineglass and putter. Julie hated Ernie, never failed to remark about him as he passed. For that reason, I'd come to like him. He was as cynically humorous offstage, I figured, as he was on.

Ernie raised his wineglass. "I see trouble. Two errant knaves off to do what?"

"Nothing," I said.

"Ah, that I doubt. How's the vending machine business, Master Timothy?"

"Don't know what you're talking about."

"Ah, never confess. But I see even through these bleary eyes. Your secrets remain safe."

"I got no secrets," Timmy said.

"Have no secrets," Ernie corrected. "You have no secrets, but you got no grammar."

Timmy said, "That a joke or something?"

"We've got to go," I said.

"Yes, I'm sure. Peter, someday we'll have to get together with your mother's boyfriend to pour lighter fluid on his chest hairs and take turns tossing matches at him."

"We've got to go," I repeated.

"Go and sin while you're young enough to repent."

Once we cleared the entrance, Timmy asked, "Why're you so nice to a queer?"

"He's okay. He's funny."

"Yeah, funny. You letting him suck your dick?"

I grabbed him by the sleeve and swung him around. "I warned you before."

He jerked his arm away. "Come on. We got something to do while the sun's high."

"I mean it. I'll let you have it," I said, but Timmy paid no mind.

We went to a nearby apartment. I was familiar with what was on the other side—showgirls from the Lido sunbathing in the nude. Since finding out about them, Tommy had been obsessed and had weighed using everything short of a battering ram and explosives to get in. There were no trespassing signs, but there was a dead bolt on the door to protect their privacy.

"I found a way." He pulled me into the alley. "Don't know how I missed it." He pointed to a telephone pole abutting the corner where the walls came together. "Saw it last night."

"I don't know," I said.

"Pussy." He grinned. "I went up this morning, up and over. Easy." He looked up the alley in both directions. "Go on. I'll keep watch."

I hesitated. He said we didn't have all day, it was now or never. "Watch out for splinters."

I climbed up, using the wall to brace myself. I sat on the edge and watched Timmy ascend. He paused so often I began to doubt he'd climbed it. But he seemed determined. At the top I pulled him onto the roof, where he sat gasping for air until he caught his breath. He nodded.

The pool was in the courtyard. We crawled along a tar roof treated with gypsum rock without making noise or being seen.

At the edge we brushed rocks aside to lie down, easing our way forward until we could see into the courtyard. Four women reclined on chaise longues some twenty feet below us, three on their bellies. The fourth, a blonde, lay on her back, everything exposed. My mouth went dry.

She encompassed all I'd envisioned as erotic—skin golden, nipples pink, limbs firm and lithe. Her meticulously trimmed pubis, almost iridescent in the warm sun, glistened like fleece. I watched the gentle rise and fall of her ribs, the lie of her breasts as she rolled over, paperback in hand, and propped herself up on her arm to read. I imagined being entwined in her long limbs, pressing against her. My groin ached. I closed my eyes and wondered if when I opened my eyes she would be gone.

Timmy went to nudge me, and as he did he brushed a rock off the edge of the roof. My heart followed it, its fine white crystals sparkling in the sunlight as it tumbled in a silent, irreversible arc toward the decking. We ducked as the stone shattered on the concrete.

Timmy pulled at my arm and whispered, "Let's get."

One of the dancers stood, aimed a finger at us, and shouted, "Dirty little shits!"

"Call the cops!" hollered another.

"Goddamn. Can't a girl have some privacy?"

The dancers' voices ricocheted behind us as Timmy and I dashed straight for the pole. I reached it first, sat down and propped my feet against it, then caution aside, hurried down. Going down, I caught a splinter, a big one from the feel of it. I fell and landed on the asphalt on my rear end, where I sat holding my hand, an inch-long sliver jammed into the palm.

I took a breath and bit down on the sliver. I clenched my teeth and jerked my hand away. I spat out the splinter and looked up at the spinning sky as blood oozed out of the wound. I told Timmy to hurry, but he was bound to the pole with both arms, afraid to move.

I said, "You never climbed a pole in your life." I should have left him there, but for unaccountable reasons, I stayed.

He descended about a foot by slipping. "Oh, shit," he said. "I gotta pee."

He began to cry. The door leading to the back opened, and two women, one a redhead, the other the blonde, bolted into the alley. They wore sheer silk robes. I gaped at the blonde's nipples, which protruded from her garment.

"Little pervert," she said.

I showed them my wounded hand, as if that somehow validated me. The blonde said it served me right and slapped the back of my head. The redhead shouted for Timmy to get off the pole, but he'd attached himself to it like an inert appliance. He shook his head, which in terms of shaking was nothing compared to his trembling legs and arms. I shouted, "Come down!"

"I'll come down when they leave," he said.

"He's scared," I said.

The redhead eyed me. "He aught'a be."

The blonde stood at the base of the pole. "Good, stay there 'til the cops come."

Timmy hugged the pole with his arms and legs. "What's the big deal? You let the whole world see it," he said as two more dancers arrived.

The blonde picked up a rock. "Say one more thing like that and I'm throwing this."

"I got money. I'll pay," he said.

"You little shit," the redhead said.

The others picked up rocks. The blonde tossed hers first, and soon as she did, the others cranked their arms back and heaved. They didn't throw much like women, but they missed him. I decided he was on his own. It was his doing and undoing. I backed slowly away, figuring to cross Sahara at Tam Drive, double back, and make it to Foxy's before any cops arrived. And it would have worked if I hadn't been looking back into the alley to make sure no one was following.

As I turned at the next apartment, I walked straight into a heavyset man, perhaps forty, in a white shirt and black pants.

Mother, readying herself for work, was painting her eyelashes when the cops knocked. Mascara brush in hand, she answered the door dressed only in her robe.

The two cops filled the doorway. "Ma'am," the lead officer asked, "this your son?"

She looked past them at me. "Yes."

"Well, may we come in?" one asked, trying to get a peek down her robe.

"Why, yes." She clutched her robe together and stepped aside so they could enter.

The bleeding had stopped, but my hand throbbed. The cop shoved me inside and told me to keep my mouth shut, which seemed needless as I'd not said one word since giving my name and address. He explained the charge, said he didn't want to arrest me, but had to if I was unsupervised.

"Well, my daughter will be home before I go to work," Mother said—a lie, followed immediately by another. "And she's nineteen."

The second officer said, "Kind of a boy's prank. Hell, a bunch of naked women by a pool, who wouldn't try to get a shot? They were damned mad, though, but said they'd let us handle it. The boy better stay out of trouble."

"You have my assurance," Mother said.

"Sorry to trouble you," the first cop said, trying for another peek. He looked at me. "Tell your pal he got lucky. Next time the both of you will go down. Got it?"

"Yes, sir."

Mother stood at the open door and watched the cops cross the courtyard before closing it.

"That was quick, telling them about Miriam," I said.

She shrugged. "I won't have it, Peter."

"Have what?"

"I just won't." She slapped my face and accidentally raked her nails down my cheek. She stood looking at me for a moment, then said she had to get dressed for work.

I sat on the couch, an open book propped on my knees. My ear rang from her slap. My hand ached. As she passed by to leave, I lowered my head and stared at the page. She paused, came over and lifted my chin. She examined the scratches on my cheek.

"I'm sorry."

"Sure."

She set my book aside and held my palm under the lamp to look at the wound. "Clean it with peroxide and put some iodine on," she said. "And use some soap on your face."

"I'm bad. I know it."

She ran her fingers through my hair. "You could pick better friends." She put the book back in my hands. "It's about time you started doing more schoolwork."

"I do."

"I'm putting you on notice. Next time the cops pick you up, they can keep you."

"Anything to make Julie happy," I said.

She twisted the knob. "I mean what I said."

I opened the door for Timmy and a kid named Louie Skyles, who pulled out a knife with a mother-of-pearl handle and pressed the button. The stainless-steel blade flickered in the light. Having made his point, he closed the switchblade and slipped it back into his pocket.

"You ready?" Timmy asked.

I nodded. We pulled up our collars in the back.

With cigarettes cuffed in our hands, we strolled Fremont from Fifteenth to Main Street where Glitter Gulch adjoined the Union Pacific depot. Sleeves rolled up to show off our scrawny arms, we puffed on our cigarettes and watched with envy as some slick-hair drove by in a freshly waxed '60 Impala ragtop.

"He ain't nothin," Timmy said as the Chevy pulled off at Sixth Street.

"Fuck 'im," Louie said and patted his pocket where the knife was hidden.

Neon exaggerated everything, especially car finishes. Hand-waxed 'Vettes were queens of the night—the hottest thing on four wheels. My dreams were fat, 'Vettes and motorcycles, but my realities were as thin as my buggy-whip arms and as few as the coins in the pockets of my frayed jeans. Triumph Bonnevilles, with their chrome spokes and purring exhausts, made my pulse run. One rode by and I stopped to stare.

"What the hell you lookin at?" Louie asked.

"Nothing," I said, watching a piece of my heart go by.

Our night led us to White Cross Drugstore, where we drank milk shakes and later stood outside on the corner of Fourth and Fremont. Leaning against the wall, we watched for girls, and when they passed, we whistled. They called us creeps and jerks. Louie pointed to his crotch and said, "Here, I got your jerk."

Friendship with Louie Skyles was tentative, for we never knew when he was going to turn his hot temper or mean talk on us. He had disgusting habits, picking pimples with his dirty fingers, which he spread on his jeans, and sucking mucus from his nose to spit while we were talking to girls. He was too mean and too much of an embarrassment to get attached to, and I was always on guard around him. Timmy had his bad points, but at least he wasn't always an embarrassment.

Bored with standing on the corner, we hiked toward the Union Pacific station five blocks west. Fremont Street pulsated with the sounds of tuned exhausts and AM radios turned high and tinny as they blared the Top Twenty. The noise from the cars competed with sounds that seemed to pounce out onto the sidewalk whenever a casino door swung open.

Goaded by opened doors, tourists in a trancelike state walked through the entrances and were met with a flurry of motion and a blast of sound. Lounge bands played, and slots jingled—*ka-chink-ka-chink-ka-chink, Ah, Getem down, a field, a come, six ways to win.* Stickmen hustled bets and shills called players to the poker room—*best poker action downtown, ka-chink-ka-chink-ka-chink.* Everywhere the eye and ear encountered sensory overload. We pushed through the crowds on the sidewalk, Louie sometimes bumping into a lone boy on purpose, turning and staring at him dangerously.

At Second and Fremont a panhandler with open palms and pained expression hard-pitched the tourists. Louie made it a point to bump into him and tell him to watch where he was going. Young women in tight-fitting shorts and sweaters stopped passersby and aimed handbills at their faces, then quickly, before the tourists could react, stuffed the handbills in their hands. Timmy whistled at one and told her he admired her breasts. She asked where his baby-sitter was.

Hookers in mesh stockings strolled the side streets of Third and Fourth, women in short skirts, women who bent down and stuck their heads in cars that paused at the curb. A crowd gathered around the penny slot machine in front of the Las Vegas Club to watch a fat man in a tropical-print shirt pull the handle and get back two pennies. Timmy said, "Pennies! What a chump."

It was Saturday night, and we were on the lookout for opportunity and, as always, cops. Nodding occasionally at tourists, two of them on foot beat swaggered down the sidewalk. They noticed a panhandler begging change and ran him off. Then a drunk staggered into their path and they helped him back inside the Pioneer Club. It was too late to cross the street, so we tried to look inconspicuous, but the cops were wise to us and told us to move on.

We looked casually back over our shoulders as we turned the next block, where we stopped and waited. When the cops entered the Golden Gate, we crossed the street and doubled back. As Louie and I stood lookout, Timmy cased the slots in the Fremont. He watched a woman march up and down a row playing five machines, and when she hit a jackpot on the far one, he dipped his hand into the tray. Before the guards could react, he snatched three dollars in nickels.

We scoured the parking lot at Honest John's for unlocked cars. While Louie and I leaned on the fender, Timmy rifled a tourist's glove box—five or six seconds to grab a roll of coins and a pack of cigarettes. Timmy found another unlocked car.

"Your turn," he said to me.

"Mine?"

"Bet you ain't got the stomach for it," Timmy said.

I swallowed. I didn't dare show fear, not in front of Louie. I grabbed the door handle, climbed inside quickly, and shut the door. Timmy put his back against the driver's window as Louie did the same with the rear door. It was as if a single giant lens was focused on my every move. My fingers trembled, my palms and forehead broke out in a terrible sweat, and my stomach soured until I thought I'd vomit. I was out of the car in seconds, claiming nothing was in there. Timmy pushed me aside and said, "Gutless." He was right. I didn't have the stomach for it. The word spun in the air like a top as he crawled in. He found a cheap camera and some coins stashed under the seat and held them up disdainfully so that I could see them.

Louie, unsatisfied with the score, used his knife to poke the sidewall of the front tire. He laughed as it hissed. "You got no balls, Pete," he said as the two of them split up the take in the alley behind the Lucky.

Timmy said we should hit the Lucky while we were there, that there was no reason it should be off-limits. It was Saturday night, and he could scam a slot tray in no time, and we could get lost in the crowd if anyone chased him. I reminded him that the one place we never capered was the Lucky. Louie picked a pimple and looked at his fingers. He said money was money. I told them again that Willy had treated me fairly and I owed him. Timmy said it was all bullshit, even if it was true, that they didn't owe anyone anything, meaning him and Louie. I argued back that there were plenty of places to score.

"Easy for someone who's got no guts to say," Louie said.

"You don't hit glove boxes either," I said.

Louie patted the pocket that held his switchblade. "Don't try me," he said.

Timmy said he figured I was full of shit about knowing Willy, and Louie said I was a faggot-bait liar. He'd made my ears burn before, but nothing like at that moment. I didn't hit Louie, because I feared him, and I couldn't hit Timmy, who was my only friend.

Timmy changed the subject, saying he'd make a big score someday and buy himself a Third Street whore for a night. I figured a real score was enough to buy a 'Vette. As we walked out of the alley, a thought occurred to me. "I met Willy Bobbins, all right," I said.

"Bullshit."

I shoved my index finger into Timmy's sternum. "You're pissin me off."

"Better to be pissed off than pissed on," he said.

"I did."

"Prove it."

We made a bet and settled on a method of proof. We'd go inside and stand by the entrance to the restaurant, and when Willy looked in our direction, I would wave. If Willy waved back, it meant he recognized me, in which case Timmy would apologize; and if Willy talked to me, Timmy owed me a dollar. If, on the other hand, Willy ignored me, I owed Timmy a dollar and had to admit I was a bullshitter. Louie said we were both a couple of faggot-bait punks and took off up Fremont Street as if he had an appointment with the governor. I was glad to see him go.

We entered the Lucky through the hotel door, made straight for the restaurant, and positioned ourselves at the entrance where he could see us clearly. I was in luck, for Willy sat in his booth talking with three men in business suits. Though I hadn't seen him in years, I recognized him immediately. He was too involved in the conversation to look up just then. A moment later a neatly dressed woman walked over and asked if we wanted a seat.

Timmy, ever quick, said, "Thank you, ma'am, but we're waiting for my parents."

She nodded and asked us to stand aside so others could enter. As we did, Willy looked away from his companion and in our general direction and afforded me the chance to prove myself to Timmy. I raised my hand and waved—an uncertain wave, to be sure, but a wave. He squinted at us, then picked up the telephone at his table.

"Told you you're a bullshitter," Timmy said.

"He didn't see me," I said and waved again, this time vigorously several times.

Willy looked directly at me and nodded.

"See, I told you."

"It wasn't a wave," Timmy said.

Determined now to get Willy to walk over to us, I started to wave a third time, but a hand on my shoulder stopped me. I was pulled helplessly away from the entrance by a large man in a uniform, as was Timmy. The two guards braced us against the wall near the cashier's cage.

"Mr. Bobbins says for you boys to find some other place to hang around," one guard said.

"But I know . . ."

He turned me in the direction of the lobby door and gave me a push. As we stepped toward the exit, Timmy cut an eye in my direction and muttered, "Bullshitter."

As I did two or three days a week, I skipped phys-ed class and walked to the self-service car wash on East Charleston. Timmy was waiting by the vacuum machine with a bundle of dry towels. When he saw me step over the cinder-block retaining wall, my schoolbooks held together by a belt hanging over my shoulder, he picked up a towel and snapped it at the vacuum hose.

"Been waitin twenty-five minutes for you," he said. "Cost us probably two bucks and no telling what I could've found under the seat if I'd had someone watching."

I slung my books off my shoulder and laid them atop the vacuum machine. "I had to make history," I said.

"School's for jerks."

A man pulled into the stall in a white Plymouth sedan with mud-spattered fenders. Timmy wheeled about and told me to get ready with the bucket and sponge. Before the man was able to open the door, Timmy was leaning on the fender ready to negotiate. In no time the man handed a dollar to Timmy, who signaled me over. The man stepped into the sun to light a cigarette.

"Do a good job," he said, "and I'll give you boys an extra quarter."

Timmy dropped a quarter in the slot and the water wand hissed to life. As I washed the car from roof to wheels, Timmy followed behind, spraying and rinsing. We were efficient and had the process timed so that it never took more than two quarters. Finished, Timmy swung into the seat behind the wheel and drove the car to the vacuum. While I dried the car, he vacuumed, and as he did he popped the glove box and rifled it, then looked under the seat. He paused and stuffed something into his pocket. He finished running the vacuum while I was wiping the windows, then he went back to ask the man what he thought.

The man, on his second cigarette by then, inhaled and let smoke drift out of his nostrils as he circled the car. He nodded, then shook his head "Didn't get it very good on the hood."

"Hey, that's sun fading. No dirt there," Timmy said.

"Not good enough, boys," he said and slipped into his seat as I held the door open.

As he drove off, Timmy hollered, "Stiff. Goddamn stiff."

"You find anything inside?" I asked.

"Naw."

He was lying. More than half the time he'd lie about finding money or short me on my share, but it didn't matter to me. We averaged forty cents a car legitimately, for we charged a dollar minimum, and it rarely took more than sixty cents to do a wash and vacuum. Timmy also knew how to jimmy the vending machine and get our money back most of the time, and it was easy to pilfer change and cigarettes when we vacuumed, as loose coins and cigarettes found a home in the seams of the seats or underneath them. He always shared the cigarettes, some of which were stale and smoked like corn-stalks.

The second car to pull in was a black Cadillac with a film of dust all over it. A young blond woman in tight-fitting blue jeans climbed out. Timmy nudged me.

"Now that's what I need," he said. "Stay here."

She didn't seem to go with the Cadillac, and it was hard to tell how old she was; she could have been anywhere between sixteen and twenty-five. She adjusted her sunglasses and lit a cigarette as she surveyed the car. Though Timmy stood next to the grille and looked at her, she ignored him. After a few seconds of staring at the car and puffing on her smoke, she read the directions on the sign.

Timmy and I went into action. "Can we help you, Miss?" She tilted the sunglasses forward on her nose and looked him up and down as he stood there with the same artificial grin on his face that had earned us thirty legitimate dollars that week. It was a stupid grin, the grin of a harmless buffoon— very disarming. No slouch, Timmy knew how to turn a buck.

After a strained moment she said, "Who're you?"

"Me?"

"No, shitface, I'm talking to the invisible mummy behind you."

Though I was supposed to wait, I approached. Up close I saw that she was still a girl, though she possessed a woman's body and carriage and had the intimidating assurance of one. She could have been seventeen or eighteen. I was no one to judge. Other than a mother and a sister, I knew women only at a distance of twenty feet looking down from a roof.

"I'm the guy, along with my friend here, who's going to clean that mess for one dollar."

"One dollar?"

"Yes, but you pay the wash. Messy as it is, it'll take half a buck and a dime to vacuum."

"One dollar?"

"Yes, ma'am, plus sixty cents for the vendor."

"I don't need it vacuumed." She shoved her sunglasses in place and smiled. "I would'a paid three. You're not very smart."

Timmy showed her an open palm. He wasn't the kind to waste time trading insults.

"Nice car," I said.

"It's ugly," she said. "It's my dad's. He warned me not to take it out in the desert. Hell, does he expect me to take my own car out for a ride in the desert?"

"No, ma'am," I said. "You have your own car?"

"Never mind. Just get this one clean."

By then Timmy had the wand in action, spraying the hood. I excused myself and began wiping the top with the sponge. A dollar-fifty was a nice score, but two-fifty would have been better. If we made enough washing and drying cars, we wouldn't have to steal. Thinking of this made me angry. Maybe Timmy undervalued our service?

When the Cadillac was completely soaped, Timmy called her over. "We'll vacuum it for nothing if you want."

Nothing! I thought. Now we're down to a dollar-forty.

She thought momentarily, then said, "Sure. Why not?"

Timmy winked. I knew what to do. As I dried, I blocked her view. Timmy kept the vacuum moving over the carpet. A few minutes later, he raised his head up and nodded to me, then shouted to her that we were finished. I buffed the rear bumper as Timmy opened the driver's door for her. She pulled out of the lot, peeling rubber, and sped west on Charleston.

Timmy and I watched her turn north on Bruce. When the car was out of sight, he rolled up his pants cuff and from his sock retrieved a woman's red-leather wallet. He opened it and pulled the bills out in a bunch, all hundreds, except for three twenties. He counted out nine hundred sixty dollars. "Jesus Christ!" he exclaimed. "I knew the bitch had bucks."

"No shit."

"Thought she could get the best of me."

I took the emptied billfold to see if he'd missed something. There was no driver's license or ID, but there were several pictures. I recognized the first— Willy Bobbins, Stetson and all—and there were more. In two of them he sat next to the girl we'd just ripped off.

I grabbed Timmy's arm. "We gotta give it back!"

He jerked his arm away. "You crazy? We're rich. I'm not giving anything back. Besides, she'll call the cops."

"No, she won't."

He tried to hand me three hundreds, but I shook my head. He always grabbed the lion's share, and I never objected, because he always took the risks.

"Hey, you don't get half."

"I don't want any. We gotta get it back to her. That was Willy Bobbins's daughter."

"Take it," he said.

I shook my head.

He let the bills drop on the ground. "That's all you get."

Timmy, faults and all, was my friend, but I couldn't let that stop me from what I knew I had to do. I wasn't much of a fighter, but Timmy was no kind of fighter. I hit him twice. That was all that was needed. He sat cross-legged on the ground and cried. I put the money back in the billfold and slipped it into my back pocket. "I'm going to see Willy," I said.

He sniffled and looked up. "No, you won't."

"If there's a reward, I'll give it to you."

"Thief. The worst kind. Steal from your partner."

I gathered up my schoolbooks.

"I'm gonna kick your ass," he said and came after me, but I warned him off with a look. He stood, red-faced, tears streaming down his cheeks, and threw a stone at me. Shouting profanities, he said, "I'm getting Louie on you!"

Timmy knew I was afraid of Louie, but I wasn't about to let that stop me.

"We're not buddies anymore!" he hollered. "You better be watching for Louie!"

"Okay," I said, but not loud enough for him to hear. I said it for me.

He threw more rocks. They were small rocks and he had no arm, so it didn't matter.

The more I thought about it as I trudged up Fremont Street, the more I was tempted to keep the money, but I didn't, though it would be a lie to say it was honesty that made me walk into the Lucky. The guard gazed down impassively and asked who I really wanted to see.

"Willy Bobbins," I said. "It's important."

He scratched his chin. "You wanna see Mr. Bobbins about something important?"

"Yes, sir."

"How old are you?"

"Fifteen almost."

He aimed me toward the door and told me to come back in six years. When I objected, he nudged me and told me to get on my way. I marched, chin up, back straight, to the front entrance, him following. He watched me enter the sidewalk crowd. I didn't look back. I crossed Fremont and kept going until I was certain the guard had lost interest, then circled back, entered by way of the hotel through the cramped lobby, and went directly to the Ranch Room Restaurant.

The room was unchanged from my first meeting with Willy—brass chandeliers and brass lamps, red-velvet brocade wallpaper, oak trim, paintings of cowboys and horses, and here and there nickel-plated spurs and horse bits. He sat chewing away with a loose-jowled frown in the same booth Miriam and I had shared with him. Hunched over a bowl of chili, he didn't seem very impressive and certainly didn't look like a legendary gangster. As I approached, he fixed an eye on me just as if he'd seen me all along.

The noise in the casino funneled into the restaurant like wind sucked through a tunnel—slot reels grinding to a stop, stickmen calling out dice, the operator announcing a page, but I heard only the voice behind me ask, "What're you doing, kid?" I looked over my shoulder at a guard, the same one. Before he could grab me, I ran to the booth and plunked the billfold down on the table.

Willy looked at it. "What's this?"

"I found it, sir."

Though he couldn't read, he took out reading glasses from his pocket and thumbed through the contents. "Where'd you get this?"

The surroundings seemed to compact into something small enough to fit inside that wallet. I stammered, "I-I-I found it, sir."

"Found it. Just like that, huh?"

His eyes seem to look at a vanishing point inside my skull. Had I overestimated his gratitude? He didn't recognize me. I glanced out of the corner of my eye for a path to the nearest exit. Time to *adios*—scram, no formal good-bye, just put the mistake behind me. I turned and ran up the aisle, headed for the first open door. No one could catch me, but still I looked back to see who followed and how close. That was my mistake.

I didn't see his leg as the crap dealer took a step back to extend his foot. I hit the carpet in this order—nose, cheek, chin, then the rest of my body. I slid to a halt eye level with a pair of high heels. My nose seemed to burst; my eyes watered. Half blind, I grabbed an ankle to pull myself up. A lady screamed as she stepped out of her high heel and called me names while I crawled about trying to stand. Bleeding nose and all, I managed to get up and say, "Tharry, ma'am."

She took a swing with her purse, but I was off again, weaving through the crowd. Two strides from Fremont Street and freedom, a hand pulled me to a sudden halt. The guard reined me through the casino by my collar. People turned momentarily to watch the show, then immediately returned to their gambling.

Blood ran from my nose down my lips and chin onto my shirt and Willy's carpet. The guard paused at the casino cage to pick up a box of tissues and stuff a handful in my palm. He warned me to hold them to my nose and not to bleed on him or Willy or Willy's booth or there would be hell to pay. Then he jerked me by my collar again, marched me to the restaurant, and stood me before Willy.

"Finished runnin?" Willy asked.

I nodded.

He held the wallet up for me to see. "Where you find this?"

I shrugged. He shrugged and repeated the question. I shrugged. He told me to stop shrugging and answer the question. I shrugged. He picked up the phone and told the operator to dial his house. He ran his tongue back and forth in his cheek as he waited and studied me.

"You're a mess, boy."

He said hello and turned away to speak in whispers, nodding here and there, occasionally glancing at me out of the corner of his eye for effect. When he hung up, he leaned forward. "Who was with you?"

I pressed the tissues to my nose and shrugged.

"Stop shruggin. You wanna be in trouble with me?"

"No, thir."

"What's your name?"

I told him my name, which came out "Peent Elkenth."

"Elkenth?" he repeated. "'At's a funny name."

In three more tries I pronounced it well enough for him to understand.

"Elkins?" He looked at the ceiling and nodded to himself. "I know . . ." he said and raised his brow. "I know you."

Through my bleeding nose, I recounted the kindness he'd shown my sister and me. He said I'd grown since, although I'd avoided getting smarter. He wanted to know if Miriam still talked like a lawyer with bowel problems and added that she'd likely grow up to make some poor man miserable. He even asked how Mother was doing. He recalled more about us than a short encounter years before would account for.

My face was swelling now. I could barely breathe.

"Hurtin?" he asked.

I nodded.

He assured the guard I wasn't a desperado and ordered a car brought to the side door. By then the tissue was filled with blood, mine. He pulled a fistful of napkins from the dispenser and passed them over. "Can't have you bleedin to death. Give the place a bad name." He held up the wallet. "Now 'at we're alone, you can tell who the boy was stole this from Betty. I don' take kindly to it. I wan'a name."

He repeated the question, but I didn't answer, and shortly afterward he dropped the subject. We sat in silence as I clamped a fresh napkin to my nose. The guard appeared, and Willy put on his hat. He told me we were leaving. I reflected on stories like Sam the Slav vanishing, no trace. The idea of getting into Willy's car for a ride didn't seem like a good one, not for someone party to stealing his daughter's money. Reluctantly, I stood. "I know about Tham the Thlav."

Willy pushed the brim of his hat. "Never heard'a him, boy."

A cop recognized Willy and marched us through the hospital waiting room where a no-nonsense nurse with clipboard in hand ordered me into a wheelchair. I told her my legs were fine, that the problem was my nose.

"Can't understand a word outta your mouth, boy," Willy said and pointed to the chair. She rolled me into a curtained cubicle, where two doctors promptly examined my nose.

"It's broken," one said to Willy. "X-rays will tell us how bad."

Willy made small talk about his broken noses, one of which came in a poker game in Victoria, Texas, where he claimed to have shot the man.

"Why'd you do that, Willy?" the doctor asked.

"Too big to punch." He winked.

When not amusing doctors, he joked with the cop who came in and out of the room to check on my progress. A nurse began to wheel me to the X-ray room. Willy walked beside me.

"That fella I shot?"

I nodded.

"He called me a cheat. Big fella, too, an a terrible poker player. Man's gotta own up to bein what he is, whether he be a hand or a thief. You wanna give up 'at boy's name now?"

I shook my head.

We waited in the hall, Willy sitting on a chair so as to be eye level with me. He leaned close. "Had more 'an one broke nose. Yes, sir. What'd you say that boy's name was?"

I shook my head.

"I'll just find out anyways. Fell off a horse once't. Broke my nose. Swear that damn horse thought it was funny. Must 'a. He kept throwin me."

"Yeth, thir."

"'At boy's probably gonna laugh at you. Ain't right, you gettin a broke nose, him gettin nothin."

"No, thir."

"You're gettin on my nerves, boy. You'd be smart to let me know."

Again I shook my head.

"Kind as I'm bein to you an all."

"Thar-ry."

"So go ahead, tell me."

"Canth."

"We'll see. You gonna have two fine-lookin shiners," he said. "That boy, what's-his-name, won't have no marks. Where you live?"

I repeated the address several times until he nodded. He tried to squeeze Timmy's name out of me as the doctor stuffed cotton up my nostrils and set my nose, attempted a bribe with a promise of ice cream. Even as he paid the hospital bill, he was still trying to break me. I didn't crack. When the doctors released me, Willy said he'd herd me on home. So that he didn't have to turn around to see me, he rode in the back and made small talk. When the Cadillac pulled to the curb, I opened the door, ready to make a quick exit.

"Hold on, boy, we got bidness."

"Thir?"

"I said our bidness ain't finished."

I figured until that point Willy had gone light and now something was about to happen that I couldn't stop. But I wouldn't give up Timmy, not after what I'd gone through.

"Thir?"

"You heard me, boy." He took out his wallet and laid two hundred-dollar bills on the seat. "That change your mind some?"

I stared at the money. It wasn't an easy decision. Timmy would have squealed. I took a slow breath so as to speak clearly. "I can'th thell, Mither Bobbinth."

Using the tip of an index finger, he pushed his hat back. "Guess that's the truth'a the matter. Take it. It's a reward."

"Really?"

"I don't like sayin things twice't."

I folded the bills and slid them in my jeans pocket. He nodded as if to say our business was concluded and told the guard to drive straight to the casino.

I stopped at Timmy's to give him the money and say I was sorry I hit him. I held the bills in my hand and knocked. He opened the door enough to stick his head out, looked at my nose, so swollen and bruised I had to breathe through my mouth, and asked if I'd seen Louie. I said no.

"What happened, then?"

I said that he and I wouldn't be stealing from cars anymore.

"Louie's lookin for you. I told him what you did, that you owe me that money. He said he'd get it from you or kick your ass."

I'd promised myself that I would give any reward to Timmy, but that was before I'd gotten a broken nose for my troubles and covered for him; that was before he'd spoken to Louie Skyles. I stuffed one of the bills in my pocket so he could see it and dropped the other. It fluttered to the ground at his feet.

He stared as if it were a fresh bloodstain on the doorstep. In one motion he scooped up the bill and slammed the door.

My luck that day was running in a pattern. The door was unlocked. I turned the knob. Hands on her hips, Mother blocked my path. She demanded to know where I'd been and what had happened. I shrugged and tried to go around. "Not so fast," she said. She claimed she had grief enough without me adding to it. None of her grief was my doing, I told her. She said she'd slap my face if it wasn't already a mess.

I said that I was hurt playing touch football in Circle Park.

"Since when do you play sports?" Shook her head. "You broke your nose in the Lucky," she said, adding that I shouldn't insult her intelligence. The telephone rang. She picked it up. The voice at the other end asked for me. She handed over the receiver.

"Thith ith Pete," I said.

"Know who this is, punk?"

"Louith," I said because he hated to be called Louis.

An unmistakable click came from his end of the line. "Know what that is, fuckhead? It's the blade that's going to cut your finger off."

5

I'd not forgotten about Louie or his switchblade. Though a year older, he too attended eighth grade at John C. Fremont. I managed to avoid him after my nose was broken, but from time to time I'd see him in the halls. He would flash a hard look and mutter a threat as we passed. After school I took a different route home or secluded myself in the school library until closing time. The week wore on, and nothing came of my worries.

Friday I walked up Sahara, figuring to spend some of Willy's money on a banana split at Foxy's. As I passed the glass window at Bertha's Fine Furniture, I glimpsed two figures following across the street. I ducked down a side street to the north, hopped a fence and ran to Santa Rita Street and from there to St. Louis, where I hunkered down behind a blue Oldsmobile in a carport.

They emerged from behind the Lutheran church and ambled across the parking lot, hands stuffed in their pockets. I squeezed between the car and the stucco wall and waited. I couldn't see, but I heard footfalls. One walked up the driveway and looked. I held my breath until he left.

Behind me the window rolled open, and a woman shadowed by the screen asked me what the hell I was doing in her driveway. I held a finger to my lips.

"Don't shush me, young man," she said. "This is my house."

"Please," I whispered.

"I'm calling the police."

It sounded like a good idea, so I nodded to her.

"Get," she said.

"Okay, okay." I moved to the edge of the car.

"Go on. Get!" she repeated.

"That's right, punk. Come on out," Louie said.

I peered out. Louie stood at the edge of the yard, arms crossed, Timmy at his side. My foot bumped a box of garden tools. A short-handled mattock caught my attention. I hefted it, felt its weight and balance, turned the handle to the ground, and banged it on the concrete.

"What're you doing?" the woman asked.

I struck the handle to the floor again, laying weight into the blow. The head slipped loose and I dropped it back in the box. The handle palmed behind my back, I stepped out.

"Well, look'a the punk."

"Get him," Timmy said.

"Won't need my blade for you," Louie said and sauntered toward me, arms cocked and fists balled, a smirk on his face.

"The old lady called the cops," I said.

"Sure."

I kept my body squared to his as he circled.

"Come on," he said.

I shook my head. We circled each other slowly, Timmy to my left waiting for a chance to jump in, Louie facing me. He feinted once with his head, thrust a quick jab at the air to intimidate me. I didn't flinch. He feinted right, and faded back, up and back, each time getting closer. We were about three feet apart when Timmy shouted, "He's got a club!" Louie's hand dived in his pocket for the switchblade.

I lunged and swung a roundhouse at his head. His reflexes were surprisingly quick. He blocked the handle with a forearm, which saved his head but cost him nonetheless. His eyes and throat bulged as he grabbed his arm. I smiled and swung a second time, planting the handle below his ribs. I wanted to punish him for the humiliation I'd endured, for his petty annoying habits, and for a long list of offenses he was unaccountable for—Julie, men who'd abused me. Louie collapsed on the lawn at my feet. I struck the next blow on the side of his thigh. He pitched about in agony, shouting curses. I pressed my heel to the side of his face to make him fully understand.

Hands trembling, I stood ready to whack his skull, to crush it if he moved, but he didn't. He just held up his uninjured arm to hide his face and begged me not to hit him again. The rage drained from me like water from a basin. I stepped back and caught my breath. He rolled about moaning, holding his wrist. I wanted to say something memorable to mark the moment.

I looked at Timmy and said, "You got something to say?"

He shook his head and backed away.

I knew then my terrible potential. Though it scared me, I felt powerful. I tossed the handle on the driveway, where it clattered to a stop, then I bent down and lifted Louie's head by the hair.

"Next time, punk, I'll hurt you." I stood and brushed my knees off. "Either of you tell the cops, I'll come after you," I said.

As I walked by I gave Timmy a shove in the chest. He didn't utter a sound. Neighbors had stepped out on their lawns to see what the noise was all about. One hollered for me to stop, but I walked on and crossed St. Louis as if I'd just won a prizefight.

Minutes later I was seated at the counter at Foxy's as police in prowl cars cruised by. My hands trembled. I couldn't stop them. I was scared and exhilarated and smiling as I wolfed down a banana split. I was too visible. I was ensnared by my own petty drama, a fugitive on the lam, a bad-ass who needed to lay low. Catercorner I saw where I could hide—the El Rancho Vegas.

Its Chinese elms parched and its remaining roofs gathering dead twigs and leaves, the El Rancho stood decaying, a season, a month, a day at a time.

I walked back and forth amidst the No Trespassing signs until I was sure no one had noticed me, then in one quick motion I hopped the fence. All that was left of the once opulent resort grounds was the few dozen trees. The skeletal remains of some plumbing protruded from the foundation of what had once been the casino, which had been destroyed in a fire. The swimming pool was filled with dirt, and the only buildings left standing were a few attached bungalows, now boarded up. I walked around until I located a bungalow where a door had been forced. I looked about until certain I wasn't being watched, then pushed the door open. It gave way with little effort.

It smelled of must. I closed my eyes to adjust to the thin shaft of light from the window, which split the room in half. I opened them, blinked, and the room came into view. It had been arranged as if its occupants were gone for the season and intended to return. In one corner a chair and love seat were shrouded in dust-covered sheets. A slightly angled full-length mirror reflected light from the crack in the board that covered the window. I felt transported, and at the same time I felt like a trespasser, violating neither the grounds nor the bungalow but the past that had once transpired here. I turned in the center of the room and bumped into a coffee table, then a chair. I pulled one of the sheets off the love seat; the fabric tore as it came off. Its cushions were propped against the back. I put one in place and took a seat.

A noise like a mouse might make came from the adjacent room. I cracked the door and looked in. It was empty except for a dresser pushed against the wall, another full-length mirror, and a mattress on the floor. Yet it seemed the room was in use. A connecting door led to the next suite. The door was stuck, but I shoved my weight into it, and on the third try, it gave.

"Don't!" a voice shouted.

I went cold. On his knees on the floor was a man bent over, his hands and arms covering his head. Again he said, "Don't." Being more scared than he was, I didn't move. Gradually he lowered his arms and peered up. When he saw I was a mere boy, he stood and pointed at me.

"What the hell? What makes you think you can come in here?"

True, I didn't belong here, but neither did he. He was, however, here first—perhaps, like me, a fugitive. I saw myself in him, sad, alone. "I didn't mean to. I . . ." My words fell off.

His brown eyes were deep set, almost hollow, and he was old and thin. The room smelled of urine and Tokay, and another odor so strong it suggested death. I turned away and rounded the corner of the cottage. The old man in pursuit, I started to run.

"Don't tell no one!" he called to me. "Please, don't tell no one."

I walked and walked, hoping not to be stopped by the cops. I returned home at sunset, long after Mother and Miriam were to have left for work. As I crossed the walkway by the pool, Ernie perked up and sat astride the lounge chair. He aimed the head of his golf club at me.

"Your mother has a visitor."

"A visitor? She's not at work?"

He shook his head. "Came in a Cadillac."

I knew who it was, but shrugged it off. "Probably no one important," I said.

Ernie glanced at the door. "She had other visitors first, young Peter. Men in uniform, the constabularies, coppers, flatfoots, the men with grim faces. Is the plural of flatfoot flatfeet? Never mind. Has that Neanderthal she allows in her life been misbehaving?"

This news was different than hearing that Willy was visiting. It hit my knees and hands like falling on ice. Timmy or Louie must have ratted me out. Ernie noticed my reaction.

"Have you been up to something, Peter?"

I didn't answer.

He rested the head of the club on the pool decking, and holding the grip in both hands, leaned toward me. "Ah, never admit a thing," he whispered.

"That's the spirit. But I do hope it's Juliana who's the miscreant and not you. Isn't that a lovely name for our Italian stud. Bet it would put some color in his face to hear that. You don't like him, do you?"

I started to shrug, but instead shook my head.

Ernie lifted his club and aimed it at my apartment door. "There, it's blessed," he said.

The walkway seemed strangely steep, and the steps almost insurmountable. I heard the muted tones of conversation on the other side of the door. It was unlocked. Mother sat at the table, Willy opposite her, sipping coffee. She wore no makeup. She didn't bother to look up, but Willy said, "Howdy. Just tellin your ma about you, Pete."

For some reason I figured he was still trying to get Timmy's name out of me. "I see, sir."

"Yep, but I ain't no sir. Well, I gotta be goin," he said and stood. "Thanks for the coffee, 'Lizabeth." He patted my shoulder as he walked to the door. Mother looked at me coldly and followed him outside. I watched through the slit in the curtains. They walked to the pool, where they conversed for a minute. From Mother's expression, I figured the worst.

When she closed the door, she pressed her back against it and slumped down to the floor. Her face seemed heavy and old. I remembered how she had once worried about each new crease in her forehead, but she'd been in a depression so long now that she'd forgotten about her wrinkles. Julie had taken more than money.

She looked up at me. "You know where he's going, Peter?"

"Beats me," I said.

"The cops were here. Looking for you."

I nodded.

"Willy said he'd take care of it."

"I did what I had to," I said.

She shook her head. "Had to? They said you beat a boy with a club. You broke his arm."

"Wrist," I corrected. Now that I knew the cops weren't coming, I wasn't so scared. I slumped down on the couch where the day before I'd sat reading the first five chapters of *Advise and Consent*, turning pages and imagining the characters' emotions as the story took shape. I wished at that moment I'd run home to read more of it.

"Why can't you be like Miriam?"

I was ashamed and didn't answer. I gathered up the book and started for my room.

"Don't you walk away," she said. "Don't you have anything to say?"

"Like?"

"I should be at work," she said.

"So you can make money to give to Julie?"

She crossed her arms while thinking, nodded twice, licked her lips, and slowly lifted herself up from the floor. "You don't care, do you? I don't know what to do."

"Why'd you call Willy?"

"Because he called me when you broke your nose and told me how you did it, told me you'd returned something someone else had stolen. He likes you. But you don't care."

"How's he know our number? I never mentioned your name."

The question set her back an instant. When she recovered, she said, "I'm the one asking questions. I said, you don't care, do you?"

What had happened to the boy who dreamed of being a man calm in crisis, moral, and confident? He stole books from libraries and broke bones with a club. I clutched the book, a thing that felt substantial in a world that seemed mostly vapor. "I want to, Mother. I want to care."

She slapped my face and walked to her room.

A guard in uniform knocked on our door to take me to the hospital for a follow-up. He politely opened the car door as if I were a dignitary. It was warm and clear, the kind of day that causes you to squint, and sunlight accented the pale rose and rusty red of the Spring Mountains to the west. I sat in the back of the Cadillac with *The Stranger* opened up and pretended to understand what I was reading.

I kept my book on my lap as the doctor examined my nose, pushing it to the side with his thumb, probing with a scope attached to a beam of light. Finished, he shook his head and told me it was fine, but I'd have a pretty knot on it the rest of my life, one that would make me appear very masculine.

"What's that you're reading?"

I showed him.

"Don't think I've read him."

"I'm an existentialist," I declared, though I had no idea what an existentialist was.

In the sunlight I paused to examine my reflection in the glass door. I tried to distinguish how I'd changed, what effect a nose with a pretty knot or slant to the left would have on my looks. I saw no improvement. Simply, I wasn't particularly good-looking.

This time the guard didn't bother opening the door. He told me to get in the back. We drove off without another word. Instead of taking Main south when we came to the intersection, he drove through and turned north on Second Street. I asked where we were going.

He caught my eyes in the mirror. "Mr. Bobbins wants to see you."

"Me?"

He turned to look this time. "I do what I'm told."

There were laws. I wasn't sure what the laws were, but I knew a kid couldn't be forced to go somewhere against his will.

"This is kidnapping," I said.

"Read your book and don't be stupid, kid."

So much for being treated as a dignitary.

Willy sat in his booth with three men. They talked in whispers. The guard told me to wait. When the men excused themselves, Willy stood and shook my hand.

"Gonna have a nose," he said, taking a close look at the damage. He told me to wait and left me standing by the booth. He returned from the kitchen with a woman in a hostess's uniform. He said she'd be in charge of me from there on. She handed me a list of rules, along with a work application, and motioned for me to follow.

"My name is Felicia, but you'll call me Mrs. Cantrell. I don't allow subordinates to become familiar with me. It's my responsibility to reprimand and punish, you understand. You're to be Mr. Bobbins's busboy. You'll have other duties too, of course."

She was a human audiotape gone amok, a sound processor that spoke without thought. She need not think, only fulfill the duties of her station. She reeled off requirements: black pants and white shirts; fingernails trimmed and clean; a haircut, short around the ears and down the back of the neck, nothing over the collar; deodorant, not too noticeable and absolutely not overpowering; and aftershave with the same limitations.

"You get all of that?"

I nodded.

"What's the book?" she asked.

"Camus," I said. "I'm an existentialist."

"I'm a Baptist and a Republican," she said. "No books at work."

"Yes, ma'am."

"Good. Politeness counts."

I was beginning to understand more than rules. This was Willy's doing, but I also saw Mother's hand in it. Now Julie and she would have both Miriam and me out of the way. Did she blame us for their problems and her depression? The hostess told me to pay attention.

"If your mind drifts that easily you probably need zinc."

I showed my most attentive face. She said a guard would drive me to the police station to get a work card, then to the health department for a card, both mandatory. She said everything had been arranged, no waiting.

I watched her sort through the papers and said, "What if I don't want to?"

She ignored the question and asked one of her own. "What happened to your nose?"

"This?" I'd invented several stories and offered the most absurd. "I jumped in an empty swimming pool."

Humorless, she asked, "The deep end or the shallow?"

No one had asked for details before. I gave her a blank expression and said, "Both."

The answer didn't faze her.

"Do you have white shirts and black pants?"

"No."

She reached over and ran her hand up and down my chin.

"Shave before work."

"I don't shave," I said.

"Start." She said that the guard would also take me to a store to buy a razor, four white shirts, and two pairs of black trousers, the cost of which would be taken out of my first three checks. The shirts were to be freshly laundered and pressed, according to the rules that governed appearance. Did I have any questions?

I was afraid she'd have the answers. "No."

I clutched my book and glanced at Willy's booth. She added that though I'd been singled out for special treatment, and even if I was a relative, which she didn't care to know, working for her wouldn't be easy. "Around here, if you jump in, it's always the deep end," she said, adding, "I hear everything."

When not serving Willy, I was kept moving, clearing tables, sweeping floors and mopping, wiping the countertop, and carting trash out to a Dumpster that smelled so strongly of decaying meat and vegetables it made me gag at first.

"Peter, take this," Mrs. Cantrell would say and hand over a wadded napkin she could just as easily have tossed away herself. "Peter, wipe the counter again, this time with elbow grease," she'd say, though it sparkled. "You, Peter, get the broom and dustpan." "Peter, don't bother the customers. Just pour their water and go."

"Peter, are you just lazy or stupid?"

"That's a rhetorical question, Mrs. Cantrell."

"Don't be insolent. Take all the trash out next time."

"Yes, ma'am."

It was hard work that sent me home exhausted, and I worked for minimum wage plus the handouts waitresses gave me from their tips at the end of the shift. When the poor-mouthing was over, I'd take home ten bucks, a fortune to a boy in 1962. Half my tips and paycheck went each week into the family coffers. Miriam made certain of this. She also opened up a savings account in my name. She demanded ten dollars a week, which she deposited for me. She loved to point out how my wealth was accumulating with interest compounding.

Willy showed me little consideration, called me "boy" and sent me on errands like counting the number of bottles of a particular chile sauce and comparing it with normal inventories or taking an envelope to the sheriff's office in the courthouse and leaving it with a secretary in the Intelligence Bureau. I was not only to go up to his office to empty the trash but also to throw it in a specific bin, then spy from inside the swinging doors and report if anyone went through the papers.

Once, when a panhandler crawled into the bin a few minutes after I'd dumped the trash, I followed instructions to the letter and reported what I saw. Two guards dragged the frightened man inside and braced him against the tile wall until Willy arrived. Willy, seeing the man's condition, stuffed money in his pocket and told him to have a free meal and a drink. I figured I'd made a mess of things, but Willy told me I'd done a fine job. Later he slipped a bill in my shirt pocket as I cleared away his coffee cup.

My station waitress, an unsmiling woman with a wide, flat face, noticed the bill. Genese was Mrs. Cantrell's favorite. She suffered from bunions so bad she limped on both legs. The only thing that seemed to pain her more than her feet was giving up money. She said, "You've got a hundred-dollar bill in your pocket."

And so I did.

At the end of our shift she said she'd been stiffed by everyone and I'd taken a tip that rightfully was hers. She made the accusation in front of others.

"Tell that to Willy," I said.

"I'm not giving up a cent tonight, Peter," she said.

"Tell that to Willy as well," I said.

I wanted to say she was too old to work, something cruel like that, but I didn't. Instead I laid my open palm on the counter and waited. She swallowed and counted out six one-dollar bills. "I guess it's yours," she said, but her tone made it clear she still felt cheated.

I gathered up the money.

The second week in May my nose was broken again when a waitress carrying a tray pushed through the swinging door to the kitchen as I was looking the wrong way. Mother accused me of getting into another fight. I didn't bother to correct her. She said I was on thin ice. Julie sneered.

That week Lana announced she'd fallen in love, but the best part was she'd fallen for a rich man and was moving to Sacramento. Mother went into a funk. Julie asked Miriam what he'd done, to which my sister replied, "You put her in debt." Money, of course, had nothing to do with Mother's state of mind. It was the ring on Lana's finger and the lack of one on Mother's, but Miriam couldn't resist the opening.

Julie reacted by buying flowers, using Mother's money, of course. His efforts were fruitless, for bouquets of the reddest roses were no antidote for Mother's mood. Only a ring would have cured her. How could Lana, who was neither young nor particularly attractive, make such a swell catch?

On May 24 Lana married her furniture retailer, a little man with a bald pate named Seymour Blumberg who had an extra thumb on his left hand. It was a hot day. Mother served as maid of honor, and Seymour's grown son was best man at the twenty-minute ceremony held in the Little Chapel of the West. Julie had gone on a binge and was too hung over that morning to put in an appearance. For the occasion Mother had bought me an autumn-brown wool suit and a shirt one collar size too small. I sat sweating off pounds and tried to be inconspicuous despite the nose splint and purple rings around my eyes.

The man next to Miriam and me, a friend of Seymour's, gave me a stupid smile and asked if I'd run into a wall. I said I was the only survivor of an airplane wreck that had killed sixty people.

"No! I'm sorry," he said.

"It's okay. I'm getting over it," I said.

Miriam jabbed my ribs and said, "He's lying."

He looked at me with indignation. "Is that so?"

Miriam leaned across me. "There were only fifty-seven killed," she said. "My brother exaggerates."

"And the pilot and copilot," I said.

"Okay, fifty-nine if you include them," she said.

"Man, are you lucky," he said.

Lana casually walked down the aisle wearing a pleated navy-blue pinafore and carrying a bouquet of black roses, which she nonchalantly tossed over her shoulder when she reached the altar. She giggled as she repeated the vows, and when Seymour kissed her, she grabbed his buttocks and winked at the audience.

When we stood to applaud the bride and groom, the man next to me said, "I hope they have your good luck."

Miriam rolled her eyes.

Outside, Mother and Lana held each other and cried as Miriam kept passing them tissues from her purse. Lana said she'd tried to wait for me, but I just wasn't growing up fast enough, though I was getting taller, and at the rate she was aging she might not do me much good if she waited any longer. "Although you could probably do me a world of good," she said. She kissed Mother, squeezed into the waiting limousine next to her bald-headed groom, and drove to the airport for two weeks in Tahiti before settling down in Sacramento, where Seymour owned a renovated Victorian mansion painted pink and white and gray.

Miriam and I were unsure whether Mother's depression came because Lana was happy or because she was gone, or because Julie wouldn't marry her, or from the combined effects of all of these. Mother's moods shifted faster than a single-wing backfield. Some days she would hide in her bedroom. Others she'd be up in the morning crying as Miriam and I dressed for school. Once she cornered us just as we were ready to leave and said, "I'll make this up to you two. You're the best children. I will. I swear I will. I'll change."

Miriam got choked up and told Mother it was okay. She didn't want to add to Mother's sorrow. I shrugged. Make what up? Our condition, it seemed to me, was what it was, and besides, wasn't everything good always waiting in the future? Outside I called Miriam a suck. She smacked the back of my head. I knocked her books out of her hands and ran.

Ruben Lee Bobbins motioned me over to the booth. I grabbed a pot of coffee and headed his way. He kept a room in the hotel. It was obvious from his bloodshot eyes that he'd not been using it.

"Kid," he said, as always, "get me some eggs over medium and bacon, and tell that screw-ass cook to make the bacon crisp without making it black." In looks no one appeared more like Willy than Ruben Lee, down to his cold-blue eyes.

"Yes, sir."

He insisted I call him sir. I poured his cup full. He watched me pour, then leaned back and pointed at the cup. "Did I ask for this, kid?"

He had none of his father's presence or charm, just the toughness that, in him, took the form of a distilled meanness. "No, sir. I can take it away."

"And waste it? Leave it."

Warning the cook about the bacon, I handed him the order. He asked, "Is he on shit?"

I wasn't sure what that meant, so I shrugged.

Ruben Lee walked to the counter where I waited for his food. "Bring it up to me, kid."

"Where?"

"Where, *sir*," he said.

"Where, sir?"

"Ask security. They'll let you through the door."

He'd been in and out of the casino relentlessly ever since Willy left for Montana. Willy claimed Ruben Lee was the best cop in the casino, had learned from the finest cross-roaders in the West and could spot a hand muck or a card switch from across the casino floor. At the time, I had no idea what a cross-roader or a hand-mucker was, only that the terms had something to do with gambling and cheating. The waitresses called Ruben Lee the lurker because he hid behind plants and pillars and spied on employees.

I poured a fresh cup of coffee and covered the plate. The guard lifted the cover, nodded and unlocked the door. "Just follow the stairs one flight and press the button by the door on the left." He stepped aside for me.

It was like entering a cavern. I climbed the stairs slowly, my footsteps sounding off the hollow walls. I reached the landing, where I balanced the tray and pressed the button. The lock buzzed. I held the tray in one hand and reached for the knob.

The door flew open and Ruben Lee bolted out. "Outta the way!" he shouted and pushed me aside. I lost the tray. Plates shattered. The cup smashed and splattered coffee on my shoes. I bent over to gather up the large pieces and put them on the tray, which I carried downstairs. As I opened the door, I stepped into the middle of three guards who were watching Clarence, a casino porter, crawl on hands and knees toward the cage, Ruben Lee on his tail, hollering, "Thieving sonofabitch, keep moving."

Clarence tried to stand, but Ruben Lee kicked him in the rear with a sharp-toed boot, which made Clarence crawl all the faster. He reached the casino cage and used the counter for support to stand up. In Ruben Lee's hand was a palette knife, commonly used by porters to scrape gum off the carpet. He waved it, shouted, "Sonofabitch!" and kicked Clarence in the shin. Clarence hopped about holding the injured leg up.

The door next to the cage opened, and George charged out just as Ruben Lee was ready to throw a punch. George stepped between them. "Whoa," he said.

"Get outta the way, George," Ruben Lee said. "He's the one. This sonofabitch Clarence." He held the palette knife up. "Used it to pry the lid to get himself a chip. Just helping himself to it like it was his own goddamn money."

Hoping that George had come to save him, the porter tried to move away, but Ruben Lee blocked his escape. "Oh, no, you don't," he said and gave Clarence another boot.

Clarence foundered, went to the floor and said, "I give up, Mr. Bobbins. I ain't fightin'."

George asked, "Clarence, how long you worked here?"

"Eight year, sir."

George shook his head. "Let 'im up."

"But . . ." Ruben Lee opened his hand to show the twenty-five-dollar chip in question.

"Leave him be. He's fired, that's all." George turned back toward his office.

Ruben Lee marched after him, demanding an explanation.

George wheeled about and said, "Get some sleep."

Ruben Lee held his gaze. "You couldn'ta caught him."

George nodded and moved on. The guards lifted Clarence up and escorted him to the front entrance, an unusual exit for someone who stole from Willy. He had gotten off easy.

Ruben Lee looked at me. "What do you want?"

I held the tray low for him to see the shattered plates. "I need a porter to clean the rest of that up."

"We got no porter, dummy." He walked the chip over the backs of his knuckles and palmed it. When he opened his hand, the chip was gone. He tapped my shirt pocket.

"Clean it up yourself and bring me breakfast," he said and walked away.

I reached in my pocket and pulled out the twenty-five-dollar chip.

6

Mrs. Cantrell reminded me of the Mother Superior in the orphanage. She hated boys and barely tolerated girls. The sins a busboy might commit were too many to enumerate and still keep a listener awake. But among them were talking back, using profanity, displaying dirty fingernails, wearing hair past the collar, popping knuckles, and paying too much attention to female customers. Then there were minor ones, like being too slow to wait on customers, insulting a customer, smoking at the counter, or reading while on duty.

As soon as I was told books were forbidden, I became obsessed by them. I sneaked them in under my apron and hid them in a crate by the loading dock, where the air smelled of garbage, cleaning solvents, and oil-stained asphalt. The concrete stoop was uncomfortable, but it was the only place quiet and safe enough for reading. On breaks I'd sit under the glare of a bare lightbulb, my back propped against the wall, my book spread open.

Old Mitch, the guard assigned night fire watch, caught me regularly with a book to my face. I'd come to recognize his labored walk and timed my reading accordingly, for when he showed up I was twenty-five minutes into my forty-minute break and knew to read no more than ten more pages, no matter how involved I got in the book.

"What'chu readin, Petey?" Mitch would ask. He was about Willy's age, but lame and frail in his limbs. In that regard, he was nothing like the other bruisers Willy employed for muscle.

"*Lord Jim*," I answered, Conrad being my latest pursuit.

"What's it about?"

I rarely had to explain a whole plot, as he was usually very quick to say it wasn't his type of book. "A man separated from his own society because of his guilt, but seeking acceptance in a new one where he is regarded as something spiritual."

"Sounds too deep. Don't you ever read westerns?"

"*The Ox Bow Incident.*"

"No, I mean real westerns."

"Guess not."

"Too bad. Damned entertaining."

I fancied myself a blossoming intellectual, having taken on the challenge of reading every book written by a Nobel Prize winner in literature, or at least the Americans. One evening I was deep into *The Sound and the Fury,* a puzzle of words and voices I couldn't unravel, though I pretended I could. Mitch came by and made his usual remark or two. He had a lonely job, so he lingered until I told him I had to read for school.

I was getting back into the novel when a second set of footsteps approached—much too light to be Mitch's. I slammed the book shut and shoved it behind my back as I stood. Mrs. Cantrell smiled widely.

"We need you to come back, Peter," she said. She refused to call me Pete because I insisted on it.

I stood with my hands behind my back and met her gaze. It would be fatal not to look her in the eye. "Yes, ma'am."

She tilted her head. "What's that you're hiding?"

"Hiding? Nothing," I said and moved quickly past her, lowering the book to my side.

"Hold it," she said.

I stopped. "Ma'am?"

"You've got a book, Peter."

I held it up for her. "Some people don't think of it as a book," I said, using a line an English teacher had used on me when I was reading *King Solomon's Mines.*

She smiled again. "Well, I'm not one of them."

I suppose things would have turned out differently for Mrs. Cantrell if she hadn't insisted on firing me. But that was her mistake. She sent me home at mid shift when dinner orders were backed up and Willy had decided to entertain two important gamblers.

A guard in one of Willy's black Cadillacs waited for me as I turned the corner from the bus stop. He motioned me over and said Mr. Bobbins was expecting me. When I explained I'd been fired, he said, "Get in. Only Mr. Bobbins can fire you."

That night George enacted a rule that any employee could read on breaks so long as it was in a designated area. After that I'd bring my books and study and read at the end of the counter reserved for employees. A week later Mitch saw me at the counter and said he'd wondered what had happened to me, that he missed our talks about literature. Though the conversations had been one or two sentences, they seemed important to him, so I occasionally took my book out to the loading dock to read under the bald light.

Thursday was the one day of the week Miriam and I crossed paths. We met for a quick burger and milk shake at Foxy's, where we sat in a booth by the window sharing an order of fries. I noticed she'd started wearing makeup in earnest.

"What are you looking at, Peter?"

"Pete. Can't you call me Pete?"

"I hate that. It's worse than boring. I repeat the question. What are you looking at?"

She reminded me of Mother. I'd noticed the resemblance before but was suddenly acutely aware of it. "Don't get like Mother," I said.

She plucked a fry off the plate and dipped it in ketchup several times. Tilting her mouth to catch it before it dribbled, she asked, "And what does that mean?"

It meant don't measure your faults in the mirror and don't blame the mirror if you find them, don't have frailties some man will exploit. I said, "Be careful is all."

"I am careful."

She didn't know what I meant, which was all the more reason for me to worry. Lately she'd been going out after work and staying out late. She'd been daydreaming, something she'd never done; I'd always been the daydreamer.

This worried me. I worried too that we'd grown too far apart already and if something happened to her our family would collapse.

I slurped on the last of my milk shake.

"That's rude," she said.

"So?"

"So, no girl will want to be seen with you."

I was fourteen, an official teenager. My sometimes booming voice embarrassed me. I was full of boundless energy that wouldn't allow me to sit still. Little tufts of fuzz grew above my lip and on my chin. My arms and legs had hardened, my abdomen had flattened, and pubic hairs spread up from my groin and surrounded my navel. Mild acne sprouted in the hollows of my cheeks and was a bigger embarrassment than my voice. And I thought constantly about sex.

Occasionally I awoke in a sweat to find a discharge on my sheets. I felt shame for all of this, and I withdrew even more earnestly into books, reading even when I wasn't interested, for when not reading I fantasized about soft, warm flesh and crevices wet with desire. I thought maybe the nuns were right about boys and though uncertain of God's existence, I asked Him to forgive me my terrible lusts.

"I don't care about girls," I said.

She looked at the ceiling in exasperation. "Why do I bother?" She fell into a moment of reverie as she held her water glass to her lips. After a thoughtful pause she took a sip and set the glass down. "Peter, I've got a secret."

"Yeah?"

"I'm going steady."

"Big deal."

At that moment when I looked at her I saw what men surely were bound to see. The light through the window made her eyes sparkle and her smooth, tan cheek glow. She was, like Mother, lovely. I was glad for her sake, for with her personality it would be a decided hindrance to be anything other than pretty when it came to men. I was certain many would lust after her.

"He's older, a pilot in the Air Force. I lied about my age. He thinks I'm nineteen."

I was reminded how she'd told the motor cop she was nineteen when she was barely thirteen. But, like Betty, Miriam could have been any age from sixteen to twenty-five. Females need wrinkles to be fully human, just as men need gray hair.

She wasn't drinking her milk shake, so I stuck my straw in it and sucked it dry. Finished, I pushed the glass aside and asked, "How old is he?"

"Twenty-four. He's a first lieutenant. But I can't tell you his name."

"Did I ask?"

"I'm not of age."

What she said gave me openmouthed lockjaw. "Are you . . . Are you and he . . . ? I . . ."

"We're not having intercourse. Do you think I'm unaware of sex? I made it clear to him."

"So, how do you feel?"

"Confused. In love, I guess. I don't know what to do. I don't want to lose him. I've never talked with anyone the way I can with him."

She'd kept friendships superficial, held people at a distance, never had a best friend. Like me, she had no one to confide in. In fact, she rarely spoke about anything of a personal nature, and never to the girls she worked with. She said they gossiped and lied, and she didn't trust them.

"Tell him the truth," I said. "Tell him how old you are. Give him the choice."

She seemed amazed. "Petey, that's very wise." She opened her purse and pulled out two quarters to leave as a tip. "Thank you," she said.

My nickname at work became "Books"—which I didn't much care for. After Mrs. Cantrell was fired, the waitresses warmed up to me, all except Genese, who blamed me for Mrs. Cantrell's departure. She just couldn't reconcile it—there was no discussing it; it was "the little bastard's" fault.

Instead of going to his booth one evening, Willy came up to the counter and swung a leg over the stool next to me. Before I could speak, Genese appeared seemingly out of the floor, just sprouted in front of us, pressing down the front of her apron. "Peter's on break, Willy. I'll be happy to serve you."

"Don't need nothin, Genese, if it's all the same."

She glared at me, but I pretended not to notice.

"What's 'at you're readin?"

"This?" I held up *The Great Gatsby*.

As his hooded eyes indicated, Willy had been up for two days, which he often was. He was unshaven. "Where the hell you been, Pete?"

"On break, sir."

He eyed the book suspiciously. "What's 'at you got there?"

I told him the title.

He squinted and looked up and over his shoulder at the chandelier. "Guess I heard'a it."

I asked if he wanted some coffee.

"Nope, no coffee. I said I heard'a it before."

"How about hot chocolate, sir?"

"Chocolate? You ever see me drink chocolate?"

I could smell whiskey on his breath. It was common knowledge that when Willy went on a binge, it was a good idea to avoid him. One waitress said his moods came from a broken heart, which sounded like romantic rubbish. All I knew was he could be mean when drunk. It was best to accommodate him.

I smiled politely. "No, sir."

"Willy. I told you a million times, boy. Willy's the name."

"Yes, Willy."

Though he seemed distracted, he shook his head at me and said, "You go on, Pete, an do your book learnin. You wanna be a lawyer someday, don't you?"

I shrugged.

"So, what's your book about?"

I told him it was about a man named Gatsby who'd gotten rich from gambling but couldn't get the woman he wanted.

"What's her name?"

"Daisy."

"A gambler, you say?"

I nodded.

"You like hot chocolate?"

"Yes, sir. I mean, yes, Willy."

He thought on this for a moment, shook his head and said, "Okay, bring some hot chocolate on up to my office, two cups. On your way tell the hostess to call me."

I replaced my book on the counter shelf. Balancing the cups of chocolate on the tray, I passed the new hostess. She told me to take my time and asked where my book was because Willy wanted me to bring it.

He stood at the door with his hat tilted back. Once inside, he flipped on the overhead lights, tossed his hat on the hat rack, making a perfect ringer, and walked behind his desk. He sat, propped his feet atop the desk, and told me to bring the hot chocolate.

He took a taste, then another. "No substitute for whiskey, but ain't near so bad as I thought. Sit down."

I took a seat opposite him.

"Start readin."

"The book?"

"Pete, don't be no dumb sumbitch. You can't read hot chocolate."

I spread the pages and began. Not just from reading, but from listening to Miriam in the backseat of Mother's car, I'd developed an ear for the rhythms and nuances of words and phrases. Though I was nervous at first, the words began to flow. Willy sipped on hot chocolate and listened. The more intent he became, the more I was encouraged to read, and soon sentences and paragraphs were gliding off my tongue. Though he'd heard news clippings and legal documents read aloud, he'd never been transported by words of fiction. Rapt, he listened for more than an hour and twice asked me to reread particular passages. Eventually he raised his hand.

"Let's stop there. You can finish tomorra."

I'd read only fifty-five pages. "Sir, it's too long a book to finish tomorrow."

"That was real fine." He waved me off with a flick of his hand. "We got plenty'a tomarras."

I carried the tray. As I opened the door, I noticed he'd closed his eyes. I turned the knob before closing the door so as not to disturb him.

Willy and I retired to his office each evening. He took no phone calls. It required six evenings to finish *Gatsby,* after which Willy leaned across the desk. "I'm gonna have a letter writ to the fella what writ *Gatsby,* tell 'im it's a perty good story, but he don't know enough about the gamblin bidness. I could give 'im some pointers for his next book."

"Fitzgerald's dead," I said.

"The fella what writ it?"

"Yes, sir."

"Too bad. It ain't a happy story, is it, Pete?"

"No, sir."

"He was too damn good for that Daisy, way too good."

"Yes, sir."

"Got any more stories like that one?"

I shrugged. "That's about the best I've read."

He nodded solemnly but asked me to keep an eye out for one he might like.

Over the next two years I would read seven novels and three collections of short stories to Willy. He liked them all, but none compared in his mind to *Gatsby.* Years later he could still quote directly from the book and describe scenes and characters in detail, and in a rare moment of nostalgia, he told me why Fitzgerald's work had so touched him: "Gatsby weren't no man's fool, 'cept his own. Ain't no bigger truth I know of, Pete. I believe everything about a man who makes his own path and stumbles on it. Man don't stumble is a man who don't walk." Just as important to Willy, I think, was Daisy. He had loved a woman as Gatsby had, with that kind of despair.

That fall Grandmother suffered a stroke, and while being driven to the hospital in Pullman, she had a heart attack. She was dead on arrival. The news came to Miriam and me through Julie, who was seated at the table in the apartment.

He twirled a tuft of hair at his collar with a finger and said nonchalantly, "Your mother's gone and she told me to watch you."

"Where'd she go?" Miriam asked.

"Washington."

"The state or the capital?" Miriam asked. She still hated Julie but had, for Mother's sake, avoided conflicts with him, so her question came as a surprise to both of us.

Julie curled his lip. "The state, Miss Prissy."

"Probably to see Grandmother. Why would she leave you in charge? Peter and I are capable of watching ourselves. Aren't we, Peter?"

"Why'd she go to Washington?" I asked.

"Her mother died, I guess." He said it as if unaware that she was also our grandmother. He pointed at an envelope.

Miriam and I looked at one another. Grandmother had been aloof, but enduring. And she'd been kind to us. I remembered that some time before Mother took Miriam and me to the orphanage I'd wandered into the neighbor's pasture and sat in a mound of dirt that happened also to be an anthill. Covered with black ants, I screamed and ran toward the house. Grandmother rushed out and scooped me into her arms. As she ran inside, ants bit her, but she never flinched, just hurriedly undressed me and put me under the water in her bathtub.

Miriam opened the envelope and read. She said it was true, Grandmother had died. Her eyes teared as she looked at Julie. "I don't care what she wrote. We'll take care of ourselves."

Too bored to answer, Julie rubbed his hand over his stubble. Miriam passed the note to me. Something of us was gone, a connection, as if a door had shut and the room on the other side had vanished and it was a room we'd barely glimpsed. I saw the old woman's sorrows fixed in her tired eyes. Perhaps her life had seen joy. Not much, I guessed, not much. I set the note down and looked at Miriam. "We've got to go to work." There was no time to talk about the old lady or what we remembered of her, no time to mourn.

As I dressed, all that was on my mind was the vague memory of the old woman who'd carried me into the bathtub and held me down as she ran water over me. I pictured her flat face, wrinkled and hard, eyes tired, and her hands, gnarled from arthritis, unbuttoning her dress front. Ants raced over her like hundreds of migrating freckles, and she smiled, telling me everything was all right, everything. She sank half-dressed into the water and submerged herself.

Except for the harsh white beam of one Malibu light it was dark as I turned the corner. I noticed a figure in the shadows by the pool. Ernie was between gigs again, half drunk and humming softly to himself. It was a pleasant night. A breeze moved a screen of smoky clouds across a white half-moon. I paused by the pool to watch the clouds. Ernie sat with his legs in the pool.

"Hello," he said. "Looks like you got here on time."

I was home early, which happened if Willy left for the night. "I'm early," I said.

He poured wine to the brim of his glass and toasted me. "To your earliness."

He got strange when he drank and spoke of things that seemed to exist without reference points. It was best to avoid such conversations. Besides, Mother had cautioned me not to keep his company, warning me he was unusual. I smiled politely and headed for the door. Even as I turned the key, I heard muffled words.

Julie looked up. His black work slacks were gathered at his ankles. Beneath him on the couch was Miriam, skirt hiked above her waist.

"Get out," he said.

But I didn't move.

"I said, get!" he repeated.

Miriam struggled under the crush of weight to free herself, but he was too heavy.

"You'll need this," a voice said behind me. I looked over my shoulder where Ernie stood with golf club in hand. He was bleary-eyed, and his face had a mischievous look as he held out his club. I took it. Julie tried to stand gracefully but his ankles were tangled in his trousers, and he fell backward on top of Miriam. Legs flailing, she twisted and covered herself with her skirt as she crawled around looking for her panties, which she found under the couch. She held them up by the elastic band and examined the rip in the side. As if this were the evidence she needed to grasp what had almost happened, she began to cry.

Ernie said he'd heard her call out, and if I hadn't showed, he would have called the cops. Julie managed to pull up his trousers. As he zipped his fly, he said, "It was her fault."

I raised the club and stepped toward him. Miriam, on her knees on the carpet, looked up and told me to stop, that nothing had happened yet, that I should think of Mother.

"That's right, kid. Listen to your sister. Think how your mom'll take it hearing what a slut her daughter is."

Julie offered a hand to Miriam, who shook her head.

"Okay, fuck it," he said and started toward the door.

Ernie whispered, "Watch out."

"Get back," I said.

Julie smiled with that same on-the-corner smile that Louie had. He took two more steps.

"I'm getting outta here," he said. "I told your mom this was a bad idea."

By then he was one step away. "Gimme the faggot's club," he said. "And you, you fucking pervert, get out of here." He extended his hand to take the club.

I guess he figured he'd somehow won, that I would simply surrender the club and take whatever punishment he chose to inflict.

"Stay," I said, meaning both for Ernie to remain and for Julie to stop.

Julie's grin widened as he extended his hand. I swung the club up and over my shoulder, my arms gaining momentum. He never saw the blur of chrome as I switched direction in mid swing. And when the head of the club leveled off and met the left side of his head just above the ear, it landed with a fine dull thud. Dumbfounded, he stood for an instant trying to get his balance, then staggered to his right three steps into the kitchen and keeled over on the linoleum.

His wound began to bleed. He rolled over on all fours, talking to himself and tried to lift himself up using the drawer handles. He collapsed and sat cross-legged holding his head. I asked if he was okay, but he didn't answer. He turned over on his side, moaned, and stretched out as if to take a nap. A moment later he was unconscious.

During all of this Ernie had kept watch at the door.

He came up beside me. "Golf etiquette, Peter," he said. "I believe you're required to say 'fore' beforehand," then added that the slob deserved it and took his club. He looked at it, its head now broken, and said, "Never learned how to play myself."

Until my heart slowed I couldn't talk or think what to do. Other than the rise and fall of his chest, Julie didn't move, and his breath was labored and raspy.

"He's a pig," Ernie said.

I nodded absentmindedly. I was only vaguely aware of Ernie telling me he hadn't seen a thing, that no one would know, as he would get rid of the club. Then he vanished.

Several seconds passed, neither Miriam nor I moving. A ringing flooded my ears, interrupted only by her muffled sobs. Gradually she uncoiled from the floor and went to her room. She came out a moment later. The bathroom door slammed shut and the shower went on. Julie hadn't moved.

I picked up the cushion from the floor where it had fallen and sat on the couch. Forgetting that I was a proclaimed existentialist, I prayed for an answer, a solution—nothing, just ringing in my ears. I sat half dazed until Miriam appeared from the hallway. She'd slipped into blue jeans and sweatshirt. Her wet hair hung loose down her back.

"Did you kill him, Peter?"

I shrugged. I didn't know.

"What'll we do?" she asked.

She'd always been the one in charge. How was I to know?

"Do?"

She looked at him. Blood stained the linoleum around his head, forming a chocolate-red halo. From the bathroom I got two towels, one of which I used to prop his head up while wrapping the second towel around it. Miriam watched.

"I wasn't going to fight anymore," she said. "I tried to tell him about Alan."

"Alan?"

"Never mind. Should we call the police?"

My wits were returning. "He tried this before?"

She nodded. "What're we going to do, Peter?"

I was scared, but hitting him had excited me in ways I couldn't understand, just as beating Louie had. No measure of consequences lessened the sheer elation of having stood my ground. Possibilities rushed about in my mind. Call an ambulance and the cops? Explain without the club, without Ernie? And the club was gone. The weapon. Why hide a weapon if there's no crime? I couldn't think clearly with him bleeding on the floor. I had to leave, had to talk to Willy. He understood these matters.

"Get a couple of blankets," I said.

"What for?"

"Just do it."

She returned, blankets in arm, and asked what we were doing. I didn't answer, for I had nothing in mind except hiding for the moment. I took one of the blankets. She followed without asking more questions. The courtyard was empty and so silent I could hear Miriam's breathing and the pool water lapping.

We waited for traffic to slow, then crossed Sahara Avenue to the wire fence that surrounded the El Rancho. Miriam asked what I thought I was doing and balked. "This is crazy," she said. "Why don't we just call the police?"

I told her I had a plan and spread the wire so she could crawl through. The plan was shaping up, and its success depended on chance, but anyone who could make Sam the Slav disappear without a trace once could do it twice.

"I think we should go back," Miriam said.

"Shut up. What about your pilot? How would he like to read about this in the paper?"

"Don't tell me to shut up," she said.

"What're we going to do? Tell Mother? And what will she say about Julie?"

Miriam had always been so certain, so audacious. She had to understand there was no going back, no more pretending innocence. She stood trembling as she considered those angles. I grabbed her wrist and pulled her along. A few steps later, her arm went slack and she followed passively, asking only that I slow down. The grounds and buildings were deserted. I was at first disoriented, having not visited the cottages for over a year.

I found a jimmied door, put my shoulder into it and pushed. It opened as if someone were expecting us. The room smelled of dust and rot. "It's dirty," Miriam said. "I can feel it." The bare walls amplified the sound of her voice. I put my hand to her mouth and said, "Shush."

She followed reluctantly.

I needed to talk to Willy in person, and I couldn't take her. Nor could I let her in on what I had in mind.

After my eyes adjusted, I searched until I found a mattress propped against the wall. I pushed it and it plopped to the floor. "Get some sleep," I said.

"On that?"

"Yeah."

"Are you leaving?"

"No," I said.

"You said you had a plan."

"I do. Go to sleep."

"Tell me," she said.

She spread her blanket and lay on the mattress. I sat on the edge for a while. Dust was everywhere. I felt dirty. I could only imagine how she felt, Miriam who treated dirt as original sin. "Miriam, I'm sorry for all this," I said. "For him doing that."

"I made a mess keeping quiet about it. I couldn't tell Mother."

"No, I guess not."

I wrapped my blanket over my shoulders and sat staring at the outline of the window on the floor. Perhaps two hours went by before she fell asleep and I slipped out. It was late, and curfew for minors was in effect. I had to be careful—everything depended on caution. I couldn't risk being stopped by cops. It was past one o'clock, and my work pass was only good up to midnight. Worse, Willy had gone home in the evening. I had to hope for some good luck.

When the downtown bus stopped, I jumped aboard. Every kid knew to take a bus after curfew. You could spend the night riding around town and never be bothered. Cops just didn't stop buses. The driver gave me a knowing look as I climbed aboard. There was but one passenger, an old man with a cane who sat three seats back. I paid the fare and swung into a seat next to the rear door for a quick exit.

That night, for whatever reason, two motor cops stopped the bus at the intersection of Las Vegas Boulevard and Gass Street. I stared at my reflection in the window. Had they found Julie? Maybe Ernie had changed his mind and called the cops? In the corner of my eye I could see that one was looking in my direction as he talked to the driver.

The driver shook his head to whatever question the cop had put to him. The stop, it seemed, had nothing to do with me. The cop said thanks but didn't leave; instead, he came down the aisle. It was Andy, still all nickel buckle and leather belt. My heart beat one-and-three-quarter time to the thud of his heavy boot heels. Before I had a chance to make up a story, he was leaning down looking into my eyes.

"You got ID, kid?"

I pulled out the curfew pass and handed it up to him.

"I know it's past time," I said, "but I work for Willy Bobbins and he wants me for a special party."

"A party?"

"Something. A function. I know you. You're Andy."

The fact that I knew his name gave him pause. He wiped his palm over his chin as he looked at the pass. "Party?" he mused aloud. He gave me the once-over, then dropped my pass on the seat.

"Better get yourself a special pass," he said.

"Yes, sir. I'll tell Mr. Bobbins."

Luck was with me. Willy was in his booth entertaining two poker players whose faces were contorted with laughter. My timing was bad, so I went to the lobby and waited. An hour passed and he'd not walked by. I returned to the restaurant to look in. His booth was empty. I looked about the casino, but no Willy. He was probably in his office. I was afraid to ask, and no one went to Willy's office without being summoned.

Uncertain as to what to do next, I stood there. What else was there to do? I might as well wait for the truth to find me. I crossed my arms and leaned against the wall.

"What're we lookin at, Pete?"

Looking over my shoulder was Willy, leaning against the wall with his arms crossed, mimicking me.

"I was looking for you, sir."

"Ain't you 'sposed'ta be in bed?"

"It's important."

"You need money?"

"No, sir, not money."

"Well, let's go have a seat."

I shook my head. "It's gotta be private."

"Someone doin somethin I should know about? You seen some feds dustin for prints or takin pictures?" He was smiling, but behind the mask was concern.

"No, sir."

"Okay, then, we'll mosey outside an have us a walk."

In front of the El Portal theater Willy stopped and rubbed his little finger inside his ear. He asked what was on my mind. I figured it best to be direct.

"I think I killed Julie," I said.

"Julie? Julie who?"

He didn't seemed at all startled, just skeptical. We walked down Fremont Street, him smiling, me confessing and wondering what he was thinking. The more of my story I told, the more amused he seemed. When I was finished, he said, "And what you want from me?"

"Well, sir, I heard you have a lot of experience in these kinds of things and I was hoping you could . . . give me the right advice."

"Who says I got experience?"

"I heard is all."

He took a cigar out and bit the end off. He sent it sailing into the gutter. "Let's see if I got this right. Some guy named Julie who dates your ma has got your sister on the couch tryin to do somethin with her an you walk in. Have I got that much right?"

"Yes, sir."

"An some sissy who don't play golf shows up with a club an hands it to you an tells you Julie's got it comin. How'm I doin?" He lit a match with his thumb and held the flame to his cigar.

"That's pretty much it."

Studying me, he puffed on the cigar until the tip flamed, and then he flipped the match into the gutter. "You take the club an beat Julie with it?"

"He was coming at me."

He tilted the brim of his hat back and blew smoke up at the lights. "Don't go tellin this story to the po-lice." His cheeks spread in a wide, friendly grin as he flicked the ash off his cigar.

"What should I tell them?"

"Tell them?" He laid a hand on my shoulder and told me not to be dumb.

In the casino he made two calls, then told me to follow him to the cage, where the cashier handed over a set of keys. He ambled casually toward the garage, cordially stopping to exchange words with a player, then a porter, and a floorman in the slot department. He held the unlit stub of his cigar between his teeth and told the floorman a joke. He seemed absolutely at ease. I was in a crisis. Didn't he understand? After they shared a laugh, Willy winked at me.

"Okay, Pete. It's gonna be fine," he said.

We took the elevator to the second floor of the garage, where Willy kept his cars.

In the Cadillac he turned to me and said, "'Is here's man-to-man bidness. Unnerstand?"

"Yes, sir."

Near the corner of Charleston Boulevard and Casino Center Willy pulled into a side lot. He rolled down his window, relit his cigar, and turned on the radio. Settling back, he seemed content to spend the night smoking and listening to Buck Owens and Johnny Cash. He didn't talk, and as I didn't know what to say, I didn't speak either. Eternal minutes later a white four-door sedan that had detective car written all over it pulled in. The driver remained in the car with the engine running. Willy said he'd be right back. When the door slammed I felt sealed in and helpless.

If I had doubts about the driver being a cop those quickly evaporated when the dome light in the other car went on. I placed the driver from when he ate with Willy, always interrupting the meal to make phone calls. He shook Willy's hand, the door shut, and the interior went dark. So much for the man-to-man stuff.

I had no choice but to wait. Soon the dome light went on, and Willy stepped out. He came to my door and leaned his elbow on it. He tapped for me to roll the window down.

"Gimme the key to your place," he said.

From the look on my face he knew my thoughts. "You need me," he said and placed his open palm on the door ledge. "I ain't askin again."

I handed the key over. He asked for the address, then left to pass the key on to the cop. When he returned, Willy was somber. He resumed smoking in silence until the radio blared an ad for an all-you-can-eat buffet. He lowered the volume and turned to me.

"Pete, you trust me?"

I swallowed and looked at my clenched hands, which had been keeping my knees from trembling. "I'm scared is all."

"Good. You'd be stupid not to be."

A half hour passed before the detective returned. The clock atop the Sahara read 2:51. Again Willy left me alone as the two of them talked in the darkened interior of the other car. All I saw of them then was an occasional glow off Willy's cigar. The clock on the Sahara registered 2:58 before the dome light in the cop car came on again. Willy shook the cop's hand, stepped away, and waved as the cop backed out onto the street. This time he was smiling.

He dropped his cigar on the asphalt, crushed it out, and slowly walked back to the car. In his hand was the key to our apartment. I sat by him without talking, remembering how he'd asked if I trusted him. That was my only choice, and I was resigned to it.

Sometime later another Cadillac pulled in. Behind the steering wheel sat Croaker, yawning and rubbing his eyes. He kept the engine running and rolled his window down. Willy got out and spoke to him, dropped the key into his hand, and backed away. As the big car pulled out, the glare of the headlights caught Willy. He seemed distorted, large and somewhat incorporeal, a vision.

He slid in beside me. "Your sister's prob'ly scared to hell an back. Does she still talk like the queen at high tea?"

"Yeah," I said and added, "I hope."

Miriam jumped up and screamed when I pushed open the door. I calmed her down and told her Willy was waiting.

"Willy?"

"Yeah. Everything's okay."

"You left me, Peter."

"Not for long."

"Does he know?"

"I didn't see any other way."

Bundled in her blanket, she followed me to his car parked at the old Strip entrance. He smiled as she slid in the backseat. When she was comfortable, his smile faded. He said everything was taken care of, there was nothing to worry about, just wait and keep quiet. "Ain't nothin happened, unnerstand?" Miriam stared as if plucking his words one at a time from the air. For once she had the good sense to appreciate her position. She nodded.

"Good."

Willy put us up in the hotel that night and the next. When Miriam and I rode up the hotel elevator with him, he said I better be ready to work that coming night. A warm bed and a night's sleep was enough to ask. I said I'd be there on time.

Two days later, when we returned to the apartment, we found it spotless, not a stain on the carpet, not a trace of a struggle, not a sign of Julie anywhere, no clothes, no car, no television—everything gone, but our deep distress.

Mother walked from her bedroom to the living room, opening closet doors, looking frantically for something left behind. She asked about a note.

"No," we answered at once.

"Okay, Peter, what did you do to make him leave?"

"Nothing, Mother," Miriam said. "He didn't do anything. He goes to work and studies and gives us money for the rent. That's more than Julie ever did."

"You never approved of him. He felt terrible." Mother shook her head several times, then sat down and had a good cry, repeating as she did, "I knew he was just waiting for the chance."

Ernie, emerging from a two-day retreat, walked down the staircase with a wine bottle and glass in one hand and a shiny new club, a pitching wedge by the look of it, in the other. He glanced at our open curtains, bowed his head in my direction, and raised the club in a mock salute.

7

Mother lost her own mother and her lover in ten days and had no time to recover from the first before facing the second. She kept asking what he'd said and looked for a note and stared at the telephone. She suspected some certain connection between Miriam and me and Julie's quick and unexpected departure. Our denials of any knowledge fell on deaf ears. Miriam, a less than convincing liar, stuck to the party line. I was proud of her for that, and when Mother cried, Miriam would hold her and assure her that he would come back, just as if she too believed it.

Ernie knocked on the door to tell Mother he'd seen Julie carrying clothes out of the apartment. "I hate to say this, Mrs. Elkins," he added, "but a woman was helping him. A blonde, showgirl, I think, tall, buxom, not nearly so attractive as you, but very strong. She moved his garments with such efficiency. Well, it's heartbreaking, but . . . Oh, my, Mrs. Elkins, don't cry. He's certainly not worth it."

And his car was gone—more proof. What else could she believe? He wasn't the first to desert her, but she was taking it badly, crying and getting down on her knees to pray for his return. I was tempted to tell her the truth, just to let her know she was wasting good prayer on a bad cause. For the first time in years Miriam and I actually wanted a man to come into Mother's life to fill the space. Of course, we hoped he wouldn't be a jerk.

Miriam called Lana, who caught a next-day flight to Las Vegas. Mother's spirits lifted when she heard the news that Lana was coming for a stay. "It'll be great. We'll paint the town," she said. "Red. Okay, pink." She hugged Miriam, then pulled away and did a quick pirouette while pretending she had castanets in her fingers. "Olé!" Miriam shouted.

When Mother left to shower, I said Miriam should tell Mother about Alan, as it might lift her spirits.

Miriam shook her head. "No, no one should know."

"Why not?"

"Jail. It could ruin him."

As Lana's plane pulled into the dock, Mother broke down and sobbed. Miriam looked at me as if I were to blame. I felt bad, but not for anything I'd done. The attendant opened the terminal gate, and the first face to appear was Lana's. When Mother ran to her, Lana dropped her carry-on. They embraced, pulled away from one another and held hands, then shrieked and jumped up and down. Remembering Lana's purple lipstick and proclivity for showing affection, I picked up the valise and kept a safe distance.

Over the next few days the apartment was stuffy; the walls seemed constricting. I gave up my room to Lana and slept on the couch. Lana went about rearranging furniture and planning activities to keep Mother occupied. During the day, while Miriam and I were at school, Mother and Lana went out. In the evening they sat surrounded by cigarette smoke and spoke in whispers.

Miriam and I suspected they were looking for Julie, and this was confirmed when a Sylvester Newberg called and left a message with me for Mother to call. I found his number in the white pages and called. His answering service answered "Newberg Investigations" and said he was out of the office on a case. I told the woman I needed to talk to Sylvester.

"Is this about a case?"

"Sort of," I said. "A missing person."

"Do you wish to leave a message?"

I told her I would call back and hung up. I'd solved part of the mystery.

On Thursday, shortly after Miriam had left for the Blue Onion, the key rattled unexpectedly in the lock. I was hurriedly getting ready for work, buttoning my white shirt, and walked down the hall to see who was there. The door flew open and Lana backed through the doorway bracing Mother, who clung to her with one arm. Lana looked surprised to see me. Mother didn't seem to recognize me at all.

"Give us a hand, Petey," Lana said.

"What happened?"

"She's a little ill."

Mother seemed drunk, face pale and wet, eyes reddened, but neither of them smelled of alcohol. Lana and I tried to guide Mother into her room, but we got in each other's way. "This won't do," I said and started to pick Mother up in my arms. She screamed, a shrill, agonized scream. Lana told me to let her down. I held her arm as she used the walls for support. She collapsed on the bed, rolled to her side, and balled up. She stared at the headboard and told me to go away. Lana nodded for me to do as I was told.

At work I spilled coffee and water, broke a plate and two glasses. The new hostess, Adele Horn, took me aside and asked if I was taking medication. I told her I was fine. She said she'd have to write me up if I screwed up another time.

"Is something bothering you?"

Again I said that I was fine.

Less than an hour later, Willy called me aside.

"Go on home," he said.

"Why?"

"Did I tell you to go, Pete?"

"Yes."

"Then go."

Willy occasionally fired employees only to rehire them within the week, mostly for drinking. It was no shame to be fired by Willy, but I didn't want to be. "Am I fired?"

He chuckled. "Wanna be?"

"I heard you're not really an employee here until you've been fired once," I said.

"Mrs. Horn says somethin's on your mind. Go on an take care of it. Don't come back till—" He looked about. " . . . Things happen we don't want to have happen," he said.

Somehow he knew.

I found the door ajar and Lana slouching on the couch as she smoked. She seemed surprised to see me and stood up.

I started to close the door. "What's going on, Lana?"

"Leave it open," Lana said.

A moan came from Mother's bedroom. Lana looked in that direction. I headed for the bedroom. She blocked my path. "It's okay, Petey. A doctor's coming."

"What's wrong?"

Lana shook her head.

"We'll get her to the hospital."

"Out of the question."

"What's going on?"

A knock came on the door. I kept an eye on Lana and reached back to open it. In the doorway stood a man dressed in a black-and-blue-checked sport coat, white shirt, and no tie. He was short and gray-haired, carried a medical bag and wore tortoiseshell horn-rims. Behind him stood a woman in her early thirties. She was taller by several inches. She wore an all-white smock, white pants, and an impatient look.

"Hello," he said.

"She's in the back room on the left," Lana said.

He thanked Lana and brushed by me, the nurse on his heels. They walked purposefully down the hall, opened Mother's room without knocking, and closed the door. Lana reclaimed her seat on the couch, doused the cigarette she'd been smoking and lit another. I asked what had happened. She told me to turn on the television and not worry. Instead I sat across from her and stared at Mother's door.

An hour passed before the doctor appeared. Lana faced him and asked how it went. He looked at me and motioned to Lana with his head. He took her elbow, guided her outside, and shut the door. I waited two, perhaps three seconds, flung the door open, and stormed out. They looked at me with annoyance that seemed to double when I insisted on knowing what was wrong with my mother. The doctor didn't acknowledge me; instead he told Lana that the nurse would stay with the patient and he'd look in tomorrow. When he turned to leave, I stepped in his path.

"What's wrong with her?"

"Nothing," he said. "I have to go."

Lana grabbed my arm and told me to relax, assured me that everything that needed to be done was being done and that Mother didn't want to go to the hospital. Inside we resumed our stations, Lana chain-smoking, me watching the door. When Miriam came home from work, Lana quickly seized her by the arm and walked her to my room, where they held a whispered conference. Too much mystery for me. I went outside to be alone.

Ernie sat at the edge of the pool drinking wine from a champagne glass. His feet dangled in the water. "Hello, young Peter," he called.

I mustered something that resembled a wave.

"How's the mother?"

The Malibu lights cast grotesque shadows of umbrellas and chair backs on the walls.

I walked closer. "Okay, I guess. No golf club?" I asked. I meant nothing by the question, just small talk, for I'd gotten so used to seeing him taking practice swings that his not having a club seemed strange to me.

"I don't like the new one—no balance," he said. "Never really played the game, Peter. Not in my whole life. Truth." He pulled out his white feet, shriveled from being in the water so long, and examined them.

I sat on the edge of a lounge chair nearby. "I didn't mean anything."

"It's okay. I'm different. You know that, don't you?"

"Yes."

"In college I had a roommate named Kirit, a Hindu. He said he'd been present when Gandhi was leading a prayer in a public square where tens of thousands were gathered. Kirit was a boy at the time and too small to see and the crowd too enormous to allow him to hear, yet he heard every word of the prayer. I asked how that was possible. He said because the prayer was silent and Hindus are good listeners."

I pondered this a moment before asking what it meant.

"I don't know, but it never left my mind. Some things don't."

"What did you say to your roommate?"

"I changed the subject. A wonderful tactic, Pete."

He sipped some wine. "Rotgut," he said and leaned back to look at the stars. "People don't ask for problems, and your mother isn't the first woman to have an abortion."

My insides seemed to shrivel, and my hands and feet felt cold and numb. I waited the feeling out, and when it passed, I said, "Mother has the flu."

"I work with showgirls, Peter. Dr. Smilnick isn't a GP. He specializes in breast implants and abortions."

I stood and backed away. "She has the flu."

"Okay, Peter. She probably does," he said. "I'm probably wrong."

"Damn right you are. What would a queer know anyhow?"

He swallowed his wine and laughed. "Right, what would a queer know anyhow?" There was pain in his eyes, but it didn't bother me. I wanted to hurt someone. He picked up his wine bottle and champagne glass and walked away.

When Mother was strong enough to walk, Lana left. Mother remained heartsick. She claimed she didn't believe Ernie about the blonde and again quizzed Miriam and me, looking for a hint of why Julie might have left. We didn't crack. We kept her hopes going because we had to hide the truth. If he'd walked into the apartment in the next instant, Mother would have taken him back, blonde or no, and worse still, if Miriam had said he'd tried to rape her, Mother would have doubted it.

"He'll be back," Miriam would assure her.

"You think so?"

"When we least expect it."

"Well, maybe."

Miriam suggested a trip to see Uncle Harve and Aunt Vivian, then drive Highway 1 to San Francisco. Mother resisted the idea, said she wanted to be home if Julie came back. Miriam mentioned surprising Lana and reminded her how much fun the four of us used to have.

"Oh, it was fun. Yes." She tilted her head in thought. "I'll have to think about it."

"I've looked at road maps. We could drive to Lake Tahoe with Lana, and you two could gamble. Remember? You laughed at road signs. Yield," Miriam said.

Mother put her palm to her forehead. "Stop a head."

We laughed—at first a spontaneous release of nerves. Then we laughed at each other laughing, and Mother gathered us in her arms as she had when we were young and she was about to leave for work. Then she pressed her head into my chest and cried terrible warm tears that dampened my shirt.

Miriam coaxed Mother to the couch. She told me to wet a washcloth in cold water and bring it. I sat on the arm of the couch as Miriam wiped Mother's tears away and told her how things were going to be wonderful, that we just needed to take a trip and look at the stars at night, and Peter promises not to get sick in the backseat, which made Mother smile. In a few more minutes Mother was talking as if the trip were her idea, saying how important it was to spend time with her brother now that their mother was dead. Mentioning her mother caused a momentary relapse, but most of her tears were spent. She sniffled and stood.

"When should we do this?" she asked.

"A week from Friday," Miriam said. "Can you get time off, Peter?"

"Pete. How many times do I have to tell you?"

"'Pete' sounds so gauche. I don't want to sound ill-bred," she said.

"Ill-bred. We're not royalty."

"Stop it," Mother said, covering her ears. "Don't do this."

Miriam and I exchanged looks. I gently pulled Mother's hands away from her ears.

"Willy will give me time off."

"How about you, Mother?"

"I have vacation coming. I was saving it to go to Hawaii with . . ." Her gaze dropped. "What if he comes back and we're gone?"

I said, "He'll wait, Mother. He has a key. You can leave a note."

Miriam sent me a knowing look. "Good idea."

Mother seemed pleased again to weigh the trip. She raised her head to look at Miriam, who waited in expectation.

"We can take turns driving," Mother said. "My kids are getting so adult. Oh, God, it was just yesterday you were reading stories to Peter in the backseat."

I didn't bother to correct Mother for calling me Peter.

"It'll be fun, Mother. Won't it, Pete?" Miriam said.

Pete, huh? I said nothing could be truer. It was a good idea. Mother felt better, and Miriam, at her best when patching things up, felt great.

"We'll do it," I said.

Miriam smiled. "Then it's done."

That following week an impalpable energy built up in our apartment as we neared the day of departure. We were like manic depressives riding atop high waves or drowning under breakers. Each day we had to find ways to reassure ourselves we were indeed going on a trip together. We had become so accustomed to disappointment that even a task as banal as taking a family road trip took on the dimensions of a major event. Everything in our lives was so patterned around hope followed by disappointment that we expected some calamity to intervene.

We did little things to assure ourselves that we had power over the outcome.

Miriam called Aunt Vivian every other day to tell her we were still coming and asked me at least twice a day if I had everything packed that I needed. Miriam, proud of her idea, wrote an essay about the importance of families traveling together and received an "A." Willy slipped me a fifty-dollar bill and told me to send postcards. I apologized to Ernie for anything I or Mother had ever done to offend him and asked him to watch the apartment. Mother brought her tips out each afternoon and counted them on the table before us, dividing the money into three piles, one for food, lodging, and gas; one for other purchases; one for gambling at Harrah's at Lake Tahoe, where we had a free room for our last two nights, reservations courtesy of Willy Bobbins. As Mother's piles grew, so did her smile, and we had our tips as well. Deciding it wouldn't be fair to surprise her best friend, Mother placed as many calls to Lana as Miriam did to Aunt Vivian.

Our timing was perfect, with spring break coming. All we talked about was the trip. Mother suggested visiting Scooter's grave. Miriam rolled her eyes. I started to blurt out that it was a little weird to visit a dog's grave, but Miriam, as if anticipating my words, quickly agreed that it was a good idea. Mother smiled. She was happy, and we were flying high because for the first time in years, we were the ones who'd made her happy. When we were alone, I told Miriam that visiting a dog's grave was a stupid idea.

"No, it's not."

"You'd think it was stupid if it was my idea."

"It would be stupid if it was your idea."

"I'll tell about Alan."

"You wouldn't."

I gave her my most cryptic smile and turned the television on.

Three days before we were to leave, as Miriam and I got ready to leave for work, Mother counted out three hundred seventy-one dollars that she'd earned the night before, a record. All totaled, in nine days she'd saved fourteen hundred dollars for the trip. Looking at it, something happened to her. It may have struck her at that moment how much money had slipped through her fingers. Her eyes misted up, perhaps from pride at what she'd done, perhaps from shame for what she hadn't, perhaps both. She shed a few tears as she stuffed the money in envelopes and marked each for its special purpose. She said as we headed out the door, "Even if he wanted to come back I wouldn't take him." She looked at us for approval.

In her eyes was the loss of her own mother, the separation from roots, and the scattering of a clan, the years of migratory escape, of chasing the elusive dream, of settling for transient love. We could see she realized we were no longer the children who sat in the backseat and played games. We'd pulled away from her. She wanted to draw us back. Miriam swallowed and put her arms around Mother's neck. She said we had to go to work and added that there would be plenty of time on the trip to talk.

Nothing was said to undermine our spirits. For the next two days, whenever we were together we talked only of good times. It had been years since we'd shared any sense of family. Mother's eyes sparkled again as they had when we used to drive to Las Vegas on weekends. The coming trip was a passage.

That Thursday a high roller from Houston lost nearly half a million at the roulette wheel. Willy sat by the gambler the whole time and told stories as the Texan forged his own downfall by constantly asking that the table limits be raised. When the man's bankroll at last flattened out, Willy put him in a limousine to the airport and slumped down in his booth.

"Pete, bring chili and lots of crackers," he said.

"Right away," I said.

"I'm a lucky man. You know why, Pete?"

"No, Willy."

He tilted his hat back with his thumb. "Neither do I."

When Ruben Lee joined him, I brought a second bowl of chili, toasted garlic bread, and a cherry Coke to the table. Willy looked up, but Ruben Lee, as was his practice, ignored me. I set the food before him and the drink near his right hand.

"I wanted a hamburger patty and fries," Ruben Lee said.

He was looking to foul the moment. He was predictable that way. "Medium?" I asked and reached for the bowl.

"Leave it," he said.

Willy was in too good a mood to have anyone upset him. He reached over and pulled the bowl to his side and told me to order a burger and bring some more crackers. When I returned, he was pointing a spoon at Ruben Lee and lecturing him. He looked at me and said, "Been tellin Ruben Lee bout your vacation. He's gonna ride you on home tonight."

Ruben Lee glanced up long enough to let me know he didn't favor the idea.

After I cleared the table, Willy told me to hang my apron up and punch out. He shook my hand and slipped me a twenty as he did, then told me to wait by the north door for Ruben Lee.

Ruben Lee showed up, putting his coat on.

"Come on, kid," he said.

His new 'Vette was a '62, red and white with a custom leather interior and a 283-inch V-8 short block with a racing cam fed by three two-barrel carburetors—everything I'd dreamed of. I settled gingerly on the leather seat and ran my hand over the dash. He turned the engine over. The sound of the tuned headers thrummed off the walls of the covered garage. I felt the vibration from my feet to my neck.

"Where you live?" he asked.

"On Boston off Tam."

He thought about this a moment, then said, "I used to screw a showgirl who lived over there. Stopped 'cause she was so tall. Hell, two inches taller than me. Great fuck, but I don't think she liked it, just did it 'cause of who I am."

"Maybe she liked you," I said, trying to be agreeable.

"You dumb about everything? The fucking expert. You ever been laid?"

I didn't answer, which he took as an admission.

He revved the engine, backed out and thrust the gearshift into first. "There's not much to know about women. Pretty ones go to the highest bidder. Ugly ones go to anyone that'll have them. That's life. I get the pretty ones. You get the leftovers."

"I never thought about it like that."

He studied me for a moment. "Never figured me for a philosopher, did you?"

"No, I guess not."

"Well, I am, Petey. I think about life a lot." He released the clutch pedal and left a six-foot streak of rubber on the parking lot.

We turned the corner at thirty and were doing almost forty on Ogden Street when a panhandler stepped off the curb into the path of the car. Ruben Lee swerved to the left and slammed his foot on the brake. He brought the car to a stop at Main Street, rammed it in reverse, and drove backward against traffic until parallel with the man he'd missed.

"What're you thinking about, old man?"

"Nothin, mister. Sorry."

"Sorry, hell. I aughta kick your ass."

The man swallowed and started to walk around the car, but Ruben Lee pulled the Corvette forward to block him.

"I don't want no trouble, mister," the man said.

"Damn right you don't," Ruben Lee said and calmly let the clutch out. He smiled and looked back through the rearview mirror as we drove to Main Street. Taking a deep breath, he tuned the radio before heading north.

"I live the other way," I said.

"Do you think I'm stupid?"

"No."

"That's good, 'cause I'm not."

We drove west on Bonanza to Highland, then north again into the West Side, the black section of town, a section that common sense told most white people to avoid. I asked where we were going. He fired up a cigarette with the car lighter and blew the smoke at the windshield.

"I've got something to do first."

"Oh."

He downshifted for a right turn. "I'm dangerous. You know why, Petey?"

"No."

"No? Why would you know. It's 'cause I don't know what I'm going to do sometimes. Hell, I could decide to let you out right here. Let some nigger shove a knife in you for your tips. What'd you earn today, Petey? Ten dollars? Enough worth getting killed for?"

He drew off the cigarette, which he let dangle from his lips.

I didn't like his game, didn't want to play but had no choice. "No, I wouldn't like that."

"'Course you wouldn't, but that wouldn't stop me. You know what does?"

"No."

"The old man."

He turned twice, once north to D Street and once east into a neighborhood where little houses constructed from cinder blocks lined both sides of the street. The houses had flat roofs and yards of Bermuda grass that had yellowed in the winter. He cracked his window to toss out the cigarette butt. A dog barked.

I thought, for no particular reason, about Clarence, the porter Ruben Lee had beaten, so I asked, "Why'd your brother let Clarence go?"

Ruben Lee looked at me out of the corner of his eye. "Don't ask what's none of your business."

He parked in the shadows of an elm in an alley by a small stucco cottage with a tar-shingle roof and chipped paint. Shades were drawn on all the windows. He reached under the seat and came up with an automatic pistol, which he laid on his lap.

"For squirrels," he said and turned up the volume on the radio, which was playing "Runaway." He waited until the song finished before shutting off the motor. He cracked open the door, looked around, and said, "Wait here."

He stuffed the gun inside his waistband, walked to the house, and knocked. The porch light came on and the door opened, partially. A black man peered out and looked from side to side, then stepped aside to let Ruben Lee enter. The porch light went out. I locked my door.

A dog barked somewhere up the alley, an alarm, one among many that were ringing in my head. Two young black men strolled up the alley, their hands shoved deep in their pockets. They ambled over to the Corvette. One ran his hand over the paint. "Oo-wee, some fine paint," he said and sidled up next to my door. His back to me, he leaned against the window and tried the door handle while the other stepped up to the driver's side. The driver's door flew open. The dome light illuminated his face as he slid into the seat without noticing me.

When he realized I was next to him, he asked what the fuck I was doing there as if it were his right to ask, as if I had somehow intruded. I swallowed and glanced out to see if the other had moved. The man beside me said, "I'm checking it out, man. You see something wrong with that?"

"It's not mine," I said, "but the guy who owns it has a gun."

He laughed and felt around for keys, running his hand over the carpet and the dash. "Don't fuck with me about no man with a gun. Where are the keys?"

"The man with the gun has them."

"Yeah? I can smell your fear."

He was about to say more, but the porch light switched on and the door opened.

Ruben Lee passed through the glare of the bare bulb and stepped down onto the half-brown lawn. In one hand he held a small paper bag. As he approached, he noticed the man sitting next to me and drew his pistol. He shouted to the man to get out of his car, but the one sitting next to me was too stunned to move.

Ruben Lee jerked the door open. "What the fuck you doing in my car?"

The man looked up. "Ah, man, don't get uptight."

"Uptight? Up fucking tight?" Ruben Lee shoved the barrel of the pistol up to the man's jaw. "Get out before I empty this sonofabitch in you."

The man didn't move. He closed his eyes and said, "Don't think I can move just now."

Ruben Lee kept the gun stuck in the hollow of the man's cheek. Neither spoke. The man, knuckles knotted, forehead shining with sweat, gripped the steel door handle as if it were a life preserver. The light went off, and it seemed the world was pitch-black.

Between pants, the man said, "Okay. Go easy, man."

Slowly Ruben Lee eased away but kept the gun aimed at the man's face. "Come on now," he said, his voice edgy. "No one here wants trouble, do we?"

I noticed that the second man had moved away, and I looked around for him. I saw him going around the back of the car.

"There's one behind you," I said.

Without hesitation Ruben Lee said, "You shoot this one, Petey. I'll kill the motherfucker sneaking up," and he swung around and fired, the sound careening into the night with a seemingly endless echo. The man shouted, "Motherfucker!" and dashed for safety in the darkened alley.

Without hesitation, Ruben Lee stuffed the gun in the other's face. "Think you can get out now?" he asked.

The man glared as he climbed out. "You ain't gonna shoot?" he stood his ground, staring.

I could envision sirens blaring, cops asking questions, no trip, Miriam telling me I'd done it again. "He'll shoot," I said. "That's Willy Bobbins's son."

The man asked if that was a fact. Ruben Lee said nothing. A step at a time, the man cautiously backpedaled. Ruben Lee swung inside and slammed the door.

"Why'd you let him in?"

"He just opened the door and sat down."

"And you just let him."

"No."

"Ah, what the hell."

He fired up the engine and let it idle, then opened the sack from which he pulled out a gelatin capsule. He separated the halves, careful not to spill any powder, and held the powdered half to his nose, closed one nostril and sniffed the contents at once. He handed me the sack and told me to put it under my seat. I did as I was told. I would have done about anything he wanted. I just wanted to get away from him.

"Petey Boy. You deserve a ride in my car after that. Yes, sir." He downshifted and pulled away from the house. Halfway up the alley, he turned on the lights.

I wanted to ask what that was in the bag, but that was out of the question. He cranked up the volume of the radio, drove up Carey Avenue to Tonopah Highway and turned north, riding the accelerator. The Corvette seemed to get lighter and lighter. Long before Lone Mountain Road the speedometer hit the century mark, and the night was a wash of black with only the rapidly vanishing white lines showing in the headlights.

At the Mt. Charleston turnoff he finally slowed to make a U-turn. He looked at me with the dull, flat eyes of an idiot and grinned. The city blinked in the distance as we drove back toward it, slower now. At the first red light he stopped and kept staring at the dash panel for several seconds even after the light turned green. I told him it was green. He gave me a dull-eyed glance and drove into the intersection at a crawl. It was a six-mile walk to the apartment, but I told him to stop and let me off, that I would walk home. He looked at me as if I were part of a tangled thought.

"Petey?"

"Yeah."

"Fuck you." He jabbed the accelerator with his foot.

The elms in the center divider ran together as the road disappeared under the tires. Ruben Lee laughed. I closed my eyes in prayer, nothing too formal, just a few panicked words begging forgiveness, a few more days of life, and a body in one piece.

We might have missed the tree if he'd not mistaken the brake for the clutch when he tried to downshift. The car shimmied, then whirled sideways again and again. The last thing I noticed in the headlights was the approach of the unyielding trunk of a Chinese elm. The stop was marked by a crunching of metal and fiberglass. I ended up on the floorboard in a tuck.

I noticed first the smells of dirt, burnt rubber, and gasoline, which told me I'd survived. I tested my body, first a digit, then a limb at a time. Though a general numbness engulfed me, I was certain nothing was broken, so I slowly crawled to the seat.

What remained of the car sat angled on the thick trunk as if prepared for launching. The engine was dead, but the radio still blared, a turn signal blinked, and the headlight beams shot upward through a halo of dust. My door was jammed shut, while the other dangled on its hinges.

I crawled over the console, braced myself with my hands, and dropped to the ground. When I landed I realized I'd injured my left knee. I sat down. The radio played "Hard Day's Night." I called out for Ruben Lee. But he was nowhere around. Cars began to stop beside the road. A man rushed over and told me not to move. A crowd gathered.

I sat looking at the splintered remnants of a dream. It was odd, the angle at which the car sat, as if it had tried to scale the tree and fell back in the attempt. And the glowing headlights, aimed skyward, seemed an act of sheer defiance. I wondered not how I'd survived, but how the headlights had come through intact.

The first cop to arrive was Andy. He asked if I could move. I nodded. He told me to stand and hand over my driver's license.

I said, "I don't drive."

He looked at the shattered side of the Corvette and said, "You sure don't." He reached inside and turned off the headlights and radio.

He and another cop measured skid marks, took statements from witnesses, and searched the car's contents. Though occasionally one would look in my direction, neither asked me anything until after the tow truck arrived. Then Andy, paper bag in one hand and pistol in the other, asked if it was my car.

"No, sir," I said.

He helped me to my feet and held up the paper sack. "Guess this isn't yours either."

I shook my head. "No, sir."

He showed the gun. "Or this?"

"No, sir."

He told me to turn around, that I was under arrest for reckless driving, grand theft auto, and possession of narcotics. He drew my arms behind me, and as the handcuffs closed over my wrists, he asked if I had anything I wanted to say.

"I'm supposed to go on a trip," I said.

"You are going on a trip," he said and led me to a patrol car pulled up to the curb.

8

Mother came, but because of the charges against me, she wasn't allowed to take custody of me or visit until the next day. I was stripped naked, dusted for lice, and left in a holding cell. Several times during the night someone passed by the cell, tapped the metal door and called, "Hey, yo, meat." The voice was high, almost high enough to be female, but definitely male.

In the morning after breakfast, I was led to a small room where Mr. Handleman, who was for some reason called a counselor, instructed me on what behavior was expected and which rules netted what punishment. There was no fighting and no loud or aggressive language. I would be searched daily, and as a juvenile, I had no rights, not even to an attorney unless I was certified as an adult. I would be housed in a dorm, part of the population until my hearing. If I made trouble, I'd be isolated. If I was violent, I would be chained and possibly moved to the county jail. In addition I had to follow rules about brushing teeth and making the bed and wearing clothes. "The rules," he said, "are in place for your protection."

I limped into the lounge, where several boys slouched on chairs and couches. There were two bookshelves with a smattering of books, a Ping-Pong table, and a television bolted to the wall, none in use. I waited by the Ping-Pong table. The boys sat segregated by race, except in one corner where three blacks my age congregated in lounge chairs with a white boy—Louie Skyles. He nodded to one of his companions. The lanky boy looked over his shoulder, sized me up, then stood and strolled by. He asked if I played Ping-Pong.

I recognized the high-pitched voice. "No."

"Well, then, get the fuck away from it, meat."

I told him I wasn't looking for trouble.

He gave an amused sneer. "What the fuck you in here for? We're all in trouble. We're all troubled. Get the pict-sh?" He jabbed a finger in my chest and walked away.

Near midmorning I was interviewed by a representative of juvenile court, who told me how my hearing was to be conducted. She said that I wasn't considered a criminal or a convict but an offender and asked if I was prepared to plead guilty and request probation or sentencing to Spring Mountain, the county camp for male offenders.

"It makes things go better that way. Understand the charges are severe enough for you to end up in Elko or perhaps prison in Carson City. Cooperation is considered. You're not even sixteen. Save yourself, Peter."

She left me with a statement form to fill out, saying it was best to keep the facts as simple as possible, just describe how I stole the car and where I got the heroin. She added that if I was a junkie, I should inform her so that the nurse would be available for me during withdrawal.

"I'm not," I said.

"Suit yourself, Peter. You won't be so tough when the symptoms hit you." She left.

I watched the clock. Exactly thirty minutes later she returned. Upon seeing the blank page in front of me, she said that it would be noted in my file. I was given linen and moved to a dorm shared with five others my age, one of who was the tall black boy. His name was Lyle.

"Rhymes with style, dig it, 'cause I'm wild," he said and sang, "Tonight you're mi-ine compl-eet-ly . . ."

The others laughed.

After lunch I was taken to a visitor's cage where Mother waited. She'd been smoking heavily, and I could smell it on her as she kissed me. I suppose she wanted to salvage something, make the previous night's events vanish and take me to the car and go.

"They won't let Miriam in," Mother said.

I nodded.

"I told them you were a good boy and this was just a misunderstanding."

I didn't mention the knock on the cell or seeing Louie, couldn't tell her anything to worry her, so told her it was okay, that people were nice and trying to help, that a woman from the court had said I could get probation.

"Then you did those things?"

I shook my head.

"Then why should you go on probation?"

I shrugged. She asked why I couldn't be like Miriam.

I said, "Mother, no one's like Miriam."

"If you followed her example, we'd be on the road right now. You've been in so much trouble, your black eyes, and I just know . . . Julie left because of you. You could've tried." She waited for me to say I was sorry. I did.

"Well, I'm sorry, too," she said. "You've ruined your life. Don't expect me to spend good money on a lawyer." She chewed at her lower lip and looked down. "Maybe this is for the best. Maybe you'll learn a lesson."

I said good-bye, walked to the door, and pressed the button. She was still seated as the door clanged shut.

I sat on the cot by myself, assessing my situation. It wasn't good. Lyle was obviously the boss, followed by Trevor, a blond kid with a crooked nose who looked meaner than Lyle. The rest seemed pretty content to follow the leader. Sammy, a kid with a booming voice, and Stewart, who was small and had a harelip and pimples, stuck together but seemed to abide by whatever Lyle or Stewart said. The last boy, Mike, whom Lyle called Michelle, was too scared to talk or even laugh. He flinched whenever Trevor came near.

Lyle walked over and propped a foot on my cot. "Know what Louie said?"

"Louie? I didn't know he could talk."

"He won't like that."

"Probably not. I said I wasn't looking for trouble."

"That's cute. Stew, don't you think that's cute?"

"Cute, very cute." Trevor stripped off his shirt and flexed his muscles. "He's a punk," he said to Lyle, who took his foot off the bunk and walked away.

When the lights went out, I lay on my back in thought. Somehow I had to prove I didn't do what I was charged with, but I had to do it without incriminating Ruben Lee. I had to consider my debt to Willy. He wouldn't be kind to someone who implicated his son in a crime.

The heater vents expired dry, hot air that muffled sound. I couldn't sleep. I listened for signs. Of what, I was unsure, breathing, perhaps evidence of others sleeping. It was too silent. They were waiting, Lyle and Trevor. Didn't Lyle have passage to the halls after lights went out, after we were forbidden to go about?

The door opened and a flashlight beam danced from cot to cot. I weighed doing something extreme, like jumping up and shouting as if I'd gone mad, but I heeded the counselor's advice and turned my head away before the guard shined the light on me. He flicked off the light and shut the door. His footsteps faded away, and silence pervaded.

Others began to stir. I lay feeling my heart try to escape my chest. Though it was almost pitch-black, I could make out forms converging. My body went rigid. Then they surrounded me.

"What?" I said, but it wasn't really a question.

"Shut up."

The door swung open, and Louie's voice whispered to Trevor and Lyle. I sat up. All at once they swarmed me and clamped their hands on my ankles and wrists. A hand covered my mouth and nose. The point of a knife pricked the flesh below my jaw.

"You talk, I stick. Dig, motherfucker?" It was Lyle talking.

I couldn't breathe. I struggled against a hand that had cut off my air, but it was useless. The weight of all five held me down. Louie told them to roll me over. I resisted, and for this I was punched in the ribs.

"No bruises," Louie said.

I couldn't appeal to their decency. So I fought them. I struggled, but they managed to turn me on my belly. Hands pawed at my waistband. I squirmed, but that seemed to aid whoever was pulling at my pants. The hand was gone from my mouth now. I said time after time, "No, no."

"I'll cut you."

The blade punctured my throat, slightly, just enough to draw blood and let me know.

"No."

The hand pressed down on my mouth again. "Shut the fuck up," Louie said and asked the others if my pants were off.

Trevor said, "Yes."

"You feel this, darlin?" Louie asked.

I felt an erection probing my cheeks, heard his panting and felt his breath on my back. As his fingers clawed at my lower back, I tightened up and for the second time in two nights prayed. I begged forgiveness and cataloged every wrong I'd ever done, especially Julie. Certain that this was retribution for that, I told Him that I was repentant, unworthy, weak, and I was sure this was what He must have wanted to hear—fear and supplication. And I wanted desperately for Him to hear me and stop this.

"Give him a couple of good ones," Lyle said.

Several hard blows landed on the back of my head. Still, I held on. Then I felt the fierce point of the blade jab my testicles, and Lyle said, "I'll turn you into a girl." Louie laughed. My prayers evaporated. I clutched my fists and closed my eyes. As he forced himself in, I felt tissue rip apart, felt my humanity dissolve.

In the morning I awoke from a fitful half sleep and remembered right away. I couldn't kid myself. There were bloodstains as proof. Mike gave me a compassionate look. I knew where I was in the pecking order and why Mike kept his gaze on the tiles. He must have had mixed feelings to see someone new come along. Now I, like he, looked at the floor. If it had been in my power to kill, I would have.

Lyle came over as I sat on the edge of my cot.

"Say anything and you'll be one sorry motherfucker. Dig?"

I didn't answer.

"I said, dig, meat?"

Still staring at the linoleum, I nodded.

"It'll be your turn when some new meat comes along. We share. Brothers, you know. It ain't all that bad."

But I knew it wouldn't happen again.

A knot filled my chest like a tangle of barbed wire. I kept dwelling on their rules, edicts that served those who chose to ignore them. Rules, rules—I had to be stronger than rules, just as Louie and Lyle were.

That afternoon, with three guards watching, I scanned the lounge for Louie; he was nowhere, but my second choice was. I limped up to Lyle, who was talking with Trevor and Sammy. He looked up to see what I had in mind, but I set my gaze on the floor like a servile creature currying favor. I said I had a question.

"Well, ask, meat."

"I don't want them to hear," I said, pointing to the others.

"No?"

I shook my head and leaned down to whisper. "About last night," I began, then before he could react, I grabbed his head and bit his ear. He emitted a howl that pierced every wall in the building and fought to break free, but I held him with that strength that came from Mother's dirt-farmer line and primal rage.

A couselor set off the alarm. Two others grabbed me by my neck and choked me, tried to drag me to the ground but couldn't. Lyle flailed about with his arms, struggling to get free, but I was locked to him. Even as guards choked and beat on me, I gouged his eyes, raked my nails over his face and bit harder. When they pried me away, half of Lyle's ear came off.

He touched his bleeding ear, and when he realized what I'd done, he came after me, punching air and shouting. By then more guards had arrived. One tackled him and took him to the floor. Blood spread over the linoleum. I held his ear between my teeth and smiled maniacally.

A guard told me to spit it out. My smile widened as he held out his open hand for me to drop it in. I looked down at Lyle, who sat holding the wound. A single guard held him down by the shoulders. Lyle had no fight left in him. I spat the ear in his face. I was still smiling as they dragged me away.

It wasn't in the rules, but it had worked. They locked me in solitary in a six-by-three-foot cell while Lyle was taken to the hospital to have his ear sewn on. After the metal door slammed, a counselor shouted that I was on my way to the county jail as soon as a judge signed the order. I would worry about jail tomorrow; tonight I'd be safe. Secure now, I lay on my cot in that cramped chamber and let fatigue take me into the night.

The third day was considerably different from the first two. Breakfast of oatmeal and a slice of half-toasted bread was served to me, after which two guards handcuffed me and escorted me to an interview room. A white-haired man in a rust-colored sport coat sat behind a bare table. The guards seated me before him. He said he was a doctor, a psychiatrist, and was to evaluate me. He asked if I would behave if he had the handcuffs removed.

"Yes, sir."

He motioned for the guard to unlock them. I sat before him with my hands on my knees.

"You know why you're here?"

"Yes, sir."

"Why's that?"

"Because of yesterday."

"And what happened?"

"Didn't they tell you?"

"Yes, but I want to hear your version."

"Mine? It's the same as theirs."

"I see."

He leaned forward. "Peter. May I call you Peter?"

"Pete."

"Okay, Pete. We're here to help you. The juvenile court is here to look out for your welfare. . . . Do you understand that?"

I had no more reason to trust them than I did Lyle or Louie. "I guess."

"We can't endanger any ward of the court. Surely you can see that, can't you?"

"Yes, sir."

"Good."

"Then, sir, you should keep me away from the others."

"Why?"

"I can't say."

"Can't? Do you mean you won't say?"

I covered my eyes for a moment and told myself not to be weak, not to speak out. And I was filled with shame, not for what I'd done to Lyle but for what I'd let them do to me. "It's the same thing, sir."

"Are you dangerous, Pete?"

"No, sir."

"But you have a terrible temper?"

"Can't say, sir."

He asked the guards to leave us alone. When they were gone, he wanted to know what I was holding back, what I was afraid to say. I didn't answer. He seemed to know already.

"Did that boy hurt you?"

I pressed my lips tightly. I didn't want to speak of what had happened, and I was afraid if I started to talk, I wouldn't stop.

"You're in for drugs. Heroin. Do you use?"

I shook my head.

"I see. You don't seem the type, and you don't seem the type to . . . bite a boy's ear off either."

I stared at my folded hands. I shook my head and told him I couldn't talk, that solitary was fine with me.

"Do you really want to be away from the rest of the population?"

I nodded.

"There will be a hearing later to determine if you should be remanded to the county jail. Should I tell them not to send you there?"

"I'm not crazy, sir. I just want to go home. We were supposed to go on a trip yesterday, my mother and Miriam, and . . . I just want to go home." Despite my best efforts to control myself, tears came. I wiped them off my nose and chin with the back of my hand. I sat crying, unable to look up. I didn't want to see another human face.

He made no effort to reassure me. When I was through, he called the guards in and said they would take me to my cell. I thanked him, for what I wasn't sure, but I felt better.

On the way to my cell, we passed Sammy and Trevor. Trevor gave me a hard look, but I stared back. I understood the rules, not the rules recited in the counselor's monotone, but the actual rules. There was only one—survival.

The next day two unexpected visitors came, strangers in charcoal-gray suits who wore polished wing-tip shoes. The taller one introduced himself as Special Agent Ruckles and the other as Special Agent Goldfarb. Ruckles told me to take a seat.

"I suppose you're wondering why two federal agents are visiting you."

"No, sir."

He raised his eyebrows to Agent Goldfarb. "Ike, we've got us a smart boy. Yes, sir."

"I bet he won't have trouble understanding what's in his best interest," Goldfarb said.

"Right. I don't think we should beat around the bush with a kid this bright. So, Petey, you've gotten yourself into a batch of trouble."

"Don't call me Petey," I said.

"No, not Petey. Peter, of course, Peter. Do you understand your situation?"

"I don't," I answered.

He thought about my answer a moment and looked to Goldfarb for approval. When Goldfarb nodded, he continued, "Here's the quick of it. You've been charged with possession of heroin, grand theft auto, reckless driving, and mayhem."

"Mayhem?"

"You bit a kid's ear off."

The crime of mayhem—hearing it reduced to one word like that made it sting. Crime, murder. And if they knew about Julie?

"What if we could guarantee probation?"

"I just want to go home."

Goldfarb winked. "Sure you do. A boy your age. This is no environment for a good kid."

"Listen to Ike," Ruckles said. "Here's how you can help yourself."

Ruckles told me they knew I worked for Willy, and that he seemed to like me. They didn't want me to testify, just keep them up to date on who came to visit. Goldfarb spread a packet of photographs out on the table and asked if I recognized any faces. I did, nearly half, but I told them I didn't. Though they kept after me for the better part of an hour, I didn't falter.

"He doesn't seem to want help," Ruckles said.

"Maybe he'd like to go back into the dorm with what's-his-name."

"Lyle," I said.

"Is that what you want?"

I looked at the door and shrugged.

"We'll leave it like this," Goldfarb said. "Think about it. We'll be back in a day or two."

Lyle, the side of his head bandaged, returned to the detention hall late the next morning. At lunch he sat at an adjacent table with his buddies and glared. The silence was broken by the sound of silverware scraping plates and occasional whispers. Mike thanked me for biting off Lyle's ear and said Lyle's mother had threatened to sue, claiming that jailing her son with an animal like me violated his rights.

A little later Mike said he was scared. I told him I was too, that everybody was probably scared and should be. Louie was still nowhere to be seen, but if he came around, he was next. Out of curiosity I asked Mike what he was in for.

"I stabbed my stepfather in his sleep."

"You did?"

He nodded.

"Kill him?"

"No. The ambulance got there too soon."

I was charged administratively with violations of rules governing violence and weapons. The staff conducted a shakedown and found the blade that Lyle had used on me under my mattress. I was informed of the charge by one of the counselors as he accompanied me to an interview room.

"Maybe this man can help," he said as he opened the door for me.

A tall man with salt-and-pepper hair and bushy eyebrows stood as we entered. A lawyer who occasionally ate with Willy, he wore an expensive Western-cut suit and a blue silk tie. His was one of the pictures in the agents' packet. Smiling, he thanked the detention counselor and asked him to leave us.

"Mr. Elkins," he said, reaching for my hand to shake, "I'm Ted Lyons. Your attorney. Do you remember me?"

I shook his hand. "Steak and eggs, medium rare, over medium, coffee, and a glass of ice. You spoon ice into your coffee to cool it. Ketchup on the hash browns."

"Very good. What do I eat for lunch?"

I shrugged. "Never served you lunch. Saturday breakfast."

He sat and motioned for me to do the same.

"Mother hired a lawyer?" I asked.

"I can't divulge who hired me, but no matter who pays the bill, I'm working for you." He smiled again.

"Did Willy hire you?"

When he didn't answer, I crossed my arms and leaned back. I was leery of all adults.

"You don't believe me?"

"I'm supposed to believe whatever adults say. They're on my side. All of them. Just ask."

He smiled. "We'll get along fine. Don't trust anyone from here on."

He asked what the court representative had advised about the procedures. I explained as best I could remember. He moved on to the charges, touching on them one at a time.

"As far as the car theft, that charge is gone. The owner refused to sign a theft form. As for the heroin, it was in the car, not on you, and the car isn't yours. The reckless driving presents some difficulty, but the real problem is the charge of mayhem. Statements from the staff say the attack was unprovoked. What do you say?"

I sat looking at my closed fist, my stomach knotted.

"From what I hear, you're not the kind who would act without provocation. What happened?"

I just stared at my hands, squeezed them tighter to stop them from trembling, and ran my tongue over my lips. Show no weakness, I thought.

"I'm your attorney, Peter. I can't repeat anything you tell me without your permission. Not a word, even if I'm ordered to by a judge."

I looked over my shoulder at the door.

"Do you believe me?"

"Willy sent you," I said.

"I can't say."

"Willy calls me Pete."

"Do you want me to call you Pete?"

I nodded.

"You were provoked?"

It seemed excruciatingly dry and stuffy in the room. I swallowed and licked my lips. He set his gaze on me, his eyes dark and kind, nothing menacing present in them.

"Yes."

"Do you want to tell me?"

"No."

He held his hands palms open before his face, then entwined the fingers. "Pretty bad, I'd say."

I balked as before, refusing to speak, out of shame and out of fear that I might cry and appear weak. I didn't want Willy thinking I was weak. The lawyer sat nodding and waiting, asking an occasional question. He prodded gently, hinting at first that he already knew the truth, until finally he said, "The sonofabitches hurt you, didn't they, Pete?"

"Sir?"

"Someone was armed. When the lights went out. When you couldn't help yourself. They did, didn't they?"

"Sir, I can't . . ." The first of the tears began.

He squeezed my shoulder. "Nothing to be ashamed of, Pete. You couldn't stop them."

I didn't realize how bad the shame was until that moment when I began to tell all.

When he'd finished his notes, he used the phone to make a call to the district court judge. Within the hour I was at the county hospital being examined by two physicians. They probed my rectum with a scope, took specimens, and asked a battery of questions, mostly embarrassing. My answers frustrated them. A counselor stood nearby, monitoring my every move, listening to my answers.

Mr. Lyons entered the examining room toward the end and told the counselor we needed privacy for a few minutes. The counselor hesitated, so Mr. Lyons quoted my constitutional guarantees and added that it appeared I was being treated as an adult offender.

"He's not likely to run away or attack us, if those are your concerns."

The counselor weighed this for a moment and left. Mr. Lyons conferred with the doctors, who confirmed what I'd said. He asked if their reports would substantiate force. Yes. Would they be willing to testify? Yes. They talked of me in the third person, in clinical terms; I was a subject that had checked positive on tests. "Thank you," he said. "I'd like to talk to Pete alone."

When the doctors left, the counselor stuck his head inside. Mr. Lyons reached to close the door and said we weren't finished. Alone with me, he explained that matters were under control, that I would remain in isolation until a hearing. He asked if I had anything more to say, and I asked if he would pass on a message to Willy. "If I see him, but only as a favor to you."

"Tell him two agents came in with photographs and asked questions."

"They did what?"

"They wanted to know who I recognized. One picture was of you."

He seemed astounded. "They can't question you without a court order and without an attorney being present. How the hell did they know you were even booked into the detention center?" He asked their names, and as he headed out the door, he told me not to worry.

I was given a new cell with two cots. The door opened sometime after dinner. In the doorway stood Mike. He was holding linen in his hands. When the door closed and locked, Mike dropped the bedding and sat down.

"Trevor says they'll kill us. They'll wait and kill us," he said.

I shook my head. "It's all talk."

Knuckles tapped on the door. "I'll see you again," said Louie Skyles's voice.

"See?" Mike said.

"He has to sleep too, doesn't he?" I asked.

Mike smiled.

I sat across from Willy in the visitors' room, his legs sprawled on both sides of the chair, hat tilted back, his face serious as walking on broken glass. He gave me a wink, but looked at me with eyes that could open a passage to the one thought you wanted to hide. He pulled an envelope from his coat pocket and set it between us. I reached for it, but he pinned it down with his hand.

"Can't take nothing from me, Pete." He nodded his head toward the counselor who monitored us.

"Oh."

"We'll get around to what's in there. So, how they treatin you?"

"Like shit, Willy."

"Watch your mouth, Pete," he said. He tapped his fingers on his knee. "Bet that's the gawdamn truth. Gotta get you back to work. You ain't no good at wipin tables and moppin floors, but you kind'a got to be a fixture."

"I only ever spilled one coffee."

"So you did."

"Willy, I don't want to stay here."

He looked at the envelope. "You know I don't read so good. 'Course, you do, readin about that Gatsby fella an all. You remember that Dan Cody, the rich fella, the one with the yacht, took a likin to that Gatsby?" He remembered better than I did. It took me a moment.

"Heard you bit a fella's ear off. Heard was all, not sayin it's a fact. They ain't no facts in a jailhouse, 'at's a fact. But I also heard he had it comin."

"What about Dan Cody?"

"I'm fixin to get to that. Just want you to know I been keepin track on you. I was about your age when the Mexicans put my pa in jail. I ever tell you?"

"No."

He removed his hat. "We was borrowin cattle, Mexican cattle, mind you. 'Bout the time America sent soldiers to kick the kaiser's butt. Good market even for mangy Mexican longhorns, so Pa got this idea. This ol Don got more cows an you could spit on in a year an he was peddlin 'em to the kaiser. So, Pa an me . . . I forgot how long a story this is. Guess I'll save 'er for later when you're out."

"I like it so far," I said.

"'Course, near as good as that Fitzgerald fella an a sight better'n some others you read me."

"Willy, some agents came to . . ."

"Shush." He picked up the envelope. "Pete, this here's got papers in it concerns you an me. I sorta went behind your back on this one—in the best spirit. I ask't your ma first 'fore I had the papers drawed up by a lawyer. The short is that if you agree, I'll be your guardian."

I stared at the envelope, which he held lightly between his fingers as if holding a winning hand. My guardian? "What about my mother?"

"Like I said, I talked to her. She already signed. It's kinda up to you."

"Why?"

He let the envelope dangle. "I ain't sayin I'm no Dan Cody, but . . . you trust me, don't you, Pete?"

"I guess."

"Somethin you wanna know, just ask. Anythin."

I thought a moment and the only question that came to mind was why Clarence got off so easy. "Why'd you let Clarence get off so light?"

The question amused him. "Weren't my responsibility. He's Croaker's cousin, come here 'cause he ask't Croaker for a job. Think 'bout that. You wouldn't wanna be Clarence."

"No."

"So, what'a you think, Pete? You wanna sign so I can get you outta here?"

"Mother signed?"

"Said it was for you. She's still your ma an you better treat her right."

I bowed my head. Too much had happened too fast for me to absorb.

Willy picked up the envelope. "Ever'thing'll be taken care of an I can take you on home."

We sat at a shiny oak table in the judge's chambers. Mr. Lyons said that I, as his client, and my guardian wouldn't pursue a rightful civil action against the juvenile court as stipulated in an agreement with the district attorney. I looked at Willy, who sat next to Mother. Dressed in a new white linen suit she'd bought for the occasion, she watched impassively. Sometimes she would glance at

Willy, who invariably met her eye. Something passed between them, something secretive. The judge asked if I understood the agreement.

"Yes, sir."

Mr. Lyons patted my shoulder; then Willy, in his first official act as my guardian, signed his mark to the stipulation, and the clerk and Mr. Lyons witnessed it.

"Very good," the judge said. "How do you plead to the speeding charge, Peter?"

Mr. Lyons winked at me.

"Guilty, Your Honor."

The judge accepted the plea. As it was a first offense, he issued a warning that I was not to appear before him again or I'd be sent to Spring Mountain or Elko. "Your record will be sealed on your eighteenth birthday. All other charges are dismissed," he said and told me I was free to leave with Mr. Bobbins.

In the parking lot Mother thanked Willy. She kissed my forehead and looked in my eyes in a way she hadn't in years. I thought she was going to cry, but she didn't. Instead she squeezed my arm like a pal and told me to come visit once in a while. As she drove away, something of me left with her, shed like the tail of a tadpole.

Willy boarded me in the Lucky, as my bedroom at the house wasn't quite ready. He'd not slept for some time. His eyes were red, and two days of gray stubble had sprouted on his jaw. We ate in Willy's booth. Steam rose from our bowls. Willy tested his chili and said it was too hot. He dropped his spoon, which clattered on the saucer, and turned to me.

"I'm puttin you in Gorman. Maybe seeing you every day'll inspire Betty to study," he said.

"I like Vegas High," I said.

He picked up his spoon, dipped it into the chili, and looked off pensively. A moment later he nodded to himself and aimed the spoon at my face. "I'm gonna let that go. Now, Gorman's a good school, an I say that's where you'll go."

"Yes, sir."

"You mean 'yes, Willy.'"

Ruben Lee joined us and tried to be cordial, calling me Petey Boy and mentioning that he'd heard I took care of business. But he'd run out and left me to take the rap, and that was the hard truth between us. So, we dipped our spoons and turned our forks and pretended to get along.

Waitresses scurried past, glancing out of the corner of their eyes. They knew I was no longer merely another busboy. Denise was gathering the plates when Ruben Lee nudged Willy and motioned with his head toward the entrance. Although I'd never seen her, I knew right away who she was. Stella Bobbins walked in holding Croaker's arm. He guided her to the booth. She seated herself next to me as Croaker squeezed in beside Ruben Lee.

"You must be Pete," she said.

A plain woman in her fifties, she had only one extraordinary physical feature—the blue of her eyes, an aqua blue ringed with flecks of gray. Some of her showed up in George, and a little in Ruben Lee, who looked far more like Willy. But I saw nothing of Betty in her.

"Yes, ma'am."

"I'm gettin your room ready, Pete. Just want to say a quick how do you do."

"Yes, ma'am."

"You wash your hands after you use the bathroom?"

I looked quizzically at Willy, who smiled back.

"Don't be lookin at him," she said. "Was me ask't the question."

"I do," I said.

"Ruben Lee couldn't get it through his head. Go in an urinate, then come right to the table." She furrowed her brow. "Damn casino sounds like a war," she said. "Too noisy for a human woman."

"Yes, ma'am."

"Betty says you're a purse thief. Any truth to that?"

I looked at Willy as I answered. "Not much, ma'am."

"He's polite, Willy."

"Yep."

She shook my hand and took a sip of water, then rubbed her palm on Willy's cheek. After saying he needed a shave, she excused herself and, her arm hooked on Croaker's, she left like a duchess leading a funeral. Willy said she was an unusual woman. Ruben Lee said, "Amen to that."

9

After I made the bed, wiped the bathtub dry, and hung up my clothes, I walked about my room, large by most standards but plainly furnished—a double bed, a desk, two dressers, all maple, and one footlocker. I ran my fingers over the furniture tops. A single French door opened onto a balcony. The closet, about the size of my room at the apartment, was empty. This was the kind of room Miriam had imagined in her stories when we were younger.

I spread the curtains to the balcony and looked out at the stables that housed Betty and Stella's three quarter horses. The house sat in the center of five acres. Much of the back was reserved for the horses; the rest was patioed sandstone or Stella's rose and cactus garden.

Betty, wearing a hat, was running barrels on her filly in the arena. After clearing the last barrel, she jerked the reins and the pinto stopped. She sat stroking the horse's neck. I waved. She pulled the brim of her hat down, rose up in the saddle, and spurred the animal. They bolted toward the barrels, her ponytail bouncing as they attacked the course.

"She be there an hour. Come in mean as hell 'cause that horse is as hard-headed as her."

I let loose of the curtains to look at an old woman, hair and eyebrows white as paper, the skin on her dark face smooth except for the web of wrinkles around her eyes. She looked at the bed and walked to the bathroom door to peer in. She shook her head at me.

"Mrs. Bobbins say make sure your hands is washed 'fore you come to eat."

I assured her my hands would be clean.

"I'm Jamita," she said and left talking to herself.

The open hallway vaulted to a ceiling supported by one laminated mahogany beam. A row of floor-to-ceiling windows faced south to view Rancho Circle Drive. As Croaker had pulled in the driveway with me in the backseat the previous night, the house had seemed large and ostentatious, and I thought Willy a hypocrite for censuring Gatsby's fancy house and highfalutin parties—"things," he said, that drew the wrong kind of attention. As I viewed the estates across the street, a Tudor-style house on seven acres and a colonial-style one on five, I realized that in his mind his *was* modest—but only by comparison.

Lunch awaited me. Stella, dressed in a man's blue work shirt and Levi's, sat at the table, which was set with plain white bone china from the stock used in the restaurant at the Lucky. She motioned for me to sit across from her and said she'd been calling Betty in for five minutes. The sandwiches were bacon, lettuce, and tomato, and the soup was bean, which Stella had made the day before. She continued to do most of the cooking for herself and the family when they were home. Cooking was the one thing Jamita allowed Stella to do around the house.

Jamita spooned soup into my bowl. "Miss Bobbins, tell this boy not to be cleanin no room."

"Peter, let Jamita do her job."

"Thank you, Miss Bobbins." Jamita looked at me to emphasize her victory. "I got things to do."

"Pete, how's your room?" Stella asked.

"Fine."

"Good. We'll get bookshelves for you. Willy says you read all the time."

"Sometimes."

"Maybe it'll rub off on Betty, though I ain't opto-mistic." She walked to the patio door and shouted, "Betty Bobbins, I ain't callin again! Put that damn horse up and come eat!"

Betty tied the horse to a hitching post and sauntered to the patio, where she flung herself down on a chaise. She refused to come inside despite Stella's entreaty to meet me.

"Met him when he stole my purse!" Betty hollered.

"He didn't steal no purse. He returned it."

"Had to steal it to return it!"

Stella shook her head and returned to the table, where she explained that I'd find out what everyone else already knew: Betty had no manners. She said this was clearly Willy's fault. He spoiled her. She told me I didn't have to apologize for returning a purse to its rightful owner; then on a note of under-statement, she said, "Betty ain't happy 'bout you movin in."

Jamita passed through, muttering that Betty was a mule-headed princess. She fixed a tray of food, which she covered with a napkin and carried to a patio table. Stella looked out on the patio, where Betty sat staring off in the opposite direction, refusing to eat.

"Tell me somethin, Peter."

"Ma'am?"

"Po-lice said they was heroin in the car."

"I don't know, ma'am."

"Was it Ruben Lee's?"

I shrugged.

She looked at the picture of her sons sitting horseback on the same saddle, George nine, holding Ruben Lee, who was two and a half. "You know what it means bein a mother?"

"No, ma'am."

"Don't call me ma'am. Do I look old?"

She looked pretty old, but I wisely shook my head.

Croaker drove me to get my belongings and warned me not to take too long. Miriam opened the door as I was carrying an armful of jeans and T-shirts to the car. She threw her books down on the couch and looked at me as if I'd committed an unpardonable sin.

"No hello?" I said.

"Sure, why not. Hello," she said.

I laid my clothes on the couch next to her books. She didn't look at them or me.

"You're breaking up the family."

"I was nothing but trouble. Now she's rid of me. Besides you're here, a perfect daughter."

"You selfish prick."

"I thought cussing indicated low intelligence and mongrel breeding."

"You heard me."

"She signed the papers."

"She had to."

"She wanted to get rid of me for years. You forget the orphanage? Remember the nuns?"

"It wasn't." She put her hands over her ears.

I pulled her hands away. "She didn't have to sign. Willy wanted her to, and she did. Besides, you don't know what happened. She could have taken me home."

Miriam picked up a book and opened it. "Go ahead, pack up and leave."

"You'll graduate and go off to college. Or marry your pilot when he gets you pregnant."

Her cheeks reddened. "I should never have told you."

"Well, you did."

I laid the last of my clothes on the couch. She'd moved to the table, where she watched over the edge of her book as I carried loads to the car. Finished, I returned to leave my key on the table. She held it up daintily, as one holds a flower stem.

"He bought you," she said.

"You don't know anything."

"Yes, I do. He paid off Mother's markers, all of them."

"Markers?"

"All over town—some Julie had lost, some from when Lana visited." Miriam palmed the key and stood, saying she had to get ready for work.

"I'll visit," I said.

"Who cares?"

I turned to leave, but had another thought. "He didn't buy me. She sold me. She just wants someone like Julie."

Miriam waited until I started out the door, then she said, "Peter, what happened? I mean, to us?"

I bowed my head and looked at my feet. "I don't know. We couldn't be kids anymore."

She tossed me the key and said, "Keep it. Come down to the Onion. You can have a burger on the house."

"Fries, double tomato, no onions."

"Sure."

But I left knowing it was for good. Neither of them could understand that night in the dorm. I was on different ground now.

Croaker was leaning on the fender, smoking a cigarette.

"Sorry, Croaker. My sister wanted to talk."

He drew on the cigarette and let the smoke swirl out of his mouth without inhaling. "My name is Mr. Crocker, not Mr. Croaker and never Croaker. Do we have an understandin here?"

"Yes, sir."

"I ain't a servant, an I ain't to be kept waitin. Are we connectin here?"

"Yes, sir."

I kept my mouth shut. Croaker tapped his cigarette out in the ashtray. "'At boy, the one you bit the ear off'a, what he do to you?"

I looked at his profile, his broad, smooth forehead, his jaw muscle that tensed at the slightest movement of his mouth, his eyebrows touched with speckles of gray like frosting, an afterthought, a boyish touch on an otherwise intimidating face.

"Mr. Crocker, there's things I don't discuss. Do we have an understanding here?"

He set his black eyes on me, looking me up and down. He'd never bothered to notice me before. Slowly the corners of his mouth turned up. "Ain't much to look at, but they may be potential." He chuckled as he hooked a left onto Charleston Boulevard. "Yeah, we got us a understandin."

I was perusing pictures in the den, the one place in the house where Stella allowed Willy to smoke cigars. About thirty by thirty feet, it was furnished with all manner of gambling equipment: five slot machines in different stages of assembly, a roulette table, half a crap table, a blackjack table, a bar with a dozen stools, one desk, a wooden Indian, a bronze horse. It was impossible to turn over a cushion and not find a loaded gun, for pistols were strategically placed so a weapon would be always be within Willy's reach.

There was a daguerreotype of Willy's mother, Betty, who had his deep-set blue eyes. Hair drawn up in a bun atop her head, she sat in a ladderback chair wearing a hand-stitched flowered dress. She held a Bible to her breast. Her lips appeared as a stern line. A second daguerreotype hung nearby, this of Clay Bobbins, dressed in black, a greatcoat and baggy trousers tucked in his boots. Willy's stone-faced father held the forestock of a rifle in one heavily knuckled hand and a Bible in the other. His back rigid, he stared from under a high-peaked hat with the contemptuous reserve of an executioner who had just performed a fine hanging.

Willy came up from behind and lit a cigar. When the initial smoke thinned, he laid the cigar on an ashtray. "Favor Ma in the face, Pa in the ears," he said and smiled that rare smile that made you open up. He slumped down in a lounge chair, puffed his cigar, and chased a faraway thought.

Finally he blinked and said, "Thing puzzles me about that Gatsby is how'd he get where he was without killin nobody? See, it don't seem true to me. Don't get me wrong, Gatsby's a good fella, but I can't see it. Don't seem natural. Deer gotta watch out for wolves, an wolves gotta watch out for lions, an both gotta watch out for drought."

"Maybe Gatsby did kill," I said.

"Maybe." He tapped his ashes into the ashtray. "Ma was a strange woman. Never approved'a Pa, not so's you'd know. That there Bible," he said, pointing, "though she couldn't read a word'a it, was her pistol and about ten cases of ammunition. She could quote the hell outta it. Memorized Scripture ever time she went to church, close enough Pa wouldn't know the differ'nce. She must'a knowed ninety-nine ways to tell him the Book didn't approve of drinkin and gamblin and stealin.

"Not a ordinary woman a'tall. Died in the influenza of nineteen eighteen. Her, my sisters, all but Codice Angela Bobbins, who married a real sumbitch named Barkum Parker, who, I swear, was nine parts Jew an one part snake, but claimed to be some descendant of English royalty. He could squeeze a nickel till it gasped for air. Now, Pa, well, he couldn't farm or ranch, thought he could gamble, wasn't much good at rustlin, but prob'ly would'a lived two hunert years if he hadn't got caught by the *federales*."

He let the cigar rest in his fingers. I looked closely at his father. On his left finger was a gold band, and above his breast pocket was a part of a medal, most of which had somehow gotten caught in the coat pocket. I pointed to the medal.

Willy held the cigar to his lips. "Guess the one thing he did was won hisself a Silver Star in Cuba. Kilt a passel'a . . ." He looked out the windows that faced that part of the veranda planted with verbena and lavender, but he stared off into the vast space beyond the Spring Mountains, lost in a memory until his cigar died out and he had to relight it.

"I never really knew Pa," he said. He pointed the cigar at the picture of his dad and said, "We were borrowin cattle in Mexico. Stop me if I tol' you this before."

"You started it once."

"Well, if that's the case, quit interruptin." He began the tale of how he and his father were separated in a storm in northern Coahuila and gradually told the story of buying his father's freedom from a Mexican officer. Finished, he snubbed out his cigar.

"What'd you say the name'a 'at boy was what stole Betty's purse?"

"I didn't."

"You sure you didn't?"

"Positive."

He nodded once as if to say he understood and let the subject die.

Betty turned off the radio and rolled up the window, her way of announcing we'd arrived at Bishop Gorman High. She parked in the student lot, where spaces were taken with shiny Impalas and Fairlanes, daddies' Karman Ghias, and a few sports cars, and now her Cadillac. She said for the last time that morning, "Can't you take the fucking bus?" She thought it worldly to use language that would shock Willy if he heard it, but she was careful not to use such language around him.

"No."

"You steal purses. Why not just steal a car?"

Betty did nothing in moderation, including disliking me. Each day she'd pick a fight or tell me she had plans as an excuse to keep from driving me to the Lucky in the afternoon. The walk didn't bother me. Along the way I'd stop at the A&W across from Huntridge Theater, where I'd sit and watch Annette Sylvestri talk and laugh infectiously. She was beautiful, thin and elegant, with amber-blond hair as straight and soft as the last touch of light at dusk. Her smile was the center of everything. Girls gathered at her booth or filled her car. Drinking Cokes and sharing french fries, they would giggle and talk, I assumed about boys. Of course, Annette had nothing to do with me. For that matter, neither did anyone else at Bishop Gorman. I was a moneyless boy, not particularly good-looking nor outgoing. Tall and shy, I had nothing to offer them, especially the Annette Sylvestris of the world. It was as if I carried the mark of Cain or, worse, was completely invisible.

"I could probably steal your purse and buy one," I said.

"Not funny."

We had a history test that day. I asked, "Who was the seventeenth president of the United States?" Betty hadn't studied; she never studied, she just paid others to do her homework or to let her copy off their test papers.

"Some asshole whose picture's on money."

"You don't know."

"Petey, you're a turd. I bet you'd float in a toilet bowl."

"Swearing indicates a lack of imagination," I said, paraphrasing Miriam.

She examined her teeth in the mirror, after which she said, "Shit, fuck, damn, bitch, bastard, turd, prick, pussy, dick, cunt, sonofabitch, motherfucker. I leave some out?"

"Twat and piss. There're more dirty words reserved for women than men. Miriam taught me that."

"*'Miriam taught me that.'* Really, pretend you don't know me." She grabbed her books. "And find your own way after school." She slammed the door and waited for me to leave before strolling through the nearest crowd of boys. Ponytail bouncing, textbooks locked in her crossed arms, back erect, she ambled by them cocksure, Willy's little girl, and their heads turned to watch.

I had nothing at stake in Betty, but Annette was another matter. Her father was a partner in Mr. Lyons's law firm. Dominic Sylvestri specialized in delaying cases until witnesses disappeared, which Willy said was a talent to be appreciated. Mr. Sylvestri, a picky eater—fruit salad with yogurt—holding each orange slice, each apple chunk, each lettuce leaf on his fork until satisfied. His habits seemed to irritate Mr. Lyons, who would turn his head away rather than watch the undertaking.

As for Annette, she went with Danny Ferguson, forward on the basketball team, tight end on the football team. Holding hands, walking together, her face tilted up to his, his aimed straight ahead, they looked the picture of young romance, minus the gilded frame. After homeroom, I hurried to English class, the first I shared with her. Settling into my seat, I opened a book and pretended to read, now and then glancing at the door.

In geometry I daydreamed; in biology I listened intently; in history I took copious notes; and in English I read every assignment twice, wrote and re-wrote essays that Sister Beatrice later suggested had been plagiarized. She awarded me B's based on this assumption. Annette received A's, not for the beauty of her prose but for the prettiness of her being. I remembered the nuns in the orphanage, their disgust toward me for being a boy.

Annette entered, willowy, her half-lidded brown eyes glinting. She'd been to San Diego, her father's beach house. Her skin was golden, nose and cheeks slightly red. She laughed at her friend's joke, and I pretended she'd laughed at something I'd said, something clever. Her long hair, cut in bangs, swayed as she crossed the front of the room to her desk. She swung into the seat and plopped her books down on the desktop.

The world reserved its joys for her kind. What was it like to live inside skin that never pimpled, to ski in Colorado at spring break, to travel Europe in the summer? Willy, with his wealth, didn't do those things, nor did his children. But Annette did. I recalled how she stood in front of the class to recite a speech about touring the great cathedrals, never once looking in my direction. The writing was boring, self-indulgent, but I never took my eyes off her. And she never once noticed me.

Sister Beatrice passed back the last assignment. She paused at my desk and looked down as she handed over my essay on the common people in Hardy's poetry. I flipped through the pages to find that she'd given me a B-minus and had written a note saying she would research until she found my sources. "Plagiarism is a sin," she wrote.

Myrna Lowell showed me her paper, a B-plus marked in the upper-right corner. A plain girl, slightly overweight, she was a good reader and writer, though she rarely received A's, a grade reserved for a selected few. I nodded. She was indignant.

"She give you another B?" she asked.

I turned the paper upside down on my desk. Though Myrna was only showing concern, my ears burned with shame as if I'd actually cheated. "B-minus."

"There will be no discussion of grades," Sister Beatrice said.

"This here's Pete," Willy said. "New fixture here." He had me shake each man's hand and told the senator to make room. Though a bit put out, the senator slid over for me. Gladhanding as he was, it was best not to offend his host.

"Ain't sayin I done nothin wrong, you see?" Willy looked from face to face until certain he'd established a gentleman's agreement. He believed in un-spoken contracts, believed every man was honorable if you held something over his head. "Tex Henderson owned the only joint 'sides mine in all'a Dallas. He'd burned me outta one place. 'Course he denied doin it, accused me of dynamitin a roadhouse of his. What was crazy was he wanted me to admit to blowin up his place, which I didn't do, but he wasn't willin to admit to burnin down my place, which he did do."

He unwrapped a cigar and slipped the band off, which he rolled into a ball and held between his index finger and thumb. "It was a misunderstandin . . ." His listeners kept silent as he lit and puffed the cigar to life. " . . . needed fixin. I went for a visit. His club bein on the top floor of the Cattlemen's Buildin, he had his own private elevator. I waited a bit, knowin he'd show, an when he did, I slipped in beside him an pressed the button.

"He was kinda startled. As a friendly gesture I took out my new nickle-plate forty-fives so's he could admire 'em." He winked at his friend, the sena-tor. "Funny thing happened, an I wouldn't'a found this out if it weren't for that little misunderstandin. Ol' Tex was tired'a runnin his joint. I offered a price when the door closed. On the second floor he wanted twice as much. Higher up we went the lower my offer got. Before reachin the top, we nego-tiated a tolerable price. If the club'd been one floor higher, I'd'a got him to knock off twenty percent more."

"The guns, Willy. That's extortion." The senator, an attorney by profession, grinned.

Willy looked flabbergasted. "Weren't neither."

"Well, Willy, if it wasn't, what was it?"

Willy drummed his fingers on the table, his expression deadpan. "Slow elevators and artful negotiation," he said. "Now, what can I do for you?"

Willy suggested the cups needed fresh coffee, which I understood to mean he was about to open his wallet.

After handshakes and back patting, his guests walked out, obviously pleased. Willy the kidder! More of a character than they'd expected, a good ol' boy. As I cleared the table, Willy asked how I liked the story. I liked them all and told him so. He considered me for a moment. I asked if he wanted more coffee or water. He told me no, then asked if I had any enemies.

I thought of Louie and Lyle. "Yeah, I guess."

He said, "Pete, don't let 'em know an try an make 'em think you're their friend."

"Okay, Willy."

"An take care'a school."

Sister Beatrice assigned a short story to be written on any subject, nothing sacrilegious or obscene, of course. It seemed every attempt I made challenged either divinity or virtue. I wrote, in flagrant profanity, "The Floozy of Fountain Valley," a story of a girl who gets drunk on sacramental wine and has sex with a boy. In "Freeing Pa" I plagiarized Willy's account of buying his father back from the Mexican Army. It read like a chapter from a bad novel, so I composed a story about a black man who hid a white man wanted by the cops under a shoeshine stand, another Willy story. I seemed destined to write the diametrical opposite of what I figured would suit Sister Beatrice. But Willy liked them, except for the foul words in the first.

"Got to make the outlaw handsomer," he said.

"Why?"

"'Cause Gatsby was handsome an so was that fella in *For Whom the Bell Tolls*."

"How do you know?"

"Women. Where'd you get a name like Gaddis Tellerman?"

I couldn't recall. It was a name that sprouted on the page.

I went to the Blue Onion and followed Miriam about, explaining the stories as she carried orders from the takeout window to the cars.

"Write about Aunt Vivian," she said. "Remember the doughnut truck and the milk and how she bribed us with treats as an excuse to . . . Here's your burger, extra tomato, one hot dog, sir, one Coke, one root beer, two regular fries, and one fried onion." She counted out change and waited with a patient smile until the driver left some coins on the tray for her.

She looked up at the light panel, watching for her number. "Mom's worried about you, Peter," she said.

"What were you saying about Aunt Vivian?"

"Why don't you at least come over and visit?"

"The doughnuts, Miriam."

"She used us as an excuse to get what she wanted anyhow. I'm not sure what it means. You're the writer."

A black Buick full of kids pulled into one of Miriam's spaces. She said she was too busy to talk and I should at least telephone once in a while. I asked what was so damned important that I should call or visit.

"She's your mother."

"She gave me away. Have you forgotten the orphanage?"

I saw by her expression that she refused to remember it the way it had been. "It was a boarding school."

"And a fucking orphanage."

"You have a filthy mouth, Peter."

"I know."

The driver of the Buick honked his horn. She waved at him and said, "I have to go."

"I'll call."

I watched her walk to the Buick, then headed up Fremont Street, hands stuffed in my pockets. By the time I'd dressed for work, a story whirred about in my head. I told Willy its title.

"'The Boy Who Drank the Holy Water'? You're gonna give up a handsome gambler hidin from the law in a shoeshine stand for a boy who drinks holy water?"

"It's about a boy put up for adoption so his mother can marry a man who doesn't want kids," I explained.

"Pete, I'm thinkin that tuition ain't gettin me no more with you 'an it does with Betty."

Willy often sat beside me as I studied. He would listen as I explained a geometry theorem or the cycle of cell growth. In his own way, he was attending school, but there was more to it. I suspected even then he had a plan in mind for me.

"Okay," he said, "read that fool story to me when it's done. We'll see."

It was about a mother who rediscovers virtue and returns to the orphanage to claim her child, only to find he's been adopted—sappy, sentimental, trite.

Willy sort of wiggled his head when I finished and said he hoped I'd get a good grade but the story didn't deserve one.

Sister Beatrice read to the class, enunciating each word with careful regard. She even got teary-eyed at the end. Resting the paper on her lap, she pointed to me and said, "The author of this touching piece is Peter."

Annette stared at me.

That night, I told Willy about my coup.

"Got an A for that?"

"Yeah."

He looked up at the light fixture. "Well, an A's okay, but the shoeshine story, now that was a good story. Tell the hostess we need these chandeliers washed."

I found her alone outside class wrapped up in Danny Ferguson's letterman jacket, her hands hidden somewhere in the long sleeves. It was a cool November afternoon. She saw me coming, folded her arms over her books, and waited, a hint of a smile on her mouth as I approached. A thrumming filled my chest. I wanted to turn away, but I'd come too far. "Hello," I said.

"Hi."

I'd never been this close to her, so close I could see the sheen of her silky skin and the specks of yellow in the center of her otherwise brown eyes. "How'd you like my story?" I asked.

The world seemed to spin on the question. She looked up, her eyes sparkling, and said, "I didn't."

She brushed past me and walked toward Danny, who waited by a bench. She gazed into his terribly handsome, terribly dumb animal face and whispered. They linked hands and looked in my direction. I was already slinking away toward the classroom door.

10

Willy had told me to pack an overnight bag and said, "Let's take a ride." He chewed on a dead cigar as we pulled into a parking space. It was December 27th and cold, and why we were at McCarran Airport was a mystery to me. He slipped his .45 under the seat and cracked his door.

"Still, can't figger that Jack Ruby. Weren't nothin but a two-bit pimp when I met him," Willy said.

"Maybe he's crazy," I said.

"No, don't think so."

I changed the subject. I'd become intrigued with microscopes and the things that fit between slides. Insects took on complex patterns and vivid detail, especially the wings. Assuming his curiosity would be aroused, I described the cell structure of a dragonfly's wing to Willy.

He listened patiently and said, "Get them classes done good, but don't get no ideas about bein no scientist. You're too smart for that stuff. No money in it."

"But . . ."

"Now, listen, Pete. I'm meetin a man who don't know I'm meetin him. It's going to be a surprise. Don't let on no different."

"Okay."

"I figger Jack, who never done nothin, wanted to be remembered for somethin is all. 'Course the whole world is crazy. People killin the President. Well, if you ain't from Dallas, you can't unnerstand." He opened the door, stood up and stretched. "Come on, an bring your bag."

The terminal was swamped with arrivals. Willy approached the United Airlines counter and asked if the flight from Dallas was on time. The ticket clerk pointed to the schedule board. "'S up there, sir."

Willy shook his head. "Didn't ask the board. I ask't you."

The man looked at Willy for a second, then quickly looked away. "Yes, sir, it's on time."

"Good for you," Willy said.

Carrying my overnight bag, I followed Willy through the maze of people to the baggage claim. He asked me to find where the baggage from the Dallas flight would be coming in. I located the sign and motioned him over.

"What other flights're arrivin?" he asked.

I looked again at the signs. "Reno."

"Good."

"Why're we here, Willy?"

"A man 'sposed to kill me," he said.

"Kill you?"

"Yep. 'At's why you gotta carry his bag."

"Me?"

"Trust me, Pete."

Willy leaned against a pillar where he could see the escalator. Looking to all the world unconcerned, he bit on his cigar. A group of travelers from Reno milled about the luggage area. As bags emerged on the conveyor, the people turned into a crowd of half-frenzied grabbers. Arms folded over his chest, Willy chewed on his dead cigar and kept watch.

Fifteen minutes passed before the passengers from the Dallas flight began to show. More and more turned the corner, but Willy's man didn't seem to be among them. The luggage feed spat bags out on the carousel. In minutes most of the tourists claimed their luggage and headed for the door, but a few unclaimed bags circled about like rafts floating in an eddy.

"Maybe he's not coming," I said.

"Probably watchin to see if he's bein watched."

Willy muttered under his breath and chewed harder on the cigar, his eyes unblinking as he scanned the escalator ferrying people to the luggage area. Then he smiled and, using the pillar for cover, turned away as the sliding doors opened. A tall, slim man of about forty wearing a white Stetson rounded the corner. He gazed about as if searching the wallpaper for enemies. His skin seemed immutably tan, as if tattooed brown, and his hawkish face had a composed, dangerous look. He'd slipped by Willy, gone outside, and doubled back.

Willy said, "I'll do the talkin."

Willy came up as the man bent over the conveyor belt. "Art. Art Mosley," Willy said.

The man jerked his head around at hearing the name. "Mr. Bobbins, Mr. Bobbins," he said and stood tall as he smiled down at Willy, almost a head shorter. He had a seducer's smile, practiced and direct, and a mouth full of straight white teeth.

"Call me Willy, Art. What brings you?" He offered his hand, which Art shook.

"It's Las Vegas, ain't it? Little gamblin, Willy," he said, hiding behind that plaster smile.

Despite the smiles, Willy and the man who'd come to kill him stared at one another.

Willy said, "Ain't this a coincidence, me here to meet Pete. Pete, this here's Art Mosley."

I shook hands with him.

"Pete kind'a lives with us. Where you stayin, Art?"

"The Algiers," he said and started toward the carousel, where his luggage was on about the twentieth trip around.

Willy followed. "Won't have it, Art."

Art stopped in his tracks. "Won't have what, Willy?"

"Won't have you stayin any place but mine."

"The Lucky? Thanks anyhow, Willy, but I got bidness. On the Strip."

"Thought you was here to gamble."

"That too."

"I wouldn't be much of a host if I ask't you to stay at the Lucky. Hell, we got all sort 'a room. Don't we, Pete?"

Willy was right—the world was crazy—him along with it. Either that, or he was kidding about Art's purpose for being in Las Vegas. "Plenty of room," I said.

Willy took my bag from my hand. "Pete'll help you with your bags, and I won't hear a no, not even a shake 'a your head. Hell, you wouldn't wanna insult an ol Texas boy."

I fit Art's two suitcases in the trunk. Willy said we'd stop for a short bite at the Lucky. Though he seemed composed, Art was beginning to sweat, as evidenced by his armpits.

Art slept at the house and received Willy's undivided attention. The first night Willy kept him up until dawn drinking sour mash and trading stories. I stayed up until midnight, when finally Willy told me to go to bed. Art objected, saying there was no reason to send me off, but Willy told me to go on.

Willy left the business to George and devoted every waking moment to Art. The more hospitable he was toward Art, the more skeptical I became. I figured what Willy had claimed about Art was a gag. I enjoyed Art's stories about his days as a vice cop in Fort Worth and started liking him, and whenever I stood to leave, he would ask me to stay for another story, and Willy would motion for me to sit.

Betty flirted openly with Art, which didn't seem to affect Willy. Art and Stella discussed old acquaintances. He complimented her clothes, her garden, her taste in furniture and drapes, her hairdo—a charmer. Stella said she'd make him a special meal and ordered Betty and me to help take down Christmas decorations, after which she sent Jamita home and told Betty she would have to help serve dinner. Betty said she had a date, which meant nothing to Stella. Willy insisted that she stay, and Art seemed pleased with the idea of her being there. We sat staring at platters of lamb chops, cauliflower, and potatoes au gratin, Willy at the head of the table, Art to his immediate right. Stella sat opposite Willy, while Betty and I sat toward the center facing one another. Betty picked at her food, alternately looking at her watch and the door. Now and then she'd mention that she had planned all week to go out.

Willy became less talkative, almost sullen. Stella seemed a bit cooler toward Art. Betty was detached. Art talked nervously and picked at his food, now and then nodding to show approval. Near the end of the meal Willy asked, "Art, how you like Stella's lamb chops?"

Art looked to get Stella's attention. "Mighty fine, ma'am."

"Thank you, Art. We miss Dallas. Don't we, Willy?"

"Sure do."

"Dad, can I go now?" Betty said.

Willy shook his head. "Not just yet, darlin. We got company."

Betty looked at Art. "If you ask me, he looks like he'd rather be somewhere else, too."

"Is 'at right, Art?" Willy asked. "You'd ruther be somewheres else?"

"Now, Willy, what kind'a question's 'at?" Stella said. "Peter, you want another chop?"

Art, thankful that Stella had come to his aid, cut off a bite of meat.

"Yes, ma'am," I said.

"Eats like he's two boys," Stella said to Art.

Art nodded, but it was obvious his mind was elsewhere. Betty watched me cut the lamb chop and shook her head. I held the meat on my fork and grinned before stuffing it in my mouth and chewing it with my mouth open.

"Disgusting," she said.

"Pete, close your mouth," Stella said. "Didn't your ma teach you nothin?"

I closed my mouth and chewed.

"Really, Dad, I'm late," Betty said.

"Darlin, don't bring it up again." Willy turned his attention back to Art. "It was a rude question I asked, Art, but I got another."

Art looked up from his plate. "Go ahead, Willy."

"You never did say what your bidness was."

"No, guess I didn't."

"Maybe I can help out. Maybe if your bidness don't go well, you can find work with me."

Art shook his head. "Got plenty 'a work, Willy."

"What exactly is it you're doin now, Art?"

Betty pushed her chair back and started to stand.

Willy aimed a finger at her and snapped, "Sit 'til I say otherwise."

She slouched down in her chair. I finished the last of my chop and folded my napkin.

"Willy," Stella said, "a handsome man like Art prob'ly sells jewelry or cars."

Willy shook his head. From beneath his coat he pulled out a Smith and Wesson .357 Magnum and held it up for Art to see. "Must be jewelry. Else why would he need this?" He opened the cylinder to show it was loaded, snapped it shut, and laid the gun before Art. "What is it, Art? Jewelry?"

Neither Betty nor I could move. Like Art, Betty stared at the revolver. Art swallowed and looked at the gun. Stella scooted her chair back and asked who wanted pecan pie.

Leaning back, Willy entwined his fingers behind his neck. "Art an me'll have some. Don't guess Betty wants any. Pete can take his upstairs an study. Boy has to study if he's gonna make it to lawyer school." Willy had taken to mentioning me and law school in one breath.

Like Betty and Art, I fixed my gaze on the revolver, while Willy and Stella seemed as casual as two picnickers discussing potato salad. When Betty and I stood to leave, Art said he had to go. Willy paid no mind, just kept his hands behind his neck, his elbows pointed to the sides. "After some pie, Art. You know, we ain't yet talked 'bout Tex. How's he doin these days? Must be a ol' man by now. Seventy or so."

His lips nearly white, Art swallowed hard. "Don't kill me, Willy. Don't." His hands were under the table out of sight, but it was obvious they were trembling.

Willy looked at the three of us. "We can have pie some other time," he said. "Ya'll go on so's me an Art can talk."

Stella and I sat on the patio with a breakfast of Western omelettes, canta-loupe, and orange juice. It was Saturday. A southwester was blowing in over the Mojave. Betty, at Brian Head with friends, was gone for the weekend, and Willy was in Montana on business. Normally I worked Saturday morn-ings, but had taken the day off with Willy's blessing. Stella ate at a slow pace, occasionally placing both hands on the arms of her chair, watching me as if she had something on her mind.

"Pete, you miss your ma?"

I felt embarrassed to confess the truth, so I lied. "Yes."

"You like it here?"

"Yes, ma'am."

She didn't pursue it. When finished, she told Jamita to clean up and take the day off with pay. "Pete an me's fixin to get acquainted." She looked me in the eye. "Turo ain't comin today, so you can help in the garden."

She'd always treated me cordially, sometimes friendly, but never warmly. Surprised, I said, "I've never gardened."

"Do what I tell you."

Gardening was her obsession. In the morning, after a leisurely bath, she tied her hair in rubber bands, adorned herself with jewelry—that and her garden being her self-indulgences. The ritual was the same: two or three cocktail rings, all yellow gold with diamonds or emeralds, on her right hand. Only the wedding band decorated her left hand; studded earrings, preferably diamonds, and a string of pearls or a teardrop tourmaline necklace around her throat. Her sole effort at makeup was the blood-red lipstick that usually wore off by midmorning and was not replaced.

After the bath, after the jewelry, she'd slip into a pair of thousand-dollar Lucchese boots, cotton work gloves, and an old straw Stetson. She then summoned Arturo, whom we called Turo. Her morning was spent with him in the back, hoeing, raking, and sprinkling water in the garden where she grew roses and flowering cactus. A tenacious weed-puller, she worked until it seemed at times she was doing penance.

In the afternoon she might ride Mabel, her mare, around the barrels several times. She rode well, but not like Betty, who assaulted the course. By the afternoon Stella normally had finished her daily labor and rested on the couch by the stone fireplace, where she watched two soap operas and took a nap until dinnertime. No one interfered with her rituals.

She pointed out various cacti, naming them by their common names—claret cup, bunny's ear, cholla. A few she'd given proper names. "'At one's Thorny. 'At's Prickly. One over there's Stickly." She pointed to a Mojave prickly pear. "'At one I call Dickhead." She waited until I asked why and said, "'Cause the sumbitch sticks me ever' time I go near."

I laughed. She said it wasn't all that funny and handed me a hoe. "Ever use one?"

"No, ma'am."

"Blister now an then's good for character. You got character, Pete?"

"I don't know, ma'am."

"We'll see." She demonstrated how to spread dirt and turn the ground for weeds. I asked why cactus and roses.

"'Cause it's differ'nt."

She had me hoe out an area that bordered the lawn, claimed it was important to keep the grass from invading. We worked until around eleven, when she told me to take a break while she went to make some iced tea. I sat on the chaise and propped up my feet.

She set the glass beside me and seated herself facing the garden. "Pete, you ever feel like somethin's crawled up your leg and bit your ass?"

"Ma'am?"

"You feel like maybe you . . . never mind. Pa was a farmer an deputy sheriff back home."

I took a sip and began chewing on a piece of ice.

"Ain't good for your teeth," she said.

"What?"

"Chewin on ice. Ruben Lee was an ice-chewer. Broke his fillins. You got any fillins?"

"Back here." I pointed to my lower left molars.

She walked to the chaise and sat on the edge. "Lemme see."

I hesitated.

"Pete, we don't know nothin 'bout one another to speak of, but you're livin under my roof an if your teeth go bad, it's my responsibility. Now, I called my dentist and made you an appointment for a checkup."

"Yes, ma'am."

"I wasn't expectin you in my home, an you damn sure wasn't expectin to be here. We was both bit in the butt."

"Yes, ma'am."

"When I heard 'bout that juvenile jail an . . . them plannin on sending you to Elko." She licked her lips and looked at her garden. "Me an Willy. What I mean is when Willy told me . . . Anyhow, you're here an neither of us expected this to be, not a few months ago."

"No, ma'am."

"See, my boys are growed up, but I liked havin 'em, even though they weren't good at hoein."

She looked into my face. "Can't blame a baby for the circumstances of its birth."

"No, ma'am." The piece of ice melted in my mouth.

"You don't waste much time talkin," she said. "That's good. Now, you're gonna show me those teeth, then I'm gonna teach you how to ride."

"A horse?"

"You see any tractors here?"

"No, ma'am."

"Bobbinses got to know how to ride. You got things to learn. We'll start there," she said and squinted as I opened my mouth for her to examine my fillings.

After dinner she asked what had been wrong with me the past few days.

"Nothing," I said.

"Well, sometimes you look so bad, if you was a horse, we'd have to shoot you."

"I'm okay."

"Like George, never say what's on your mind. Hell, that boy broke his arm onct an didn't say a thing 'bout it till Willy told him to put up 'is horse. Boy took a fall an was ashamed to tell us. In Montana at our house a mile south'a Butte. If you're lucky, you'll never see Butte."

"No, ma'am."

"Now, what you so dog-faced over?"

"Ma'am?"

"I ain't stupid, Pete. You wanna get along here, never think I'm stupid. Can't read books, but sometimes I read minds. You're moonin over a gal. I know signs. Went through 'em with George, though the girl was hardly worth a second look. She's married an got four boys now an a husband who works half a year an gets drunk the rest. Next year George got Elaine in a fix. But he got hisself a fine wife."

"Yes, ma'am," I said. George was her obvious favorite.

"Yours worth a second look?"

"Mine?"

"Don't toy with me, I got no time. Her name." She patted a cushion and told me to sit.

It came out before I had a chance to think. "Annette, Annette Sylvestri." I seated myself.

"Lawyer's daughter. Got a snoot full. Worse 'an Betty."

"Yes, ma'am."

"Been out with her?"

"No."

"'Course not. Sometimes I ask dumb questions. Am I gonna hafta pry this out a piece at a time?"

I guess I felt like talking and somehow trusted her. I told her about approaching Annette, at first expecting her to laugh. She didn't. Instead, when I finished, she reached over, brushed a loose strand of my hair, and said, "Heartache's a slow, hard pain." She pondered this a moment and said, "Don't be tellin no one 'bout ridin. Though it can't hardly be called ridin. You'll be old enough soon. Let's hope you're a sight better at drivin."

11

A line of humanity curled out the front door, over the walkway, and into the parking lot. I asked Croaker why Willy didn't make a call to arrange for us to go straight in.

"Why he wanna waste a favor on a punk like you?"

I said that was a good point.

He said I should shut up and think about what I had to do because if I flunked, I wouldn't get a second chance. "Someday I'm gonna remind you on this an then we'll see. You just remember a Ford."

Having coached me as Stella wished in the fine points of driving for a week, he felt he'd devoted enough time to advise me on the purchase of a car. He'd taught begrudgingly, but well.

"Yes, sir."

Though I'd saved enough for a used Ford, I didn't intend to buy one no matter what he suggested. I had dreams.

"Willy got some fool notions over the years, but you 'bout take the cake, Pete."

"You don't like me, Mr. Crocker."

"Ain't that. It's just hard to judge your worth."

I was moderately comforted by Stella's assurance that if Croaker really didn't like me, he would pick me up and drop me on my head.

For three hours Croaker mumbled about inefficient clerks and squawking kids who ran around their mothers' legs. Finally we were at the counter, where I faced a formidable woman who said, "Birth certificate and consent form first. Look at the chart and read the first line second line third line. Place your hand over your left eye and read the numbers next to . . ." She looked up at Croaker. "Are you the parent?" she asked.

Croaker looked at me, at the backs of his dark hands, at her, then at the ceiling as if thinking about it. "You really want me to answer that?"

"Well, if you aren't, then why're you here?"

Croaker cracked his knuckles. His nerves were getting brittle. "I was wonderin the same thing myself."

"He's my licensed driver," I said, "who drove me here, in the car I'll use."

"Why didn't you just say so?" she asked Croaker.

"'Cause you ask't if I was the parent."

She handed me a booklet and an answer sheet and told me to sit at the first open desk and answer all the questions. I was not to mark on the question book, but use the answer sheet. After I completed the exam and filled out the forms, I had to wait again, this time for the driving test.

"Pete, you're gettin on my nerves."

"Sorry, Mr. Crocker."

"Sorry don't mean nothin if you don't make amen's."

"How?"

"I'm thinkin on it."

His eye narrowed. "Those books you read put anythin in that head 'a yours?"

"Mr. Crocker, that's a rhetorical question. My sister's noted for rhetorical questions, famous the world over for them. In fact, the queen of England knows my sister asks rhetorical questions. The only fact more widely known than my sister's penchant for asking rhetorical questions is my own habit of never answering them."

His eyes narrowed as the corners of his mouth turned up. "Guess you could say I don't much like you. Yes, sir, you could put it that way."

I was about to add something, but he raised his finger as a warning. "No sass, boy."

Fortunately for me the examiner called out my name. He had a full mug of coffee in one hand and a clipboard with a white form in the other. A man of around forty with a pendulous paunch, he raised his cup about an inch and motioned with his head for me to follow. "You make me spill the coffee, you flunk automatically. Other than that, you have a chance," he said.

"Can I get you to drink most of it first?"

He glanced back. "You have the keys?"

After first checking lights and brakes and horn, he handed me the keys and slid into the passenger seat. "Know where the bank is in Commercial Center?"

"Yes, sir."

"Drive me there and back without spilling my coffee and without running a red light and do one parallel park and you pass. Got it?"

"Got it."

The Cadillac, nimble as a falling tree and swift as an iceberg, worked to my advantage. I signaled a turn and pulled slowly onto Sahara Avenue. It was midmorning and traffic was light. Using both hand signals and blinkers, I changed lanes. The examiner sat holding the coffee mug between his legs while filling out a check. If he noticed my driving at all, he gave no hint. I kept the car moving at a steady forty miles an hour heading west. I drove without incident to the bank, where he told me to keep the engine running while he made his car payment. He left the coffee behind. A few minutes later he ambled out of the bank, swung open the door, and told me to head back; all that was left was the parallel parking. He sat down and lifted the mug to his lips.

As we pulled out, the air splintered with the sounds of sirens as three sheriff's patrol cars came from three different directions and hemmed us in. A deputy crouched behind the door of his black-and-white, pointing a shotgun at us and ordering us to get out with our hands in the air. I came out first and was quickly taken to the pavement by another officer, but when the examiner stepped out in his khaki uniform and silver shield, his trousers wet-stained by coffee, the deputies looked questioningly at one another.

A sergeant pulled up in his patrol car and stuck his head out the open window. "It was a false alarm, boys. A teller hit it by accident."

A deputy said we could go. At once they slammed the car doors shut and rolled out of the parking lot. The examiner still stood with his hands in the air, one clutching the clipboard and the other the empty cup. When we entered the Department of Motor Vehicles lot, the examiner told me to just park and go inside. I took a seat beside Croaker, who asked how it went. I told him I did everything just the way he'd instructed.

"What took so long?"

"Traffic."

"Well, now you can run your own damn self aroun," he said. He seemed pleased, but I could never be sure. He stood and began pacing. A few minutes later the examiner showed up and handed me a slip. He said I could try again after thirty days. I began to protest. He said, "Thirty days," and walked away.

"Just a minute," Croaker said.

The examiner placed his hands on his hips. "I have people waiting. Bring him back in thirty days."

Croaker cussed under his breath as he snatched the form from my hand. "We'll see," he said over and over as we crossed the pavement. At the car he asked what had happened. I told the whole story. When I finished, he puffed his cheeks and slowly released the air.

Two days later Croaker picked me up on the sidewalk of Maryland Parkway as I was walking from school to the Lucky. He scooted across the seat and told me to get behind the wheel. Then, pointing toward Sahara Avenue, he said, "Le's go see a fat man."

The examiner politely apologized for the confusion and handed me a slip that indicated I'd passed the test with a score of one hundred. He escorted us ahead of everyone else to the counter, where a clerk typed a permanent license on the spot. When the license was in my hand, Croaker got nose to nose with the examiner. "Weren't no confusion," he said. "You done the boy wrong."

The examiner's Adam's apple bobbled. "Yes, sir. My mistake."

Croaker nudged me. "Le's go." He opened the door to leave and let me pass first. "You one big pain in the ass, you know that?"

"Yes, Mr. Crocker," I said, "a big pain in the ass."

He tapped me gently on the back of the head. "Bet that weren't just coffee on 'is lap."

I fondled the license. Willy had come through, again.

I opened the door and walked directly to the T-120TT displayed in the showroom window. The motorcycle was more than a two-wheeled machine with a 650 cc heart, more than a shiny red finish, more than chrome. It was an expression of disgust at all things pedestrian. It was a dream I awoke to in my room at night when I'd feel the shadows approach, when the voices whispered in the dark. I'd see myself on it, leaned into a turn, its pea-shooter exhausts thrumming. A sign on the bars warned patrons not to sit on it. I removed the sign, threw my leg over the machine, and straddled the Triumph's soft leather seat.

"Hey! Get off." The salesman stood at the door of his office. "I've been patient, kid, but I'm going to ask you to leave. Can't have you sitting on the bikes. Insurance and all."

I ran my hands over the tank and climbed off. "Sure like this one, Tom."

He replaced the sign. "I've put up with you taking my time with questions, but . . ."

"I've got my license and the money."

For months I'd entered the showroom and pestered Tom until he told me not to come back except with cash in hand—eleven hundred twenty-seven dollars—and for months I'd kept my desire secret for fear that I'd be forbidden to buy it.

I opened my jacket and pulled out the cash from an inside pocket. "I want it."

"You're underage, aren't you?" he said, but his eyes were locked on the wad of cash in my hand and his face said everything could be arranged.

I said I had permission and handed him a typed letter with Mother's forged signature granting me permission to contract for the purchase of a motorcycle. "You can see it's notarized." For a fee of ten dollars a bail bonds-man friend of Willy's had notarized the forgery.

Tom went through the motions, placed his glasses on the bridge of his nose, held the letter at arm's length, nodding as he read. He needed just enough to cover himself in court. He slipped his glasses off his nose and dangled them before me as if they were proof of his acumen on such matters. "As a technicality," he said, "the title will be in your mother's name too." His eyes went right to the money in my hand.

Under Tom's delighted gaze, I mounted the Bonneville again and told him to start the paperwork. I walked it outside, kicked the starter twice, and let the engine idle. It trembled under me like something alive. Tom asked if I was sure I could ride. I'd learned to ride a horse, sort of, in a few weeks. Why not a motorcycle? "Sure."

"Hottest production bike in the world."

"I know."

Though no Corvette or drop-top Impala, it could rip a 120-mile-an-hour hole in the air. A library book claimed a rider who could handle a bicycle could ride a motorcycle, but books don't mount the world's hottest production motorcycle and twist the throttle. The Triumph reared up and soared across the parking lot on its rear wheel, my hand locked to the throttle, Tom hollering at me: "The fence! The fence!"

I can't be certain what captained my reflex—probably sheer desire to not damage the motorcycle—but I closed the throttle. The front wheel dropped almost instantly. I navigated a tenuous stop with a little aid from the fence— one short rebound. Then I set my feet on the ground.

Tom ran over, asking if I was okay, then seeing I'd done no damage to myself, the bike, or the fence, said, "I thought you could ride."

Never, in any fantasy, had I fathomed such a gut-pulling thrill, a surge that washes away good sense. My lips spread in a smile, I said, "That *is* riding."

"Do us a favor," he said, "use the gate."

A bit rough on throttle and clutch, I slipped out on the road and headed toward Fremont Street and the Blue Onion. I wanted Miriam to see it first. I circled slowly, getting a feel for the machine. The drive-in was filled with its afternoon crowd, high-schoolers in Dad's wheels, a couple of airmen, a low-rider in a chopped '49 Ford two-door. I pulled in beside the low-rider and set the kickstand. Miriam didn't come to take my order. I swung off the bike, caught a carhop named Sissy, and asked where my sister was.

"Pete?" she asked. A gum-munching girl of seventeen with bottle-black hair, she looked admiringly at my bike, then at me, trying to merge the two pictures into one.

"Yes."

"Nice motorcycle."

"Just got it. Where's Miriam?" I asked again.

"In a play at the college."

I asked Sissy if she'd like a ride sometime. She smacked her gum and considered the offer, then said she never went out with a man who didn't have to shave.

Cars squeezed into the A&W parking spaces. I backed off the throttle and pulled into a space beside a blue Thunderbird. Annette sat in the front passenger seat of the T-Bird with Rachel Steinmetz, who said something to her as I cut the engine. Rachel opened the door, lifted the tray off, and set it on the curb. Annette glanced at me as Rachel slammed the door. They laughed. Annette flipped me a finger and Rachel backed out over a speed bump, scraping the car's undercarriage as they drove off.

"Bitches." Betty stood an arm's length away. I hadn't noticed her car when I pulled in.

"I just wanted a Coke," I said.

She shook her head. "You want to impress Annette Sylvestri. You'd go for the type."

"You think so?"

Betty nodded thoughtfully and ran her fingers up and down the handlebars. "She won't give you a look, dumb shit. You'd think those books would make you smart. Shiny. You steal it?"

"I don't steal."

"Just purses," she said. "It's nice."

"I bought it. Bet your dad has a cow when he sees it."

"He'll get over it, but Stella will be pissed."

This was getting close to the longest conversation we'd ever held without her belittling me in some way. Suddenly aware of it, we both fell silent as she looked at the gas tank. Finally she said, "Start it up, Petey."

I kicked it to life, and Betty climbed on.

"Who said you could ride?"

"Don't be an asshole, Petey. Let's go."

None of the fantasies I had of the Triumph included her on the back. But there she was.

At the corner of Fifteenth and Bridger I panicked and braked for a car that crossed in front of us. The bike squirmed to a stop and died.

"Too much for you, Pete?"

She got off while I started it. Some kids from Vegas High drove by and told us to get a horse. Betty did her imitation of Annette and flipped them off.

She climbed back on and leaned into me. She slid her arms around my waist and pressed herself against me. "Go," she said.

We rode to the Tonopah Highway, where I turned the throttle. More relaxed now, she leaned back and held my waist. The desert took on startling clarity, each living thing distinctly carved, each creosote bush, each yucca. Now and then as she moved about, her breasts grazed my back, which was both exciting and troubling.

I pulled over at the Mt. Charleston junction, where she lit a cigarette. She turned in a slow circle, swallowing everything in. A truck rumbled past, churning the air and tousling her hair. She removed her hair ribbon and ran her fingers through the long strands. I'd never seen her with her hair loose before. It made her appear remarkably different, angellike. Resting her hand on the handlebars, she said, "If I was you, I'd ride to Florida or Alaska, ride until . . ." She didn't finish, just gave me a patient smile and crushed her cigarette underfoot.

We cruised until the sky faded into twilight, then rode toward Red Rock to watch the city light itself up. She stood beside the bike, subdued and remote, and stared at the bejeweled basin.

I reminded her I had to go to work.

"Sometimes I hate it," she said.

"What?"

"Everything."

I didn't want to talk. "We have to go."

"We could go to Montana. Wait till you see the ranch."

I'd seen a few photos on Willy's wall. Twice yearly he went to his spread to bury money, according to rumor. I asked, "Do you like the ranch?"

"Petey, don't be stupid."

I watched her stare at the city. I couldn't guess what she wanted, but I knew what I wanted—endless miles of road to travel and amazingly her on the back of the motorcycle.

I let her off at the A&W, where the manager rushed out and said he was about to tow her car. She unlocked her door and said that if he did, her dad would buy the drive-in and fire him.

After work, I parked on the edge of the driveway. I was slipping the key in when the door opened. Willy stood at the threshold. He grabbed my sleeve, pulled me inside, and dug a finger into my chest. "I ain't sayin don't ride her, but if she gets hurt, find a gun an shoot yourself."

12

On his desk lay several black-and-white photos, some yellowing. Willy motioned for me to sit, but kept looking at the photos unhurriedly as if deciding which to select for purchase. I sat as he quietly pored over them.

He sported a three-day growth of beard. Eyes red and tired, he smelled strongly of bourbon. He had reason to drink and go without rest—the Internal Revenue Service. As the probe had gathered momentum, he'd become reclusive, keeping to his office, where he held lengthy late-night conferences with his attorneys and sons, or resting in his suite, where no one was allowed. His appearances on the casino floor were ceremonial, as he tendered all management to George.

Minutes went by before he finally looked up. "Pete, you ain't visitin your ma."

No point denying it. "No, Willy."

"I told you 'bout my ma, how she died of the influenza in nineteen an eighteen, her an my sisters. Pa died too an there was just me and my cousin Luther, we called Luke. An he died, near Galveston, drowned in the ocean."

"I'm sorry."

He aimed an index finger at me. "Did I say talk? I'm tellin you that people don't hang around for you to see 'em in your own sweet time." After considering me at length, he picked up where he'd left off. "I got one sister left. Her an me don't see things the same. Ain't her blame or mine. I ain't the nicest sumbitch to trod foot on this damn earth, but I ain't the worst. Thing is, I take care'a family an friends. You unnerstand?"

I said I did.

"I got my mind on things an can't be spendin time fixin your affairs," he said.

Willy opened a drawer and pulled out a bottle of Jack Daniel's. He twisted the cap off and picked up a photo, which he held like a flower stem between his finger and thumb. The room was silent but for the hum of traffic from Fremont Street. He laid the picture down gently and said, "Get outta here. Tomorra you gonna visit your ma an tell her you're sorry."

"Yes, sir."

He looked up. "I told you 'bout that."

"Yes, Willy." I stood to leave.

"Get your bidness done in the mornin 'cause in the afternoon you'll be buyin clothes."

"Clothes?"

"Can't have you at the ranch dressed like that, boy. Be a damn embarrassment. How you an Betty gettin on?"

"Okay, I guess."

He nodded, took a swallow directly from the bottle, and returned to his snapshots. I walked to the door.

"Pete, find a good book you can read me."

"What one?"

"If I knew, wouldn't I be readin my own damn self? Why the hell am I payin for schoolin if you don't know?"

I closed the door and exhaled.

In the morning we headed off to Montana in one of Willy's Cadillacs, to the West I'd fancied as paradise when I'd seen movies like *Red River* and *High Noon*. We drove northeast through the Arizona Strip and Virgin River Gorge, past the Iron Mountains and stretches of Utah farm and ranch land, stretches of the West I'd never seen before. I was reminded of my mother's photos. Images weren't specific enough for me to recall exact details, but I remembered her snapshots and my sister's imaginative tales, and the general impression of Gaddis Tillerman's West that had fixed itself in my head was much like the one we were passing through. I wanted to stop here and there, to drive slowly and savor the trip, but Willy liked to drive straight through to the ranch, a few stops for gas and food, no more.

He wasn't talkative. Whatever occupied his thoughts drew his mind away from the drive. About two o'clock I had to remind him we'd not stopped for lunch. He uncapped his bottle of sour mash, took a sip, and handed it to me in jest.

"Here, this'll put your stomach at rest, if it don't kill it entirely."

He stopped at the next truck stop and bought us sirloins, medium rare and smothered in onions. When finally we turned west off the highway a few miles south of Dillon and entered the Big Hole, it was dark. We'd traveled seventeen hours straight. Minutes later the sun tipped the horizon and filled the side-view mirror with a blinding glow. It seemed to happen all at once. That was my first impression of the landscape; everything about it was large and sudden, like a deep breath held in painfully and then released with a whoosh.

In the deepening gloom Willy started to talk—and didn't stop. He told story after story about Dallas, his unlikely climb to power in the underworld, which he didn't speak of as an underworld. Around midnight he fell silent again. Ten miles north of Twin Falls he'd told his last story, about a hitchhiker he'd once picked up nearby. Then he turned on the car radio, set the volume, and sank into the seat. Occasionally he would unscrew the cap on his bottle and take a sip. I dozed off and on until one time I opened my eyes and said the sun was coming up.

He said, "Pete, you been a good road partner so far, but it ain't a good time to be tellin me what my eyes is smart enough to figger out."

Ranches spread on both sides of the highway. A herd of horses turned and charged away at the sound of the car, tails flailing as they ran. I pictured myself racing them on my motorcycle, but Willy didn't even look. We came to the sign that read "7-11." Even the sight of the gate didn't shake Willy's mood; if anything, it tightened its grip.

Gravel clattered against the fender wells as we bounced over the shallow ruts. We rode for miles without catching sight of a house. Then we came to a rise that inclined to a meadow of sage and clump grass, balsamroot, lupine, and western larkspur. About a mile ahead a cottonwood grove cradled three houses and a barn. We stopped.

A breeze rustled the clump grass at the shoulder of the road. Willy took a swallow of whiskey before opening the door. He left the engine idling and walked into the hardpan, where he navigated slowly through the sage, picking wildflowers. Seeing we were going to be stopped a while, I got out to stretch my legs. He gathered flowers until both hands were full. When he walked back, he seemed not to notice me. He got into the passenger seat, then told me to get behind the wheel. He laid the flowers between us and said, "Drive."

He kept the bottle in his lap and remained silent. I knew he wanted no conversation. I drove at a steady pace and kept my eyes on the ranch houses. The car smelled of whiskey and wildflowers. The grove was not so far off after all; the illusion was merely an effect of the Montana landscape that exaggerates features and dwarfs subjects. The ranch houses sat atop a knoll. We drove through the open gate.

"Don't care much for that motorcycle," Willy muttered.

I didn't answer.

I stopped the Cadillac in front of the largest house. Willy shook his head.

"This here's the bunkhouse," he said. "Ain't where I sleep. That's the ranch house." He pointed to a square white house built on a stone foundation and surrounded by a white ladder fence. It had a wide porch and an upstairs half again the size of the ground floor. A garden spread out from both sides of the flagstone walkway. The door opened and a man dressed in a denim jacket and chaps waved and ambled down the stairs.

I parked by the hitching post in front.

Willy rolled down his window. "Cal."

The man said, "Willy, it's ready." His left hand was thumbless. He squinted at me. "Who's your driver?"

"Pete. A genuine tenderfoot, Cal. All yours." With that Willy swooped up the wildflowers and walked to the house.

"Ride a little rough, Pete?" Cal asked.

"No."

He nodded. "He'll be okay in a day or so."

Though I didn't recall him from the Lucky, Cal seemed familiar. He rested his hands on his knees as he leaned inside to ask for the car keys to unload the luggage. After toting Willy's bags into the main house, he had me back the car up to the bunkhouse.

I had to look up at Cal. His weathered face gave his deep-set blue eyes an almost startling effect. He looked a cowboy from head to foot—scuffed boots, faded jeans, scarred hands. In new jeans, shiny boots, and a wide belt with a silver buckle, I felt conspicuous.

We stood on a floor covered with yellow linoleum. He pointed out the hallway to the rooms. The first on the right was to be mine. "Don't have but six hands right now," he said. "We're rounding up spring calves for branding. Willy says you never been on a horse. That true?"

"True," I said, keeping my promise to Stella.

"You will. This is a working ranch." He let this register, then asked if I liked chili.

"Yes, sir."

"Be a good idea to stay away from the house till Willy comes out. He'll hole up for a day or two." He told me to get some sleep, shut-eye he called it, and he'd wake me up for lunch.

After lunch Cal walked me to the stables, which from the ridge had looked like a barn. As we approached, bedlam broke out as four beagles barked and jumped at the fence. Cal shouted for them to shut up. He picked up a clod and heaved it at the pen. He said, "Something to clean up after, never mind them ripping clothes off the line now and then and me catching hell for it."

He removed his straw hat, exposing a deep scar on his forehead. From his shirt pocket he pulled out cigarette papers and a pouch of tobacco, which he poured as if it were gold dust. Using one hand, he rolled the cigarette and lit a match on the seat of his jeans. He noticed I was looking at what remained of a left thumb.

"Looped the running end around the pommel roping a steer. Horse stopped, steer didn't. Don't have to worry about getting it caught the second time. See that one?" He pointed to a muscular animal feeding at a trough on the far side of the coral.

"Yes."

"He's a Leopard Appaloosa. Name's Lead. Climb up a cliff if you can handle him."

"Big horse," I said. On his white hindquarters the horse had several large gray spots that looked like painted paw tracks. The rest of his coat was gray.

"He's a gelding. Got his winter coat. Looks best in the summer. He'll kick your head off if you give him half a chance, Pete. You listen to every word I say tomorrow 'cause you got one-half day to get to know him."

"What if I don't want to?"

He avoided the question. "In the kitchen you'll find a bag of apples. Give him a couple so he'll know you tomorrow."

The big Appaloosa pushed hay around with his nose. He was nothing like Stella's mare and a bit scary. Well, I'd tried a motorcycle the hard way.

It took a half hour of coaxing to get Lead to come; even then he kept his distance, sniffing. He had one blue eye and one brown. The brown one seemed kind; the other looked to have a touch of dementia. I held out an apple. He sniffed the air, ears twitching.

"Go on in, boy," a voice said from behind.

I turned and faced a short, sun-crispened man with a graying beard and a bulbous nose mapped with broken capillaries. He had tiny brown amused eyes. He shook my hand before I had a chance to recover from my initial astonishment.

"Didn't mean to scare. Name's Jiggers, Jiggers Phee from Dandy Ridge.

You're a tall one, near as tall as Cal," he said, his paintbrush eyebrows rising. "What's your name?"

Like Cal's, his was a familiar face. I figured they were just types I'd seen before. "Pete Elkins from Palouse. That's in Washington."

"Alliteration. Peter from Palouse. I know about such stuff, being a cowboy poet and all."

"Cowboy poet?"

"Busted that horse. Smart, I'll tell you. Broke him five or six times, so I thought, but he threw me over a fence and rode me into a rail. One day I looked him in the eye and said, 'I'm going to ride you or shoot you,' and brought the rifle along to make my point. Can't say it was the rifle. Maybe he was just tired of throwing me." He held up an index finger and looked at the sky, then began to recite:

Ol' Lead, a horse of distinction,
couldn't be rode so I heard.
He was driven by primal instinction,
crazy to fly like a bird.
Cowboys come from Dillon, Fargo,
Cheyenne, and Laramie,
tryin to break what couldn't be broke,
that is, by no one but Mr. Jiggers Phee.

I smiled. "Is 'instinction' a word?"

"Is in my verse. Think you could do any better?"

"I don't think so."

"Good, 'cause there's room for but one poet on a ranch, and here I'm he."

"Yes, sir, Mr. Phee."

"Jiggers. Looks like you got a hungry horse."

Lead snorted, his muzzle so close to me I could feel his breath on the back of my neck. Tentatively, I offered him an apple. He sniffed, but backed away.

"Put it on the rail," Jiggers said.

Lead snatched the apple with his large yellow teeth and immediately crushed it.

"He'll take the next one from you," Jiggers said. "Got god-awful snouts, bigger hearts. Nothing like a big Appaloosa climbing a hill, surefooted as a jackass and strong as an elephant."

"You like them, then?"

He motioned the idea off with a wave of his hand. "I wouldn't have one of the mean sonofabitches. Well, take it easy there, Peter from Palouse." Humming, he swaggered off on his short legs, favoring his left. Every few feet he'd pause to rub his fingers and thumb together as if kneading verse off his fingertips.

I met the hands at the supper table. The cook, a woman named Conchita, supervised the meal. "Supervised" was the word to describe what she did, for the men served themselves, and her primary obligation seemed to involve keeping them from breaking knuckles and plates as they reached for food.

They talked sparingly, especially Pearl, a slender blond boy, who at nineteen was the youngest. They ate at a frenzied pace, stuffing biscuits in their mouths with one hand while spooning in chili and forking in bites of meat loaf with the other. Conchita enforced manners by occasionally slapping at a hand that reached for a platter or bowl she'd not yet set down.

Afterward they broke out a deck of cards to play hearts, all except Sarge, who sat and watched from a corner of the room, and Jiggers, who brought out a pen and a composition book filled with thick, frayed pages. Cal asked if I wanted a seat. I said I didn't know how to play.

"Got money?" Oso, a burly vaquero from Chihuahua, Mexico, asked. His English was broken, but he understood every word that passed across the table.

"Some," I said.

"Hey, we teach you. *No hay problema.*" The others laughed, even more so when I wisely shook my head.

Cal, who seemed popular with the others, said he was going fishing after the branding. Lon, a lanky man in his forties with a front tooth missing, claimed the boss gets first crack at the brook trout, but privilege didn't matter as Cal couldn't get a minnow out of a toilet bowl with a box of dynamite. Cal winked and said Lon was ready for a month of riding fence. Jiggers said the only fisherman on the ranch was Sarge, who acknowledged the compliment with a nod. A quiet man who wore wire-rim glasses, he had said grace silently at the table before eating. He hadn't asked questions of me but had paid particular attention whenever someone else did. He too seemed like someone I'd seen before.

Lon slapped down a card on the table and cackled when Leon got stuck with the queen of spades. Leon was muscular, with a face that looked carved from stone, and he had two fingers missing from his left hand. Though he looked hard, he was good-natured. The game appeared to be a ritual wherein the only point was to rib each other. Pearl went to his bunk and returned with a bottle of schnapps. He uncorked it, took a swallow, and passed it on.

Leon wondered how long Willy would recluse himself in the house this time. Cal nodded his head toward me. They went on slapping down cards and trading mild jibes. The conversation shifted to Willy wanting me to ride Lead the next morning.

Jiggers looked up. "Should be some poetry there."

"You know what you're in for, Pete?" Leon asked.

"No."

He clicked his tongue and shook his head. Pearl looked at me with sympathetic eyes. Oso raised his eyebrows and looked at the ceiling. Cal told them to stop teasing.

"He can be rode, Pete. Don't let these boys get to you," Cal said.

"Ain't been rode lately," Pearl said.

"Not lately," Leon said.

"*Pues,* he naber kill no one," Oso said.

Jiggers smiled at me. I pictured Lead's demented blue eye and excused myself to go for more apples. The dogs howled as I passed and the horses whinnied and skittered nervously as they watched my approach. I climbed the rail. "Look what I brought." I held out an apple. He didn't waste time stepping back, just seized it like a purse snatcher.

The night was silent save for a few boisterous crickets and a westerly breeze snapping branches. I strolled past the main house. A light glowed in a window. Curious, I walked nearer. The back of Willy's head showed as he sat in a chair at a dining table. To his right was a fifth of Jack Daniel's. He seemed entranced as he stared at an oil painting hanging on the wall . . . of a slender woman with strawberry-blond hair and walnut-brown eyes.

Her long hair hung over her shoulders, and she had a certain youthful grace. Beside her stood a palomino Arabian with a white mane, her hand cupping its neck. As is the case with beautiful faces, hers seemed ageless.

"What're you doing, Pete?" a voice asked.

Startled, I wheeled about. I was in the light, and the speaker in the dark, so I couldn't make out his face.

"Nothing. I just . . ."

"Didn't mean to scare you. It's me, Sarge."

"Oh." I took a last glance at Willy to see if our voices had disturbed him, but they hadn't. I stepped out of the light and toward the shadow that was Sarge.

"I took some apples to Lead."

"Why'd you do that?"

"I've got to ride him tomorrow."

"Ever ridden before?"

Again I kept my promise to Stella and said, "No, sir."

He scuffed the ground with his toe and looked up at the stars. "Well, don't worry. He's a good gentle mount." We shared an awkward moment of silence, then he pointed to a cluster of stars. "Orion," he said. "Your name's Elkins."

"Yes, sir."

"Elkins, an unusual name." He explained he liked to walk alone at night to think, said that he had some magazines if I liked to read, and excused himself.

I went directly to my bunk.

The card game wound down, and soon boot heels resounded on the linoleum as the men strolled to their quarters. They chided each other, their voices warm and congenial. After trading good nights, each shut his door and the hallway light went off. Sarge came in later, paused at my door, then moved on to his room.

Sometime past midnight I drifted off, sleeping soundly until barking woke me. I spread my curtain and looked out. Willy was leading a saddled horse out of the stables. He walked with a noticeable stagger and took two attempts before mounting the saddle. He flicked the reins and rode off.

The hands were showered and dressing as I entered. Pearl said I looked hung over and told me the best cure was a shot of schnapps, which might also make my ride more pleasant. They talked cheerfully as Conchita served scrambled eggs with onions and green peppers, and heavily buttered tortillas.

After the others left, Cal called me over. "Don't have to ride him if you don't want to."

"Well, I do."

"Good. That's the spirit."

He had me mount and dismount a saddle strapped to a nail barrel. I pretended complete ignorance as he showed me how to position and bend my legs, explained the way a horse responds to pressure from heels and knees. Reins were more complicated. Gentle on those, he warned. No rough movements, steady back to slow, heavier to stop, but don't keep pressure on once the horse is under control. Forward, soft on the rein and pressure from both knees to gallop or run a horse. Don't give the horse much head at first.

He walked me to a stall, opened the gate, and told me to watch as he rode. The horse was skittish and jerked away. Cal grabbed an ear and twisted it. The animal hung its head as if sedated. He said, "I've seen riders break their hands on a dumb animal's head to control it. Not much smarter than the horse."

Cal unstrapped a saddle and tossed it to me. He laid the bit and harness on top of the saddle and motioned for me to follow. Then I was alone in the stall with Lead. Cal coached me as I slipped the bit in Lead's mouth and set the bridle. The saddle was easy. Cal told me to hop on so he could adjust the stirrups.

"Let me know when they're right," he said.

"How'll I know?"

"When your knees are sore, the stirrups are too high, and when your ass gets sore they're too low. But when both your knees and your ass are sore, they're just right." He smiled. "For now we'll just guess."

I dismounted. Cal took the reins and walked Lead out to the arena, where the hands were waiting. "You ready, Pete?"

Instead of answering, I placed my foot in the stirrup and swung over the saddle as Cal held the reins. Lead stepped sideways. It felt good to sit atop a powerful animal. He looked back with that blue eye as if forming a plan. The men loafed by the fence, smoking or chewing tobacco.

"He'll take you hard left first, Peter, then rear. Be ready!" Jiggers called out.

"Stay high in the saddle!" Leon shouted.

"*Tengas cuidado, Pedro!*" Oso hollered.

"No need being afraid, Pete. Every cowboy gets throwed," Cal said.

I received the reins. Lead shivered. I looked at Cal, who showed traces of a smile.

"Give him some rein and knee pressure," Cal said.

"Open the gate," I said.

"What?"

"Open it," I said and nudged Lead with my knees to get him moving.

When the gate opened, I hit his flanks with my heels, leaned slightly forward, and slapped Lead's hindquarter. Oso shouted, "Andale, vaquero!" Jiggers took off his hat and waved it. Sarge hollered the joke was on them. Then I was racing through wildflowers and sage, wind in my face, Lead lengthening his stride into the onrushing landscape.

Willy came out that afternoon. I was hunched over on a stool outside the bunkhouse peeling a bucket of potatoes Conchita had given me. He went first to the dog pen, where he opened the gate. The beagles circled him and nipped and growled playfully. He petted them for several minutes, calling each by name. Finished, he walked directly to the porch where I sat.

"Them's some worthless dogs, but . . . Well, you got the boys. Least that's the report."

"Yeah."

"Stella been teachin you?"

"Stella?"

"Good horsewoman. What's doin with them taters?"

"Conchita told me to peel them."

"Well, finish up an get the Cadillac. You an me is goin to Butte."

Dropping the last potato I was working on into the water, I laid the peeler on the stool and wiped my hands.

"What the hell you doin, Pete?"

"Going for the car."

"I only own the ranch, Pete. Conchita runs the show. You be gettin both 'a us in trouble."

I sat back down. Willy went inside and returned a moment later with another stool and potato peeler. "She made me wash my hands," he said.

Willy drove. It was dark by the time we reached Butte, and the temperature had dropped several degrees. He took me to dinner downtown where the maître d,' a silver-haired man with a robust face, greeted Willy with a British accent and a vigorous handshake. Willy introduced me. At the table the maître d' hung about, lamenting the once splendid city he claimed was in decay.

"Food's still great, I bet," Willy said.

"This is the only spot of civilization left, sir, a true inn, if you will, in terms of nourishment, and of course drink. Your usual, I presume?"

"You bet."

"Remember, Mr. Bobbins, the establishments here and in Meadorville?" He looked at me. "During the war we served elegant food despite rationing. Scruffy miners dressed up on Friday to bring their ladies—trying so to act like fine gentlemen. I remember Mr. Bobbins and the lady . . ."

Willy motioned with his finger to cut off the words.

The headwaiter cleared his throat. "Yes. You'll find the food as always. Your usual, then. Right away."

After the maître d' left, Willy said, "I like the fancy way he talks, always did. Fine fella for someone so highbrow."

"You lived here?"

"After the war started an after bein run outta Dallas an Tulsa."

"We lived here, but I don't remember."

"You was too young, Pete," Willy said knowingly, and that was all he said on the matter.

At the Finnlander Hotel he traded small talk with a desk clerk who'd earned a limp from his days as a miner. As he handed our keys to Willy, he said something about a room being kept the same. Willy thanked him, saying he might look in on it in the morning. As the elevator doors closed, his expression changed. He'd had only one drink before dinner and was both sober and somber. "Pete, soon I'll be goin to prison. Promise you'll see Betty don't get in trouble."

I was too taken aback to answer right away.

"I 'spect it's a big thing to ask, her bein so spirited an not much for makin friends. I want you to promise you'll spend time with her and your ma, too."

"Betty doesn't like me."

"She'll get over that. Say the words. A promise means somethin to men like us. Like that Gatsby fella, we got us a bed a nails when we was young. That's past." He pressed the button to the third floor. "You promise?"

"Are you really going to prison, Willy?"

"Say it, Pete."

"I promise."

He held out his hand for me to shake.

After a breakfast of biscuits and gravy washed down with black coffee, Willy drove the streets of Butte, a city of wounded old houses and red brick buildings soiled orange, like a city with cancer. He drove unhurriedly.

"It was different back then. War bidness."

He told the story of a company of black soldiers, army engineers, brought in to speed up production. The miners refused to work with them, not because of race but because the mines were theirs, and they stood up to threats from the president, the military, and the U.S. attorney. The company of soldiers was pulled out of the mines.

I asked Willy the point.

"Maybe they ain't one. It just happened is all."

We paid a visit to the Five Mile Bar, an abandoned two-story roadhouse, its white paint weathered and chipped. It had been Willy's until 1950, along with the casino in Meadorville. We walked the perimeter. The panes had been smashed, the windows boarded up. He pried a half-rotted sheet of plywood off a window and tossed it to the ground. Inside smelled of dust. He shook his head and looked in.

"Like seein something dead, Pete."

He tossed the keys to me and told me to drive. I was seated and turning the engine over when he slid in beside me. "What'd you say that boy's name was stole Betty's purse?" he asked.

"Don't remember ever saying what it was."

He took a puff off the cigar, which he held out as if admiring it. "No, guess you didn't."

From there he directed me to the highway to Helena. He had me stop at an overlook. He took off his hat and tossed it on the seat before he opened the door. A wind swirled up from below, and his thin hair rustled. "Berkeley Pit," he said. "Takes the breath away, don't it?"

And it did. I stared at a gaping excavation that took on mythical proportions with its walls carved into tiers, seats for giants, a colosseum, a hole-diggers' hole, a pit hollowed out by madmen who'd not yet given up. Below, four gnome-size tractors spat diesel smoke and churned dust about like ocean spray.

"Used to be towns there, Finntown an Dublin Gulch an Meadorville." Willy pointed behind us. "Highway used to be there, two lanes into Helena, an from Friday night till Sunday cars lined up, like Fremont Street on a weekend night. Cops had to direct traffic." Arms folded over his chest, he stood on the overlook and stared out. A while passed before he spoke again.

"Thing about change is it damages people an ain't nothin they can do. Like me gettin old. Anaconda owned this—biggest copper-mining company in the world—owned land the miners built houses on an raised families on. Dollar a year for a lot. Hell, my rent was a buck. Company needed casinos an whorehouses, wanted all the vice an churches an parks you could pack in a small city. Idea was to give miners what they wanted. One day the deep mines run outta copper. They started this hole and tore down the towns, casinos, ever'thing.

"I was gone by then. Kefauver was closin down men like me, so I left. Some didn't. Runnin outta copper got to them miners. Some killed theirselves. Takes a brave an crazy man to go down there knowin it may be his grave. Men what risked them holes, men what took on the whole of the United States couldn't stop what bidness brought their way. Nothin more fearsome 'an bidness, Pete.

"What we're lookin at is a big open grave. Communities down there. You just can't see 'em." He let this sink in, then said, "You prob'ly lived some-where 'round here, Pete."

"Really?"

He smiled an ironic smile. "Just guessin, son."

He'd never called me son before. My imagination soared for an instant. He ran his fingers through his thin hair and took a last look at the giant hole. "They's things best left in the past, Pete. Can't fill that hole in and build them houses again. Gone's gone."

He lit a cigar and walked back to the car. I stood a moment gazing at the open pit, wondering what it meant and why Willy had told me what he had. I was sixteen facing seventeen, certain of very little, but some things seemed assured—Willy knew more about my story, and part of it was somewhere in that huge bowl of Montana dirt.

Two days later I was packing my bag when Sarge knocked and asked if he could come in. He sat down on the springs, but didn't speak. I'd rolled up my mattress and, following Conchita's exact instructions, tucked my sheets and towels inside the pillowcase. She was fastidious about such things. I wasn't sure what he wanted, so I kept silent and packed. When he cleared his throat, I looked over. "Guess you'll be coming back this summer."

I said I didn't know.

"You fish, Pete?"

"Never have."

He nodded. "No one here . . . Well, sometimes Cal, but the others don't. Maybe. Well, if you'd . . . like it, I'll take you fishing."

"I would like it."

He stood and fidgeted with his cuffs, realized what he was doing and shoved his hands in his pockets to stop himself. "You need help with that bag?"

"No, sir."

"The boys call me Sarge."

"You want me to call you Sarge?"

"No. I like . . . 'Sir' will be just fine." He walked to the door. "Don't worry about a pole or tackle. I got all you'll need." Again he nodded and wished me well.

13

That spring, pressure from the IRS kept Willy inside the casino, where he met with politicians and poker players, told stories, walked among the patrons and shook hands, and smiled when a player with a million-dollar credit line asked to bet it all on a spin of the roulette ball.

"You want to spin the ball yourself?" Willy asked.

The gambler said, "No, I want you to spin it, Willy."

A pit boss stacked ten hundred-thousand-dollar marker buttons on the even. Willy set the ball on the rim of the wheel head and spun it so hard it whined for the first six rotations. When it finally descended twenty seconds later, it ticked a fret and dived into the six. Willy took eighty piles of greenbacks, twenty-five thousand in each, from three security guards and laid the money next to the million-dollar lammer button. "Care to let it ride?" he asked.

The high roller shook his head.

"Care to count it?" Willy asked.

"You ain't no banker, Willy. I trust you."

The event made headlines as the single biggest wager in history. Willy said he'd lost bigger bets than that, but those were in back rooms, and he wouldn't want revenuers to know about them because they might be business deductions. Reporters laughed at Willy's joke and took down every word.

Sin City, by B. Lawrence Karras, a best-seller in its first week, was published in May. A chapter devoted to Willy's exploits in Texas claimed he was connected to the underworld and had paid the Mafia to make hits, including the one on Sammy "the Slav" Lukovic, who once owned five percent of the old Sierra Club. The book didn't help Willy's image with the feds, but people flocked to the Lucky just to get a glimpse of him. For his part, Willy defended himself by saying that if anyone needed killing, he wasn't about to put up good money just to do public service.

I was the one who had to read to Willy the part where the author called him a splendidly ignorant hick and a splendidly stupid boor. Willy raised his finger for me to stop. "Man's a New Yorker. Never seen one who could play poker. Don't know how to bluff. They get the upper hand, they let you know right away. I never lost a penny to one in bidness, but many's the New Yorker lost to me. You keep the upper hand by lettin 'em think they got it."

He laughed at the part about the Slav choking to death on a billiard ball held in place by a gag, said he always did bite off more than he could chew. Of course, the mystery to me was the same as the mystery to the author—why?

When I finished reading the last page of the book, Willy took it in hand and examined the dustcover. "He ain't no F. Scott Fitzgerald an this ain't no *Gatsby,*" he said, picked up the telephone, leaned back, and waited for his attorney to come on the line. He told the lawyer to draft a letter to B. Lawrence Karras telling him not to worry about a lawsuit, even though he'd told a few splendid whoppers, because business was up a splendid five or six points due to the splendid publicity. Willy added an invitation for Karras to come visit the Lucky at the casino's expense and, of course, sign a copy of the splendid book.

Betty drew on the cigarette and held the smoke in as she looked at the intersection. The waitress asked if we wanted to place our order yet. Betty shook her head.

"Just bring another Coke," she said.

"What about Einstein?" the waitress asked, meaning me.

I looked up. "Do you have grappa?"

"What's that?" the waitress asked.

"Don't pay any attention to him. He's weird," Betty said. She thought for a second and added, "When he gets here, why don't you move to another booth?"

Her remark hurt, but I nodded and pretended to study. Though I'd begun to have feelings for her, she was in love with Richard Forsby, a twenty-seven-year-old guitarist with wispy blond hair, a narrow aristocratic nose, and deep-set eyes. His one claim to fame was picking a guitar with Elvis Presley while both were in the army in Germany.

He played backup gigs with different bands, performing at the Saddle Club or the Nashville-Nevada—forty-bucks-a-night gigs. Betty and I would wait in a booth at Denny's at Five Points East, where she'd watch the door to the Saddle Club. Sometimes we'd wait hours. She would smoke cigarettes and stare through the darkened window, her biology book open but unread.

"Why watch? His breaks are at the same time," I said.

"Petey, read your book."

Before the waitress returned with the soft drink, Rich came out of the Saddle Club and waved. A sparkle came to Betty's eyes as she moved over. When he pushed the glass door open, I scooped up my books. So lanky that his limbs seemed to move in shifts, he sauntered to the booth, slipped in beside Betty, and took her waiting hand. I stood.

"Petey, you don't have to go," he said.

"Got to, Rich. Got to study."

I moved down two booths, which was just as well. She acted as giddy as the high school girls she mocked. She paid for meals and listened as if mesmerized whenever he spoke. And I had to watch it. I buried my face in my schoolbook as the waitress dropped off the Coke to Betty and took their orders.

She walked to my booth and said, "I need these tables."

I stared at the open page. "I'll have a corned beef on rye, please."

"You could sit at the counter."

"Can't study there."

"One corned beef on rye."

"Yes, and I changed my mind on the grappa."

She was looking at herself in the darkened window and didn't hear.

"Petey, you're too skinny," Rich called over. "Order a vanilla shake." Which was what Betty often told him, as he was even thinner than I.

"One vanilla shake," the waitress said and walked away.

He spoke in between bites, Betty hypnotized by the motion of his lips and his Adam's apple. He *could* confuse and hypnotize. In twenty-seven years he'd accumulated an amalgam of facts and philosophies to use on his audience, believing that the world was nearing a condition he called stasis and California was the new Babylon, only its decay would begin at its metacultural peak. He explained a metaculture as a money/image-based society copied from pieces of previous cultures with nothing profound, worthy, or original to its credit. In essence, we were all living a Monopoly game. His ideas came from Kerouac and Sartre, with a few from Eastern seers.

I chewed on my dry sandwich as my eyes blundered back and forth over the same three sentences without finding sense in the written words. Rich was talking about Peter the fisherman as a metaphor for the spread of religion and decline of society. I found my attention straying from the book to what he was saying.

Rich stopped and lit a cigarette.

Betty asked, "You mean our Petey?"

"I'm talking about Simon Peter, the man Christ chose."

"Oh. Well, why don't you ever talk about Petey?"

He saw me watching and winked as if we were in this together. I tried not to like Rich, but his friendly manner and sense of humor made me feel as if he and I were sharing a private joke, though I seldom understood anything he talked about. "Okay, here we go." He set his cigarette in the ashtray. "Pete, why are you here?"

"Here, here?" I pointed to the booth. "Or Las Vegas?"

"Either."

"I moved here with my mother."

Rich puffed on his cigarette and watched the smoke rise, after which he turned to her and said profoundly, "People seek Las Vegas when they don't have a home."

Betty paid the bill.

Betty and I rehearsed a script in case Stella asked questions. Whatever I decided *was* the story—saw *The Naked Prey*, great; burger and fries at the Blue Onion. Stella merely nodded as she always did and told me I was getting to be quite a liar, a skill that came quickly to those who hung around Miss Bobbins. Betty ran up the stairs, thudding her heels on every other step. I was left to look at Stella until I could look no longer.

Betty sat on the edge of her chair and told me I must convince Willy it was okay for her to go out, as she was ready for finals.

"You're not ready," I said.

"I will be."

Three weeks before, she'd been desperate, knew none of the material. She resisted her books the way cats resist swimming pools. So, as she smoked cigarettes, I'd drilled her on Dickens and Brontë, Shelley and Byron, the Crusades and the Knights Templar, food chains and bioms. She was passably ready for everything but Algebra I, and we needed the weekend to study.

"You can't add two columns of numbers, much less find the value of three *X* if *Y* is seven and two-thirds and *Z* is twenty when *X* is divided by two."

"I can get the answers."

"Sure."

She tapped my forehead and repeated, "I said I can *get* the answers."

As what she said sank in, I shook my head. "If you're caught . . ."

"Follow me."

I followed her to the arena, where we sat on the top rail. She lit a cigarette and ran her fingers through her hair, which hung loose over her shoulders and breasts. She looked toward the patio door and handed me the cigarette.

"Petey, I need something," she said. "It means my life. You know Miss Margaret."

Miss Margaret, the toughest teacher at Gorman and the most boring, taught math, and her exams were as secret as a Soviet code. I took a draw and handed the cigarette back.

"You ready to hear this?" she asked.

Already half afraid, I listened as she explained Miss Margaret's Friday bingo ritual at the Nugget, followed by a shrimp cocktail and a glass of champagne at the Golden Gate. "I know where she keeps the tests," Betty said. "I need someone who can recognize the right one."

I knew where this was leading and shook my head.

"All you have to do is copy the test answers and I'll take them in with me."

"No way. I'm no thief."

"You stole purses out of cars. What's the difference?"

"I didn't either."

"Come on. If I don't pass, it's summer school. Would you want to take her again?"

Richard had a gig in Reno, and Betty had been brooding ever since he left. Worse, Stella had restricted her from travel if she flunked a class. No matter how much Betty pleaded with Willy, Stella would say no. "You'll have to take her for geometry anyhow," I said.

"Petey, I've arranged it."

"I won't do it." I jumped down from the rail.

"You're chickenshit."

"Okay, I'm chickenshit." I started for the house.

She sprang down and followed. "Petey, you're my only chance. You've got brains enough to spot the right exam."

I stopped. "Why should I?"

"A thousand dollars."

"You have a thousand dollars?"

"I'll have five thousand if I pass."

"You get five grand for passing?"

"And a thousand more for every B."

"No way, Betty."

She flicked the cigarette away. "Two thousand."

I swallowed, imagining what it would be like to have that kind of money to throw around.

She smiled. "You should be flattered. I'm giving the burglar five hundred is all."

"A burglar. Jesus, Betty, you can't trust a thief," I said, thinking of Timmy.

"He's a professional."

"Why tell me?"

"I trust you."

"I'll still say no."

"Don't be pigheaded." Again she pulled the cigarette pack out of her pocket, tapped one out, and lit it. She looked across the patio to the door, smoke drifting from her mouth. "Promise you won't tell a soul?"

I envisioned the woman she would become, the frown that would come to her mouth and the lines that would frame her eyes, a lovely, sad sketch of a girl who resembled the woman in the portrait Willy admired. "How'd you find a burglar?"

"Can't say."

"Ruben Lee, I'll bet."

"Hell, you'll probably go to the old man and tell him."

"I wouldn't. Never."

She took a drag, tossed the cigarette to the ground, and crushed it out. "Guess I'll have to depend on him to write down the answers."

"Hope he knows more about algebra than you."

"Fuck you, Petey. I'm getting drunk." She turned toward the house.

"What time?" I asked.

She strolled back and playfully pulled at my arm. "I wouldn't ask if I thought there was any other way."

We walked toward the house leaning into each other, her breast brushing against the side of my arm. A pleasant warmth crawled down from my head to my belly, where it curled up like a kitten too stupid to know any better. She chuckled. When I looked at her, we burst out in laughter, the kind that cloaks fear.

Miss Margaret's, a two-bedroom white stucco house on Sweeney Avenue near Fifteenth Street, lay in the shadows of four huge elms whose roots cracked the walkways and whose boughs interlocked over the roadway. It was a quiet street.

I parked my motorcycle on Fifteenth and walked to the black Ford pickup where Betty and her burglar waited for me. The closer I got to them, the more my guts stirred. The passenger door swung open as I approached, and Tennessee slipped out. He asked if I was ready. He smelled rank. A tall man in his twenties, he looked older, and dangerous. I nodded.

The old broad, he informed me, had left in her car fifteen minutes earlier. Everything looked good. He told Betty to be ready, in case. She wished us luck. We had a plan—walk past the house as if out for a stroll, see if any neighbors pay attention, circle around into the backyard. As we neared her house, a car came up Sweeney from Maryland Parkway, illuminating us in its headlights. I wanted to turn and run. Tennessee must have sensed this. "Stay cool," he said.

The car passed by, the driver taking no notice of us as he pulled into a driveway near where Betty waited. We passed Miss Margaret's, dark except for porch lights in the front and rear. The neighbors seemed otherwise occupied, so Tennessee nodded and we circled back, jumped her fence and ducked behind the oleander bushes. He had me wait as he went and unscrewed the light. Then he stood in the shadow of the porch. Before I realized what he'd done, the lock was picked and the kitchen door pushed open.

He signaled. I started to move, but I just didn't have the courage. This wasn't a bungalow at the El Rancho. He came over, grabbed my arm, and shoved me up the porch steps and through the open door. In the kitchen he forced me to the wall, his forearm under my chin.

"Don't fuck this up, kid. If the old lady comes in on us, I'll take care of it." His spittle sprinkled my face.

He held me against the wall until his exasperation abated, then shook his head slowly as he released me. "Crazy idea," he said. "Never should'a said yes."

Using a penlight, he walked down the hall to a small bedroom used as an office. He handed me the light to hold while he went to work on the file drawers. He inserted pick and turning wrench in the key well and manipulated them, repeating the same deft motions to line up the tumblers. He couldn't get the lock to give. Muttering that he wasn't getting paid enough, he slammed his palm into the drawer. Three cars drove by. Their lights swept down the hallway. Each time headlight beams crossed the window, my thought was that she had come home early and Tennessee would kill her.

A patrol car swung down the street, slowed, and shot a spotlight beam into the living room. Tennessee reached up, gripped my hand, covered the light, and whispered for me to get down. I suddenly had to go to the bath-room. His hand remained clamped over mine. The darkness seemed to mag-nify sound, especially the idling engine and the radio sizzling intermittently with static. I imagined them rattling the kitchen door and finding it un-locked. Finally the patrol car moved on, east to Fifteenth, where it turned north. All the while Tennessee kept a grip on the penlight. My fingers were numb. He let go of me and immediately returned to the cabinet.

"More light," he said. A metallic click, and the drawer slid open. He smiled. "Okay, kid, get it done fast."

Miss Margaret, the methodical mathematician, kept orderly files. She stored papers marked "Tests" in the second drawer. Now it was Tennessee's turn to hold the light as I pulled out the sheet marked "Algebra I Test." She'd even been kind enough to mark down the operations. I copied fast, flipping sheets back and forth, confirming each note. It took twenty-five minutes to complete three-fourths of the copying. All the while I thought my guts were going to burst. I looked at him pleadingly and dropped the pen as I couldn't go on.

"I've got to go," I said.

"What?"

"I've got to go. I can't hold it."

"You mean you gotta shit?"

I nodded.

"Jesus H. Christ. Stupid fuckin kid. I should'a knowed better. Goddamn, go, but take the test with you."

I copied as fast as I could while Tennessee stood at the door telling me the place smelled putrid. I finished and handed him the original. He was in-stantly gone. The cabinet slammed shut.

He waited at the back door. "No one never pulled nothin like that on me," he said.

I gave him the notepad with the answers and he told me to get lost. After looking up and down the street, he walked to the truck. I took the sidewalk on the opposite side. The truck door opened long enough for me to glimpse Betty as he tossed her the pad.

I was still warming the engine on my bike when sirens sounded. How far off I wasn't sure, but near enough, it seemed, and getting louder. I circled on Fifteenth and headed for Charleston, sirens converging from everywhere. I was almost to Second Street when a siren burped behind me.

I glanced over my shoulder to see a motorcycle cop motioning me to the side of the road. Although scared, I stood tall. He asked for license and reg-istration, all the while looking at my bike. My hands shook as I lifted the seat.

After checking the registration against the plate, he asked how long I'd owned it. I remembered Willy's advice about getting along with cops and relaxed. "A few months."

"Where you coming from?"

I said the first thing that came to mind. "Church."

"Which church?"

I knew only two by name, St. Anne's Catholic Church and Christ's Church Episcopal. "Christ's Church," I said.

"What were you doing there?"

My wits provided. "Training to be an altar boy."

He nodded and looked in the direction of some oncoming emergency lights. An ambulance blared past, driving east. We watched it race down the street, lights flashing and fading.

"Accident on the highway," he said. "County. I was an altar boy," he added and told me to wait by the Triumph. He read my name to the dispatcher. The radio crackled—voices using code, static, dispatchers passing on information. A dispatcher informed him I had no record.

He handed back my ID without explanation and said, "Be careful. Had my eye on one like it, but I'm just too tall. Shame, isn't it?"

I swung my leg over the bike. "Real shame, yes, sir."

14

Betty flunked algebra and refused to pay me. Miss Margaret had smelled an odor when she came home, and though she found nothing missing, she wrote all new tests for her classes. Betty had enough good sense not to use the cheat sheet. Though mad for two days, she finally found the humor in it and we shared a good laugh. But the laughter ceased when Willy said she would have to take summer classes and turned a deaf ear to her appeals. She locked herself in her room, refused to talk, eat, or come out. Arguing that George and Ruben Lee had gotten whatever they wanted, though neither was much of a scholar, she tried to convince Willy to let her have the summer off. What came of her arguing was he bought her a car. Willy favored big, expensive Cadillacs, preferably black. Betty wanted a pink Mustang convertible. The Ford seemed reasonable, as he was under the impression that it was tame, being dainty and pink and all, but under the hood it housed a wind-busting high-compression 289 short block with a racing cam and tuned headers.

The first day she picked up her new wheels, Betty drove me out on West

Charleston toward Red Rock. We crossed Jones Boulevard at forty in third gear, then she downshifted to second, drove the gas pedal to the floor, and snapped my head back. Half a mile later the speedometer was buried and her long hair looked like a streamer in a hurricane. We slowed to fifty before sound returned to my ears. "What'a you think, Petey?" she shouted.

An embarrassment to be seen in, it was a monster at the gas pedal that could spray exhaust in the windshield of most any stock car around. "Too light to go that fast!" I shouted back.

She took this as a challenge, braking the car and slowing to about ten, then swinging a U-turn headed east, ripping through the gears. She finally braked and pulled under the aluminum awning at Pappy's Drive-in. "We'll take it to Reno," she said.

"Reno? But your dad . . ."

"Doesn't count. I promised I'd try. The ol' man just wants to hear me say it, that's all. Besides, I told him you'd get rid of your motorcycle."

"You did what?"

"Two cherry Cokes," she said to the waitress. Then to me, "He worries."

"About me?"

"No, stupid. About me. Says you can't handle it and I should have the good sense not to ride with you."

"You don't have to ride on it."

She gave me an arrogant smirk. "You don't know Willy." When he wasn't present, she usually called him Willy. She asked me to open her purse, said I should be pretty good at finding a ring case, since stealing purses was once my profession.

"Wasn't either."

"Just what was your criminal profession?"

"Rifling glove boxes," I said, though it was a lie.

"Hardly qualifies you as a public nuisance."

By then I'd found the ring case and opened it. It was an eighteen-karat-gold man's ring made in the image of a saddle, and on the pommel was a garnet. "Pretty gaudy," I said.

"Willy would love it if it was carved out of soap."

I snapped the lid down and dropped the case in her purse. "For his birthday?"

"Petey, you're not so dumb."

Two hundred people were invited to Willy's party—three hundred came. No one was turned away if a Bobbins recalled the face. A Western band, largely ignored, played on a platform stage. They seemed content, as from time to time someone would request a tune and leave a dollar in the fishbowl at the foot of the stage. Like everyone else at the party, the musicians ate and drank their fill.

Stella recruited me to serve hamburgers. Atop the table next to the mustard and ketchup I put a tip jar and primed it with two five-dollar bills. If the band could earn an extra dollar, so could I. An hour later I'd earned some three dollars. On her way to see the caterer, Stella noticed the jar with the measly earnings and swooped it up. "They'll be none'a that," she said and burrowed her way through the crowd with thirteen dollars of my money.

Smiling and shaking hands, George wandered in and out of the crowd with his elder boy trailing him. Since taking over management of the casino, George ran it like a fortress under siege. He tracked how many times a porter emptied trash baskets and calculated how much could be saved by replacing liners twice a day instead of three times. Beyond a "Hi, Pete," he rarely spoke to me.

Willy's case was before the grand jury, but he showed little evidence of pressure as he mingled with guests, regaling them with homey anecdotes. Betty wore a silk-print ankle-length dress, her hair curled, tied back in a matching burgundy bow. Bound to get to Reno, she played the dutiful daughter, greeting new arrivals and guiding them to the bar. Whenever she glided by my station, she'd smile and whisper, "Reno." Ruben Lee skulked around with a drink in hand. On one occasion I glimpsed him talking to a card cheater who had once tutored him in the trade. It was easy to see he was in a foul mood. He avoided me most of the evening, for which I was glad. But eventually he approached, flipped a cigarette on the lawn, and set his drink on a nearby table.

"They got you earning your keep, Petey."

I asked if he wanted his rare, medium, or well done.

He stared in my face. "Don't give a shit. Meat in a bun, Petey Boy. You know about that. Didn't someone slam some meat in your buns? That's what I hear."

I slapped a patty between two halves of a bun and handed it over on a paper plate. He showed a bare palm, twirled it twice, then whacked the tabletop and slowly pulled his hand away. Two dollars sat faceup on the table. "For you."

"Can't take tips, Ruben Lee. Your mother's orders."

He offered a wry smile and picked up the bills. He was standing there when Willy climbed up on the platform, Stella at his side, and took the microphone. The gathering slowly hushed.

"Well, 'spose I'll start by thankin the Lord for one more year, an then thank ya'll for comin. It's my—what is this, Stella?"

"I'm thirty-nine, so you must be forty an a half."

The audience laughed.

"May not be here next year if Uncle Sam has anythin to do with it."

"Where you goin, Willy?" someone in the throng shouted.

"Vietnam. Ain't you heard? They's draftin me." He wrapped an arm around Stella's waist and pulled her close. "What we're up here for's to announce we had us a board 'a directors meetin today, me bein the board. The Lucky's fixin to have a new general manager. He's ready for the job, cause his car motor's a runnin out front." He pointed to George, who stood by the stage. "Y'all know George Bobbins, who'll be bossin things."

George joined his parents on the stage. "Hope you're enjoying my father's sixty-second birthday. I had the boys at the ranch butcher a steer for the hamburgers and I don't want any leftovers." Taking their cue, the audience hooted and whistled. Ruben Lee held the unfinished half of his hamburger at arm's length, spat out what was in his mouth, and tossed the remainder in the trash. "Shitty meat," he said and stomped off toward the patio doors.

George came by with a whiskey bottle in hand and a half-full glass, which he held in front of his chest, but never drank from. He asked if I'd had a chance to eat.

"Yes. Well, sort of."

He looked about at the clusters of people. "Willy," he said, "tells me you're doing well in school. That right?"

"Okay, I guess."

"Good, good. When he's gone, Pete, you come to me if you need something."

He'd never addressed me other than the polite hello or when ordering a meal. "Sure. I mean, yes, sir."

"When no one else is around, I'm George. Okay?"

"Okay."

George shrugged. "I've got to see a few people. Remember what I said."

The celebrants turned from food to drink, their voices blending into one low-pitched growl. The band played. A few couples danced. Stella scooted in and out of the house directing servants like a first sergeant while George and Willy wandered about, each with a bottle of whiskey, patting backs and refilling drinks from their stock. I'd been standing for hours and needed to urinate. I went to find a bathroom. Those downstairs were in use, so I ran up the staircase, hurdling every other stair, and hurried to my bedroom, where I jerked open the bathroom door.

Ruben Lee sat on the stool, sleeve rolled up, a belt cinched around his biceps, a charred spoon on the lid of the water tank. "Hey, Petey." He looked up for an instant, then jabbed the needle in a bulging vein on his forearm.

"I have to piss," I said.

He drew on the plunger until a drop of blood swirled in the syringe, then pressed the plunger and loosened the belt. The syringe dangled from his arm. "Petey boy, reason I haven't run you over is 'cause the old man likes you for whatever fucking reason. Now get the fuck gone."

An instant later his eyes went opaque, his head bobbed twice, and he muttered something unintelligible. I closed the door and backed away, but the image of him with the syringe tacked to his arm by the needle stayed. I went to the bathroom down the hallway. Nervous and hurried, I fumbled with my zipper and nearly urinated on my leg. I locked the door, turned off the light, and slumped down on the cool tiles.

15

Willy decided I'd work at the ranch over the summer. He said it would make a man of me, though he'd said that about several other things as well. For my part, I was glad to go. I needed to get away from Betty; my feelings for her were changing. Willy wanted me to fly up, but I suspected he would get rid of the Triumph while I was gone. Backpack over my shoulders and a wallet stuffed with twenties in my back pocket, I threw my leg over the saddle and rode to the Big Hole, a trip that took three days.

Strange looks greeted me that Sunday as I rode in pulling a trail of dust behind the Triumph and came to a stop near the bunkhouse. Jiggers asked what the hell kind of horse that was I was riding. Cal told me not to scare the livestock with it. Sarge ran his hand up and down the handlebars admiring it. Conchita shook her head and said, *"Tonto joven,"* young fool. The rest of the hands were working cattle. Conchita gave me a sandwich and a list of chores to follow. Sarge, fishing pole in hand, took a look over my shoulder at the list. "I'd rather fish, myself," he said. "You fish yet?"

"No, sir, never had the chance."

He looked off toward the foothills. "Too bad. I'll teach you sometime." That said, he shouldered his pole and marched off.

The next morning before dawn Jiggers shook me awake and said we were riding out in an hour. After pancakes, bacon, and eggs, we saddled up and rode southwest. It was early summer and the clouds slipped gracefully over the mountains; breezes flowed out of the arroyos and cooled the Big Hole. The land smelled fecund, and on horseback the lie of it was rough and unforgiving. Thus I began my apprenticeship as a cowhand.

I traveled as vaqueros had for a hundred years or more, learned to ride the horse and not the saddle. Riding was a continuum, more a state of being than doing, for the ranch stretched twenty-seven miles west to the foothills and from the foothills east eight miles, where the earth was soft and creeks and gullies marked the boundaries of the other great ranches. We covered much of the range, prodding cattle toward better pastures or searching for strays.

My mentors were many and patient. They knew I was no cowboy and likely never would be, but they took pride in their trade and instilled in me that notion of pride. They taught me to keep dust out of my mouth with a damp bandanna and I learned half a dozen other uses for one, which included holding berries or straining dirt out of water taken from a pond. I rode with a round pebble in my mouth to keep it moist. Every day added to what I'd learned the day before. Though tolerant, they were demanding. Every man did his share, no slackers.

Lead proved a steady animal that compensated for my lack of skill in the saddle. I rode fence under the wise gaze of Jiggers, and when not mounted, I was down mending wire. Fifty-five acres was seeded in alfalfa. I learned to operate a tractor and cut hay. Sometimes my job was to ride remuda, water and feed the horses, so I learned how to talk to horses and walk among them without making them skittish. I became familiar with the use of a rope and sensed when a steer was going to run or make a turn into the flanks of my mount. My hands blistered the first week and callused the second, and in four weeks hardened into palms that could feel the burn of a rope without bleeding. It was hard work. It was quiet work.

The men, often boisterous in the bunkhouse, became a silent bunch out on the range, but they still found opportunities to tease me. They kidded me about pimples and inexperience, about being too tall and too thin, about being a city boy, and about being a virgin, though they were only guessing about that because I never let on one way or the other.

We worked until dusk, then curried horses and tied down the remuda before eating beef and beans prepared on a chuck wagon if luck was with us, or beans warmed over a fire if it wasn't. We'd circle around a crackling campfire to eat. Rough men with rough language, they held opinions that were as hard-worn as their chaps. Talk centered on the next day's work or how it was sad the honest whores had left Butte for better pastures and sadder still that they took the rest of the whores with them. Talk was also about getting too drunk to walk and maybe finding a good fight if they weren't lucky enough to find a woman—which, they assured each other, was always a possibility, no matter how remote.

A superstitious bunch, they prized luck and embroidered notions of their hardness. It was manly to get drunk and crack knuckles on hard skulls, but helping a cow with a difficult calving was just work. They boasted on their faults while disavowing their compassion and the basic goodness of their humanity.

After the meal, they smoked and told stories, stories that unified them as a community, stories that might be ten words, no more, like the one about Johnny Dawkins who rode that mare with the stockinged fetlocks. It said everything that needed saying: Dawkins rode a hard ride and broke a mean animal. These stories were as reassuring as the quiet pride the men took in their labor. Cal and Jiggers told more stories than the others, while Sarge never offered any. When the fire was at last embers, it was doused with water and the smell of wet, charred wood marked the final minutes before sleep. Those so inclined went off to urinate or take a last look at a horse or maybe have a smoke.

I'd seen Western epics, movies about gunslingers and good guys who could be at once the same guys, and townships saved from evil, and sexless women who waited for a valiant man to make things right. The world of the cowboy in film was sliced into the righteous and the despotic. The world of the cowhand was divided into hard work and rest. The parts, however, weren't divided equally. We started before sunrise and kept at it until the sun set behind the Bitterroots. Cowhands are men who need a horse under them and work ahead. They know the elements, how to judge a steer on the run, how to get off a galloping animal, how to turn a cow with her calf. Much like the silence of the range at night, their humility about their work was reassuring and made for reflection when the crickets sang and the clouds passed through the moon's reflection.

The rituals of the day done, they rolled up in their saddle blankets and snored and farted and dreamed about that next ride up a rocky arroyo or the next drunk or the chance of a woman finding them, for they, themselves, knew neither the path to a woman's door nor the words to touch her heart. By the end of my fourth week I'd discarded the myths of the West. This hard, tiring labor and brotherly union was how the West was and, I assumed, always had been.

My body heavy and sore from a day in the saddle, I moved mechanically around the site. Each man found a flat piece of earth and groomed it with sagebrush, then tossed down a bedroll. Crickets chirped and night creatures called out over the rolling land. Before fatigue overwhelmed me, there was time for pondering and looking up at stars that seemed a fingertip away. The lustrous night sky kindled a certain quality of introspection.

I should have been content, and I was, except for a terrible sense of longing. Betty was on my mind as I gazed up at the stars. She had become my picture just as Willy had his. I'd framed her in sunlight and blue skies, in mountain woodlands and on the banks of a churning brook. A steer bleated its terribly lonely call. Finally exhaustion took me. The last things I remembered were the night air and the smell of horses and sage and dust and thinking of Betty.

We were riding the east fence line. It was a dry, cloudless day, so it was a pleasure to ride where the grass was high, the ground was moist, and the occasional willow or cottonwood shaded us. We turned our horses and crossed a brook. A strand was snapped on the wire where the range fence crossed the water bed. Jiggers's many falls had left him with arthritis and sciatica. He dismounted tenderly and pressed his hands on the small of his back, stretched his arms skyward, and looked around. "Here's where old Garstadts' stud jumped the fence. Cut himself up doing it," he said.

He knew everything there was to know about everything that didn't need knowing and talked more than the rest of the crew combined. He loved facts, especially those he'd invented. Figures and dates established his expertise. "John L. won the first heavyweight championship by whupping a fella named Paddy Ryan," he'd say, and someone would ask how many rounds, to which Jiggers would respond, "Nine, February seven, eighteen and eighty-two." As he had the figures and names together, he added that Sullivan wore pink-and-gray knee-length shorts and at the time slept with a woman named Martha after whom Martha's Vineyard had been named and she was a fourth cousin, once removed, of Queen Victoria.

No one seemed to care if he was lying, for Jiggers entertained. Full of shit, the boys would say with a wink, but none of them ever challenged him. His memory was deadly accurate. Cal told me not to let Jiggers get on my nerves. I didn't. I let him talk, but he preferred me coaxing the story out. I asked, "What kind of stud?"

"Horse stud, Pete. Bring me some more wire."

I handed him wire and watched him twist the strands before he went to work splicing.

"Had muscle like a draft horse, but he was quarter horse, mean as a bobcat. That chestnut filly Rita was so proud of was a Thoroughbred, skittish and kinda dumb. She caught that stud ready to mount her Thoroughbred." He grimaced as a barb punctured his glove. He slipped off the glove to check his finger for blood, then went back to work.

Even then I'd begun to tie truth and speculation together. Now I had a name to match the strawberry blonde in the portrait. "Willy raised Thoroughbreds?"

"No."

"So why that one?"

"She liked it, liked riding high."

The window to the story open now, Jiggers told how the stud kicked in the gate to get to the filly. Rita fired a shot, but the stud merely mounted the filly. Rita walked to the stall and put the next bullet between the stud's eyes.

I imagined the woman in the picture, long hair flowing as she walked purposefully toward the animal, calmly lifted the rifle to her shoulder, and squeezed off a round. Blood flowed from the horse's nostrils as he bellowed, then collapsed, his organ still snug inside the filly, dragging her to the ground and breaking her leg. Her business done, Rita had called out to the hands, who charged over in response to the shots. She handed the rifle to Cal and told him to do what had to be done with the filly, but never to mention it.

"There, we got it," Jiggers said as he completed the splice. "Let's tighten 'er."

Using cut willow branches, we wound the strands until the fence was secure and the wires taut. Jiggers tested it, seemed satisfied, and got on his horse.

As we rode north, we crossed the brook again and stopped in the middle so our horses could drink. Jiggers leaned over his pommel and asked if I wanted to hear the rest of the story. Without waiting for me to answer, he began telling how Garstadts raised hogs during the war, so meat, any kind, was precious. Willy had the stud butchered and sold most of the meat to Garstadts to feed his pigs. The remainder went to feed Rita's beagles.

Jiggers winked. "Sometime later Garstadts figured it all out and come looking for damages for the stud and his money back for the meat. Rita aimed that same rifle at him and told him hogs would eat human meat just as easily."

"Sad thing when a good animal dies doing what nature intended." He measured my reaction, kneed his horse, and climbed the bank.

Whistling off-key as we rode the fence, Jiggers spoke no more about Rita or the horse. I acted as if he'd told just another story. We rode the fence line until an hour before dusk. When it was time to head to the ranch house, he stopped his mount and took hold of my reins. He caught my eye directly. "When you partner up with a fella," he said, "you listen and let it go." I nodded twice, slowly, letting him know I fully understood. He released the reins. We pushed the horses to a gallop and rode to the bunkhouse for the first table meal and bed sleep in three weeks.

The next payday Cal said we needed a weekend in Dillon. Pearl asked Cal if it was okay to ride south to Twin Falls instead. Lon said that he and Pearl had had enough of Dillon, that they planned to find a couple of whores and have a time. The bare truth of their intentions, so heedlessly laid out, caused Pearl to drop his head and blush.

There was nothing to do in Dillon, a cattle-shipping town of modest one-story homes on sprawling green lots sandwiched between equally modest two-story homes on similar lots. Much of the town had been built in the latter part of the nineteenth and the early twentieth centuries. Downtown were a few bars, a movie theater, and several cafés. It was a clean and orderly business center of predictable brick buildings and somber trees, mostly old elms with flowing canopies and tall evergreens with alligator-skin bark. All suggested continuity, a place that saw generations of families grow up.

We roomed at a motel north of town. While the others went off to do their drinking, I stayed behind and read and watched TV. For a while Sarge watched television, which he did half-interestedly. Something seemed to be troubling him. He asked several times what I had planned. When finally I convinced him I had no plans, he nodded as if he understood, then said we should have stayed at the ranch and gone fishing. After that he looked at the door as if waiting for it to open until he became restless enough and excused himself, saying he knew a woman who served a fine lunch downtown and would enjoy seeing her again. He asked if I cared to come. I was uncertain whether he truly wanted companionship and declined. "Well, okay, Pete. You've had enough of our company. Too bad Pearl took off to Twin Falls. He's kind of quiet, but closer to your age."

It was ironic, his saying that Pearl was quiet, for this was about as much conversation as I'd ever gotten from Sarge. He excused himself, and I was left to ponder what usually governed my thinking when I was alone—Betty. The room seemed to shrink. I was restless, used to working the entire day. My body resented inactivity. It was best to leave. Get up, move, now, the room seemed to say. I slipped on my boots and stepped out.

I had chosen to ride the Triumph rather than sit in the bed of a pickup, and it started on the second kick. I turned the throttle and rode the highway with nothing in mind but to chase away annoyances. It was in the mid-eighties. Sunlight glistened on the handlebars. Alone on the highway to Butte I found myself smiling at nothing at all.

Once there, I rode aimlessly around the streets, up steep roadways, crossing rusted-out railroad tracks between the soot-stained brick walls of deserted buildings that appeared too stubborn to realize they were dead. Largely empty, the streets seemed stark. I parked the bike at a café for lunch. The patrons were three men at one table and a family of five at the other. I swung onto a stool at the counter and picked up the menu. An elderly woman asked if I wanted coffee. She was thin and dressed in a straw-colored smock and light-blue apron and seemed utterly taxed. I turned up my cup.

"How're the hamburgers?" I asked.

"Cooked and served on a bun."

"Lettuce and tomato?"

"Sometimes."

I waited for her to add more, but her face was a blank. "How about the apple pie?"

"Crust with cooked apples."

"Homemade?"

She shook her head.

I said I'd have the hamburger. She wanted to know if that was with everything. I nodded.

"Want fries with that?"

When I looked up from the menu, she was smiling. "How much?" I asked.

"Ketchup's twenty-five cents. The fries are free."

"Done," I said.

As she poured the coffee, I told her I'd worked in a restaurant in Las Vegas and asked how long she'd been at it. She said when she started out the world was still flat and she'd probably still be doing it when the world returned to being flat. I asked her name.

"Amanda, but if you've got something in mind, forget it because you're too old and I have to go home and build an atomic reactor."

She came by and checked on me more often than her job called for, and her conversation turned to friendly chatter. She'd lived in Butte for thirty years and had seen it go from boom to bust, but couldn't bring herself to leave. She asked if I was going to college. I was too flattered at the idea of looking like a college man to tell her I was only entering into my junior year of high school; instead I answered that I was working on a ranch near Dillon.

"Best get your butt in class," she said. "A war's going on. Wouldn't want to go myself. What ranch?"

"Seven-Eleven," I answered. "Willy Bobbins's ranch."

Her brow wrinkled as she lipped the name. She tapped twice on the counter. "Owned a casino in Meadorville and a roadhouse. He left after Anaconda closed down the mines . . . or before." Her voice went flat for a moment, and she muttered as she walked behind the counter to take the coffee-pot off the burner. When she turned, she tilted her head and said, "The ranch where the woman was shot back after the war, an accident."

We were generally immune to events that shaped the world beyond the fence line. Sometimes news would break through the barriers of our isolation. Work and the whim of nature dominated life, which flowed one day into the next, marked occasionally by an event worthy of conversation, like Lon spraining a wrist when a steer turned into his horse or Pearl receiving mail and taking a pickup and leaving for two days without permission or explanation.

Idle times were never truly idle. We played horseshoes or cards and raced horses over the alfalfa fields, which of course was strictly forbidden. The realms of work and play were often undemarcated. The television in the bunkhouse went largely unused, as most of the men couldn't relate to the programs. They'd watch a John Wayne movie and guffaw at the stereotypes, but never at John Wayne, who touched a fundamental part of them that no other character seemed to.

Sarge, who subscribed to *Time* and *Newsweek,* was my link to the outside. I'd whipped through the six books I'd brought and craved reading. He loaned me his magazines, but only after he'd digested the information in each. He and I alone shared awareness of that world outside the Big Hole, but some speechless thing inside him kept us from discussing anything, even the news. The magazines let me know that the world was rapidly changing. History as I now understand it was divided by the single event that had occurred the previous November, the John F. Kennedy assassination. A rock group called the Beatles from England now dominated the consciousness of the younger generation, of which I was and wasn't, at the same time, a member. President Johnson was propagating legislation that would be the foundation for his Great Society and at the same time forming the policies that would send my generation to Southeast Asia.

These events all seemed distant and perhaps exaggerations of life, for on the range we existed in the immediacy of our own calm. At least this was true until Pearl disappeared again and returned after two days to bundle up his belongings. He took off his hat and held it over his chest when he entered the bunk house.

"Boys, it's been a pleasure cowboyin here. I come here hopin to learn and I did. Now I gotta go. I been drafted."

We were stunned by the news. Certainly the war in Vietnam seemed too remote to touch us. Though Sarge, a veteran of WW II, refused to agree, Jiggers claimed it was no war at all, not compared to the big one. But now the reality of it confronted us in a very personal way, and it seemed terribly real. It was sad, for Pearl's leaving seemed preventable. Lon and Oso both asked if he couldn't find some other way, like joining the National Guard.

"No, boys. It wouldn't be right."

There was no more discussing the question. What was right was just that. They acquiesced with a nod. Cal said they'd keep his job open, not because the law said so but because he was a good hand. Jiggers fell into a funk after hearing the news, and Sarge pointed out that it was a damned shame taking a young man away from his family. Pearl appreciated the kind thought, but said he didn't have much in the way of family. He didn't see that we were his family.

"You'll do fine," Leon said. "We'll keep your horse in shape, Pearl."

"Name's Edmond," he said. "Never liked the name, so I went by Pearl 'cause it was different."

He apologized for taking the truck without permission, but the letter said to report immediately. He was a very literal young man. He packed his gear and asked if he could store it at the ranch, as he had no place to send it, then Cal drove him to the bus station in Dillon. We pitched horseshoes that evening and avoided conversation.

16

On a day pushing ninety degrees with no breeze to speak of, Willy showed. It was the last week in July and time to round up the spring calves for branding. The previous evening he'd called unexpectedly from Twin Falls, where, too tired to continue alone, he'd laid over for the night. As if to mark the moment, a redtail hawk sailed the thermals near the foothills just as Willy's Cadillac came over the swell and down the incline, its tires spewing up dust that hung thick over the road.

Cal rushed through a last inspection of the house to make sure it was ready—fresh linen, bottle of Jack, shot glass on the dining table—his worrying needless, for Conchita had attended to every detail the previous night. She waited by the front door from time to time looking toward the screen and shaking her head, obviously miffed by his inadvertent affront. The rest of us lined up outside as if awaiting a visiting dignitary.

The Cadillac slowed as he passed by. The windows were darkened. The tires chattered to a stop as the car pulled in front of the house. He got out, waved without looking, and marched in carrying a bottle of Jack D. at his side. It was obvious he'd been at it. I was disappointed that he'd ignored me. No one else seemed bothered by it. Jiggers said we'd see him in a couple of days when he sobered up.

That evening I slipped up to the house and peered in the window from a safe distance. He sat facing the portrait of Rita, a shot glass to his left, the bottle to his right. He was polishing his .45 with a white cloth, which seemed to me a strange thing to do, as I'd never before seen him attend to anything in this fashion. I always assumed someone else did such things for him. I noticed something else, though I thought at the time I might be mistaken, but there by the whiskey bottle was a black leather-bound book. Willy, who couldn't read, had a book.

As few things went unnoticed on the ranch, especially when Conchita was up and on foot, I moved on before being discovered. It wasn't a good idea to spy on the boss. We had a new hand named Cyrus Peeples, whom Cal had hired as a wrangler two days after Pearl left to be inducted. That night I sat behind Cyrus and watched the others play pinochle, the game that had replaced hearts since Pearl left. They talked about the weather, the coming roundup, the barbecue that was sure to follow, and a mare that had strayed onto the ranch and needed to be returned before we were all hanged for rustling. Willy went unmentioned, but occasionally Cal, Jiggers, or Lon looked up from his hand and fixed a gaze on the one lighted window in the big house.

I'd adjusted to the hard work and the dead sleep, but that day we'd done very little. Restless, I tossed and turned. My bed seemed terribly small. The sound of boots stirring gravel woke me from a light sleep, and the beagles broke into a frenzy of howling. I spread the curtain and looked out to see Willy staggering about. In his hand was the .45, its nickel finish flashing in the moonlight. He talked to himself and waved the pistol around as if using it as a pointer. For several minutes he stood moving in a small circle in the space between the big house and the cottage out back, then staggered back to the house and slammed the door.

In the morning Willy emerged from the house ready to ride. Dark circles ringed his eyes, but he was sober and clean-shaven. He saddled his horse, let the beagles out, and rode south and west at a steady trot, the beagles baying as they ran free in front.

He returned two hours later and after penning the dogs, shook every man's hand and saved a special hello for Cyrus, who was so tall Willy had to crane his neck to see him. When he reached me, he said he'd gotten good reports, but figured all along I'd be better at cowboying than cleaning tables, which wasn't saying much. Squeezing my calloused hand, he asked if Cal had toughened me up. I'd gained weight and had shoulders to show for all the hard work. "Yep," I said.

"Good." Without further comment, he held the reins, slid his boot into the stirrup, and swung into the saddle.

Cal ran the roundup while Willy, as if just another hand, filled in where he could, turning away a cow so that her calf could be roped or chasing into a thicket after a calf. He didn't malinger or complain and, like the others, he didn't drink on the range. You'd think he was simply another old hand smoking a cigar while spurring his cutting horse in and out of the herd. Soon he had color in his cheeks, his eyes sparkled, and his lips invariably met you with a smile.

Willy took command of the campfire at night, stirring coals with a stick and telling stories. The food was better and more abundant. Conchita rode out from the ranch house every night to serve up chili with sirloin chunks, and potatoes fried with jalapeños and onions. She slept in the pickup. In the morning she made bacon and eggs to go with stacks of pancakes. After breakfast she returned in the same pickup to the ranch house, only to come back out and feed us again that night.

Willy bedded down once the fire was doused. In no time he'd be snoring, a rattling noise that carried like the sound of a diesel engine. He tired out early, but come dawn he was the first up, full of energy, saying things like, "We prob'ly aughta slow down or we'll finish early and have to get drunk and eat a cow or two."

Jiggers, Lon, and I cornered some cows that had slipped away and found a route through a rocky arroyo into the foothills. A white-faced bull had taken charge and had no intention of letting us turn them back. He snorted and lowered his head. Lon held a hand up.

"Pete, soon as I get that bull's attention, you head up that bank and circle behind them cows and push them to us."

That said, he swung his pony about and hollered at the bull. I spurred Lead, who was surefooted and strong enough in the hindquarters to climb an iceberg, but we hit loose dirt and rock that broke away like salt underfoot. He fought to find his footing, but we slid backwards until I thought he was going to topple. I threw myself off the saddle, grabbed the bridle, and tried to lead him up.

I was unaware of anything but getting him up the incline. Lon shouted something. When I turned I saw the bull heading up the bank not twenty feet away. That crazy blue eye of Lead's looked the size of a plum as he dug his hooves into the soft dirt. I let go of the reins.

I found myself staring at the bull, who'd pulled up a few feet away. He turned his head and looked at me with one eye, his tail flicking back and forth slowly.

"Don't move, Pete!" Lon called.

I stood my ground and held my breath. Gradually the bull lost interest in me and turned away. Lon came up and asked if I was okay. I waved my hat signifying I was fine. And I thought I was, until I put weight on my left ankle. It was sprained.

Lon and Jiggers pushed the herd out of the arroyo without me, then Jiggers came back and helped take off my boot. The ankle was throbbing. He moved it in a slow circle, listening.

"Not broke," Jiggers said. "I busted so many bones I can tell one better than an X-ray machine. Try standing."

I could rest on it, but that was all. Jiggers took my arm. "Twisted ankle feels worse than it is. Ride in and get some ice on it. Day or two you'll be fine. 'Sides, we're all but done out here."

Lead had found a patch of juicy clump grass the cows had missed and was doing his best to accomplish what they hadn't. Being more interested in filling his stomach than being ridden, he wouldn't let Jiggers get a hand on the reins. "Damn dumb animal!" Jiggers shouted. A few minutes later Jiggers appeared above me leading Lead.

Conchita, loading the truck with food, was too busy to take notice when I rode in. I walked Lead in and unsaddled him. He eyed me as if waiting for me to brush him. I told him to curry himself and limped to the bunkhouse. Conchita, seeing I was hobbled, called me *pobrecito,* but went on loading the truck.

Seated at the table, I buried my ankle in a bucket of ice and was just getting used to the numbness in my foot when I heard the sound of a car. I pulled my foot out and hopped to the window on my good leg to spread the curtains. It was Betty's Mustang, top down, bounding over the hard road in a swirl of dust, striking every rut and bump. She brought the car to a sliding stop in front of the big house, and before the dust dissipated, threw open the door and jumped out.

"Meez, Meez!" Conchita shouted from the cab of the pickup, then ran up the walkway flapping her arms to intercept Betty before she reached the ranch house.

I hopped to the door to see better. It was impossible to hear them, but Conchita seemed intent on getting Betty away from the house, and Betty seemed equally determined to go inside. I went out and shouted hello from the porch. Betty, at first, seemed not to recognize me, then raised her hands to her cheeks and ran toward me, leaving Conchita standing flatfooted at the doorway, with her arms held stiffly at her sides. "Petey, where's Willy? Where's my dad?"

"Out branding calves."

She looked at my bare foot. "What happened?"

"Twisted the ankle."

"Petey, remember your promise?"

"What promise?"

"About Rich."

I remembered my vow of silence on the matter. "No."

"Don't," she said, sounding desperate.

"I remember."

"Swear again you won't tell anyone."

Conchita labored toward the bunkhouse. I looked off, thinking. Was I nothing but someone to substantiate her lies? To be used? She stepped up on the porch and looked at me with pleading eyes. "Promise?" she whispered.

"Okay."

"Meez," Conchita said, aiming a finger at Betty, "you stay in the cottage."

Betty said, "Okay. In fact, that'll be nice, but tell my father I'm here. Can you do that?"

Conchita pointed to the truck bed, filled with food, and said she wouldn't be back until morning. This seemed to satisfy Betty, who wrapped her arm in Conchita's and walked off with her. As she carried her suitcase to the cottage, Betty turned and took a last look at me. I nodded.

Willy arrived in the pickup shortly after as Betty and I sat eating cold hot dogs and canned vegetable soup. He slammed the door of the truck and clomped into the bunkhouse. His face red, it was obvious he was displeased.

"You're 'sposed to be in school," he said.

"Hello, Daddy," she said. "We've got more cold hot dogs if you want some."

"Excuse us, Pete," he said.

He pulled her up by her arm. I'd witnessed how easily she'd charmed him in the past and figured she'd be in control soon enough. Holding her in tow, he marched to the cottage, his voice muffled, scolding. He opened the door and drew her inside, then the door slammed. Intermittently his voice rose loud enough to set the beagles to barking. Once she shouted back, but he drowned her out. Finally the door opened and slammed shut, and he toiled over the gravel up the walkway to the porch of the big house. He slammed that door as well.

The branding finished, it was nearing time for a barbecue at the ranch. As he waited in ignorance of his future, the animal munched calmly on some hay. Neither sound nor movement came from the big house, where Willy was still holed up, or the cottage, where Betty was held prisoner. I sat, a bucket of potatoes at my feet, on the porch facing the corral, where a huge steer was tethered. Marty Robbins sang "El Paso" over the radio and Conchita, preparing enchiladas, hummed along. Just then Willy's black Cadillac appeared on the road, churning up gravel and dust as it bounded over ruts. I stood, careful of my tender ankle, and watched. Conchita turned down the radio and stepped out beside me as the car pulled in. "Dios mios, la señora," she said.

Leaving its engine idling, Croaker opened his door and looked over the top to ask where Willy was. Stella waved from beside him. I waved back and said the big house, adding that he was sleeping. Stella remained seated as Croaker hurried to the front door of the big house, but he didn't have to knock. The door opened, and Willy, unshaven and barefoot but boots in hand, stepped out. Croaker whispered something. Willy slipped into his boots and the two of them walked to the car, Willy tenderly. The atmosphere was brittle as an icicle. He looked at me and said, "Don't you have things to do, mister?" and leaned in the window to confer with Stella.

I sat back down on my stool and picked up the knife as Croaker moved the Cadillac to the cottage. Croaker held the door open for Willy and Stella to enter, then followed. Betty shouted, "Not her!" Then the door shut. Conchita stepped out, crossed herself, and returned to her kitchen.

I peeled "spuds," as Willy called them, and managed to avoid cutting off a finger, but all the while my mind was imagining the drama in the cottage. Neither Stella nor George ever visited the ranch. But here Stella was, inside the cottage with Betty. Whatever the difficulty was, it involved Richard and my promise. I felt akin to the tethered steer who just then lifted his tail and dropped a paddy in the hay pile.

Willy stepped outside, lit his cigar, and walked over. He paused and looked at the midday sky, said it looked like a day in paradise and it was a shame to make the boys stay around when the weather was so fine. He took out his billfold and told me to dry my hands. He counted out six hundred-dollar bills, which he handed over. "When they come in, give this money to Cal and tell 'em Willy said for the boys to go to town for a couple'a days."

"A couple of days?"

"You ain't usually hard of hearin."

"Got it."

"You know that fella Shakespeare?"

"Yeah."

"I brung a book. They's a story 'bout Julius Caesar. You know the story?"

I said we'd studied it in school.

"Good. Come on over to the house tonight an read me it."

"It's not easy. The language . . ."

"Didn't ask, did I?"

"No, Willy."

He turned on his heel and headed back to the cottage. Sarge rode in a few minutes later, stopped his horse a hundred yards from the ranch houses, and walked it in. I hobbled over to the corral fence as he was unsaddling his horse. He slung the saddle over the fence and removed the saddle blanket as I lifted my bad ankle and rested it on the first slat in the fence. "Sarge."

He looked over his shoulder. "Ankle better, Pete?"

"I guess."

He slipped on his eyeglasses and peered over the fence at me. "Best give it time."

"Willy's canceling the barbecue," I said.

"Well," he said, looking to where Stella was leaned against the Cadillac, smoking.

"She came in today with Croaker," I said.

"So I see."

"Sarge, how long you worked here?"

"Since the last year of the war. Came home with a discharge and a limp. Spent a three-day drunk in Willy's roadhouse, gambled away my pay, and took up wrangling."

We watched Stella drop her cigarette and crush it underfoot. "She doesn't come here often, does she?" I asked.

He took off his glasses and cleaned them on his shirttail, then tucked the shirttail back in his jeans. He looked at me for a moment as if he had something important to say but didn't know how to start. He took a breath and looked away at the mountains. His eyes followed Stella as she opened the cottage door. He said, "C'mon, let's sit on the porch and I'll bandage that ankle."

He wrapped my ankle slowly, asking me several times if he was causing me pain. When the job was done, he helped me slip on my boot. "Pete, where were you born?"

"Washington. Palouse. Why?"

"Just wondered."

"We lived in Butte when I was a baby," I said. "I've seen pictures."

"Well, better get to that steer."

The hands seemed disappointed that the barbecue was canceled, but the idea of going to town at Willy's expense soon caught hold. They began making bold and boisterous plans, as if they were going to Paris or Rome. They showered and changed clothes quickly. Sarge held back until the others were in the two pickups, then he pulled me aside and told me to stay off my ankle.

"Pete, I like it here," he said, which I took to mean I was to keep what we said to myself.

"I know."

Cal honked. Sarge looked over his shoulder. "Been watching. You're getting to be a buckaroo," he said and backed off the porch. I had the impression there was more, *much* more, that he wanted to tell me. Soon the only sign of them all was a stream of dust running north.

Conchita scrambled eggs and peppers with the potatoes and served them on tortillas with a red chile sauce. She filled four plates, covered them, and wrapped them in towels. She gave me two to carry to the cottage. Betty took the plates and asked how my ankle was doing. I told her it was okay. She mouthed a question. "Did Willy ask anything?" I shook my head.

Stella came out of the back and said in a raspy voice, "Hear your horse went down, Pete."

"Yes, ma'am."

"Ankle okay?" She looked deprived of sleep, her face slack and her eyes puffy.

"Better."

"We're all a little tired. You'll hafta excuse us now." She reached over Betty's shoulder and shut the door.

Conchita watched me eat, appraising my expression as I chewed. She squinted as I dipped my fork in the food. "Too mush salt," she said.

"No, perfect," I said.

"I thin' too mush oil."

"No, didn't notice it."

"Ah, *pues,* maybe it's not so bad as I thought."

"It's wonderful. Really."

"All food can be better, no?"

"I don't think so." This was as much conversation as we'd ever had. I decided to push her. "How long have you worked at the ranch?"

"A bery long tine," she said, an ambiguous answer that told me to drop the matter. She left me to clean up while she went to the big house after dirty dishes. When she returned, she told me to dry my hands, that Willy wanted me.

This marked the first time I'd ever entered the big house. Croaker opened the door and walked me to the dining room, where Willy sat nursing a bottle of sour mash. He signaled for me to take a chair. Between us lay the black leather-bound book and two shot glasses. He clasped a shot glass in one hand and poured with the other. After he set the bottle down, he pushed the book over using two fingers.

"Want you to read 'bout Julius Caesar."

I finished the first scene and began the second. Willy raised a palm for me to stop and poured a shot into the second glass and another into his. He pushed one to me. "Drink up, Pete."

He swallowed his without expression and said, "It's what men do onc't in a while. Drink together an talk."

I held the glass to my lips. The fumes burned my nostrils. He encouraged me with a nod, so I swallowed the whiskey down in one gulp. It landed like an unexpected punch that spread throughout my stomach and chest. Unable to swallow or breathe, I grabbed the table and looked at him as if hooked to a bare electrical wire. He grinned.

When finally I bent over and coughed, Willy came around the table and slapped my back. "See, ain't so easy doin men's things, Pete. Takes gettin used to. For instance, a man and a gal. Things happen, but they's a price."

I took a few slow breaths and started to stand.

"Don't get up just yet." He laid a palm on my shoulders and pushed me down.

By then the alcohol had numbed my tongue. I sat silent and motionless.

He pulled his hand away. "You been doin anythin I wouldn't approve of?"

"Sir?"

"Willy," he said. "Call me Willy."

"I don't understand."

"Betty tells a different story, Pete." He swung me about in my seat, gripped my chin between his fingers and thumb, and tilted my face up. I was amazed at the strength in his hands. "You two sleepin in the same house, goin ever'where together. Plenty'a opportunity. She's fine lookin. Boy could be tempted. Ain't that so, Pete?"

"Yes."

"Was you tempted?"

"I didn't."

"You know who, then?"

"No."

He squeezed a little harder, his thumb pressing just above the chin until the pain brought water to my eyes. "You lyin to me, Pete?"

"I can't say, Willy."

He let go and walked back to his seat, where he slumped in the chair. He stared off until I asked if he wanted me to leave. He shook his head. "Way I figure it, they was some Roman lords who was jealous of Caesar, is 'at right?"

"Yes."

"Well, pick it up an finish. I knew it wasn't you. Just had to hear it was all."

Just after dawn Betty trudged to the bunkhouse. She leaned on the porch rail and smoked a cigarette before she came in and knocked on my door. She stepped back when I opened it.

"I'm out of prison," she said. She wore a blue-and-white-checkered shirt with pearl snaps, tight-fitting blue jeans, and boots. Her hair was tied back into a ponytail with a yellow ribbon. "Let's eat and ride, Pete."

Conchita fixed buttermilk pancakes, which we smothered in homemade blueberry syrup. Though she left us to eat, we didn't talk. Betty held her fork away from her lips and looked at the far wall. I watched until she asked what the hell I was staring at.

"I'm sorry," I said.

"Sorry? Everyone's sorry," she said. Then as an afterthought she added, "Your sister called. She wanted to see you. Didn't say about what."

We cleared the table, as Conchita got upset if dishes were left for her. Betty said she'd saddle the horses. I asked if Willy said we could ride.

"Not that it matters," she said, "it was his idea that you go."

I sat on the top rail of the stall so as to slip my leg over Lead. He shivered and stepped sideways as if sensing I was hobbled, but settled down as soon as I reined him through the gate. Though I had a number of questions, Betty seemed content to keep silent. We rode at an easy pace until we reached a field of grease brush and clump grass. Cattle hadn't yet grazed the area. We stopped near some boulders below a granite shelf.

She circled once, smirking as she did, then dismounted by a boulder. "Know what's funny? He expected it to be you. You probably disappointed him."

Lead shifted to the right and stood at a slant as if he'd sunk into the ground and grazed the clump grass.

"What?" I asked and slid off, careful of my bad ankle.

She climbed a squat, flat-topped boulder. She faced the sun, untied her yellow bow, and let her hair flow free as she ran her fingers through it. Then she unsnapped her shirt, one snap at a time, and spread it open. She wore no bra. Her breasts were as I'd imagined, white and full, and crowned by delicate pink nipples.

"I went to a nude beach in Saint Maarten when I was fifteen," she said. "It's natural to have the sun on your body." She closed her eyes as if in a trance. When she opened them, she looked at me with a challenging expression.

"You didn't break your promise?"

"No."

"You'd like to fuck me, wouldn't you?"

I couldn't speak, out of fear and embarrassment. I turned away.

"Not an offer, Petey, just a question. I'm pregnant. Still want to fuck me?" She smiled. "I told them at school you aren't a homosexual. That's what they think, you know. They know about biting the ear off and the reason why."

"How?"

"Nothing's secret."

I felt ready to cry. I drew in the reins. It wasn't easy to mount up, as Lead kept turning away, but I eventually pulled myself into the saddle. I took a quick glance. She leaned back on her arms, her breasts pointing skyward, the blond tips of her long hair brushing the flat granite.

Halfway to the ranch she eased her horse beside me. She'd been crying. "It was Annette Sylvestri. Her father told her," she said. I said nothing, which was probably best. I hated Annette.

That afternoon the relentless hum of cicadas drowned out all other noise. The heat was oppressive. Stella's Cadillac was gone. Stella remained inside the cottage with Betty, while Willy recluded himself inside the big house. The two were like enemy camps planning strategies. In the middle of the battle lines was Betty—both the cause of and the resolution to the campaign. I sat in the shade of the porch and read Sarge's old magazines. The only activity in evidence was in the hurried trips Conchita made back and forth from the big house to the cottage. Normally collected, she seemed frazzled by the demands laid on her as she carried lunch and dinner trays, mumbling to herself along the way. My eyes often strayed from the page to the door of the cottage. As inconspicuously as possible, I watched the passing of the day.

At dusk the cicadas fell silent and gave over to the crickets, and it became obvious that nothing was coming to a head. Had it not been for the sprain, I would have been in Dillon with the others and spared this grief. It was better not to know. I limped to my room, where I lay thinking I might collect my pay and leave, and I would have, but my ankle was too sore to shift motorcycle gears.

I drifted off to sleep. When I awoke, I heard Conchita. It sounded as if she was muttering novenas. Then I realized what had awakened me was not Conchita praying, but Betty screaming profanities at Stella, who raged back at her. The next noise I heard was a car door slam. I hopped to the window to see the Cadillac parked and two men standing outside it, one being Croaker. As they paused beside the car, I recognized the second one. A nurse accompanied him, a new one, but it was the same scene, different place. Then Willy stepped out to greet them. After the exchange, Willy walked to the cottage with the doctor and nurse as Croaker ambled up the path to the big house. The cottage door opened and Stella welcomed them in. Willy stood at the door until it shut, then he lit his cigar and walked back toward the big house. Betty hollered for her daddy, but Willy didn't look back. That was the last sound to come from the cottage.

I lay back down to escape my own helplessness, thought of Mother, her heartbreaks, and of Miriam. Lights glowed in the cottage past midnight. After the doctor and nurse walked to the big house, the lights went out and I fell asleep.

Sometime later the beagles began to harp, which wasn't unusual. I buried my head under the pillow, but their howls grew to a sustained exasperating noise that refused to die off. A door slammed. Footsteps plodded across the dirt. The dogs yelped anxiously. In a fragment of a second a gunshot fractured the night. A whimper was followed by a second shot. The crickets paused.

Except for the sound of my breathing, there was a dangerous silence that reminded me of the night in juvey. I lay arrested, every sense on alert, until I heard footsteps march back. I swung my feet to the floor and lumbered to the window. Willy passed by, in one hand a whiskey bottle, in the other a .45.

It was a warm morning. Though my ankle throbbed, the livestock needed feeding, so I went to the stalls and gingerly forked hay into the feeding troughs. A bit later I heard Croaker humming "Rock of Ages" as he approached the stalls. Then he entered, pushing a wheelbarrow in which lay the dog, stiff and smelling rank. Bluebottle flies swarmed its blood-crusted eyes and tongue. The horses whinnied and retreated to the far corners of their stalls, where they stood sideways, shivering as if struck by a winter gust. I gagged, but managed to keep my breakfast down, for which I was thankful.

Croaker had laid two gunnysacks and shovels alongside the dog. "You eat yet, Pete?"

"Yeah."

"Good. You can help. Don't be throwin up no breakfast, though."

Though I was in pain, I shoveled alongside him and didn't complain. Behind the stalls we dug a cavity about three feet deep. Finished, we laid the dog in, covered him with the gunnysacks, and dumped dirt on top, after which we piled rocks on the grave to discourage coyotes from digging it up. Sweating and obviously annoyed, Croaker crossed his hands over the handle of his shovel and leaned on it as he stared at the grave. I asked if he was going to say some kind words over the grave.

"Pete, I was thinkin 'bout using you as a grave marker."

"I'll record that as a no."

"Record what you want." He tossed his shovel on the wheelbarrow.

I did the same. For some reason I felt free to speak up. "Bet it's not the first grave you ever dug."

"You got a smart young mouth, Pete. Maybe Willy's right. You'll make a lawyer if someone don't break your head open fust. Let's go 'fore I lose my humor."

Willy leaned against the doorjamb smoking a cigar as he waited to intercept us. Except for bloodshot eyes, he showed little effect from the night's drinking. He winked at me and told Croaker the doctor had to leave right away, then said, "Pete, go inside while I talk to Croaker."

The doctor waited at the landing by the handrail. I nodded politely, but he was distracted by the nurse, who descended the stairs, overnight bag in hand. He asked how she'd slept, to which she answered, "How do you sleep in a place where men get drunk and shoot dogs?"

He clutched her arm and whispered in her ear.

"Fine. Then I slept like a princess on twelve mattresses and no pea." That said, she rushed down the stairs, the doctor following hastily behind and grabbing at her arm to slow her down. He paused as he shut the door, nodded to me and wished me a good day.

Willy entered and motioned for me to follow him to the small office beside the dining room. He opened a drawer and tossed me an envelope. He said it contained six hundred dollars that I was to deliver to Cal in Dillon at the train station. "Tell 'im to keep the boys in town for a bit an when he comes back get rid'a the dogs." He added that Croaker would drive and leave me for a bit while he dropped "our guests" off at the airport in Butte. He asked if I had any questions.

"Why'd you shoot the dog?"

"Ain't a question to be asked."

"Then I don't have any."

I headed for the door.

"Pete, when you get back, you'll be eatin here with me. I want you to finish that story."

Stella asked me to sit next to her. As I seated myself in the backseat, the doctor smiled, then looked out the window. He didn't remember me from the night he came to the apartment, probably didn't even remember the apartment. The nurse crossed her hands over her lap and stared straight ahead, ignoring the conversation Stella and I carried on about nothing important. Stella just wanted to talk after being imprisoned in the cottage with Betty for two days.

Croaker waited outside the motel where the hands were registered and told me to run the money up. Cal, alone in the room, didn't like to hear that the men were to stay in town. He took the money and counted it down, said it was all there. "Pete, you be a good hand and keep ranch business on the ranch," he said. On the ride back, Croaker listened to a blues station. Once he looked over at me and asked if I knew who Blind Lemon was.

"No."

"Leadbelly?"

"No."

"You ain't so smart after all," he said and went to humming.

The ranch looked deserted. Conchita remained in the cottage with Betty. Willy opened the door and motioned to us to join him. He set down three large bowls of Texas chili and a knife and a raw onion on a plate. We ate. Between bites, he and Croaker reminisced about Dallas during the Depression, their stories parading colorful characters across the room—Stencil Bob, the counterfeiter who etched the plates backward but still tried to pass the bills; Black Thomas, who shot himself in the foot once by accident and again on purpose because he was mad over shooting himself in the first place. From the club in Deep Ellum, they knew Blind Lemon and Leadbelly, legendary blues singers, and they spoke of bootleggers and gamblers, each one his own story.

After we ate, Willy filled a water glass with sour mash and told me to pick up the book and read. He sat at the table as Croaker rocked on a chair by the window and smoked his pipe. Soon the room smelled of hickory tobacco. Shakespeare's lines sometimes confused me, and certainly Willy, but the story and the drama captured him. He liked Mark Antony and Brutus, but said Cassius reminded him of a bootlegger from Fort Worth who wanted to run the world but wanted everyone else to do the dirty work. Finished, I set the book down.

"What you think of it?" he asked Croaker.

Croaker puffed on the pipe. "Fella can tell a story, but he's got a way of makin words get lost. 'Cept for them words, don't sound no different 'an Dallas."

"How you see it, Pete?"

"I'm not sure, Willy."

"'Bout loyalty, Pete. Loyalty. That Antony fella was loyal. Stuck by Caesar after he died." He was staring as he said this. "Bet he didn't keep no secrets from Caesar."

Somewhere in the cloud of blue smoke Croaker's voice said that Antony was loyal, no doubt about it.

"You loyal, Pete?" Willy asked.

"Me? Yes."

"No, you're not. I'm a fair man when it comes to family, an you're family. I won't shoot you in the foot."

He said they could wait me out. I didn't know what he meant until Croaker brought two pitchers of water and one glass. Willy sat across the table, smoking a cigar as Croaker took a seat next to me and set the glass and pitchers directly in front of me.

"I want a name," Willy said.

I shook my head. Willy said it was painful to have a full bladder and not be able to let loose. He described a man forced to drink two gallons of water after his penis had been tied off. He claimed the man went crazy.

"Not like food, Pete. You can't throw up."

Thereafter, each time Willy asked and I wouldn't tell, he'd tell Croaker I needed another sip and Croaker would guide the glass to my lips. I tried not to think about my bladder and the terrible discomfort I began to experience.

But with nothing to distract me, the pain intensified. I asked if promises and loyalty weren't important. He said that was certainly true and told Croaker to give me another taste of water. When the room began to swirl about, when my abdomen was a knot and I felt certain the next sip would kill me, Willy patiently asked, "His name?"

I'd downed two pitchers of water and was staring at a full glass that Croaker dangled in front of my eyes. I decided to wet my pants. It just didn't matter anymore. As if reading my mind, Willy said he knew what I was thinking and that we'd just start over again, but this time they'd tie off my penis. Willy didn't make idle threats. I lowered my head and thought.

"He's lasted longer 'an I thought, Willy," Croaker said. "If'n he was our age, he wouldn't'a made it. Hell, that Kyle what worked for Henderson didn't make it no hour."

Willy motioned with his head. Croaker held the glass to my lips and tilted it, telling me to drink it down like a good boy. I closed my eyes and turned my head away.

"Had enough?" Willy asked.

I remembered the humiliation I'd suffered at the sound of her and Rich whispering nearby as I pretended to study and once overhearing their lovemaking coming through the walls of the Blue Angel Motel as I sat in the parking lot with the windows rolled down on Betty's Cadillac. Tell the truth, name the name, I thought. I was reminded of my promise. Wouldn't Willy expect me to honor a promise? Wouldn't a promise take precedence? My bladder seemed ready to explode. I was desperate. I was about to give up Richard Forsby when out of the blue another thought occurred. I hadn't thought of the burglar or his foul breath for weeks, but it was suddenly as if it was coming at me at that very moment. I blinked and looked back and forth. They looked at me like men hauling in the catch of the day. I licked my lips and took a long slow breath, which I released at once, then before I changed my mind, I blurted out, "His name's Tennessee. That's all I know." I said it only because the name seemed a safe one—a nickname, a nobody.

I stood without permission and ran to the toilet.

17

The morning of the Saturday I was to meet Alan Holder, Miriam's pilot, the lead story on the local news in the *Las Vegas Review-Journal* was about an ex-con found dead in a car by Sunrise Mountain. Below the headlines was a mug shot of a man identified as Raymond Oliver Bandy, the man I knew as Tennessee. I bought the paper and read the article, not once but several times, as if by my reading it the facts would change. But nothing was going to change the fact that he was dead. He'd been assassinated somewhere, then driven in his car to Lake Mead Road and abandoned. There were no leads at the time of the story. I tore the picture out and folded it neatly and put it in my wallet. When I'd given Tennessee's name to Willy, it had been an impulse. I wanted only to keep my promise to Betty and to pee. I meant no harm. Now he was dead.

Willy arrived from the casino unexpectedly and knocked on my door as I was tying my tie. My first thought was that he was going to take me on a ride and I'd go bravely. He leaned against the jamb and said that I wasn't to go to work the next evening. Once dressed, I went downstairs, where he was drinking a whiskey in the dining room. "You need a wardrobe," he said.

I looked at my ensemble, a white sport coat, blue-and-red-striped tie, and beige chinos. "What's wrong with this?"

"Nothin, Pete. You're a damn fashion plate. Your ma could'a ate at the Lucky," he said.

I said she preferred to go up the glass elevator seeing the view from the top of the Mint. He swallowed his whiskey, then talked about Dallas, his downtown club that had an elevator that went to a restaurant that was a front. He seemed too calm for someone who had recently ordered an assassination. I wondered if he knew what was on my mind. I looked for hints in the conversation that he no longer trusted me. Did Betty know? Or would she put it together? It didn't occur to me that Betty couldn't know I'd given a phony identity for her lover. He told me to take one of the Cadillacs. I was glad to leave.

The maître d' saw me coming and greeted me with an amused smile. Through two rows of faultless white-capped teeth he asked the name of my party. I told him the Holder party.

"This way, sir," he said, the "sir" sounding like a steel bar dropped on concrete. I followed him into the air-conditioned room where Mother and Miriam sat with Alan Holder at a window table. Beyond them the Strip bled into velvet night. Plates and glasses tinkled as waiters scurried about pouring wine and serving food. George Liberace's band played on the stage, and a few couples danced to the slow music.

I looked at Mother and gave her a smile, which she returned. She seemed more like someone I once knew, an acquaintance, perhaps someone who'd once interested me but no longer did. Alan rose and offered his hand. He was what I'd expected—twenty-five, a graduate of the Academy, tall, cereal-box handsome, athletic—impressive. He said, "Glad to meet you. I'm Alan."

"I'm F. Scott Fitzgerald," I said.

The maître d', his caps shining phosphorescently, held my chair and waited for me to sit. He asked if I wanted to order a drink. I said I'd have a gin and tonic with a twist and a touch of ginger. He asked if I'd prefer something with a little less alcohol. "Bring him water," Miriam said.

Alan addressed Miriam. "He's like you said."

"Eccentric."

The maître d' kept holding the back of my chair.

"Call me Peter," I said. To the maître d's relief, I took my seat.

We sat measuring the awkwardness and searching for words to end it. He said something like being glad to meet the man of the family, and I said he was lucky he hadn't met the others. Miriam scowled, while Mother looked down at her napkin. Alan let the comment die. I asked how he had become a pilot. It was something he'd dreamed of as a kid, even though his father had discouraged it from the beginning, as the family owned three retail stores. He was expected to study business and help run the stores.

"You sound normal. Why'd you pick Miriam?"

Miriam said, "He says things like that to aggravate me."

Mother set her martini down and said, "Behave, Peter."

Alan said, "Miriam says you have a motorcycle."

"A Triumph. Six-fifty," I said.

"I had a Beezer. Drove Mum crazy with worry. She says a jet is safer. She worries less."

I looked at Mother. "I worked for mine."

"So did I, after school two days a week, Saturdays, and over the summer. I showed up one day straddling it." He moved on to discussing his first sailboat and sailing.

I behaved and listened as we ate. Mother ordered cherries jubilee for four. When the dessert came she said it was nice to have the family together again. I said it was too bad Julie wasn't here. Mother spilled her first spoonful on her lap and glared at me, then looked down. "My dress," she said and rushed to the ladies' room.

"Why'd you have to say that?" Miriam gave me a distressed look, kissed Alan on the temple, and followed after Mother.

"If it's not too personal, who's Julie?" Alan asked.

"The reason we're in Las Vegas. Mother moved us to be with him."

"Oh."

We stared in the direction where Miriam and Mother disappeared, as if our looking in that direction would draw them back. Alan cleared his throat. "Do you mind if I'm six years older than your sister?"

"Miriam? Are you kidding? She was born thirty years old."

He smiled.

He was asking if I'd like to go up in a fighter jet when Miriam and Mother returned. Miriam placed her hand on my arm and asked me to dance. I said she should dance with her fiancé. She grabbed my arm in both hands and pulled. "I said, let's dance."

I complained about my ankle.

"Doesn't stop you from riding a motorcycle," she said.

The band played the theme from *Mondo Cane*. Miriam and I danced as we had as children when she forced me to follow her lead while she practiced a new step. She leaned close and said that bringing up Julie's name was cruel.

"She's had plenty of time to get over him."

Miriam shook her head. I hesitated in the middle of a step and came down on her toe.

"Ouch! Shit, Peter!"

Couples and even band members looked at us.

"Listen," she said and explained that the night I was arrested for drugs, Mother went into a funk and Miriam had told all. She wanted Mother to know what Julie had tried, that he was no good, and that I'd defended her. "Mother didn't say a word. Doesn't that mean something?"

Mother knew. That explained why I was at Willy's. "What about our promise to Willy?" Meaning our promise never to speak of that night.

"She wouldn't tell. They knew each other in Butte. Don't be cruel to her."

Mother and Alan danced next to us. He asked to change partners. I let go. My sister's face glowed as she entered his arms. Mother seemed eager to sit, so I walked her to the table. I reached over to sip from her martini, which tasted like pine needles. I grimaced and swallowed. She placed her hand on the back of my forearm and squeezed. "The sonofabitch needed it."

I nodded. Whatever had been our relationship before, it was changed now. She was an accessory to covering up my crime. We were equals in this. I suspected her silence was a wise choice, which had as much as anything to do with Willy's involvement in covering it up. We watched Miriam and Alan dance. They floated under the soft lights. Remarkably rare and distinct from the other couples. It seemed obvious that they were intended to meet, to be lovely, and grow old, sip tea, and brag about grandchildren—everything together. I realized that Miriam, always so adult, had all along been the fictional heroine in books she'd read on those long rides and stories she'd contrived to fit Mother's photos. *Little Women, Jane Eyre, Wuthering Heights*—the sadness, the smiles—the Princess and Gaddis Tellerman, more sadness, more smiles. She'd met her big-novel hero. They entwined fingers and walked to the table.

One night in September while I was on break at work, Betty showed up dressed in blue jeans and a red shirt. She'd been crying. She said she had to talk to me. We walked outside and up Fremont toward Main Street. She'd been with Richard. They'd taken a room at the Blue Angel.

"I told him what happened, the abortion. He called the Lucky. I told him not to, but he insisted. He said what Willy did was wrong, that only he and I should make that decision."

"Did he tell Willy?"

"No, he was tied up on business. George asked if Rich wanted to leave a message. Rich hung up." Hand shaking, she lit a cigarette.

"So what happened?"

"He said he was going to see Willy in person."

"No." I felt a lot older than my sixteen years.

She nodded. "I've got to stop him."

She blew smoke up into the neon haze. Her eyes glistened as she looked up. I wanted to tell her just how serious this was, tell her Tennessee was a dead man. But I told her to go home and not to worry, that I'd take care of it. She squeezed my forearm and left.

I hurried back inside, hoping that in the meantime Rich had found the good sense to abandon his moronic plan. At first I wasn't sure, as I hadn't seen him in months, and he was thinner and had bleached his hair. He floated into the restaurant like a buoy, filled with self-righteousness and not much good sense. Willy wasn't one to listen to gab about ideals or social theories. I set my broom and dustpan behind the counter, hurried over, and said, "Follow me." When he hesitated, I grabbed his arm and pulled. He protested all the way to the loading dock.

"What'a you want, Pete?"

"I'm running this by fast and you're going to listen."

He took a step back. "I got no time for kid shit, Pete. I'm on a goddamn mission here."

"Look," I said and pointed at the ledge of the roof.

When he looked up, I threw a punch to his jaw. I'd gained fifteen pounds of muscle over the summer and used all of it. He hit the ground, dazed. I straddled his chest, hands clutching his collar. He tried to free himself and hit me a grazing blow to the forehead.

I lifted his head up. "Forget your mission. Willy asked who got Betty pregnant and I gave another name." He tried to break my grip. I bounced his head off the asphalt. "I'll keep it up as long as I have to. Don't make me hurt you," I said. "Social theory doesn't matter here."

"Let go." He threw another ineffectual blow.

He had to take this seriously. I slammed his head into the asphalt again. "Listen!"

He grimaced. "Jesus, that hurts." The fight left him.

"The guy I named was killed. You'll get hurt or worse. You understand? Do you?"

His eyes were a bit glazed, but gradually he came to understand. "You're not kidding."

I shook my head.

"Get off, Pete."

I slowly got up, helped him to his feet, and showed my open palms to indicate the fighting was over. He asked why I gave the wrong name.

"I promised. If you tell her what I said, she might slip, and if you mention it to Willy, worse could happen."

Just then a voice called my name. A guard stood on the loading platform. I said hello, and he asked if there was a problem. "Just talking," I said.

"Looked like wrestling," he said.

"It's okay. We're friends."

The guard stepped inside. If he reported the incident, I'd have to make up a story. I asked Rich if he understood.

"What can I do?"

I shrugged. "Stay away."

He rolled his tongue in his cheek and touched the back of his head. "I got a knot."

"Sorry."

"You sucker punched me."

"Yeah, I did."

To salvage something of his pride he clenched his fists and threw a feeble punch, which I sidestepped. I said he should be thankful I wasn't Willy, but he squared off as if he wanted more. I told him to go on. He told me to fuck myself, then trotted down the alley and vanished. When the chief of security asked about the scrape, I said it was over money owed me. He informed me that Willy wanted personal matters kept separate from work, that the next time he would have to write a warning slip. He was so earnest in thinking he was doing me a favor that I had to stifle a laugh.

Miriam's wedding was held on a Saturday morning in the chapel of All Saints Episcopal Church. The Holders' daughter, Victoria, and a slew of aunts and uncles sat stiff as models at a morticians' convention and looked straight ahead to make it clear they'd come because to do otherwise would have been discourteous. Alan, in dress whites, arrived ten minutes late because his best man stopped to wash the car. They hurried to the altar.

Victoria, a nondescript college sophomore whose single ambition appeared to be breaking the world's record for continuous yawning, had a boyfriend attending the Coast Guard Academy. Her only desire was to get the wedding over with. I leaned forward and looked in her direction to get her attention. When she finally looked at me I opened my mouth and pointed at my cuspid, indicating she had something caught in her teeth. When she understood what I was conveying, she covered her mouth and began to probe with a fingernail.

Stella bounced an elbow off my ribs. "Behave, Peter."

I'd been given the chore of driving the Holders around when school was out. I drove them to Red Rock Canyon, Lake Mead, and the Valley of Fire. I hadn't been much of a guide, but I kept them occupied while the wedding details were being handled by a woman whom Willy had hired. Their itinerary had been planned in advance, but Mrs. Holder had insisted on changes each day. She disliked having people assume they knew what she would enjoy doing.

Willy had arranged a three-day package of entertainment to keep the Holders busy. With Alan and Miriam escorting them everywhere, they saw Sammy Davis, Jr., at the Sands, Connie Francis at the Sahara, Errol Garner at the Tropicana; they ate at Don the Beachcomber's, the Regency Room, and the Dome of the Sea. Mr. Holder said it was delightful. In between yawns, Victoria called it exciting. Mrs. Holder called it exhausting. About the only thing Mrs. Holder seemed to approve of was Willy, who called her "the fine missus" and charmed her with stories, toned down for Easterners' ears.

Mr. Holder, tall, composed, an affable smile for everyone, stood patient in the face of everything. A self-made retail merchant, he spoke in a soft but assured manner and pretty much seemed to disregard his wife while nodding in agreement to everything she said. Called Mum by her clan, Mrs. Holder was a woman with the bulk and disposition of a German field marshal. She abhorred, to degrees, almost everything she was made to endure. At various times Las Vegas was too crass, too warm, too middle class, too gaudy; the food too bland, too seasoned, too middle class, too expensive, too cheap; the desert dull, barren, ugly, uninviting, bleached out, isolated—and somehow middle class as well. Alan would simply give her audience an understanding smile and later say, "That's Mum."

Miriam and her bridesmaid, a carhop name Darla, reached the church fifteen minutes late. She'd asked Willy to give her away, as Morin Samuel Elkins, the man whose last name we bore, didn't answer her request and

Uncle Harve was in the hospital. Before the brief rehearsal on Thursday, Willy had claimed he was practicing for Betty's wedding, except hers would be at midnight if he had any say, and he hoped he wouldn't need a shotgun. Betty stared at him blankly.

Miriam and Willy joined arms at the back of the chapel and waited for the organ music. He wasn't much for mornings. But as they marched down the aisle, he tried to look dignified and managed to keep his eyes open and walk straight, if with a bit of a bowlegged swagger. Miriam held her chin high and appeared to be on the verge of laughter. Though she'd attained a woman's poise, she seemed both woman and girl, and the veil and the flowers braided in her hair created the illusion that we were beholding something of a fairy-tale nature.

When the priest asked who gave this woman away, Willy said, "Me, by default," and sedately offered Miriam's hand to Alan. He offered a light-hearted smile. The congregation chuckled, and he took a seat between Betty and Stella. The ceremony was generic, the beautiful bride and handsome groom repeating vows as they gazed into each other's eyes, oblivious of us. Mother, dry-eyed but dazed, held on to my arm and watched her daughter pass by locked arm in arm with Alan. As we filed out, the Holders behind us, Mother still hadn't cried. I was waiting.

Miriam and Alan passed under the crossed swords of officers from his squadron.

Stella, who'd been cool throughout the ceremony, said, "It was a beautiful wedding, quick and, well, elegant." She handed me a fistful of tissues and nudged me toward Mother.

Mother said, "I feel so old." Her face seemed to drop.

Mrs. Holder, her makeup streaked with mascara, took Mother's wrist and said, "You are *much* too young, Elizabeth, as is your daughter, but welcome to the family." That said, she smothered Mother in her bearlike breast, and they both had a good cry. I handed them the tissues and was immediately assaulted by Lana, who hooked her arm in mine.

"I haven't kissed you yet, have I, Petey?"

I saw the purple lipstick and hard lines at the corners of her mouth. She hadn't, but I lied. "Sure you did."

By then Miriam and Alan were off. Plans tossed aside, the rest of us loaded randomly into the limousines to drive across town to the VFW lodge, where a band, a bartender, and three waiters stood by. Betty rode with Stella, Lana, and me, as Mum had asked Mother and Willy to ride with her and Mr. Holder. Stella and Betty sat at opposite windows and didn't speak. Lana lit a cigarette and said she hoped she didn't burn a hole in her dress. I sank into my seat.

At the dinner Mother and Mum traded places with others to be together.

They seemed the best of friends, leaning into each other, talking intimately and sharing private laughter. Jealous, Lana excused herself to go outside for some fresh air. The music began. Miriam and Alan took the floor and floated together as they had that night at the Mint, gazing secretively into each other's eyes long enough to make hearts swell. We loved them, loved their love for each other, and loved the future they owned. We felt privileged. When they finished, everyone applauded, except for Lana and Betty, who were outside smoking and commiserating.

The families were called to the dance floor. Willy stepped out with Victoria, who suddenly came to life. Apparently dancing didn't bore her; she even tapped her toes before the music began. Mr. Holder slipped his arm around Miriam's waist and guided her to the center of the floor. Aunts and cousins found a few spare pilots. Their partners in tow, they spilled out onto the dance floor. Too late for me to make a graceful exit, I saw Mrs. Holder approach. She stood before me, her great girth swaying to "The Tennessee Waltz," and said that if I were a gentleman I would ask her to dance, but since I wasn't she was taking matters into her own hands.

She placed my hand at the small of her back and enveloped me in her mammoth body, which radiated heat like an incinerator. Amazingly smooth, she guided me about the dance floor while thanking me for being a patient tour guide. She said Mr. Bobbins reminded her of the men in her family who were, as she put it, New England seafarers, for she hailed from New Bedford, but his language was less salty. Near the end of the song, she said Miriam was a lovely young woman and Mother had done a fine job raising us. I wished I could see the world through her eyes.

At her insistence, I danced with Betty. I couldn't dance, so I tried to talk. She looked about the room as if annoyed and said, "Shut up, Petey."

With a drink in hand, Willy walked by us, winding a path through the dance floor. "Now, 'at's what I like to see. Two young people havin a time."

"Willy! Let 'em be," Stella said. She was on Willy's tail as he worked his way to the bar. She turned and shook her head. I wasn't sure if she disapproved of me, of Betty, or of me being with Betty. Stella didn't like social affairs, and it was obvious that she was ready to leave.

Betty pulled away and asked me to walk her outside, where she handed me her lighter as she placed a cigarette in her lips. The flame illumined the contours of her face. She puffed the cigarette, leaned against the rail, and looked up. "Why do others get the happiness, Petey?"

I didn't answer.

"Good. Don't talk. It doesn't need an answer. There isn't one." She drew on the cigarette.

I thought of her leaned back on the boulder, shirt unbuttoned, breasts arched toward the sky. I wanted to kiss her, to feel her weight against me, to touch her. I stared at my shoes, then squinted into the darkened sky as she puffed on the cigarette.

"Rich called," she said.

"Oh," I said trying to show no concern.

"He's in Oregon. Says you warned him to leave."

"What else did he say?"

"That he loves me."

It seemed she wanted an apology, so I offered up a feeble one, though unsure what it was I was apologizing for. She blew cigarette smoke in my face. "Fuck you, Petey."

"You're underage," I said, "and he's in his twenties."

She studied me through a plume of smoke. "Fuck you anyhow," she said and crushed her cigarette on top of the rail. She left me in the shadows. Stella came out on her way to a waiting limousine. She paused and asked what I was doing in the dark.

"Nothing."

"Be careful now, Pete. Don't try to saddle no horse when it's gallopin. Good night now."

"Yes, ma'am."

"You're a good boy."

I waited a minute before going back.

Mum, a few drinks under her belt, took the microphone from the bandleader and wished her son and daughter-in-law the best of everything. She gave a special thanks to Mr. Bobbins, who was much more like a New Englander than a Texan. Willy slapped his thigh and laughed. She invited Mother to visit and asked that she bring Mr. and Mrs. Bobbins. From the stage she went straight to the bar, where she and Willy downed a shot of Jack each, which he proclaimed made her an official Texan.

Except for Lana persistently asking me to dance, I was left pretty much alone. I tried to get Mother aside and tell her to take Lana home, but by then Mr. Holder, more than a bit tipsy, was trying to hustle her. Victoria, sur-rounded by three pilots and wearing parts of each one's uniform, sat cross-legged atop a table and downed shooters. New Englanders took a while to thaw out, but they knew how to heat up once the chill was gone. Finally, the bride and groom left for the airport to enjoy a weeklong honeymoon in Ha-waii, a present from Willy.

That night as I lay half asleep, my door opened, then closed. My heart jumped and I asked who was there. She padded across the tile in bare feet and stopped at the edge of the bed. She lifted the covers. The mattress moved as she crawled in. Then I felt the delicate touch of her silk nightgown and her body heat radiating through it. We lay in dead silence, except for our breathing, during which I became aroused. It took a while to find the courage to touch her, and when I tried, she pushed my hand away.

"No, be still and let me hold you."

I did as she said. She didn't speak after that, and I couldn't. She began to sniffle and apologized, said she couldn't help it. I asked what if Stella caught us.

"Don't mention that name, Pete."

Before dawn she awoke, and I watched with slitted eyes as she sat up on the edge of the bed, brushed her fingers through her hair. The sight of her bare back as she walked to the door lingered long after she'd gone.

18

Willy's tax lawyers, specialists from Los Angeles, started off optimistic about the case, then at a meeting in his office he berated them, saying he wasn't paying for optimism but results and so far it looked pretty sad to him. They made the mistake of looking to George for support. "Who you think's payin the tab here?" Willy said. Briefcases in hand, the lawyers skulked out of the casino. By firing that team and hiring a new firm from San Francisco, Willy was able to buy time. The next batch of attorneys focused on delays and legal maneuvers, a strategy that frustrated those around Willy, but not him. As the climax of the case neared, he acted as if nothing other than the next sunrise was pending.

His second team of lawyers weren't optimists, but they were arrogant. During dinner at the house he told them that income tax violated the Constitution and he aimed to stand up for the law. One asked how Willy had become an authority on the Constitution. He grinned and said he wasn't yet, but he sure would be by the time he got out of prison, which was where he was going because his lawyers "didn't know squat about the law." He laughed and poured himself a shot of whiskey. He was the only one who found this amusing.

Agents in their plain four-door Fords tailed Willy everywhere. After months of watching, they served warrants at the casino and the house. The case went to a grand jury, but the feds had missed records hidden at the house, transactions that could put Willy away for several years. The books created a bit of a nuisance, for they implicated George, and George was needed to run the Lucky. And since Willy was under surveillance, he couldn't get the books out of the house to be doctored.

Willy came home from the Lucky with two attorneys and George. He told me to take my homework upstairs and stay until he called. I did as told at once. I couldn't see Willy now without remembering the mug shot of Tennessee and the headline declaring his murder. I would have doubts, wonder if I'd jumped to a wrong conclusion, then I'd picture the beagle, tongue hanging out, flies feeding off it, and that's how I'd see the burglar. I was afraid that one day Willy would look at me and say, "'Bout that Tennessee fella . . ."

Cars came and left. Croaker and Ruben Lee arrived. Meetings went on into the afternoon and early evening. Feds were parked out front and up the street. Stella knocked on my door and told me to come down for dinner. Conversation at the table was lighthearted, Willy telling about a Mexican don who ruled a hacienda like a king. After dinner I returned to my room to wait. The lawyers left, but Willy still didn't call for me.

Sometime later Ruben Lee knocked on my door and said, "Petey, the old man wants you."

Ruben Lee looked at me as he usually did, half resentful, half amused. The week before, Willy had found him passed out on the catwalk in the "eye in the sky" and had him flown to Cancún with twenty dollars in his pocket. Surf tickling his feet, Ruben Lee had awakened on the beach with no idea where he was or how he'd gotten there. He'd phoned Willy, who said he could find his own way home and if he wanted to take drugs, he could stay in Mexico, where they were inexpensive. Of course, Willy had employed a Mexican police chief to safeguard his son, who came home five days later after a dozen apologetic phone calls to Willy.

Ruben Lee didn't like me, but he dared not go against Willy's wishes. I didn't like him either. I hadn't forgotten the night he used my bathroom to shoot up or what I'd gone through at juvey. I flipped off the desk lamp and went down.

Croaker and the family, except for Betty, waited. Though the dining table would have been better suited for such a gathering, they sat at the kitchen table. Willy motioned me to a chair next to him. A bottle of Jack D. sat in front of him. He filled Ruben Lee's and Croaker's glasses and asked if I wanted a shot.

"Don't start, Willy," Stella said.

"Boy can make up his own mind now. 'Sides, he tried it at the ranch. Didn't you?"

I looked at Stella, who shook her head. I said I didn't care for any. Willy swished whiskey around in his glass. "Pete, figure me and you'd do a little fishin and golfin. I always wanted to take up golf. How you feel about that?"

"I thought I was going," Ruben Lee said.

Undaunted, Willy winked. "Might have to send you to Mexico again, or maybe Siberia. 'Sides, I can't mix the two of you, can I? Like pourin lemonade in milk. Pete's goin. Stella'll call the school on Monday if we ain't back."

"We going to the ranch, Willy?"

"No, sir."

It instantly entered my head that this was about Tennessee, that I could link Willy to a murder and was in danger. "Sounds okay to me," I said in a display of bravado.

"We'll share drivin an you can bring books along an maybe read a story. Get some shut-eye."

Ruben Lee eyed me. I excused myself and stood up.

"Sure you won't have a nip 'fore bed?" Willy said.

"Now, Willy," Stella said.

Croaker woke me before dawn to help load the trunk. Along with suitcases, we packed a bag of never-used golf clubs, two Garcia rods, and spinning reels. He laid three bottles of Jack D. on the floorboard on the passenger side and shut the door.

"Don't be lettin him drive if he's drunk," Croaker said.

"But what if . . . ?"

"No what-ifs."

"Yes, sir," I said.

Stella fixed French toast and coffee, filled a thermos and told me to bathe and be sure and brush my teeth.

Willy smelled of whiskey. His left eye drooped as he said he'd sleep once we were on the road. He looked up and down the street. "Take 'er outta here with the lights off an when we hit Rancho, go north an put some fire to 'er."

At Rancho I turned and flipped on the headlights. He adjusted the side-view mirror. He was smiling now. I saw why when I looked in the rearview mirror and found two cars speeding up from behind. As we neared Lone Mountain on the highway to Reno, we were doing eighty, and the other cars were gaining. Willy kept watch out of the side-view mirror. He told me to slow down. After we passed through Indian Springs, he pulled the brim of his hat down and said, "I'm gettin some shut-eye." A minute later he was snoring. He snoozed until Tonopah, where I stopped to gas the car. I got out to check the oil as the attendant filled the tank. It was past nine and so cold I could see my breath. Willy cracked his door and asked if I had money. I nodded. He shut the door and pulled his hat down again. Our company gassed up at the other pumps.

Without raising his chin, Willy said, "Be ready to pull off if I give a say."

I didn't ask what he had in mind. As he instructed, I pulled onto a deserted road that led to the foothills. It was rutted and got rougher as we drove on, the undercarriage scraping bottom several times. When I looked doubtfully at Willy, he said, "Keep drivin," and drew his .45, which he laid on the seat.

My thoughts went to Tennessee. I gripped the wheel and looked straight ahead, steering away from ruts when possible. The road flattened to hardpack, ground crusted with gravel-size rock. It was lifeless here except for a few withered sages and tumbleweeds piled against the boulders and here and there cans and bottles and broken glass. He said this would do fine.

He came around with the automatic in hand and stood studying the terrain. He wobbled slightly. "Perty damn isolated, Pete," he said. "No one'll hear a shot here."

"No, Willy." Placing a hand on my shoulder, he pointed to a white rock fifty feet ahead.

"Watch 'ere," he said and lifted the pistol.

There was the blast that clogged my ears, then the bullet struck the white rock and ricocheted. The sound traveled over the flats until it was washed away by the wind. He smiled a half-stuporous smile and asked what I thought. I was ready to beg for my life if necessary, but he had to ask the question. I wasn't about to volunteer anything. I said it was an impressive shot.

"Open your hand." He laid the gun in my palm. "Got a hair trigger. Don't go crazy, point like it's a finger an aim. Go light on that trigger and let it happen."

I sighted over the top. The gun fired, recoiled, then the slide slammed back and forward, and I fired a second time without realizing it. He was right about the trigger. He reached for my hand to steady it.

"I said easy on the trigger."

The next one I squeezed off, and though the bullet struck the sand five feet in front of the rock, Willy seemed satisfied. He told me to get in the car as he emptied the magazine into the rock. When finished, he leaned against the center post, snapped in a fresh magazine, and slid the gun into his shoulder holster.

"I wanted to make sure you could use it without shootin a foot off, yours or mine. You done fine." He looked in the direction of the highway. "I'll do the drivin."

"I'm fine. I'll drive," I said.

He shook his head. "I'm ready to drive now."

"Can't, Willy."

"Can't what?"

"Can't drive. Croaker told me not to let you if you . . ."

"Croaker, huh?"

"Croaker."

He made a clicking sound with his tongue and acquiesced with a nod.

We met a surveillance team on the way out. Willy waved to them and told me to do the same. The road was too narrow to accommodate both them and us, so they had to back up to let us go on. Willy smiled as we went by. They proceeded up the road even after we were past, to search, I assumed, for evidence. Willy didn't say much after that until we reached the town of Mina. As we passed through, he studied the land ahead. A mile north, he raised a hand for me to stop. We stepped out onto an isolated stretch in a brisk forty degrees.

"This'll do fine."

To the east were railroad tracks, to the west, sage and a few old mining claims. He had me get the golf bag, then snatching up a bottle of Jack, he threw open his door. He dug through a side pouch for a ball, which he held between his thumb and first two fingers and looked at the lay of the land. "Where the hell's the best place to hit these?" he asked.

"On a golf course," I said.

Willy shook his head. "Ain't one around here," he said and told me to follow. I shouldered the bag. Wind gusted, surly and unpredictable, sometimes from the north, sometimes from the west, stirring up sheets of sand that stung our eyes. About fifty yards in from the highway Willy dropped the ball at his feet and called for a club.

"Which one?" I asked.

"Big'un. It's a big desert."

I handed over a wood. He took it with a smile and balanced the club against his hip as he took a swallow from the bottle, which he handed back to me. He addressed the ball and said, "Kind of a stupid game, Pete."

Though his swing was stiff and he held the club like a bat, he put his thigh and hip into the motion. The club whipped forward, Willy smiling. His swing came to a startling halt as sand, half a pound of it, shot into the wind and immediately back into his face. He stepped away spitting and wiping his eyes. The ball hadn't moved. "Maybe this ain't a good idea," he said.

When his eyes cleared, Willy examined the head, joined to the shaft now by a mere thread. He looked at it, me, and then the club again. "Guess I'll be needin another."

He took another swig of Jack D. and moved the ball. He scraped away the top layer of sand to check for rocks. He said, "This ain't no easy course, Pete," and lined up over the ball this time, the wind at his back just in case.

"Must be a hole out there somewheres," he said and swung his six iron, this time ripping a divot in the sand. Again the ball hadn't moved. He took another swing, this time topping the ball and rolling it about thirty feet.

"Maybe you're doing this wrong," I said.

He squinted at me. "Pete, do you see a golf course?"

"No, Willy."

"See any grass?"

"No."

"Except for 'at mine shaft, you see any holes?"

"Not yet."

"Hell, boy, I'm doin ever gawdamn thing wrong. Don't matter."

He motioned for me to follow. Addressing the ball, he moved his hips back and forth, then swung again. Some sand went sailing, but this time he lofted the ball straight ahead about seventy-five yards. He turned and winked. "Nothin to it. Think I got the hang now," he said.

So he played an imaginary course, and every time he managed contact and sent the ball aloft, he said it was a hole in one. I followed behind, handing clubs and replacing lost balls. By the time he'd finished, the Jack was half gone, he laughed and declared himself the winner of the Greater Mina Open Golf Championship. When we reached the highway, he set a ball in the center of the white lines and called for a wood.

He picked a line of sight directly south, where agents in two cars sat clicking pictures. This time his swing looked smooth. The head barely scratched asphalt as Willy drove the ball about two hundred yards down the center of the highway, and when it hit, it caromed off the hardtop and bounced until it went out of sight near where the agents were spying on us.

Willy smiled broadly. "I'd call that the shot of the day." He exchanged the club with me for his bottle and told me to put the bag away.

He sat behind the wheel, the bottle between his legs, and told me he'd drive for a while. I hesitated. He motioned with his finger and told me to toss him the keys.

"It might give them an excuse to stop us," I said, pointing toward our escorts.

He focused on me with one eye closed. "Good thinkin," he said. "Now, gimme the keys."

I shook my head.

"You more scared'a Croaker 'an you are'a me?"

I nodded.

"More good thinkin," he said and slid over.

As I locked my door, Willy turned down the radio.

"Now, just what the hell does George see in that game?"

That afternoon we sat on the bank of a dry creek bed south of Battle Mountain and fished for nothing with poles and line but no hooks or bait. We tied sinkers to the line so that we could cast. I told Willy this made no more sense than the golf game. But Willy claimed it made sense to fish this way, as there was neither water nor fish. "Why waste bait and hooks where they ain't no fish?" He kept track of our catch. He declared himself winner in terms of poundage as he reeled in a sixteen-foot shark named Stumpy. He said he was going to send Stumpy to J. Edgar Hoover because it looked enough like him to be his son, "if J. Edgar had the stuff to father a boy."

All the while, federal agents followed us. They escorted us to Jarbidge, where it snowed; to Elko, where the wind blew cold off the Utah plain; to Ely, where there was nothing much to remember; to Wendover, where Willy knew a casino owner; and to Alamo, where we visited a rancher who showed us two ostriches that he claimed were the future of Western ranching. The agents took pictures and stopped at pay phones to make dispatches while Willy napped in the car. They ate hot dogs and hamburgers as we dined on steak and baked potatoes or lobster. Willy spared no expense for our comfort so as to magnify their own discomfort.

We stopped, we visited, then we gassed up and took off again over highway, down dirt roads and over dry lake beds. All the while the agents followed.

When Willy passed out in a motel room in Alamo, I called Stella to tell her we were okay.

"He's drunk, ain't he?"

"Yes, ma'am."

"You don't let him get you in no trouble, Pete."

"No, ma'am."

"You're a good boy," she said.

We left Alamo, Willy heading north again. In Ely we took a room in a highway motel with a sign that read CLEAN SHEETS, GOOD BEDS. IF YOU CAN'T SLEEP HERE, BROTHER, IT'S YOUR CONSCIENCE. As he sipped whiskey from a water glass, I read the first three chapters of *Sea Wolf* to him until his eyes shut. Thanking me, he rolled on his side and passed out. His snoring kept me awake for an hour or so. At 2:00 A.M. he woke me and told me to get the car started, as we were heading to Elko. I pulled the car up to the motel door and waited. A couple of seconds later Willy ran out of the door hiding his face with his hat. "Make sure the boys is followin us," he said.

We pulled out of the parking lot slowly and onto the highway. Soon the cars followed in tandem, three of them now. Willy pulled his hat down over his head and dozed. I yawned and thought about my own bed and a full night's sleep.

In Elko we pulled into the Cattleman's to eat. Willy told the hostess some men in business suits would arrive soon. He gave her a five-dollar bill and asked her to seat them nearby, which she did. We ate steak and eggs, drank coffee leisurely, and all the while Willy talked about his favorite sports— rodeo and golf. He said that polo came close to combining them, but that any sport played by a bunch of dethroned dukes wasn't for him. He singled out one of the agents sitting at the next table.

"What'a you think'a tryin to putt from the back of a buckin bronco?"

The agent looked at his companions, shrugged and left for the men's toilet.

"Must be a Easterner," Willy said.

He told the waitress to bring the agents' bill to him and tell them they were good sports. While they were trying to figure out a graceful way to refuse Willy's generosity, he whispered for me to pull the car in front with the back door open and be ready to leave. When he came out, he slid in the backseat headfirst and shouted, "Hit it!"

The door slammed as I made the turn out the front entrance, screeching tire rubber. Willy crawled over the seat and told me to spare no gas, that he'd pay the ticket if we were stopped. "Let's see how good these fellas is." An hour later they passed us as we waited on a side road. Willy told me to pull in behind and follow them. "See how they like it," he said.

He was having a great time at the expense of my nerves, which seemed constantly on the verge of splintering.

The game entered a new phase the next day. Willy had me stick the accelerator to the floorboard for a mile or two and then double back. Traveling in the opposite direction, we passed the agents as they stared at us, mouths open, eyes wide. Willy pointed in our direction and motioned with an arm for them to hurry. We watched until we saw their brake lights. When the second car made the U-turn, he told me to slow down and swing about. Again we passed them going in the opposite direction, Willy hooting and screaming and taking another slug off his Jack. This time they didn't turn around right away, and we lost them for twenty minutes. We parked in a wash under a clump of rabbitbrush. They drove by at about a hundred miles per hour.

"Havin fun, Pete?"

"I guess."

"Take 'er on out slow like and head home."

They pulled us over near the entrance to the Test Site and showed Willy a search warrant for the car. As we stood in the shivering cold, they stripped the insides out and went through every possible hiding spot. Willy bumped his shoulder to mine. "You're a good pardner," he said.

On the evening of the fifth day, I pulled the Cadillac into the driveway. Willy, balled up in a blanket, was leaning against the door snoring. I shook him awake. He opened his eyes and squinted to make sure where he was. He told me not to bother with the luggage just yet and fumbled about in his jacket pocket until he found what he was looking for. He handed over a letter-size envelope.

"Just don't spend it on another motorcycle. One'a them damned contraptions is enough."

I opened the envelope, spread the bills, and counted them. One thousand dollars.

He pressed the door handle and said, "Would'a made it two, but you lied to me. Don't ever lie to me again, Pete."

I didn't ask him what it was I'd lied about. I assumed it was Tennessee.

While we led the IRS and the FBI on the senseless pursuit, Willy's lawyers negotiated and his accountants cooked his books under the watchful eye of George. Still, the IRS had a case; it was a matter of degree and what kind of deal his attorneys could walk before a judge. The next day he surrendered to marshals, who said he'd be kept in isolation and closely observed until his case went to court. He was booked into the county jail and given a private cell with a television and a telephone. Two days later Willy pled guilty to one count of income-tax evasion.

Three days later in Salem, Oregon, two unknown assailants cornered Richard Forsby outside a club where he was performing and, using a cut-down baseball bat, crushed his hands. Stella received a call that night from a hospital clerk in Salem who said Betty had been listed as next of kin on Richard's admission slip. The clerk asked if someone would guarantee payment on the bill. Stella said the bill would be paid, but Betty Bobbins was not next of kin. An investigator uncovered a marriage license issued to Richard Forsby and Betty Ann Bobbins. The marriage, performed in Reno in June, was annulled in early December in district court on the grounds that Betty Ann Bobbins had lied about her age.

19

It was disturbing to see Ruben Lee slouched in Willy's booth, legs sprawled out insolently, holding court with a consortium of thieves, pushers, and shylocks—gone the poker players, cowboys, and politicians who'd gathered to seek favor or enjoy a story. Laughter became a rare thing. Matters were better when George was around. He treated me politely, if coldly, and sat by himself discussing business on the phone. He never mingled with Ruben Lee's friends.

I waited the table, as was my responsibility, but no longer enjoyed the work. I missed being summoned to Willy's office and having a bowl of chili with him as he balanced figures or told stories. I missed reading him stories and hearing his reaction. I felt vulnerable. Nightmares of my experience in juvey returned, twofold, threefold. Conditions were worse at the house, where Stella and Betty cold-shouldered one another. Since the annulment they spoke only through a third party—Croaker if he was around, but usually me—an insufferable situation. I was thankful when work kept me away.

Word of Willy came through Stella. He was asking for a bail release until his sentencing, but the attorney general fought every effort. If he'd asked about me, Stella didn't say, so I assumed he hadn't. He had good reason. Tennessee dead—my doing—when Rich Forsby was the guilty party. I figured Willy had discovered my deception and let me off because I'd honored a promise and he understood honor. Then the week before Christmas Croaker handed me a tray and told me to take a bowl of chili to the jail.

"Willy?"

"He says that jailhouse slop is killin him. I said if his own chili don't kill 'im, nothin will. Wouldn't you say 'at's about right?"

"Chili that could eat a hole in the bathtub," I said.

"Eat up the whole damn plumbin." Croaker pulled me aside by the arm. "If he tells you somethin, will you recollect it?"

"I suppose."

"Word for word?"

"Yes."

A deputy patted me down and ran the plastic spoon through the bowl. When I asked if he was looking for a file, he told me to quit watching movies. He motioned for me to follow him through a dull iron door. It clanged shut and echoed off the concrete floors. My neck hairs bristled. The deputy told me to be careful and led me down a recently waxed corridor. We passed several tanks, each crowded, rough-looking men in jail overalls, some of whom hung on the bars and stared at us. Others released catcalls that echoed down the corridor. The deputy stopped before a four-man cell. Willy sat on a bunk playing solitaire and watching television. He alone occupied the cell.

"Well, well, Pete." He set his cards aside as the guard unlocked the door. "Smells like Texas chili."

The deputy motioned me inside. I placed the tray on a small table beside the bunk.

"Get that damned TV, will you, Pete?"

As I shut off the television, Willy lifted the cover off the bowl and sniffed. He said he was glad to see me and motioned for me to sit opposite him. He withdrew *Winesburg, Ohio* from under a pillow and passed it to me.

"Been goin crazy," he said and told me to read.

I read, he ate. I finished the first story as a trustee arrived with the timing of a French waiter to bring two cups of coffee. Willy asked him to take a taste first, which the man did willingly. In exchange Willy passed a dollar through the bars.

He sat sipping coffee. I did the same.

"Maybe I'll learn myself how to read in here," he said.

"That's a good idea."

"Maybe I won't. I like listenin to a good story. Tell me what's goin on in my casino. They restricted my visits to lawyers an family. Croaker ain't around to tell, an I know those boys 'a mine is paintin fairy tales."

I told him about some firings and a memo George had written threatening workers with their jobs and a few other incidents, but I avoided talking about Ruben Lee or George directly, especially about Ruben Lee consorting with drug dealers in Willy's booth.

"This is costin you tips," he said.

"George and Ruben Lee don't tip," I said.

He smiled. "No, they don't. Stay clear of Ruben Lee for the time bein. Unnerstand?"

"Yeah."

"My pa didn't do his family right. I learn't from it," he said, but as soon as he said it, he stared off as if someone was saying something to him and he couldn't quite make out the words. I asked if that was all.

"I ain't produced much in the way 'a sons," he said. "Can you memorize a number?"

I nodded, and he gave me a telephone number to call if something came up I couldn't take to George or Croaker. He said I was to use it in only an extreme case, and I was to say my name and that I was calling on Willy's behalf. I repeated the number twice. Pleased, he said. "Go on, Pete. We'll have a time at the ranch next year."

In the morning Willy was fined eighty-five thousand dollars, which he paid on the spot, and sentenced to two years at the La Tuna Federal Corrections Facility north of Roswell. A reporter, granted an interview in the county jail that night, asked how he felt about going to the same prison as Joseph Valachi. Willy said he'd met Joe once and didn't think much of his card playing, and he should have been sentenced to hard time for passing himself off as a poker player. The reporter said he was sentenced to life. "Well, then

when he does die, they should bring 'im back to life and sentence 'im again."
His statement made national news.

Betty and Stella, in a moment of truce, were decorating the Christmas
tree when the phone rang. I was on a ladder stringing lights over the staircase
and unable to answer it. Stella grabbed the receiver. "It's probably for me,"
Betty said and hovered nearby.

Stella put a finger to her lips and demanded quiet. "It's Willy," she said
and listened intently. She closed her hand over the receiver and announced,
"Willy'll be comin home for Christmas," then put her ear to the phone again.
She nodded a few times, looked at the star atop the tree, and said, "He
means Christmas next year."

The day after Christmas a letter came from Jiggers that Sarge had come
down with cancer and Pearl had been assigned to the Eleventh Air Assault in
Fort Benning, Georgia, training to go to Vietnam. The news hit hard, especially with Willy in jail. I asked George for the week of spring break off, as I
wanted to go to the ranch. He told me that he would arrange it.

20

The week before spring break when I was to go to the ranch, Miriam left for
Philadelphia, Mother flew to Hawaii with some mystery man, and Stella
rode the train to Roswell for a month to visit Willy. Betty hid in her room or
sat in the den and stared at the television, refusing to talk. She blamed me
for Richard's hands. I told her I had nothing to do with it. Her answer was that
I was a purse thief and she was sorry she'd ever thought I was anything else.

When the time came to pack for the trip, I found George had overlooked
giving me time off. According to the hostess I was scheduled to work the
following day, when I was supposed to leave. With Willy away I'd lost my
privileges, and George was nowhere to be found that night. I worked four
hours waiting for people to vacate my tables and then I asked to leave early. It
was slow, so the hostess let me go.

I pulled into the driveway and set the kickstand. Though Betty's Mustang
was parked in the driveway, the house was dark except for one light in the
hallway. Jamita had long since gone home. I figured Betty had finally decided
it was time to go out, so I changed clothes and flopped down on the couch in
the den. Watching television was a luxury. I flipped the set on and propped
my feet up, hoping to catch the late news, but a running faucet upstairs
distracted me.

I lowered the volume and called out for Betty. There was no answer. Reluctantly, I went upstairs and listened outside her room. The sound of running water came from inside. There was no light. I started to knock, thought better of it, and turned to leave. Halfway down the hallway I stopped and turned around. This time I knocked and called her name. The only sound that came from the other side was running water. I tested the doorknob. Betty, afraid that Stella would snoop through her belongings, never left it unlocked when going out. Sure enough, it was locked. I shrugged and turned to leave a second time, but heard a distinct splash. I called out, but still got no response. I didn't like the situation, but I had promised Willy to watch over Betty. I had to make a decision, even a wrong choice. I slammed my weight into the door.

Willy believed in dead bolts and solid wood doors. I used my foot the next time and the next ten after that before the door began to buckle. I hit it again with my shoulder and bucked backwards. I was breathing pretty hard by then. I turned the knob. The door opened. Her room smelled of whiskey. I flipped the light on. A bottle of bourbon sat atop the nightstand. Her bed was unmade and clothes were strewn about the floor, shoes and boots and jeans, brassieres flopped over backs of chairs, hats tossed on the bedposts, evidence of her sense of disorder. But no Betty.

The bathroom door was closed and water seeped under it onto the carpet, spreading out into a darkening ring. I jiggled the doorknob. I called, then stepped back and kicked the door open. She lay in the tub, her arm hanging limply over the edge. On the vanity lay two prescription bottles, both empty, and a vial with a filmy powder.

Water up to her mouth, she rested against the wall of the tub. I turned off the faucet, shoved my arm into the bath, and pulled the plug. Then I grabbed a towel and hollered at her. She blinked and offered a wan smile like a baby awakening as someone picks it up. I lifted her out. She lay in my arms—dead wet weight—her long hair dripping on the tiles. Here she was, naked and lovely as I had often imagined, but there was no time to reflect on it.

I wrapped her in the towel. Her eyes opened, and she tried to speak but produced nothing other than low, guttural sounds. She beat on my arms and shoulders with her fists as I lowered her to the floor. I grabbed the vial and prescription bottles, noted they weren't in her name, and stuffed them in my pocket. In the closet hung a terry-cloth bathrobe. She fought blindly as I slipped her arms through the sleeves. I tied the waistband, propped her against my shoulder, and lifted her. A set of car keys sat on the dresser. I scooped them up as I passed by.

I set her in the seat and got behind the wheel. As I fired the engine, she leaned over and vomited. "Good girl," I said and backed out.

She slumped against the passenger door, holding her belly, and said, "Oh, Jesus." She looked over at me, her eyes glassy, but I felt she at least recognized me.

"Good," I said, put the car in first, and laid my foot to the accelerator.

She passed out on the way to the hospital. I parked where a sign said AMBU-LANCES ONLY and shouted for help, that I had a girl who'd overdosed. It was cold, and she shivered as I lifted her out. I told her it was going to be okay. Coming out of her daze, she struck me on the nose.

"Careful, now, you'll break it," I said and lifted her onto my shoulder, then hurried toward the white lights of the emergency room, hollering for help. At the steps a nurse and an orderly rushed out. The attendant helped me get her onto a gurney. Her robe opened as we laid her down, and I covered her. The nurse asked how long it had been and what she'd taken. I said within an hour, which was just a guess, then fumbled in my pocket and came out with the bottles and the vial. Did I know if she had vomited? I said yes, which seemed to please the nurse, who told me to get the car out of the ambulance zone. Then they rolled her away.

After moving the Mustang, I went to the registration desk. The clerk asked who was responsible for the bill. "Guess I am," I said.

"Are you the next of kin?"

"Not exactly."

"Are you twenty-one?"

"No."

She said I'd have to contact a responsible adult, placed a form on a clipboard, and told me to fill in as many of the spaces as I could. I found a chair in a corner. I got no further than Betty's name. The woman behind the counter spied on me over the rim of her reading glasses. I looked around. Near the swinging doors was a pay phone. I felt in my pocket for a dime. "Hello," a man's baritone voice answered. It had a slight drawl, not as pronounced as Willy's, but similar.

"My name's Pete. Willy told me to call this number if I had a problem I couldn't take to anyone else."

"Where are you?"

I told him the emergency room of the hospital. He didn't ask for details, just calmly told me to stay put, not to talk to anyone until he got there, and not to sign anything. I asked how I would recognize him. "I'll know you," he said and hung up.

About ten minutes later a doctor and a policeman pulled me aside. The cop wanted to know where Betty had gotten the drugs. The doctor wanted to know how much of what she'd taken. I did as instructed, not that I would have done otherwise, for I had no answers. About the only thing I could have told them was Betty's name, but I didn't. I gave mine and explained I was waiting for someone to take care of matters. The cop said he was losing his patience and left me with the doctor, who said saving the girl was more important than protecting myself.

The cop returned and ordered me to stand and lean into the wall with both hands. As he frisked me, he explained to the doctor that I had a juvenile record for possession of heroin. He pulled my hands behind my back and handcuffed me. The doctor, concerned that I would hold back information, protested, but the cop said that would change when the detectives arrived. Just then one did.

I recognized him immediately. The uniformed officer greeted him as lieutenant and briefly told him of Betty's overdose and my record. The lieutenant thanked him and asked that he remove my handcuffs. When they came off, the lieutenant pulled me aside. "Pete, my name's Frank. Just nod or shake your head. Did you have anything to do with this overdose?"

I shook my head.

"Good. Is that Betty Bobbins in there?"

I nodded.

"Have a seat." He left and told the cop to watch me, nothing more. After a word with the doctor, the two of them walked through the swinging doors, where Betty was. Two more detectives arrived. After a conference with the uniformed cop, they entered the emergency room, only to step back out a minute later, mutter something to the cop, and leave. The man in uniform looked at me with disdain but said nothing. Frank stepped through the swinging doors and called the cop over by his name, Jess. They leaned into their words and made little gestures with their hands until Frank patted him on the shoulder and thanked him. The cop left. Frank sat down next to me. "They pumped her stomach. She'll be here overnight. The flu. You understand?"

"Yes, sir."

"Frank. I'm just Frank." He studied me for a moment.

I asked if I could go.

"No. What's at the house?"

"I brought what was there to the hospital."

"Barbs. Probably heroin in the vial. I can guess where that came from."

I told him I'd broken the doors in to get to her.

"Good thing you did. I'll get someone to repair them. Was there a note?"

"A note?"

"Yeah, did you see a note?"

"No."

"Willy says you'll be a fine lawyer someday, so start using your head now. You have a place to go for a few days?"

I remembered the ranch and wanting to go. "I planned to go to Willy's ranch."

"Been there. God's country, Montana."

"I can't go because of work."

He nodded. "You want to go?"

"Yes."

He told me to stay put. He walked to the pay phone and stood with his back to me as he talked. A moment later he returned and sat beside me.

"Wait here. George'll be coming. He's got some questions. Afterwards, you go on to Montana. If you need anything, call."

George arrived to sign the papers. He didn't say much at first, but when we were in the parking lot, he told me to have a seat in his car.

"You can't let Ma know about this," he said.

"No, sir."

"Or Willy. Is that understood?"

"Yes."

"Good. I forgot your schedule. I'll take care of it. And don't worry about Betty. She'll stay with me for a while."

"Okay." I started to open the door.

"Pete?"

"Yes."

"Any chance it was an accident?"

I thought, then shook my head and shut the door.

In the morning, as I was loading the trunk of one of the Cadillacs, Frank pulled into the driveway in a plain blue Mercury, a detective unit. Behind him came a red Ford pickup. Frank waved as he parked beside me. "I brought a carpenter," he said.

I asked how she was.

"Groggy, weak, pigheaded, if you want to know."

I slammed the trunk. "Need keys to get in," I said.

"No. I've got a set." He stepped out of the car. "Well, say hello to Cal for me."

As I backed out, a question bubbled up in my mind and percolated there. Since Frank was the one who had come the night I went to Willie for help, he knew all about Julie. How much, if anything, I wondered, did he know about Tennessee?

21

I drove Willy's Cadillac straight through to the ranch. Cal came up as I opened the trunk, looked me over, and said I looked worse than a cow coming out of a bad calving and I should get some shut-eye. He claimed things were pretty much the same, but he missed Sarge, who had been taken to Butte two days before. He said it was strange how a man who rarely spoke could leave such an empty spot at a table. "I've been ridin with Sarge . . . well, it seems about a hundred years."

He ran his hand across his cheek, as he often did when thinking. "Probably lucky you missed him. He kind 'a begun to waste away. Well, maybe you ought to get some rest." He looked as if he was waiting for me to say something.

Other than Sarge and Croaker, Cal was probably the quietest man I'd ever met. He'd just spoken to me more in three minutes than he ever had before. "Maybe I'll go see him."

"Suit yourself."

I gathered up my bag and went to the bunkhouse, where I tossed the suitcase on the floor and threw myself down on a bare mattress. Jiggers appeared as if summoned. Seeing me seemed to please him. He carried a brown paper sack, had been drinking, and smelled of whiskey. He took a seat at the foot of the bed. "Gonna unpack?"

"After some sleep."

"I saved this," he said, handing over a cold chicken sandwich. "Figured you'd be hungry."

"Thanks."

"You got my letter?"

Answering with a nod, I unwrapped the sandwich. Until I bit into it, I didn't realize how hungry I was. Right away Jiggers began to talk about Sarge, as if the conversation had been about him. "Worked with him all those years and thought I knew him. Well, I didn't. No more than I knew anyone, though I thought I knew them all. Sarge was a hard one to crack. Kept his business close, real close. Last week he up and says before the war he went to Stanford and studied history. I asked why he didn't do something better with his life. You know what he said?"

I swallowed a bite. "No."

"He said, 'I thought I would when I grew up.' Isn't that a strange thing to say? He asked me at the same time if you was coming up."

Me? I remembered our uncomfortable conversations, silent breaks that seemed like blank spaces on a test page that needed filling. Did he want to see me? Or was it *why* did he want to see me? I knew then I had to go to Butte. "I'm going up to Butte. You want to come along?"

Jiggers shook his head. "Said our good-byes. He told me to take good care of his horses, keep them fit and don't let any tenderfoot ride them. Fact is, not too many wanted to partner up with him. Man who keeps his thoughts too private makes other men uneasy. On the other hand, a man who blabs his business . . . Ah, you're too tired to listen to some busted-up old buckaroo."

I wanted to see Sarge for more than one reason—curiosity perhaps, but about what I wasn't at all sure. "Thanks for the sandwich."

"Sure. May as well tell him we're thinking about him. Guess that's the damned truth of the matter if it were to be known. Just be fussy about what you say." He brushed his hands over his thighs as if drying them. He seemed more bent from his arthritis than usual as he moved to the door. "Imagine," he muttered. "Stanford." He closed the door.

I didn't bother undressing. My eyes fluttered and I was asleep.

In the morning over an after-breakfast coffee, I told Cal I'd be freeloading a few days. He said he'd squeeze some work out of me over the summer, but I could exercise Sarge's horses if I did any riding. He pushed himself up from his seat. "What you got in mind to do?" he asked.

"Take a ride to Butte."

He nodded. "Real name's Sylvester Armstrong. Shame," he said. "Damned shame." He shook his head and left me at the table.

It was a brisk Montana day, overcast and threatening. As I pulled onto the highway, the droplets began to fall. I turned on the wipers and the radio, sank into the seat, and let the big car carry me. The drive to Butte made me pensive, and as I pulled in, I had a twinge of doubt. Sarge probably wanted to be alone now more than ever. Who was I? A kid he'd shared his magazines with, an ineffectual tenderfoot who had no right to call himself a hand, much less a wrangler.

The hospital, just off the highway, was easy to find. Sarge, however, had checked out.

"But he's dying," I said to the woman behind the reception counter.

"I wouldn't know about that," she said impatiently.

I thanked her and turned to leave, then had another thought. "Did he leave any messages? Maybe in the ward?"

She sighed and motioned me over. "We're not supposed to, but hold on." She dialed a number and asked for Anna, then handed me the receiver. "Tell her he's your uncle," she said.

When the nurse spoke, I told her my name and said I was looking for my uncle, Sylvester Armstrong. "He goes by Sarge Armstrong."

"He checked out yesterday," she said.

"Did he leave a message?"

"No, but he took a room at the Finnlander," she said. "You're his nephew?"

"Yes."

"You should know he refused radiation."

I told her I appreciated the information, then thanked the receptionist and left.

He sat on a couch in the lobby, newspaper opened, reading glasses propped on his nose. He kept reading even as I settled down on the cushion next to him. I leaned over to see what he was reading. He closed the paper. "You can buy one for yourself right around the corner, Pete."

"I kind of like yours."

"Then you'll just have to wait," he said, opened the paper again, and read.

When he closed the paper, he folded it neatly and handed it over. "Enjoy it," he said. I tucked the paper under my arm and told him I'd read it later.

"You come all the way here just to borrow my paper?"

His body was lost in the folds of his clothes, and he looked too weak to sit upright. The wasting had begun, and the disease had chewed away his vitality, but his eyes remained clear and intelligent. "No. Came to see the sights."

"Well, I'd expect that from a blind man or a fool."

"They said you didn't take treatments."

He removed his glasses and looked out the lobby window. "They had no right to tell you."

I was a bit ashamed for having said it, and more so for having violated the nurse's confidence. I changed the subject. "Jiggers and the others told me to say hello."

Still looking out the window, he nodded. "I saw no point in it. And the drugs. Hell, I couldn't read. Three words and I'd drift off. I'll miss not reading the news. Gets me angry reading it and angrier still if I can't." He laid his mottled hand on the arm of the couch. His wrist was thin as a woman's. "Will you give me a hand up, Pete?"

"Sure."

His grip was too weak for him to hold on, so I held his forearm and gently raised him. I wondered where he'd found the strength to get to the hotel. He needed to use the toilet and reluctantly asked if I'd help him to his room. In the elevator he leaned against both me and the wall as we went up to the fourth floor. When we reached his room, he handed me the key and said he didn't think he could manage the door. His hand trembled. I held the door open for him.

ream of wheat, thank you."

he looked at me as if to confirm the gag.

'm still in high school," I said. "This is Sarge. I worked with him at the

h."

'leased to meet you, Sarge. I'm Amanda."

How do you do?"

he asked for my order.

Buckwheat pancakes and two strips of bacon."

he set my pancakes down right away, but took her time placing Sarge's
as if waiting for him to speak. But he just squinted at his paper. She set
owl down and left.

think she likes you," I said.

e poured honey in the bowl and stirred his cereal. "She's curious. Proba-
onders . . ." He winced and let go of the spoon, which clattered on the

ou okay?"

e took a shallow breath, picked up the spoon, and started eating.
nda arrived with fresh coffee. "How's everything, gentlemen?" She filled
nugs.

ine," I said.

ter that, except to check our coffee, Amanda pretty much stayed away.
read, passing sections of his newspaper to me as he finished them and
ng occasional comments. He came to the classifieds and folded the
paper. "No point reading them," he said. Excusing himself, he stood to
the toilet. "Hope I can do this without having an accident."

manda warmed our coffee. "Your friend okay?"

wish he was."

le's dying, isn't he?"

vasn't willing to say. She said she understood.

rge was pleased with having used the toilet without an accident. He
if I would ride him around, so I did for an hour. This exhausted him, so
turned to the hotel where he stretched out on his bed and stared at the
g while I put in a collect call to the ranch. Conchita answered the tele-
e. He told me not to tell her anything about him, so I just said he seemed
doing fine. Later he slipped into a troubled half sleep that he drifted in
ut of. Not knowing what else to do, I sat beside him so he wouldn't be
By midafternoon he was in pain and gasping for every breath. I asked if
nted water. He blinked and opened his eyes.

never held a man's hand before, nor a dying person's hand, but I held
was like holding a child's. Sometime before noon his hand went limp.

"Why don't you go back to the hospital?" I asked.

"No dignity there, Pete."

It took several minutes for him to come out of the bathroom. It was obvious from the stain on his trousers that he didn't make it to the toilet in time.
He said he couldn't stand, didn't have strength enough, which was evident
when he crossed the floor to his bed. He flopped down on the foot of the
bed, trying to catch his breath. "Spent a considerable time on the hard
ground or a flimsy bunk. Always had a problem sleeping. When I was a kid,
my little brother died in his sleep. I was afraid of sleep after that. That was
how I became a reader."

I walked to the door, which was still ajar.

"You leaving me, Pete?"

"No, just shutting the door."

"There's a glass in the bathroom. Would you bring me some water?"

I did as asked. Setting the glass aside, I propped him up so he could drink.
He took a swallow, then waved the rest off. "They drug you up in the hospital," he said. "Don't want to go out drugged up. Seems like the last thing a
man does he should experience it. Jiggers told me he wrote you. He figured
you and I sort of became friends because of the magazines. Tell you the
truth, I was glad to have you read them. No one else ever did."

"Is there something I can get?"

"No, I feel like talking is all. I haven't felt that way in years, and I don't
want to go to sleep. I want to be awake when it happens."

"Nothing's going to happen," I said.

"Pete, I'm a smart man. I know what I've got." He winced and held his
breath, then slowly let it out. He asked for another sip. He insisted I pull a
chair up next to the bed so he wouldn't have to shout. I laughed. This
brought a smile to his lips. Except for three trips to the toilet he talked for
two straight hours. The pain was at times too severe to allow him to speak.
He held his breath then and seemed to count to himself. He never complained.

He ventured into all manner of things, but always the tales were autobio-
graphical. He started out to be an engineer, but changed his mind after he
took Greek history at Stanford under a professor who made him love the
ancients. Then the war had come. His father, who sold farm equipment,
went bankrupt because of the Depression and died of a heart attack when
Sarge was fighting in the South Pacific. His mother worked in a plant building B-17s. His sister married and moved to Alaska. All of them had died.

Though each word sapped his strength, he kept talking. It was as if he
were trying to free himself of his own history so he could move on. Occasion-

ally I'd prop him up and help him drink. Whenever I asked if he needed anything, he told me not to interrupt. Finally he got to talking about the ranch.

He was wounded in the war and returned to the States. He'd needed only a year of college to complete a degree, and so he came to Butte to work in the mines and start back to college. He'd worked the mines, but mining was in a slump. He was nearly broke when Willy put him to work, first as a dealer. But Sarge hated dealing, hated the confinement and wasn't good at it, so when Willy gave him a chance to work at the ranch, he took it. He'd intended it to be a summer job.

I asked what kept him there. From the change in his expression, I knew I'd triggered something. He was slow to answer, then said he'd just let things take him, that the pace of the ranch seemed to arrest time. This, I could tell, was only part of the truth. I assumed he had good reason for not wanting to tell me, so I didn't pry.

A bit later he drifted to sleep. I sat and watched his chest struggle. This was more than I'd counted on. I don't know how long I watched him before I realized how hungry I was. With every intention of returning, I stood up. His eyes blinked open. "Pete, are you leaving?"

"I was going to get some food."

He looked toward the window. "It's dark out."

"Yeah."

"You'll come back?"

"Yeah. You want anything?"

He thought a moment. "Fresh-squeezed orange juice."

I went to the restaurant where Amanda waited tables. She was off for the day, and the new waitress said their orange juice was from a frozen mix. After eating, I purchased half a dozen oranges, got my bag from the car, and registered myself into a room across the hall from Sarge's. The clerk asked if I was a friend of Mr. Armstrong's. I told him yes. He said they'd made a mistake letting him stay, that if he died there it would look bad for the hotel.

"Do you know who Willy Bobbins is?"

"Why, yes. Mr. Bobbins keeps a room with us. Pays for it year-round."

"You'll be doing him a personal favor if you don't disturb Mr. Armstrong."

He perused my face. He said, "I see. I'll inform the manager."

In my room I squeezed the oranges into a fresh drinking glass. Sarge seemed pleased to see me. He asked if I had something to read, that he'd like to be read to. I had a paperback copy of *To Kill a Mockingbird* in my suitcase. A few sips of orange juice was all he could handle, though he insisted it tasted just wonderful. In the middle of the third chapter Sarge dozed off

again. I gave him several minutes to awaken, and when he book on the nightstand and left him to sleep. Certainly the last few hours with would wake up if it was time for him doubt he would, and I took that assurance with me as I cr

In the morning he seemed not only in better spirits, bu He'd dressed himself in clean clothes and was waiting knocked on the door. I asked if he had the strength for a car

"A restaurant where this nice waitress works."

"We can give it a try. I'd sure like some coffee and a ne

He allowed my help to the elevator, but once the door op he held himself erect and passed the front desk. Though I to walk, he nodded to the desk clerk and said good morning heels, just in case. He seemed to gain confidence, even sug the restaurant until I said it was four blocks uphill, and always steep.

Amanda stood behind the counter. I grabbed a seat and who'd stopped to buy a newspaper. As she set menus do recognized me, though the memory was dim. I explained I'd mer on a ranch near Dillon. Sarge saw me and headed over. too thin to support his head.

She winked. "Oh, yeah. How's the college boy?"

"Fine."

"What'll you have?"

"Two coffees to start."

Sarge sat down. "What's this about a college boy?"

"She thought I was in college. I didn't correct her."

He shook his head and opened the newspaper.

It bothered me that he seemed disappointed in me. "It

He squinted. "It's exactly like you lied."

When Amanda arrived with coffee, Sarge said withou the print, "So, Pete, how's that course you're taking in bra

"What?"

"Oh, hello, ma'am," he said to Amanda. "Pete's studyin Youngest student in Harvard Med School."

She looked at me. "Must take them really young."

He kept up the gag, and though raspy, his voice was su he talked without hesitating. "He's an exceptional boy. Ta about the medulla oblongata and the corpus callosum."

Amanda didn't quite know how to react at first and as have?"

I tucked it under the bedding and called the desk clerk. I suggested it would be wise to call an ambulance and be discreet, adding that I'd make certain Willy Bobbins picked up whatever expense was involved.

Afterwards, I slept in the room where Sarge died, not on the bed but on the floor. The sleep was fitful, disturbed by a dream of Rita and Willy and Sarge, in which the three of them were at a dance and Willy shot Sarge. I awoke wondering why I'd had such a dream. I sat in the chair and waited for the first glimmer of sunlight to touch the windowpane. And when the sun broke the horizon, I picked up the telephone and asked the clerk to give me long distance.

George deplaned and walked into the terminal, where I stood half embarrassed. He wore a light brown silk suit and a thin dark brown tie. He seemed the usual George, all business. I was uncertain what to expect. He'd sounded harried when I called, but said he'd fly up right away, that he'd be in the air within the hour. He saw me standing in the lobby and walked straight to me, extending his hand as he neared. He asked if I was doing all right.

I nodded and said, "I didn't know who else to call. I've never . . . This is the first time I ever had to deal with a dead man." I was lying. I thought of the night I'd confided in Willy about Julie D'Rittio. But that was different, I told myself.

He carried a thin leather briefcase in his left hand. "If you're trying to apologize, Pete, there's no need to. You did the right thing. He's our responsibility. He was a good man."

"Didn't you bring luggage?"

"No, Pete."

"They have clothes at the ranch that'll fit you," I said, as if I were somehow in charge.

He smiled. I couldn't recall seeing him smile before. When he smiled, he looked considerably more like Willy than I'd ever noticed. The smile faded, and once again he was the George everyone else saw, the tight-faced general manager of a lucrative casino. I wondered why he didn't smile more often. "I won't be going to the ranch. I never go there," he said.

"Oh."

"Let's get this business done, Pete. I've got to fly back today."

I drove him to the hotel, where he spoke with the manager. The man nodded occasionally, letting George do the talking. When they were finished, George motioned for me to follow. We went up to the room. It was as I had left it, the bed unmade, the blanket I'd wrapped myself in at the foot. George opened the dresser drawers. They were empty except for two recent newspapers and one change of underwear. When he finished with all the drawers and the closet, George turned to me.

"Did you see any papers or valuables?"

I shook my head. "I don't think he had anything."

"Okay, let's get a bite to eat and we'll head over to the lawyer's office."

"Lawyer?"

"Yes. We've got legal matters to take care of. Sarge was a good man. Willy won't have the State of Montana burying him. I called the ranch, and arrangements have been made. We just have to make it legal."

"Okay. I think Sarge would like that."

He looked me up and down as if trying to figure out what to do with me. He smiled for the second time that day. "Let's eat. Seems to me we've never talked, have we?"

"Not much."

I thought we'd go to the café and see Amanda, but George told me to find a grocery store. He bought a package of buns and a dozen hot dogs, a bottle of relish, one of mustard and one of ketchup, napkins, plastic silverware, and two Cokes. When we got back in the car, he took off his suit coat, removed his tie, and unbuttoned his collar. He pointed across the highway to a hill south of Butte proper. After we crossed the highway, he brought my attention to the first cemetery. "That's the Jewish cemetery. Always struck me as strange that they'd have their own, but it was their choice. The next one's for everyone else, or was until it was filled. There, pull over there." He pointed to a gravel road on the left.

The road inclined for about a half mile, then forked. He directed me to turn right. I followed a washboard dirt road until we came to a brick and stone house with windows and doors boarded up. He told me to stop and wait in the car. He got out and walked around the house, not once but twice. On his way back he stooped over, picked up a stone, and heaved it across the road, then turned around and took a long look at the place. When he finally slid into his seat, he told me to drive straight down the road until it dead-ended.

We came to a clearing, not a meadow exactly but a smooth, sloping knoll overgrown with wildflowers and grease brush. Here he told me to stop. He carried the grocery bag and motioned for me to follow. We trekked down a narrow trail to a dry gorge. He stopped at a shaded clearing surrounded by boulders, where a wild patch of tamarisk was encroaching on some ancient cottonwoods. The thick trunks of the old trees were black.

"Hasn't changed," he said and told me to gather up some dry branches.

Within minutes we had a fire going in a well-used ring of rocks. Using his pocketknife, he cut some branches off the tamarisk, skinned away the bark, and sharpened them to a point.

"I've always liked hot dogs like this, over an open fire and kind of charred," he said as he pulled his first from the fire. "My wife won't let me eat like this at home. And I don't get to go camping. The boys would like it, but there's no time." He placed the wiener in a bun and liberally poured mustard, ketchup, and relish on it.

I fixed mine with considerably fewer condiments. As I was about to take my first bite, George raised his open palm. I stopped. What had I done?

"Pete, we're gentlemen, right?"

"Yes, sir."

"George. Call me George."

He sounded like Willy. "Okay, George."

"As a gentleman, you promise never to tell my wife about this?"

"As a gentleman. Never," I said.

He stuffed a third of his hot dog in his mouth and bit down. I bit off somewhat less of mine. He nodded at me as he chewed. Sometime before our fourth hot dog, George stopped as he was pouring ketchup on his and looked at me quizzically. He wiped his mouth with a napkin. "Pete, tell me something."

"What's that?"

"Why didn't you call me on Betty?"

Strange question, I thought. One that evoked a dozen more. Betty wanted to die. Sarge wanted to live, spend his life wrangling cattle, reading periodicals, and fishing cold-water streams for brook trout—hardly the stuff that stirs novels, but a life nonetheless. A life should be lived. Isn't that what Willy would say? "Willy. Because Willy told me what to do."

George looked at me and nodded his head twice.

I held my hot dog away from me and let some mustard drip on the ground, then scraped some dirt over it with the toe of my boot.

"Like you never mentioned taking the blame for Ruben Lee?" He took a bite of his next hot dog and leaned against a rock as he chewed. He swallowed and took a sip of Coke. "You're okay, Pete. Ma was right about you."

22

Willy was granted a reprieve in late May before school let out. A judge determined he could complete his term in the county jail, so he was returned to Las

Vegas and settled in as if setting up camp—private cell, television, radio, phone privileges whenever he wanted, and no jail garb. He wore a denim shirt and jeans and paid two inmates to launder his clothes and polish his boots.

Because of these circumstances, I became Willy's regular visitor. Assigned a special three-hour shift at the Lucky, I clocked in at five-thirty in the evening, dressed in a waiter's jacket, and at a quarter to six met a guard in the kitchen, where I picked up Willy's call-in order. If George wanted to relay a message, he would wait on the first floor of the parking ramp and whisper to me, "Tell him the Bishop wrote seventy-five," which I was not supposed to understand. In response, Willy might tell me the Bishop's good for it, cut him off, or extend twenty.

I used the entrance for arriving prisoners, where I buzzed the metal door and waited. A moment later the door would open. A deputy waited to frisk me, then checked the contents of the tray before he escorted me to the third floor, where Willy waited in a cell, the door unlocked.

That first evening Willy lifted the napkin from the bowl of chili and breathed in the aroma. "Makes jail almost tolerable, Pete," he said. He was allowed spoon, fork, and knife. I was surprised he wasn't allowed to carry his .45. When I mentioned this, he beamed. He asked about Sarge, wanted to know brief details of what happened in those two days. I gave him a synopsis.

"Wouldn't stay in the hospital. Did he say why?"

"Didn't want to die there. He wanted to be lucid when he died."

"Was he?"

"Sleeping, I guess."

"Funny fella. Bright as a new sheet. Liked cowboyin. Well, I told Cal to give him a grave on the ranch. It was all he asked. Did you like him?"

"Sure, I liked him, Willy. He was a nice man."

"And you got to spend time with him. 'At's good."

It seemed a strange thing for Willy to say. As an afterthought, he said, "Heard Betty was in the hospital with food poisoning?"

It was a question. "Yes."

Disappointed that she'd already gone to San Antonio for the summer, Willy reconciled it by saying the riding school she attended was a good one and he was pleased she was finally taking riding seriously, though it meant she would miss summer school. At best, if she'd stayed home, she would have been an infrequent visitor. "You took her to the hospital, didn't you?" he asked.

"Yes." I wasn't about to volunteer information about that night. Records had been altered to indicate food poisoning in order to justify pumping her stomach.

"You mad at me, Pete?"

"No, Willy."

"Then why ain't you gawdamn talkin to me?"

"Nothing to say."

"You think a lot of that gal, don't you?"

"Maybe."

"'S 'at why you're always lyin for her?"

I didn't answer. He ate and talked about prison life, but seemed preoccupied and at times lost his train of thought. When he'd emptied the bowl and plate, he looked up and suggested I bring a book next time, saying that he missed hearing stories.

I gathered up the tray. "I'm glad you're back, Willy."

"You mean that, don't you, Pete?" He dropped the napkin on the tray.

"Yeah, sure do."

"Pete, did Sarge die good?"

"I don't know what you mean."

"Some men squirm, you know. How was it for him?"

"He talked a lot. I mean, a lot for him." I turned to go but had another thought. "At first I think he wanted to die, then he wanted to live. He . . ." I didn't finish. I was in uncomfortable territory, and Willy didn't press me. I wished him good night and carried the tray outside, where the deputy waited to escort me away.

Summer set in, and despite continuous legal maneuvering on his behalf Willy remained incarcerated. He was made trusty without duties and allowed free rein of the third floor of the jail. Every afternoon he went outside and sat with a towel draped over his shoulder and smoked a cigar while other trusties washed and detailed patrol cars. Four evenings a week I brought him dinner and kept a book at hand to read. I wanted to go to the ranch for the remainder of the summer, and though I badgered him to let me, Willy wouldn't allow it. Wasn't I obligated to help out now that he needed a friend? Sometimes he asked about the Lucky, if I believed this or that. He said George had a lot to learn about people and Ruben Lee had everything to learn about everything. He asked what I thought about Ruben Lee catching two slot thieves who were stringing a machine and having the guards beat them up.

"Wouldn't it be a good idea to have them arrested and the story printed in the paper?"

"You think word don't get out on the street?"

"If they went to court and were convicted, wouldn't the message last longer?"

206 ♠ *The Lucky*

"You're askin like a natural-born lawyer."

I blushed, but was flattered that he put any stock in my opinion.

From Willy's bunk, where we would watch prisoners being processed, we once saw the jail sergeant slap a prisoner, who broke down and cried like a baby. Another time a prisoner went berserk as he stepped off the elevator and the bars slid back. It took two cops and three jailers to subdue the man, who fought even as they dragged him to the rubber room. "Place like this brings out the worst in a fella. Once't they was a man beat his head against the bars 'til he kil't hisself," he said. He thought a moment and added, "Sorry, plum forgot you had your own experience, Pete."

The sound of metal clanging on metal was like slapping an exclamation point after the word "irreversible," and the closing of the doors never ceased to disturb me. Each and every time I heard the clang, I'd sit a little more rigid. Only death seemed more lonely and absolute than the clashing of metal door against metal frame, followed by the echo of footsteps.

One evening as Willy was eating lamb chops and wild rice, six cops marched a prisoner past the cell. A tall, thick-bodied man with a mane of wheat-colored hair, he had a menacing look to him even though handcuffed and surrounded by half a dozen cops on his way to the booking cell. He looked, in fact, as if he was in charge of the procession. As he passed, he glared at me with his pale blue eyes. It was like looking at two blue dots in the hollow sockets of a skull.

When the cuffs were unlocked, he told one cop to keep his hands off and another to fuck himself. After that he stood silent and defiant as his belongings were inventoried and sealed in an envelope. When the booking officer asked his name, he said, "John Satan."

"Your real name."

"Lick my balls."

Willy was so well liked by inmates and the jailers that when it was slow, a cop or two would stop by for a little chitchat. A deputy named Fred Osterhaus strolled over after the prisoner was locked down. He carried a copy of the booking sheet, which he showed to Willy, apparently assuming Willy could read. Willy pretended to, but when he didn't react, the officer asked if he didn't think it was funny. Willy said show it to me. I knew to cover for him and read out loud the line where the deputy pointed. The booking officer had written in the prisoner's name as "Lick My Balls, a.k.a. John Satan." Willy offered up a belated laugh and said he missed that part. He asked what the man was booked for.

"Murder, Willy," Deputy Osterhaus said. "He robbed a dry cleaners and tied up the owner and two employees. Doused them with cleaning solvents and set fire to them. He hung around to piss on the wall. Told two witnesses he was trying to put out the blaze and laughed about it. Meanest sonofabitch I ever saw."

"Burned 'em alive?" Willy asked.

"Yes, sir."

Willy pushed the tray aside and shook his head. "Two of 'em just worked there?" I'd seen him angry before and knew him well enough to see he was upset.

"That's about it," the deputy answered.

Willy looked at the empty plate on his tray and back at the cop. "Fred, see if those folks had family. They did, get the names to George an he'll give 'em some money, say ten grand."

"You're serious."

"Serious as one of them atomic bombs they keep settin off."

"That's mighty generous, Willy."

"Never mind. Just do it an don't go tellin it around."

But Fred told, and maybe Willy intended for word of his generosity to circulate. I was never certain. He seemed to have some motive behind everything he did. No matter, the papers carried the story on the front page of the local section, and Willy's beneficence sparked others to initiate a trust fund providing support and college tuition for the victims' children. After half an hour of covering the first mass bombing of Hanoi, Cold War tensions, and a Titan 3 missile being launched with the thrust of 2,400,000 pounds from solid rocket fuel, the network news closed with a piece on Willy, who, though a prisoner, the anchorman said, "acted selflessly to help two families of men he'd never met."

The story captured the public's imagination for a week, and the publicity set off a chain reaction. Gross revenues at the Lucky increased forty percent the weekend following the broadcast. A man interviewed for the evening news said he knew he was going to lose and he'd rather it go to a gentleman like Willy. The governor, both senators, and the lone congressman from the state wrote on Willy's behalf to the U.S. attorney general and the judge who'd presided over the case. Included was a statement by Deputy Fred Osterhaus, who insisted he'd defied Willy's wishes to keep the donations confidential.

The judge agreed to reassess Willy's sentence and asked the U.S. attorney and Willy's lawyers to submit briefs. While his sentence was under review, Willy was released on bail and went home with every confidence that he would never again see jail from the inside. In one masterful stroke, he'd done for himself what a battery of high-priced attorneys couldn't accomplish.

Miriam flew into town to visit Mother and called me to meet her at Foxy's. She filled in news of her life. She'd finished her sophomore year at Villanova, paid for in part by her in-laws and the rest by Willy. She'd made the dean's list and was in line for a scholarship. Her husband wrote weekly and called whenever he could. In August before fall semester began, they planned to meet in Japan for a week. She missed him, but was happy.

I had little to say. I ate my banana split, listened, and thought about Betty. By then I was missing her again and jealous, of what I had no idea. It was just a feeling. Everybody in my life seemed to be floating about. Or was it me?

"The reason I came into town is that Mother's planning on marrying."

"So."

"So you should know. You should go to the wedding, Peter."

"Pete. What's he like? Another Julie?"

"He's short and European, Corsican, I think, and has money. Leonardo's his name. And he owns three jewelry stores."

I remembered all the traveling on the road like fugitives, the hurried packing and panicked runs to the car, all the while chasing some dream—or were we running from something? Mother had scored. Isn't that what Las Vegas was about? The score. I was bitter, at least at the moment.

"Good."

"That's all you have to say?"

"I won't go to the wedding."

"Peter!"

"Pete. And don't try to convince me otherwise."

We sat locked in our own thoughts for a long while as the afternoon sun beat through the window. The old El Rancho was still there across the street, its Chinese elms cracked and dying, its fences bent or broken. The elusive dream. She asked what was new in the love department.

I looked over at her. "Love department?"

She nodded. "Have you done it yet?"

"Oh, Jesus, Miriam. Nice try. Where're you staying?"

"Friends. Don't change the subject. I figured you and Betty would be doing it by now."

"Yeah, what made you think that?"

"Willy. He . . ."

The waitress filled Miriam's coffee cup and asked if we cared for anything more.

"No," I said, and when she left, asked Miriam, "Willy what?"

"Nothing. Forget it."

"Miriam, I held a man's hand while he died. A cowhand named Sarge. He was all alone."

She leaned back. "Why'd you tell me that?"

"Who else would I tell?"

"Really? It must have been terrible."

"No. No, it wasn't. I was glad to be there, and he wanted to die. I spent his last day with him. He probably talked more that day than any other day of his life."

She came around the table and sat beside me to kiss me on the temple. She said she was proud of me. We sat absorbing the feeling of being together, brother and sister, conspirators and rivals, sharers of secrets and now friends. She asked me to drive her to the airport in the morning.

Willy changed my mind about not going to the wedding. I would go, he told me, because my mother was a decent, good woman and would want me there. No matter what she'd done or what I thought she'd done, I owed her respect. He stared as only he could.

"But she's marrying for money," I said. "Like Daisy in the book."

Willy nodded twice and began unwrapping a cigar. "Fine book, but it's a book, Pete. Your mother's life is in the flesh. You'll go an don't never let me hear you talk bad about her."

23

By mid-July the mood in the house was as uncomfortable as the temperature, which had hit 105 on July 1 and never went lower. At first Stella enjoyed Willy's attention, but soon her tolerance faded. She turned testy and sharp-tongued, treated him as she did the help when they got on her nerves. He followed her about, talking as she worked in her garden or from the fence as she rode her horse. He spoke of matters that meant little or nothing—rare steaks, salt in chili, women in jeans, bluebonnets in bloom in East Texas. He talked as if gorging himself on conversation after having been starved for it for months.

Stella, who had often complained that Willy spent too much time away, was drained by his company. Two days before Betty's return, they were in the garden. I was in my room. Willy said he was thinking about turning everything over to the boys and retiring to the ranch. "Yep, be a pleasure just to worry about horses and cows, have a few friends visit."

"Willy Bobbins, you're free to do what you damn well want, but I ain't leavin. I'll go to Texas, where it so happens you can't 'cause you got too much history there, but I ain't followin you to Montana, specially that place. Maybe that crazy daughter of yours would like to go. Not me."

I peeped through the shutters.

Stella, who'd been cutting off dead rose blossoms, threw her shears at his feet and told him to make himself useful.

"No need gettin mad an bringin up things from then," he said.

"I ain't mad, but I'm fixin to be." She stood with her hands on her hips, staring at him.

He picked up the shears and clipped a bud.

"Not that far down, Willy. Jesus. An what are you going to do about Ruben Lee?"

"Ruben Lee?"

"Our son, you know him."

"Do?"

"Willy, don't pretend." She snatched the shears away and turned her back to him.

"I'll talk to him."

"Talk, talk. Do somethin. If it was Betty, you'd be doin somethin fast enough."

"I'll see to it."

"Seein ain't enough."

Willy looked up at my window. I was screened from view by the shutters. Nonetheless, he lowered his voice so that he couldn't be overheard.

"I ain't forgot, nor forgiven," she said, took the shears from him, and went back to cutting off dead buds fiercely, as if severing the heads of ghosts.

Willy backed into the shade. A moment later the door slammed and he stomped up the stairs. His voice, though barely audible, came through the walls as he talked on the telephone. When he hung up the house went quiet and the only sounds came from Stella's shears and sparrows in the Chinese elms.

It was best to leave when Stella and Willy were warring. I picked up my boots and slipped into the hallway, figuring a ride to the mountains would serve as a good getaway. The door to Willy's office was ajar, so I tiptoed to the stairs and almost tripped over Willy, who was seated on the second stair, sipping iced tea. "What you stalkin, boy?"

"Nothing, Willy."

He set aside his glass and ordered me to sit. Lighting a cigar, something sure to stir Stella's anger, he fanned the match out. "Where you fixin to go?"

"To the mountains."

He pointed with the amber tip. "On that contraption?"

"Yeah."

"Go on. Hell, I would if I wasn't a gawdamn prisoner in this gawdamn house."

"Thanks," I said.

"For what?"

"Nothing, really, just thanks."

"You're welcome for nothin. When you get back, pack some clothes and be ready to go."

"Go where?"

"Does every gawdamn person in this family need to question me?" He chewed the wet end of the cigar and looked at me as if trying to memorize my face. "If I wanted you to know, I'd say."

"I can pack now," I said.

"Later's fine. But be ready to go on the click of a second, tomorrow, day after, an don't kill yourself on that contraption." He drew on the cigar and flicked the ashes into his palm. He was in violation of Stella's rules. He glanced about, looking for a place to hide the ashes, and finally settled for putting them in his trouser pocket. "I'm just damned tired of bein cooped up."

It was clear he wasn't going to be anyone's prisoner much longer.

Willy woke me at seven in the morning and told me to carry his bags down to the Cadillac, that we were on our way to the ranch, but we'd be taking company. Something metal clacked in his pocket as he bounced down the stairs, overnight bag in one hand.

Ruben Lee's house was in the Scotch 80s, a square half mile of high-priced ranch homes. Willy put his ear to the door, then stepped back and rang the bell. We waited. No answer, and it was obvious after a half-minute wait that there would be none. He slipped a key in, gave it a quick turn, and pushed the door open. A pair of shiny chrome handcuffs came out of his pocket.

He knocked once on the door to Ruben Lee's bedroom, turned the knob and said, "Good mornin." Ruben Lee, on a bare mattress, wrapped in a blanket, didn't seemed to recognize us or mind very much that we were there. Willy told me to find a suitcase and toss in enough clothes to last a week. "Come on, son," he said and yanked the blanket off.

Ruben Lee came up groggy but swinging. Willy stepped aside and floored him with a smooth uppercut to the abdomen. He then picked out a shirt and a pair of jeans from the closet. "Your ma's upset. Now get dressed." He tossed the clothes to him and grabbed socks and undershorts out of the dresser drawers, which he slung at Ruben Lee, who didn't move.

"Get with it, mister. We's scheduled to pull out." He gripped Ruben Lee's arm and tugged. Again, Ruben Lee came up punching. Willy tripped him and caught him as he was going down. He saw I'd stopped packing the suitcase. "You wanna do this while I pack?" he asked.

I was tempted to take over, but shook my head and stuffed another shirt in the suitcase.

Ruben Lee tried to kick as Willy slipped the shorts over an ankle. Willy said he didn't have much choice and hit Ruben Lee squarely on the jaw so hard I was sure he'd broken it. Unconscious, Ruben Lee was awkward to move, but Willy managed to dress him. He said we could forget putting on his boots for now, then handcuffed him and lifted him over a shoulder. Willy tottered down the hallway, stopping occasionally to adjust his load. He stuffed Ruben Lee into the backseat as I packed the suitcase into the trunk, then he went back and locked up the house.

Once seated, Willy said, "Gonna be a bear when he comes to. Never mind nothin he says. If he gets too crazy, I'll sit on him all the way to Montana."

At times when Ruben Lee came to he was feverish and mumbled words, slurred and disconnected. Willy and I took turns driving. South of Salt Lake Ruben Lee finally came around. He sat up and asked, "Dad, why am I in these?" meaning the handcuffs.

Willy said, "'Cause you're ruinin yourself, boy."

"I'm hungry," he said in a dejected voice, "and thirsty."

"We'll fix you up, son," Willy said.

Ruben Lee lay back down and curled up. "I don't do drugs," he said. "Promise I don't."

"Didn't mention drugs, son." Willy told him it would be okay, just rest and he'd get some food soon.

We stopped at a McDonald's. Willy kept Ruben Lee handcuffed and sat in the backseat feeding him an apple turnover and a milk shake. Afterward, he wrapped an arm around him and talked to him tenderly, saying things will be a lot better for everyone, especially him, when the drugs are gone. They rocked back and forth, Ruben Lee listening like a little kid. The only time he spoke was to say, "I hope so, Dad. I hope so."

We drove on through the early night and arrived at the ranch in the deepest blackness of dark. Clouds blocked the sky. Conchita met us with a flashlight and guided us up the steps to the house, Ruben Lee leaning against Willy, who threw the door open, then looked at Conchita and sighed.

When I awoke in the morning I found Willy gone, where, I had no idea. I saddled up Lead and got directions to Sarge's grave from Jiggers. The high rolling clouds and humid air reminded me of the previous summer's roundup. I wanted nothing more at the moment than to spend life as Sarge had. This was as close to a home as I'd ever had, and during the ride I decided to tell Willy that I wished to stay here to finish school.

The ride took an hour. As I neared the rise Jiggers had mentioned, I slowed Lead and looked for a path through the combe. Lead perked his ears, and I became aware of the sound of a horse and rider heading east. The scrub was thick bramble, wall-like, and the trail followed a narrow creek. I rode down and found the grave in a clearing in the pine, just as Jiggers had described, and there to the east was the second trail, which could amply accommodate a truck. I sat the horse and looked at the granite headstone, "Sylvester 'Sarge' Armstrong, 1919–1965." He was forty-six, younger than I'd thought.

I hadn't come to say holy words or whatever is muttered over the dead. Graves, though unequivocal, somehow soften death. I was curious; I merely wanted to see the name engraved on stone, as if that and not the last heartbeat somehow finalized death. His death absolute now, I circled the grave, ready to leave when I noticed a second headstone fifty feet away, wildflowers neatly arranged at its base. I rode there, dismounted, and let go of the reins. Immaculately carved in the white marble was the name Rita Ann, no last name, born 1922, died 1949. Her, no doubt.

The sky was closing in, bringing long-awaited rain. I mounted and took the trail east. It was raining when I reached the road to the ranch house. It was slick with mud, and water had puddled in the ruts. I saw a rider in a slicker coming my way. I waved, and as soon as he waved back, I recognized Willy. "What'cha doin, Pete?" he asked, pulling to a stop.

"Enjoying the rain, Willy."

He tossed me a slicker and said, "Can't have you comin down sick."

We rode side by side at an easy trot, splashing mud. At the stalls he handed over his reins and told me to brush the horses and bed them down, then come inside the house. I noticed, as he walked away, there was no spring to his bowlegged step. He was aging. It bothered me to see it.

Croaker opened the door, turned away without comment, and let me shut it behind us. The place smelled of dampness and smoke. Willy sat at the table drinking coffee. Ruben Lee lay on a cot under several blankets, his hands cuffed, his ankles and chest tied to the cot. Next to him was a nightstand with a pitcher of ice water, a glass with a straw, a pack of Lucky Strikes, and an ashtray filled with cigarette butts. He didn't seem to recognize me.

"Sit, Pete," Willy said and from a thermos he poured me a mug of coffee, which he pushed across the table. He lifted his cigar from the ashtray, puffed it to life, and pointed toward Ruben Lee. "I need you here for a bit. He's havin a go of it. Can't ask the boys to help. You, me, an Croaker'll take spells."

Ruben Lee, his lips dry and ashen, shivered under his many blankets.

"Conchita has soup cookin. He'll be needin it." He noticed I was looking at Ruben Lee. "Somethin the matter?"

"He doesn't like me."

"Sure he does, Pete."

"No, he doesn't."

"You're right at that. He don't much. But Croaker needs rest, an I was up all night. I'm countin on you."

Croaker excused himself and said he was off to bed.

Outside, the wind had come with the rain and it whistled over the eaves and tickled the shutters. Willy clomped across the hardwood to the cot, where he poured an inch of water in the glass. He held Ruben Lee's head up and guided his lips to the straw. Ruben Lee sucked until the water was gone. Willy asked if he wanted more. Ruben Lee lay back and closed his eyes.

Willy sighed. "You'll prob'ly have to feed 'im," he said. "Maybe take him to pee." Scraping its legs on the hard floor, he pulled a chair up and straddled it. He spoke in a near whisper. "Pete, I do right by you, unnerstan?"

I nodded.

"When he comes to, he'll be wantin a cigarette. Leave 'im have one, but be careful. No calls, an keep them handcuffs on."

"Okay."

He patted my shoulder, said I was a good boy, then swung his leg off the chair and left me with Ruben Lee. Thunderheads came in and the sky exploded. Ruben Lee floated in and out, talking in his sleep. He awoke, saw me, and shivered violently. I pulled the chair up to the cot.

"Pete. Do me something," he said.

"What?"

"I know a place in Butte, a house in Dog Patch. It's worth a thousand dollars to pick something up for me. All I have to do is make a phone call."

"Can't. Willy said no calls."

"How much is he paying?"

"He's not."

"Two thousand."

"Can't do it, Ruben Lee."

He licked his lips and swallowed. "Three thousand."

He saw from my expression I was considering the offer. I recalled how easily Betty had offered money to get the test questions. I'd never really understood how money meant so much and yet so little to Ruben Lee and Betty and probably George. It was for the asking—two thousand dollars, three thousand—figures they knew could buy people.

Whatever my price, I didn't have to worry about it very long. A knock came at the door. Ruben Lee watched closely as I crossed the room. Conchita greeted us. Water dripped from her as she handed me a basket and shed her raincoat. She took the basket and spread bowls and spoons on the table as if we were going to dine, plates and silverware clattering. She poured soup and spooned out fried chiles. Since she never again looked in his direction, it became obvious she didn't want to acknowledge the fact that Ruben Lee was tied to his bed. Table set, she backed away. "Leab the plates for me outside." She slipped on her coat and said, "*Buenos noches,* Pedrito, you boys eat ebrythin."

Left to feed Ruben Lee, I filled his bowl and asked if he wanted a tortilla. He shook his head. I popped a chile in my mouth and immediately broke out in sweat.

He looked up as I set the bowl on the nightstand. "All that sweat pouring out, you'd think you were dying."

"I am." I propped his head up with the pillow, spooned some soup and offered it to him. Some dribbled down his cheek. I daubed it off with a napkin.

He shook his head. "I'm not a baby. Undo the rope and let me feed my-self."

"Willy said no."

"Willy's not here." He smiled.

I held the spoon to his lips.

He smiled and sipped. Like his father, Ruben Lee had a disarming smile, impish and playful. "I've treated you bad, Pete, and here you are feeding me."

"Yeah. It's what Willy wants."

"Oh, hell, go on ahead and feed me, then."

I filled the spoon. He took the soup again.

"I feel like a baby. Come on. What can I do?"

"No."

"I could eat up, and then we could play cards, double solitaire."

"I wouldn't play cards with you."

"You're smart. That's one thing we all agree on." He gave me another imp-ish smile.

The wind ripped against the shutters. He asked how long it had been storming. I told him since midday. "May as well be tied up, then. Where the hell would I go? But if I had to piss, wouldn't you untie me?"

I shrugged.

"What's the difference?"

He had a point. I set the bowl down. "The cuffs stay on."

"You have a key?"

"No."

"So, what's there to worry about?"

He was certainly too weak to escape. And where would he go? "You won't tell Willy?"

"Tell? Tell what?"

We stared at each other for a moment. I looked for malice or deceit in his eyes, saw none, and untied him. I had to help him sit. He set his feet on the floor and thanked me. His hands were handcuffed in front so he could use them. I handed over the spoon and held the bowl. His hand trembling, he dipped the spoon in. His eyes closed as he swallowed. "Conchita sure can cook, huh? Hold it higher, Pete," he said.

I raised it to his chin. Thunder cracked and the windows turned white as lightning struck nearby. We both looked. The lights flickered. I saw the flash of chrome too late. The blow landed on my chin and toppled me backwards. A second came down on my forehead. The ceiling swirled, then everything went black. I heard the door open and shut and crawled to my feet. All I could think was how disappointed Willy would be. Blood ran down my cheek. I stumbled to the door and threw it open. He was trying to unlock the car.

I charged out and splashed through the mud. He didn't see me coming. I tackled him and we went down in the mud, rolling over and over. For a moment I gained the advantage and I told him to give it up. He tried to knee me in the groin, so I drove a fist into his face and started to throw another blow when somehow he ended up on top, using the chain on the handcuffs to cut off my wind. After a short struggle I went blank.

The next thing I knew I had my elbow jammed under his jaw and was shouting, "I'll kill you! I'll kill you!" as someone was pulling me off.

"Stop it, boy."

I felt weightless. That someone was Croaker, who lifted me up and set me aside. He reached down and pulled Ruben Lee to his feet and said, "You ain't killin no one, Pete. An you ain't goin nowhere, Ruben Lee."

We stood there, our lungs sucking air and the rain washing over the three of us. Ruben Lee shivered. Blood streaked down my forehead. Finally, Croaker said, "Come on, Pete. It's over." He grasped Ruben Lee by the arm and pushed him toward the open door.

Inside Croaker removed the handcuffs and told Ruben Lee to undress. Ruben Lee reluctantly dropped his clothes in a pile by the cot and, naked, sat down. His pale skin and thin arms belied his strength. He glared. "Don't forget this, Petey. I won't."

"Shut up with that talk, Ruben Lee," Croaker said and turned to me. "Go upstairs and get this boy some clothes."

Ruben Lee was dressed and fed and tied to his cot before Croaker turned to me. He brought out a first-aid kit and went to work on my forehead as Ruben Lee glared from his cot.

"Could use some stitches," Croaker said as he touched it with iodine.

I tried not to flinch. I didn't want to show pain in front of Ruben Lee. So I stared at the wall as Croaker cleaned the cuts. He handed me a compress and warned that I'd probably bleed for a while unless I wanted him to stitch me. The grin on his face hinted that I should be content to use the compress. "'At'll do, I 'spose," he said softly. "How much he offer?"

"Huh?"

"Oh, he'd try money. How much?"

"Three thousand." I took the compress and pressed it to my cut. "Thanks, Croaker."

"Mr. Crocker. Shut up. You're more trouble an you're worth, I say."

"Yeah, guess I am."

Croaker scratched the back of his neck. "You turn down three thousand? You ain't so smart as some people thinks." He looked at the soup and tortillas. "Well, let's have us some soup an I'll go on upstairs. You be outta here in the mornin so Willy won't see that mess on your face."

He poured a bowl of soup and rolled a tortilla, which he dipped in the soup.

"It's not over, Petey Boy," Ruben Lee said.

Croaker pointed his tortilla at Ruben Lee. "You give it up, boy. Can't you see I'm eatin? Next time I won't pull 'im off, no, sir. Not next time, no, sir."

In the morning Croaker drove me to Butte. He said that it was for my own good, that Ruben Lee had made threats and was the kind to carry them out.

The first week in August, ten days before expected, Betty called. Her hello had a chime to it as she asked, "Pete, how's your summer?" She sounded like the old Betty, brassy and tough. I told her my mother had married a man named Leonardo.

"Weird name," she said.

I said I'd gone to the ranch with Willy and Ruben Lee, but didn't offer up details. She'd talked to Willy and had figured out what was going on since Willy, Croaker, and Ruben Lee were staying at the ranch until September. Ruben Lee, it seemed, was doing fine, but Willy thought it best to stay a while to make sure.

"I want you to pick me up at the airport and don't mention it to anyone."

I didn't want to be her accomplice. "Why not?"

"Pete, don't ask."

"I'm spending my life meeting people at airports," I said.

She gave me the flight number and said good-bye.

Betty deplaned from the Dallas flight, her hair, longer now and sun-streaked, bouncing as she walked up. She came to an abrupt stop a few feet away and looked me up and down. We'd not seen each other since I'd carried her into the emergency room.

"You've grown."

It was true. I'd gained twenty pounds and started shaving. All this had happened since April. The changes seemed more pronounced to her, because we'd been separated. She entwined her fingers behind my neck. She smelled of cigarettes and perfume. The kiss was hardly passionate, but something desperate was in those warm lips. I held her a moment, holding on to what, I wasn't sure. I wanted to say I missed her, but that would prove her power over me. I let go and asked if she'd enjoyed the riding school. She said I was a jerk.

"I take it you didn't enjoy it."

"You didn't tell anyone I was here?"

"No."

"Good, take me to the Tropicana."

I tried to pry out the reason for all the secrecy, but she switched subjects. After gathering her luggage, we drove to the Tropicana, where she pecked my cheek, told the bell captain to hold her luggage, and hurried inside. Again I had been made an accomplice. To what, I had only a vague idea. I shifted into first and started to leave, then decided I wanted to know.

I parked near the tennis courts and crossed to the pool, where several sunbathers lay on the chaise longues. One well-endowed woman peeled down her top and caught my eye. I tripped going up the step, smiled sheepishly, and disappeared inside. I grabbed the first available house phone and asked the operator to ring Richard Forsby's room.

"Do you know the room number, sir?"

"No."

"One moment, please."

An instant later the line buzzed and Rich answered, "Hello."

In the background I heard Betty ask who was on the phone. It seemed she wanted me to know, had set it up so that I'd discover her. I heard Rich again, his voice hollow and distant, indistinguishable from what echoed in my head. I lowered the receiver. My pulse drumming in my ears, I walked past the pool, this time without noticing women in bikinis or puddles of water reflecting the sun off the deck. This love stuff was a hard rock. I resolved to stop thinking about Betty, but I wasn't sure I knew how to go about it.

24

It was a warm September day and the air smelled of autumn bloomers in Stella's rose garden. We sat at the edge of the courtyard and watched as George played catch on the lawn with his sons, Willy Jay and George Thomas. Elaine, George's wife, smoked and watched from the courtyard. George's boys, rarely allowed to associate with other children, played hard, often until George collapsed, which they were trying to make him do.

We'd had our fill of ribs and potato salad and were just enjoying the soft sun. Ruben Lee, sipping on a whiskey and soda, had come home tanned and considerably thinner, but no more pleasant. The barbecue had been in his honor. If he appreciated the gesture, he didn't show it. Stella, knitting a shawl, seemed pleased, though it was hard to say whether it was because Ruben Lee was better or because her family was together.

Willy propped his feet up on a chair. He said Cal had worked Ruben Lee like a dog and it showed. He asked Betty what she thought of her brother now. Betty, in a blue tank top and jeans, ran her fingers through her sun-streaked hair and stared absentmindedly as she sat cross-legged on a lounge chair. Her blue eyes and silky hair were striking against her summer tan.

Willy said, "Well, I ask't a question."

Adjusting her yarn, Stella leaned back in her chair. "You should ask who she's seein."

Betty let go of a strand of hair. "I'm not seeing nobody."

"You're always seeing somebody," Ruben Lee said.

Willy looked at me and winked. "You got any idear who, Pete?"

I dared not look at her. "No. No idea."

"I don't see why who I go out with or don't go out with should concern anyone," Betty said. "It's not like I'm out shooting dope."

"Careful," Ruben Lee said.

"I just wish people wouldn't mind my business."

"I wish we could all get along," Stella said.

Elaine looked over her shoulder, snuffed out her cigarette, and walked away to be with George. Stella watched her cross the lawn. Quiet and private, Elaine always seemed detached from the family. She was attractive, had a walk that was almost a dance, a way of sliding forward while her hips swayed. The light shone through her sheer skirt, outlining her fine legs. As she sank down onto the lawn, Elaine radiated sex. I wondered how she felt about George, for it was common knowledge that he never looked at another woman, the casino being his mistress.

Ruben Lee, still upset, stared disdainfully at Betty. She matched him stare for stare. Willy blew an ash off his cigar. "I been back six hours an ever'one is goin at each other like buzzards fightin over a carcass," he said.

"She can keep her remarks to herself," Ruben Lee said. "Not like she's perfect. Isn't that right, Betty?"

"I haven't the slightest idea what you're talking about, Mr. Ruben Lee Bobbins."

"You haven't?"

"I have," Stella said.

Betty held her hair off her shoulders and asked, "And what's that?"

"She's seein that musician," Stella said.

Betty shot me an accusing look.

"Is 'at true, Betty?" Willy asked.

"'Course it's true," Stella said. "Too old for her and a smelly hippie to boot."

Ruben Lee's expression slackened. Betty flipped her hair back and said she was leaving, that she had plans. She flashed Ruben Lee a final look of contempt.

"I told you it was true," Stella said.

"You're goin out the night I come home?" Willy asked.

"You never punished that girl," Stella said. "Let her run wild all the time."

Willy pointed his cigar at Stella. "If you'd done right as a mother . . ."

Stella glanced at me. "Watch what you say, Willy."

By then Betty was through the French door heading in full stride toward the front door. Willy sprang up. He called to her, but she'd already stormed out. The sound of tires squealing on asphalt marked her departure. Willy stood at the door to the courtyard and motioned for Stella. Ruben Lee smirked as they went inside and closed the door. I sensed I'd be next. He leaned back on his elbows and squinted in my direction. "Ready to try it without handcuffs, Petey?"

I shook my head.

"Scared?"

"Can't win, Ruben Lee." I left him and sat on the lawn with my back to him.

He called me a coward. "No, you can't."

George ambled up to ask what was going on with Willy and Stella.

Ruben Lee shrugged. "Betty again."

George handed me his glove and said the boys had worn him out, it was my turn. Grateful, I slipped my fingers into the glove and walked out on the lawn. The boys and I tossed the ball back and forth until George came out and told them it was time to go. George Thomas moaned, while Willy Jay just sat down on the lawn and refused to budge. George swooped Willy Jay up and threatened him with a whipping if he cried. An instant later Elaine, George, and the boys marched by. Thanking me, he took his glove and headed inside.

Stella stood in the courtyard with a lit cigarette. Her hands trembled as she inhaled. Then the door opened and Willy, .45 in hand, motioned for me. Stella didn't look at me as I passed by.

"Pete, what's goin on with Betty?"

I shook my head.

"You're lyin?"

"No."

He turned away. "You know what she's been up to, aw'right. I aim to give that boy a good scare."

A thought occurred. "Breaking his hands didn't stop him," I said.

He faced me. "Pete, don't accuse no one of nothin you don't know."

"I know."

He looked me over. "Fair enough. Now, forget it."

"I've got an idea," I said to Willy.

Ruben Lee came out of the kitchen and stepped behind Willy. "What the hell does he know? We're wasting time."

Willy swung about and faced Ruben Lee. "Shut up. Ever heard of *The Great Gatsby*?"

Ruben Lee furrowed his brow. "I don't watch sports."

"Ain't sports. It's a book."

"I don't read either," Ruben Lee said, and he seemed proud of it.

"Better be good," Willy said to me. He sat down on the sofa and motioned for me to join. He rested the gun on his knee, ready to listen. I kept my eyes on him and explained my idea. He nodded occasionally and when I finished, he said, "I told you he's smart, Ruben Lee. When Betty grows up, she'll come to her senses and be a good woman," he said.

One phone call set the plan in action. I took the extra set of keys to Betty's car and rode with Ruben Lee, who didn't talk until we were almost at the motel. We turned off Industrial Road and onto Tropicana. He asked, "What's with this Gatsby guy? I mean, I never heard of him." I said Gatsby was a gambler shot by a bereaved husband, because his wife was run over by a woman driving Gatsby's car. "How come I never heard about that?"

"It was kept secret," I said.

He turned onto Las Vegas Boulevard and headed south, then pulled into the parking lot of the El Mirage Motel where a Samuel Forster had rented the room where Betty's Mustang had been spotted. Ruben Lee backed into a parking space by her car. As soon as I shut the door, he pulled out. I stood in shadows under the walkway until a pea-green four-door sedan pulled in and caught me in its headlight beams. It parked two spaces away, and Frank stepped out and asked if I was ready.

"I guess."

"We'll handle everything. You just get her out of here as soon as she's in the car. Don't look back and don't ever mention what you saw."

"Yes, sir."

Frank waited beside me until two detectives arrived and parked by his car. He went to the office, flashed his badge to the clerk, and came out with a room key, which he showed to the other cops. He told me to get ready. I unlocked the Mustang using the second set of keys and slid behind the wheel.

The cops stationed themselves on opposite sides of the door, one with a drawn weapon. Frank slipped the key and the three of them charged into the room. Betty screamed, a light came on, and for an instant I glimpsed her in bed, a sheet drawn to her chin. She shouted, then someone shut the door.

Several minutes afterward, shadows moved about on the flat drapes. Frank stepped out and looked around, and I saw Betty in the pale light, shrugging into her shirt. He went inside again and left the door ajar. I heard footsteps on the gravel and glanced over to see Rich strolling up with a plump yellow bag from a burger stand in his hand. He looked at the door and froze. Involved in deciding what to do, he didn't notice me open the car door. Before he could react, I'd pulled him to the ground and pinned him. He tried to hit and at the same time hold on to the hamburger bag. Rich was no fighter.

"Let me go, Pete. I love her."

I told him that he wasn't very smart coming back.

He sat sullenly on the ground, leaning against the door of the Mustang. "Hope you're happy about this, Pete," he said. The next instant two cops surrounded him and lifted him to his feet. They marched him to their car, where they shoved him gently into the backseat, one sitting on either side of him.

Holding Betty by the arm, Frank walked her to the Mustang. As he opened the passenger door, she told him she would tell Willy, that Willy would have his fucking badge. He said that was fine. I sat behind the steering wheel with the bag of hamburgers in my lap. She flung her back against the seat and folded her arms as Frank slammed the door. He stuck his head in the window and said, "Take her home."

I handed her the bag. She wouldn't take it, so I dropped it on her lap.

"Fuck you, Petey," she said.

The bag rolled to the floor as she bent over sobbing. I took a last look at the cop car. Two detectives, little more than shadows, were working Rich over, slowly, methodically, as if to a cadence. Frank leaned against the front fender, smoking a cigarette. He waved. I pressed the accelerator down slowly and gently, wondering what my real intention was in doing all this.

25

Willy's sentence came up for review in November. Outside the Federal Building a reporter asked if Willy's benevolence to the families of the victims was a ploy to get his sentence reduced. Willy's lead attorney said that was absurd, that Willy was being a conscientious citizen. The reporter retorted that conscientious citizens pay taxes. Other reporters attempted friendlier questions, but Willy just smiled and let the lawyers talk. In his brown silk suit, white Stetson, and ostrich-leather boots, with the family, including me, walking behind, he marched into the courtroom. With another smile and no comment for the reporters, he stood confidently beside his attorneys.

Despite the full gallery, the deeply varnished walnut tables and paneling, and the judge's austere bench, the courtroom seemed hollow and cold. The bailiff called for the court to rise, and the black-robed judge strolled in from his chambers. After the court was seated, the clerk announced the case.

We sat behind Willy and his attorneys. He turned and winked. The judge sipped his water, looked at the lawyers, and asked that they make brief statements, adding, "And I mean brief, gentlemen." The U.S. attorney remained at his table and said that the Justice Department was not in favor of total clemency but would not oppose leniency. Willy's lawyer was equally brief. He held up a box of letters and said the judge had copies of them and knew they spoke of Mr. Bobbins's good character. He asked that Willy be credited for time served and be allowed to return to his position at the Lucky. The judge considered the remarks before he looked at the defense table. "Mr. Bobbins, do you care to address the court on this matter?" he asked.

Willy stood and cleared his throat. "Your Honor, I never learnt how to read or write, but I put men to work during the Depression. I was a gambler an I run whiskey when runnin it was a crime, but it's no crime now, an neither's gamblin in the state a Nevada. When I come here, I didn't come intendin to break no laws. I put men an women to work an done right by 'em.

"I got nothin against no man what never did nothin to me, an I've forgivin a whole passel who did do me wrong. I owed the gover'ment more an I paid. I did, an I'm shore sorry for that. Now, I did the gover'ment wrong, an I won't deny it. All I'm askin is that the gover'ment do for me what I done for others—show some forgiveness. That's all I got to say, Your Honor."

He meant every word he'd said, and I was sure very few in the courtroom doubted him. But I also knew of Tennessee and Sam the Slav and others unknown that Willy hadn't forgiven.

"Does the government care to respond?" the judge asked.

"No, Your Honor."

"Then I'm to assume you do not oppose the motion?"

The U.S. attorney looked at Willy. "That's correct, Your Honor."

"Mr. Bobbins, all the letters mentioned intone the same theme: that you are an asset to this community. I hereby vacate the remainder of your prison term and order that you serve one additional year of probation, after which the case will revert to a civil tax action and you may petition for full restoration of rights. The court has no objection to Mr. Bobbins returning to his business if it isn't in conflict with the interests of the State of Nevada. Court adjourned."

We were called to our feet as the judge stood. Willy shook his lawyers' hands, pecked Stella's cheek, and walked out. The reporter who'd challenged Willy as we entered asked for a comment. Willy said, "Soon as I get back to work, you're welcome to come have a bowl a chili with me." As we sat in the Cadillac, Willy asked if Gatsby could have done any better.

"No, sir," I replied.

Myrna Bloomingthal stood behind me in the physics lab and set her books on the countertop. She was one of Annette's friends, and because we attended the same classes we were acquainted, but not well enough for her to approach me in physics class. I tried to pretend she wasn't beside me, but Myrna was the type who demanded to be addressed. "Don't pretend I'm not here," she said.

"Why would I do that?"

She shook her head. "Pete, can I ask you a question?"

"*May* I ask a question," I said.

"Okay. *May* I. I told her."

"Told who?"

"Annette. I said you were too conceited."

I asked which Annette.

Myrna put her hands on her hips and said, "Only the best-looking girl in school."

I remembered the torment, how her eyes looked away whenever she caught me looking, how she sneered at my story. "Ah, I remember her."

"Well?" Myrna said.

"Well what?"

"Every guy in school wants to take her," Myrna said. "She's not interested in any of them."

"There's a point here."

"God, do I have to draw a picture?"

My project involved disassembling an electric motor and converting it into an electromagnet. I was diagramming the components. I held the chart up. "Well?"

"I told her you were conceited." Myrna scooped up her books and walked away.

I began bumping into Annette in the hallways, the cafeteria, and occasionally the practice field. She would smile coyly and say something innocuous. "Why don't we have a class together this year?" I regarded her politely. I had Betty on my mind.

Annette had been through two boyfriends since Danny had left to play football for Northern Arizona College and dumped her for a girl from Phoenix. He'd brought the girl to Gorman that spring and they'd walked around campus hand in hand, which sent shock waves through Annette's circle of friends. Afterward, Annette had missed a week of classes.

One day at the drinking fountain, she asked me, forthrightly, if Myrna had talked to me.

"About what?"

"Oh, then she didn't?"

I drank and stepped aside for her. "I remember something."

"I'll be honest, Pete. I wasn't very nice to you."

"Sure you were."

"I was?"

"Yeah."

She held her hair aside to drink from the fountain. She looked up flirtatiously. "You're joking."

"No, I'm serious. You were very nice to me."

"When?"

"I'll have to think about that."

"Think about this. I'm sorry about how I acted."

I stood nodding and doubting her motives, as well I should. She wiped the corner of her mouth and asked, "Do you have a date for homecoming?"

I appeared indifferent. "Betty, I think."

"You're kidding."

"Okay, I'm kidding." I shrugged.

On Saturday Betty knocked lightly at my door. She stood, hands on her hips, and said, "I hear we're an item."

"Really?"

"That's what I hear, Petey. All over school."

"Must be true," I said, grinning.

"What you did to Richie's not enough?" She ran her fingers through her hair. "I wish you'd never come into this house. You're no good." She reached in and slammed my door.

I lay and stared at the ceiling. I didn't go down to eat, didn't study. When I came out it was nine and Betty was in her room, her television casting shadows under the door. Downstairs Stella was in front of her own TV. I went back to my room and got out an envelope with the story about Tennessee's body being found. I opened it, threw the envelope away, and wrote a note explaining how this could just as easily have been Rich. I sealed the note and newspaper copy in a fresh envelope and slipped it into my leather jacket. On the way out I shoved the envelope under Betty's door.

The bike was cold. I kicked it several times without luck until it finally rattled to life. Black smoke spewed as the noise of the exhausts rumbled off the walls. I pushed in the choke and the engine settled into a steady idle. I engaged the gears with my left foot. Betty stood in the garage, the envelope in her hand. She held it up and asked what it meant. I looked away and rode out. She hollered and ran after me. It was my petty drama, and she had no right to interfere.

At the front gate to Rancho Circle the guard stepped out of his hut and motioned me over, but I turned my head away from him and passed by. His name was Earl, and I didn't mean to ignore him. He was a friendly enough guy who had to answer to dozens of rich people and simply took his job guarding an entrance too seriously, but I didn't want him to see the tears streaming down my cheeks.

Leaning into the handlebars, I turned north and got on the throttle right away. I had no intention of ever returning. Houses and fences and curbs whistled by as I rolled on the throttle. Speed seemed to lighten the world. I turned my head away from the wind and wiped my eyes with the back of my hand. When I looked forward, the light at Washington had changed to red.

Two slow cars filled the intersection. Down-gearing from fourth to third, I leaned left and swerved around the first. The second slammed on his brakes, leaving only a small seam for me to get through. My calf barely grazed the bumper, but it was enough. The bike and I separated. For an instant I watched the bike tumble toward a light pole like a reckless acrobat. Then everything rushed at me in a sequence of intense images—glistening asphalt, splintering stars, and blinding lights.

26

I was awakened by a nurse who asked if I could see her. I could, though she was a bit of a blur, a sort of head on an equally unformed body. I tried to move, but found myself in traction, my left arm and leg in casts, and my head bandaged. My mouth was dry. I nodded.

"Try not to sleep," she said and walked away.

A doctor entered, grabbed the chart at the bottom of my bed, and leaned over until he appeared as one large, glowing face about four inches from my eyes. He asked how I was doing. I told him my head ached and that I was terribly thirsty. He said that was natural, that I'd suffered a concussion and two bad fractures and should consider myself lucky that worse hadn't happened.

"We get kidneys, eyes, you know, spare parts from kids like you. Motorcycles are a boon to the organ-donor business."

He sat on the edge of the bed and held a scope to my eyes. As he swept a light back and forth in front of my nose, he instructed me to follow it with my eyes. Emitting an occasional grunt, he examined me, touched my forehead and cheeks, and pressed my fingernails. Finished, he nodded, smiled again, and stood. "Do you remember what happened?" he asked.

I vaguely remembered entering the intersection, and the strange sensation of thinking I was about to die, but not being afraid. I asked if my motorcycle was okay. He said he didn't know, but that it was probably in better shape than I was. He found this amusing. "How bad am I?" I asked.

"Well, Peter, you're young. When your bones mend in three or four months, you can get back on your motorcycle and do it again." He then asked if I was up to seeing a visitor or two.

"Yes, sir."

When the door opened, I had three: Willy, decked out in a fine wool suit and silver buckle, Stella in her favorite wool dress, and Croaker, who looked me over with a stony eye before nodding. Stella leaned over and kissed my forehead. She smelled of mint and lilac and faintly of cigarette smoke. She'd never before demonstrated affection toward me, so both of us were a little embarrassed by it. I told her she smelled nice.

"Well, thank you kindly, Pete. It's damn nice to see you ain't kil't yourself, though someone aught'a."

There were but two chairs. Croaker remained on his feet by the door while Willy and Stella pulled up chairs next to the bed. "Weren't 'sposed to be ridin that thing," Willy said.

"I knew somethin like this would happen," Stella added. "I never liked them damn things."

"No one gonna ask how's he doin?" Croaker said.

I looked in his direction. "Fine, I guess. I'm fine."

Willy looked at my casts and my bandaged head and smirked. He said, "Then we're free to call you a dumb sumbitch."

"Where's Betty?" I asked.

Willy swapped looks with Stella. She answered that Betty had something planned, but she'd be along. Willy asked about the accident, but as I couldn't remember much, I had nothing to add to what they'd been told. Stella searched her purse for a card, which she handed over. It wished me a speedy recovery and was signed by George and his family. Willy mentioned George would have come by, but he had to watch the shop.

The nurse brought in a pitcher, poured some water in a glass, and held the straw to my mouth. I held the water in, enjoying the luxury of it. After the nurse left, we passed small talk. Stella had arranged with my teachers to have my assignments delivered to the hospital. Willy chewed on a dead cigar and talked about going to the ranch in the spring. Croaker commented on how good the waiter was who'd taken my old job and added that the food even tasted better, which might be because it was reaching the table before rotting.

When it seemed conversation had run out, we struggled to keep it going. We seemed obliged to do so. Finally, Willy said he'd like to talk to me alone. Stella kissed my forehead again, took the card from my hand, and propped it on the nightstand. Willy waited for the door to close.

"Pete, you ain't done much to disappoint me," he said, "but this time you done it. How 'bout them plans for law school an all? You wanna lose that?"

"I never said I wanted to go to law school, Willy."

"I'm fixin to get mad. 'Course you did. What else would you be? Too smart to be a doctor, way I see it."

"I didn't mean to have an accident," I said.

"What do I have to do to keep you off it?"

"Probably too wrecked to ride," I said.

"Was after I had it crushed. What'll it take?"

From his expression, he wasn't joking. I remembered how he'd made me sweat until I blurted out Tennessee's name. That intensity was in his eyes now, too intense to take in. I looked at the ceiling and said, "A Corvette, a red one with lake pipes, and a blonde."

He rolled the unlit cigar from side to side in his mouth, studying the situation. "How you feel about Betty?"

I shrugged. "It doesn't matter."

"She says it ain't her fault you hurt yourself. What you got to say?"

I swallowed. "Nothing."

He patted my leg cast and left.

Except for a slow-knitting fibula, I healed pretty much as the doctor had predicted. Irritable, I hobbled about on crutches with little to do but study and read. I tried to stay awake. Old dreams plagued my sleep. I'd go nights without the dream coming, but when it did, it came forcefully. I'd writhe away from my assailants in panic and feel about in the dark, my heart driving against my chest as if to escape it. Once I dreamed Tennessee was one of them. I could smell his rank breath, and that alone woke me.

In the midst of a conversation with Stella, I thought of that night in juvey and went blank. She asked what I was thinking and I answered, "Nothing." She appreciated privacy. I blanked again when Willy was talking. He asked if I'd been listening and repeated what he'd said. "Look at you. You'll be thinkin different 'bout them machines now, I figure."

"It wasn't the bike," I said. "It was me."

"Same difference."

He didn't mention the accident again, but it was a bad fact that sat between us in every conversation.

Betty drove me to school and home. She'd turn up the radio and sing along, fix her lipstick in the mirror, and smoke, but she wouldn't talk. If at home, she left when I entered a room or wouldn't come in if I was already in one. Stella delighted in this, while Willy simply made believe it was a passing thing. Bobbinses, he admitted, were pigheaded. He was convinced time would straighten out whatever was wrong.

The last week in November the principal interrupted class with an announcement. He said he was sad to say that Ronald McPherson, a former Bishop Gorman student, had been killed in Vietnam's Ia Drang Valley. He asked that we bow our heads and led us in prayer. The news had little effect on me, McPherson having graduated my freshman year. I couldn't remember what he looked like, and Vietnam seemed very far away.

That evening I ate with Willy and Croaker at the casino. Willy was in good spirits. The Nevada Gaming Commission had granted him a temporary operator's license to run the Lucky again. Profits were up. George was doing well managing the day-to-day affairs, and Ruben Lee had been off drugs for months. Willy was biting into a sirloin when his phone buzzed. "Damn," he said, set down his fork and picked up the receiver.

His expression hardening, he listened. After he hung up, he took a swallow of water, then another, and waited before speaking. I'd seen him handle crisis with such calm I couldn't imagine what the caller had said. I was sure it had to do with Betty. He asked if I'd gotten to know Pearl very well. I said not as well as I knew the others at the ranch.

"Was kill't. Somewhere in Vietnam. Damn good cowboy. Damn good."

I recalled Pearl's embarrassment as he stood before the hands and gave up his true name and said he wanted to be a good soldier. Now he was a dead soldier. I remembered *his* face well, and Vietnam seemed very close indeed. We ate slowly after that. No need to hurry.

On Christmas Day the Bobbins tribe was at the house. Mother and her new husband, Leonardo, were invited as well, but didn't show. A blue spruce with red and white ornaments filled one corner of the family room. Surrounded by gifts, it nearly reached the ten-foot ceiling. Upon arriving, the grandsons counted packages to make sure each received the same exact number. George, clad in a Santa Claus suit stuffed with pillows, killed five cinnamon rums by noon and walked around burping and shouting "Ho! Ho! Ho!" as if he'd coined it.

I sat in a corner and watched while Betty sat in another and looked at everybody but me. George passed out presents. His boys attacked the packages, tearing paper and tossing ribbon aside to get to the prize. There were Erector sets, G.I. Joes, cap pistols, water pistols, baseballs, basketballs, skis, tennis rackets, toy trucks, model airplanes, board games, two footballs, and pictures of two four-year-old geldings that were awaiting the boys in stalls at home. Stella took a picture of each present as it was unwrapped. When the last of their gifts was opened, Willy Jay tilted his head and looked at his father, who by then was groggy. "Dad, didn't I ask for a pinball?" George looked befuddled. He pulled the beard down, gazed at the ceiling, and muttered, "Shit."

"But didn't I?" The boy was not to be denied.

"I've got one ordered," George said. "A special one."

"Two, Dad," George Thomas said.

"Got two ordered." George belched and offered the same deadpan smile to everyone in the room.

Pleased, the boys set their presents neatly by the tree and took one of the footballs to the backyard. Almost unnoticed was Croaker, who'd arrived at the tail end of the presents. Willy got out of his chair, slapped my thigh as he passed by, and signaled with his head for me to follow. I limped behind on my walking cast. Ruben Lee too fell in line. We marched to the front door.

The instant I stepped outside, I saw a 'Vette, just as I'd imagined in my fantasies, a red Stingray convertible with lake pipes and a red interior. I hurried past Willy and Croaker, thudding my cast on the concrete. I threw open the door. The interior smelled new, but better. I reached in with my good arm and gripped the wheel. It was like touching a dream. I turned to thank Willy.

"Like it, Pete?" he asked.

"It's perfect, Willy, the perfect Christmas present."

"Betty always liked red. You think maybe it'll get 'er outta 'er mood?"

The car was for Betty. The truth grabbed me by the throat and held me numb as Willy repeated the question. Finally I said, "It should," but I didn't look at him as I let go of the steering wheel. Pretending that I wasn't disappointed, I stood beside Willy and nodded. I decided I needed another motorcycle.

The casts came off and I asked for my job back, but Willy said he was happy with the new waiter. I said I'd work another station. He shook his head. "I'll put you in the count room," he said.

"I have to be twenty-one," I said.

He smiled. "You start right away."

Willy woke me at four A.M. with a call and said it was time I learned the business. I met him in the booth, where he was having coffee with Ruben Lee. They walked me down to the count room. Willy said I'd work with the small, meaning coins from slots. I'd work three-hour shifts four days a week at a wage of forty dollars. He patted my back and left me with Ruben Lee.

Ruben Lee handed me a key. "If gaming agents show up, you duck through here," he said, referring to a metal door. He pointed to a red light above a table where four pasty-skinned men dressed in knee-length leather aprons diligently separated cash by denominations. "If that flashes, it means agents are on their way down in the elevator. Got it?"

"Yeah."

"You start tomorrow. Follow me."

He watched as I used my key in the metal door to make certain it worked. The door led to a staircase, which led to the eye in the sky, where spotters monitored the daily activities in the casino. We took the stairs to the first landing and stopped by a stool. He told me to look through the periscope. it was aimed at the count table, where the four men were busy, their quick hands laying out bills in even stacks of twenty-five ones, twenty fives, ten tens, twenty-five twenties, twenty fifties, fifty hundreds.

He said, "You can see everything. I watched for days and can't catch them."

"Catch them?"

"Stealing. Someone's getting us."

I caught his eye.

He shook his head. "Wasn't my idea. The old man thinks you'll see something I can't. I told him you couldn't see your dick with a flashlight and a magnifying glass."

We climbed more stairs to the eye in the sky, which Ruben Lee referred to as "the peek." A series of catwalks overlooked two-way mirrors. A man often seen with George and Willy sat on a stool and viewed the casino with a pair of opera glasses. He ignored our approach. "Gus, this is Pete," Ruben Lee said.

Gus grunted and went back to his work.

"Gus is about the best cheat ever was," Ruben Lee said. "Taught me everything. Dad wants him to work with you. I told him you didn't have the instinct. Do you?"

I shrugged.

"That key's good for the other doors up here and the old man's office. I said it was crazy, but . . . fuck it." He thought a moment and said, "Follow me."

The coins and cash were called the drop, and my job was to weigh and record the buckets. Each was numbered corresponding to the slot machine it came from. I worked with Croaker's nephew, Bobby Sands, lifting galvanized buckets, some weighing seventy pounds, onto a scale. We poured the coins into canvas bags, which went to a back room in the cage to be machine-rolled into wrappers. I wore steel-toed boots, which I soon learned was a good idea. I banged my shins on buckets, dropped buckets on my toes and on Bobby's, spilled quarters over the floor and swept them up, clattered, clanged, and generally created havoc, but the count men never seemed to take notice.

The "soft count" came in steel boxes and was separated and recorded as each was opened. Old men with deft fingers and deadpan faces, the counters seemed oblivious to all but the piles of green they counted like Cistercian monks chanting before an altar. They clipped bills into stacks by denomination, stuffed those into cylinders, and immediately sent the money to the cage through a suction tube, for cash was blood to the casino. They were merely a chamber in the heart that kept cash circulating.

As I lowered the bucket and waited for the scale to settle, I watched Jules, Chas, Mickey, and John separate and count. All were dapper dressers and had been with Willy since he'd reopened the Sierra Club as the Lucky. For three weeks I never noticed them lose rhythm or stray from the task, and to his frustration, neither did Ruben Lee. So which one? Were all of them in on it and so clever they couldn't be detected? Every day there was a five-hundred-to seven-hundred-dollar discrepancy.

I'd figured out pit bosses were keeping track of the drop on certain games and reporting figures to George, who compared those numbers with the count. Willy had me relay everything I saw, which was always approximately the same. He said he had no doubts that the boys, as he called them, knew I was a plant, but one was so bold and clever that he kept the scam going.

"Pete, we're gonna nail the sumbitch. Stay with it."

Sunday morning of the fourth week, I arrived ten minutes early, about five minutes before the boxes were brought down. The elevator door opened and three security guards stood beside the cart containing the swing-shift table drop. They seemed a bit surprised to see me, as they were usually gone by the time I came in. One dropped a key ring, bent down to pick it up, and slipped the keys in his pocket. They pushed the cart in, and another guard took a set of keys off his belt to unlock the storage vault. They stacked the boxes on the shelves. As they left, one adjusted his holster. The keys on his belt jingled.

When the count men arrived, they entered the cage and, using a single set of keys, unlocked boxes one at a time. The count went as usual, including a six-hundred-dollar variance on craps one. I followed Jules and John into the elevator. Both smiled and wished me a good day as the doors slid open. I watched them turn in the keys to the drop boxes at the cage and leave the casino. I went to the door and climbed to the eye in the sky.

It was dark on the catwalk. I found Ruben Lee bent over a rail smoking a cigarette as he watched a roulette game. He looked up nonchalantly and said, "Don't say you saw anything. I watched the whole time and didn't see a move."

"It's the guards," I said.

He squinted. "The guards?"

"Is the money missing from a swing-shift box?"

"Yeah."

"One box?"

"Sometimes two or three. That's why we don't know which one."

"I saw keys. They somehow got keys to the drop box."

Though skeptical, he listened.

That afternoon Willy summoned me to White Cross Drug at Fourth and Fremont. He acted like he'd just won a big poker hand as he ordered two vanilla shakes. He told me it was going to be an interesting morning and not to miss work. I said I never missed work, which he said could be taken two ways. We laughed together and drank our milk shakes, and he told me to come in early.

An hour before the count was taken, Ruben Lee climbed up through a trapdoor to the elevator. He'd had a peephole big enough to accommodate a scope drilled through it. I was readying my scale and canvas bags for the count and the guards were unloading boxes when Ruben Lee dropped through the trapdoor and coolly walked to the door that led to the stairs to the eye in the sky. Willy led five other guards through the open door and said, "'Mornin, boys."

The guards exchanged glances. One said, "Good morning, Mr. Bobbins."

The elevator doors shut and the elevator ascended.

"Don't bother to finish," Willy said and walked into the cage room, where he calmly took away the gun of the nearest man. "Tommy, I'm disappointed," he said.

Ruben Lee and the five guards disarmed the others. The elevator doors opened. Bobby Sands held the button for Jules, Mickey, John, and Chas, who seemed not to take notice.

One of the thieves pulled out his two hundred and held it up. "Here, Mr. Bobbins, I . . ."

"No, Spence, keep it. You earned it," Willy said.

The four count men filed by, each in turn removing his coat and exchanging it on the hook for a leather apron. They helped each other slip into the heavy aprons and tie the straps in the back. Once fitted in their garments, they went into the cage room and began removing boxes from the shelves, logging each in as if nothing else were going on. "I want the cops," one thief said.

"No need," Willy said. "You unnerstand, boys. You been there."

Willy told them to have a nice day and walked out.

Half an hour later, when they'd finished with the thieves, they took them out the back way. The room smelled of blood and sweat. It smelled of violence. When the door closed we released a collective sigh as if we'd held our breaths the whole time. Blood was splattered on the concrete walls and the steel cage and on the floor and on the shelves. The elevator cranked and the door opened and two porters with soapy water in buckets, sponges and mops in hand, entered, escorted by a guard. One of them whistled. The guard said someone had spilled ketchup.

"Ain't that the truth," the porter said and swished his mop in a bucket.

27

Willy sat at his desk, Gus opposite him. "Was right here," Willy said, "Hugh Stample took a gun to his own head and said he'd kill hisself 'cause he'd lost his money. I was sittin where Gus is an I told him to go ahead. But he didn't. We made a deal an he lived another six years. They was stealing him blind from the inside an he was losin the rest to poker."

Willy lipped his cigar. "Gus caught them what was stealin. He's gonna teach you, Pete."

"Me?"

"Ruben Lee learnt at your age."

"But why?"

"'Cause it'll help when you're a lawyer."

"I just want to work on the ranch."

Willy picked up a crystal paperweight and tossed it to me. It felt heavy and cold in my warm hands. "You wanna be one of them with legs? A paperweight with legs? Now, I been damned patient with you, but I'm fixin to get mad."

I laid the paperweight on the desktop and gazed out the window at the Vegas Vic sign. Nothing was in my favor, going up against the house, Willy might say. I knew what he'd advise—always take the house odds. He watched with that poker player's stare, untouchable, indifferent. There was nothing to be said that hadn't already been. I shrugged.

"'At's better. Now, go on with Gus an pay attention."

And so I began, at age seventeen and two months, an unusual apprentice-ship. Gus showed me a false shuffle and how to spot it, then watched me try for an hour before he was satisfied that I understood the move, though I couldn't execute it.

"Like lobster claws," he said and handed over a deck of cards to take home. "Shave with it in your hand. Tie your laces with it in your hand. Wipe your butt with it in your hand. Make the damn thing a part of you." He told me to practice in front of a mirror and sent me out of the room, said he couldn't bear someone with fingers like a snow cone.

After hours of practice, I was doing fine—I thought. I demonstrated the move for Willy, who seemed pleased. But when I showed Gus the following week, he shook his head and told me it was crude, that he'd seen an amputee handle cards with his toes better. Telling me not to come back until I could do the move as well as a three-year-old, he sent me away to practice some more.

For four weeks we repeated the same scenario. He'd shake his head, I'd leave dejected. Then one day, though I felt I was no better than I'd been at the end of the first week, he nodded. "You ain't gonna make no livin at it. But you ain't exactly a hammer thumb neither."

He shuffled a deck and showed me the top card, a deuce of diamonds. He pitched the cards, dealing each of us a hand, and told me to turn mine over. I had a ten and an eight. He showed a six. "Feeling pretty good about it, Pete?" he asked and flipped his hole card over—an ace.

He hit the soft seventeen with the two of diamonds and scooped up my cards. "Now," he said, showing me the card on the top of deck, "we'll learn to deal deuces, though I ain't got much faith in those things on your hands that you try and pass off as fingers."

Willy decided I'd been living too easy too long. I was bound someday for the best college in the country, which he insisted was the University of Texas, though George told him dozens of universities ranked higher academically. Nothing swayed Willy. The best lawyers he knew had graduated from U of T, "an the best crooks as well." That was proof enough for him. It mattered nothing to me where he wanted me to go. My mind was made up that I was best suited to ranch work. In time, I felt sure, Willy would discover this to be true and dispense with the talk about law school. Meanwhile I'd play along.

His next grand decision didn't go over so easily. He insisted that I accompany Betty to the junior-senior prom, a decision made without first consulting us. He wouldn't let the idea go, even though Betty and I protested, I because I didn't know how to dance and she because I was "a pimply-chinned creep and an embarrassment." He said there was no arguing the matter since she didn't have a date and neither did I. Along with a photographer to record the night, he'd arranged a prom dress and corsage for her, a tuxedo for me, and a limousine to transport us to the prom, then to Don the Beachcomber's and a show.

Willy announced his idea over the Sunday dinner table. While I was on the mend, Betty had sunk into an even more morose mood. She resented Willy's part in running Rich out of town, but it was me she hated. She never mentioned the newspaper clipping or the comment I'd written on it, and no amount of talk could convince her that Rich had been discovered by a detective Stella had hired to follow her. I was the betrayer. When Willy made his declaration about the prom, she gave me a look that could scald and set her fork on the edge of the plate. "It's bad enough everybody thinking Pete and me are . . . an item," she said. "I'm not going."

"You're goin," Willy said.

"There's things I won't do, Dad."

"Most things you won't do," Stella said.

"'At's right, ain't it?" Willy said. "It's about time you did somethin.'"

"I won't," she said. "Not with a dickhead like him." She lifted her chin and marched away from the table.

"Kind'a sure of herself, ain't she?" he said. "Pete, be a good dickhead an pass on some'a them mashed 'taters, would you?"

Despite a threatened hunger strike by Betty if he insisted that she go to the prom, Willy enrolled me in Arthur Murray's for ballroom lessons. He drove me to class and watched me practice the fox-trot and the waltz with a limp. My ankle hadn't yet healed and at night needed a long soak in hot water. All the while I was still Gus's pupil, so for weeks my daily regimen consisted of school followed by school followed by school. I didn't learn to dance well, but Gus was proud that I could finally slip the top card back and pop a second, though he added that I should probably take up being a short-order cook or an assassin.

"How about wrangling?" I asked.

"Well, you got the hands for it, but I'm not sure you got the brains. Don't you have to be smarter than a cow?"

Five days before the prom, Betty threatened Willy with all manner of warnings, insisting that she would run away before she would go to the prom with me. When he'd finally had enough, he took her car keys away from her and refused to give them back until he saw her on her way out the door in her prom dress.

Four days before the dance, Croaker came to escort Betty for her final fitting because she was without her car. She sat on the bottom step and said she could drive herself there just fine, that she wasn't a child. Stella informed her that the only way the Corvette would ever get out of the garage was if Betty got up off the stairs and into the car with Croaker right away, and no comments. Betty walked out downcast and slipped meekly into the passenger seat. She loved that Corvette.

The day of the prom I sat in a corner studying for finals. Occasionally Betty, her hair wrapped in a blue towel, would look up from filing her nails or whatever labor of beauty had her engaged at the time and shoot me a ten-second stare just to prove her feelings hadn't changed any. She was readying herself, as she'd refused Willy's invitation to a beauty parlor, saying that she didn't want to owe him for it, nor did she want to be made up like some silly bitch, like that stupid Annette Silvestri, who Petey has the hots for. Willy offered an expression that said everything—loving her was exhausting.

Willy woke a little after noon, grabbed a cup of coffee, and sat at the table. He had figures to go over and didn't want to be bothered. The housekeeper dusted. I studied. Betty ignored us now as she sanded and polished and brushed and looked at herself in the mirror. Willy looked up and said that for someone who didn't want to go, she was sure going to a lot of trouble.

"I'm not interested in your opinion," she said.

Willy took the keys out of his pocket and jingled them.

That afternoon an orchid corsage the width of an elephant's foot arrived. Betty answered the door, took one look at the corsage, and told Willy she would never wear anything so hideous. She huffed, carried the corsage to the kitchen, and put it in the refrigerator between the milk and the leftover lamb chops.

As she passed by Willy, she said wearing such an ugly corsage would make her a laughingstock. He looked up from the balance sheet and said, "Glad it makes you happy, honey."

He hired a photographer to accompany us and record the night. When Betty heard from Stella about our companion, she was seated cross-legged on the couch plucking her eyebrows. She tossed her tweezers on the coffee table and muttered she didn't know what had gotten into her father. Stella warned her not to scratch the furniture. Betty gathered up her instruments, said her whole family was crazy, and marched upstairs to her room. That was the last anyone saw of her for the day.

In the midst of all the contention Stella went about her daily rituals, worked her garden, rode her horse, and watched television. On occasion she would come inside and float by Willy, pausing long enough to say he was trying to break a fox from eating eggs by feeding it a chicken, or trying to get a waterfall to go uphill. Willy asked why the women in the house couldn't get along.

My tuxedo arrived at 5:30. By 6:10, hair slicked back and shining and two new pimples on my chin, I popped out of my room and limped downstairs. Mitchell, the photographer, arrived at 6:23 and took two quick shots of me before he positioned himself at the foot of the stairs for Betty to make her entrance. At 6:41 the chauffeur pulled up to the front door in a white Cadillac limousine. Stella opened the door and said she hoped he was patient. At 6:43 I retrieved the corsage from the refrigerator. At 6:46 Willy downed his third shot of sour mash and stomped up the stairs. Betty told him to go away, that she wasn't dressed. He said if she wasn't down in five minutes, he'd drag her down naked if necessary.

We waited in silence as he descended the staircase. He smiled and said, "Just wants to look 'er best." He sat down, poured another shot and offered a drink to Mitchell, who declined, saying he never drank on the job, but he'd certainly be proud sometime to have a drink with a man like Willy Bobbins. Willy smiled and asked if the fee just went up, tossed down his whiskey, then stared at the second hand on his watch. No one spoke, except for Stella, who mentioned that it was a nice night for a long walk and she wished she was in Texas where a person could do exactly that. Willy poured another drink, toasted her, and, downing the last drop of Jack Daniel's, stood and started for the stairs.

Betty's door opened and shut quietly. Her half heels tapped as she walked through the hardwood hall. When she turned the corner, Willy halted in his tracks and backed down the stairs using the handrail, his expression one of amazement. Her white-gloved hand resting on the rail, she stood atop the landing. The other clutched a lavender purse that matched her chiffon gown. Her hair cascaded in loose waves over her white shoulders—a stunning likeness of the Rita in the portrait. The resemblance was not lost on Stella or Willy or me, though I dared not show it. I stood and held the corsage at my waist in both hands.

She arched one eyebrow and said to her silenced audience, "What's the big deal?"

Mitchell knew his true subject when he saw it. As she took that first light step down, he went to work. She smiled at the lens and blinked when the flashes went off. I'd never thought of her as beautiful, not as I'd thought of Annette Silvestri, anyhow. But she was. I said hello, removed the corsage from its clear plastic box, and held it out. She sniffed the orchid. She nodded for the first time in days as I fumbled about trying to find the right spot on her gown to place the corsage while at the same time trying to avoid her breast. Willy said my hands were as clumsy as Gus had claimed.

"Petey! He's laughing at us," Betty said and snatched the corsage away. She pinned it on above her heart and said we were ready. She looked at Willy. "Where're my keys?"

"They'll be on the table. You ain't out the door yet."

She nodded twice and motioned for me to take her arm. "I am a lady, Pete."

The chauffeur introduced himself as Jonathan, opened the door for us, and lifted the lid to a small ice chest containing champagne, wheat crackers, two shrimp cocktails, and a jar of caviar. He uncorked the champagne, which he mentioned was compliments of Mr. Bobbins. The snacks were for our pleasure, he said, then shut the door.

I leaned near to her and said, "You're beautiful."

"Petey, let's just get this over with," she said, poured herself a glass of champagne, downed it, and poured another.

At the door a greeter took our tickets, warned us that alcohol was not permitted inside. Betty removed her glove reluctantly to have her hand stamped. Mitchell followed us inside. Couples were already dancing. Hundreds of purple and gold streamers flowed from the overheads and down the walls. A seven-piece band occupied the stage, playing soft ballads as a spotlight scanned the dance floor isolating couples for a few seconds of distinction before moving on.

Tables were reserved for students, so Mitchell sat by the stage with a group of volunteer chaperones. He told us to enjoy ourselves, that he'd do just fine. He opened his case, hung the light meter from his neck, and tinkered with his flash attachment. He had a gift for gab and immediately recruited assistance from the parents on either side of him, handing one a lens to hold and the other a gray card off which he took a light reading. Our table abutted the dance floor. At the next table over sat Annette Sylvestri and her clutch of friends. She pointed us out. The others glanced in our direction, bowed their heads together, and whispered. Betty, who'd polished off two glasses of champagne, pretended not to notice being noticed. She was good at pretending. I was not.

As the band played, we sipped punch and watched couples glide across the floor or scanned the tables—anything to avoid our mutual discomfort. Annette had come with Felix Streiger, a reporter on the school paper who, using the pen name El Thesaurus, wrote like a bad imitation of Milton. He sat beside her, his hand resting on her thigh. She would push it away, and he would promptly set it back in place. I told Betty to look at them. "Why would I care, Petey?" she said.

A few boys who'd come alone asked Betty to dance. She refused all but one, and him she left on the dance floor and stormed back to the table. "He thought he could rub my ass," she said.

When our glasses were empty, I went to the punch bowl for refills. Mitchell called me over and said, "Mr. Bobbins expects pictures of his daughter on the dance floor. With you." I told him not to worry. She seemed distracted when I returned with the punch. I asked if she was okay. About to cry, she merely shook her head and, before I could get another word out, she rushed to the door. I glanced at Mitchell, shrugged, and went after her.

She was smoking a cigarette on a bench.

"This wasn't my idea."

"I know. Want a cigarette?" She offered me the pack.

"No."

"Suit yourself." She took a drag and blew the smoke at the night. "You spied on me at the Trop."

"Guilty."

She took another drag and let the smoke waft slowly out of her mouth as she flicked ashes off the tip. "I don't like being spied on," she said. "Do you know what it's like to be the daughter of a man who can have things done?"

I leaned against the back of the bench.

A light illuminated the nearby walkway. It caught her face as she sat forward, her eyes searching. "What was the newspaper picture all about?"

"Tennessee? I wanted you to know what happened."

"I knew he was killed. Ruben Lee told me. But why?"

"Willy asked me, you know, at the ranch. He wanted to know who you'd been with. I told him Tennessee."

"Petey?" She held my chin and made me look her in the eye.

I nodded. "It's true."

She looked away. We fell silent as couples strolled by and boys walked out to their cars for a shot of whiskey or to smoke a joint. Some looked at us. Others pretended not to notice. She crushed the first cigarette underfoot and lit another. When the last of the kids passed by, she said, "Rich doesn't care who I am. It doesn't matter that Willy Bobbins has money."

"And it doesn't matter that you were underage," I said.

At first the comment upset her, but gradually she nodded. "No, it doesn't, but I chased him, Petey." She smoked her cigarette and looked off. Her chest rose, then fell with a sigh. She licked her lips in thought and smoked and fondled a lock of hair. Her skin was iridescent where the moonlight hit it, but the shadows took the girl from her face. I waited, afraid to speak. Call it moonlight madness, but she seemed the stuff of poetry and song. She had appeared mature and confident when I first sighted her as she stepped out of Willy's black Cadillac. Now she seemed womanly and damaged.

"Look," I said, "I took two hundred out of savings. Let's get Jonathan to drive up and down the Strip until it's spent."

She crushed her cigarette on the concrete. "Two hundred?"

"Yeah."

"College money?"

"Maybe it's for another bike. Maybe I won't go to college."

She smiled. "You will, Petey. You're smart."

"What do you think?"

She looked at the limo parked by the curb. "I got some money too," she said.

"Willy wants a picture of us dancing."

"Do we have to?"

I offered my arm. She said what the hell and took it. I told Mitchell to snap shots as fast as he could, as we were only dancing one dance, then I led her to the floor. She entered my arms and tentatively rested her cheek on my chest. Until I was holding her, I hadn't realized how short she was. I'd always imagined her taller, just as Willy had always seemed bigger than he was.

"You're a runt," I said.

She smiled and rested her hand in mine. The band played the song from *Mondo Cane,* the same song I remembered dancing clumsily to at the Mint. I stepped, she followed. What had been torture for me and the dance instructor translated to something quite different once I held her. It took a moment to meld the patterns of our bodies, but we found the rhythm and moved to the center of the dance floor. I could see myself with her dancing, could see what others saw, what Mitchell was capturing on film.

One dance became two and then three. A couple of boys asked to cut in. I stepped aside for them, but she declined. Not because of me, but I pretended it was. After three more songs I asked if she was ready to go. "One more," she said, and my chest swelled. As we left, I felt Annette's eyes on me. I reached for Betty's hand. She started to pull away, but just for an instant, then slipped her fingers into mine. "That ought to burn the bitch's ass," she whispered.

We met Mitchell at the door and asked if he'd gotten a few pictures. He seemed pleased to say he had to change film twice. "How'd you like to go out on the town with us?" Betty asked.

"Absolutely. A great idea," he said.

Jonathan drove to the Stardust. We insisted he come inside and eat with us. It mattered to no one that we were underage; it was Las Vegas in 1966 and the town celebrated prom nights. Young people in formal wear were, if not welcomed, tolerated. Betty gave her name to the head waiter at the Aku Aku. He looked us over and said he had no table reserved for a Betty Bobbins.

"Oh, there's been some mistake. That's Bobbins, Betty Bobbins. My father took care of it," she said, which was a lie.

"Bobbins?"

"Yes."

He picked up the telephone and turned his back to us as he spoke into it. Hanging up, he told us he was checking it out. A few minutes later a man in a blue silk suit and narrow black tie walked up. He looked at us, nodded to the head waiter, and gestured as if writing on his palm. The head waiter smiled and said, "Thank you for your patience. The dinner for four will be compliments of the house. Follow me. I'll take you to your table."

It was the same wherever we went that night: There was always a table and someone picked up the tab. By four A.M. we'd worn out both Mitchell and Jonathan, who sat at the bar drinking coffee as Betty and I danced the last dance at the Top of the Strip. Holding hands, we walked to the passage to the elevator, where we waited for our escorts to finish their drinks and join us. We could see out the windows. The beaded streetlights and casino signs of the Strip twenty-odd stories below lit the path to downtown, where dealers were picking and paying bets at the Lucky, which would someday be Betty's, or part hers anyhow. I asked if she ever thought of that.

"It's been fun, Petey. Don't ruin it with stupid questions."

On the ride home we offered to let Mitchell sit in the back with us, but he said he enjoyed Jonathan's company. At the house, we offered them a fifty-dollar tip apiece. Jonathan took his, but Mitchell refused, saying that Willy was paying him handsomely. Though it wasn't that funny, his answer caused us to laugh. We stood at the door and watched them drive off.

"Well, was it all that bad?" I asked.

She leaned into the door and looked up at me. "I'll never forget this night, Petey."

"Me either."

"A guy shows a girl a time like this on prom night has earned a kiss."

I wasn't sure how to go about it, so I placed one hand on her waist and the other behind her shoulder. As I was about to kiss her, she said, "You ever kiss a girl?"

"Huh?"

"You ever kiss a girl?"

"Sure, lots of them."

"You're lying. I'll be your first." She laughed.

Too embarrassed to do anything, I stood back and stuffed my hands in my pockets. She reached up, held my neck in one hand, and stood on her toes. She pecked my cheek, released my neck, and said that I was sweet. An instant later the door opened. I hadn't even noticed that she'd turned the doorknob. Like a spark, she flashed out of sight.

I sat on the porch step until the blush of dawn outlined Sunrise Mountain and the streetlights lost their glow, then I went to my room.

I spent the first week of summer struggling under the tutelage of Gus, who claimed he'd seen dog turds with more dexterity than my fingers had. I said I lacked the instincts of a good thief, that I'd tried to rifle glove boxes but didn't have the nerve.

"That shows a flaw in your character, but it don't explain havin hands like catcher's mitts," he said and took a swallow of schnapps, chasing it with lemonade. I told him the truth of the matter was that I wasn't interested in being a card cheat.

"Don't say 'cheat,' say 'crossroader.' It's a gentleman's profession. Guy who cheats is one who steps out on his wife. I know many a crossroader who never cheated and many a cheat who never picked up cards or dice. Dice? You wanna learn dice? Is that it?"

"That's not what I meant."

He thought a moment. "You got a girl in mind. That's it." He tossed down another shot of schnapps and quickly chased it. His face screwed up at the taste of the lemonade.

"Why do you drink the lemonade?" I asked.

"Makes the taste of schnapps tolerable."

"If you don't like the taste, why drink it?"

"You ain't here to ask questions." He studied me a moment before adding, "Doctor took me off whiskey. Now pick up the deck and show me you can change your hole card."

I went through the motions for Willy, who insisted I stay with my tutor, though Gus said it would be easier to teach a cactus to ride a horse. Occasionally Ruben Lee dropped in. He took pleasure in watching me fumble about, but Gus would defend my progress. "Boy's just not a quick learner like you. Got books and school on his mind. Plans to be a lawyer someday."

One thing I was good at was bending the cards, not in nice neat patterns the way skilled crossroaders do, but in interesting tangles and dips and twists so that no one could read them. Gus found this amusing. To pass time he drank slugs of schnapps, for his cough he said, and told stories about the old days in Montana. He mentioned a woman who'd worked at a casino in Meadorville. She'd learned the business in Pocatello, from a man named Dixon Row.

"Remember the gal, the one from Pocatello?"

"Yeah, I think," I said. "But you've told me a lot of stories about women."

"She'd smile at them copper miners and switch a hole card. Her moves were okay, not great. Didn't hafta be too good. She was so pretty, it just didn't matter. Miners lined up to get to her game. Hell, they'd fight each other. Probably knew she was takin them, but it didn't matter. They were gonna lose the money or drink it up anyhow."

He stopped as if that were the complete story, but I knew better. I asked what happened to her. He said Willy hired her away and told her she didn't have to cheat in his place.

"A waste of talent, but Willy ran an honest store. Never cheated no one. Never wanted no one cheating him."

"What happened after that?"

"Happened?"

"To her?"

Gus's face had the expression of a base runner caught off base, and he stumbled through his answer. "She went her way. Probably married a miner. Maybe took off when the clubs went bad. Lookee here, when're you gonna learn to slide that card out with the thumb?"

"Why'd you tell me about her?"

"You're full of damned questions. 'Cause the point is she was pretty and could get by on that. You, well, if you were a surgeon, you'd be hung."

"Hanged."

"What's that?"

"What was her name?"

He took a shot of schnapps and held it in his mouth before swallowing. "Damned stuff might kill me. Should'a stuck to whiskey. Can't recall her name. Kind'a reddish-blond hair, real pretty gal. Face I can remember now, which is unusual if you realize an old drunk like me's got a lot to forget and has forgot most of it. I'm a drunk. You know that, don't you?"

"Let me show you something," I said and shuffled the deck. I showed him the top card, a seven of diamonds, dealt out three hands, and turned up a nine, not a bump in the delivery. He smiled when I hit my twelve with that seven of diamonds. "I've been practicing," I said.

"Well, well. Good, but not near the best. The best was a deuce dealer with one arm named Jackson Lowery. Lost the other in the war and had to relearn with one hand. He could do more with one hand and his eyes closed than you'll ever do with two good hands and eyes. Got by with it for four years after the war, then one mornin he showed up on the porch of the club he was workin at the time, his throat slit."

I reshuffled and slid the second card off the deck and turned it over.

He winked. "Not so rough, smooth it out before you go for speed. Bubble the top card for now. I'll show you the heel peek later." He unscrewed the cap on his pint. "Them miners were tough old boys. Anyhow, Jackson was so good he got twenty percent of the table take. Some, like me, got ten."

"Gus, was that woman's name Rita, by chance?"

He chased the schnapps down, ran his tongue over his molars, and squinted. "Can't say, Pete. Drank one too many whiskeys in my youth."

My ankle improved, and though it meant leaving Betty for the summer, I was eager to get to the ranch. For a time Willy refused to let me go, saying he needed someone he could trust in the count room. I finally began to wear him down.

"How're the lessons comin?"

"I'm about the best cheater you ever saw."

"Can't shuffle the deck, from what I hear."

"I'll try harder. But I'd make a good wrangler. I'm getting muscle."

He looked me over and smiled. "I was thinkin you'd take up golf, somethin where you don't need no muscle."

"I went golfing with you and didn't see much that appealed to me."

"Why, I thought we had us a time, Pete."

"We did, Willy."

He smiled. "Bet them fool agents still talk about that one. How much pay you expectin?"

"Hand's wage."

"You ain't worth that much, but I'll think on it."

Betty told me not to leave without saying good-bye. I went out back to the stalls. Stella stood in her garden smoking and staring at a weed called hog's potato like it had just killed her mother. I asked where Betty was.

"I use poisons on this bugger an it keeps comin at me. I got a damn war here, Pete. No time to keep up with her," she said, stomped out her cigarette and leaned into the spade. "You better get on to Montana 'fore I have you diggin. They's a turkey sandwich. Fixed it myself."

She shook her head, muttered, and planted the point of the spade in the dirt. I left without seeing Betty.

28

I drove up in Betty's old embarrassing pink Mustang, arriving on Sunday morning as the sun came up from my back. Shadows spread over the wide bowl, and landmarks touched by sunlight began to take on character. I turned off the all-night all-rock station and listened to the tires sing on the pavement until I came to the turnoff.

As the tires touched gravel, I felt a sense of homecoming. A small herd of whiteface cattle lolled in the flats. A bull raised its head and bellowed. The mountains, capped in spring snow, jutted into a vast blue; oily sage, thick as winter fur, covered the ground, and clumps of wildflowers ran up the foothills like splashes on a paint palette. I rolled the windows down and let the sweet Montana air blow in, dust and all.

As the car bounded up the road, its springs bottoming under the load, I could almost feel the boys shaking my hand, hear their roughhouse chatter as they played hearts or pinochle. I felt the wonderful release from ache as I tossed down a bedroll and lay on my back staring at stars.

But the hands weren't there to greet me. Cal and Conchita stepped down from the porch and waved as I braked. He shook my hand, looked the Mustang over, and asked where I got the fancy pink car. I told him Betty got a new Corvette, that this was her old car. I made no claim to it.

"Where's the motorcycle?"

"Wrecked it."

He said, "We expected you earlier."

"Couldn't come."

"Cal," Conchita said, "*el niño necesita comer.*"

"She's teaching me Spanish." He fell silent and stared at the car. At length he said to her, "There's things need to be mentioned." He addressed me. "You heard about Pearl?"

"Yeah."

"We buried him here. Pearl wrote it up in his will. Willy gave permission." Conchita tugged at my sleeve. "I got son biscuits and graby, Pedro."

I grabbed my bags, slammed down the trunk lid, and headed for the bunkhouse. Cal didn't move. "What's the matter?" I asked.

"Can't stay there," he said. "Got no room, Pete. We hired three men on."

I looked at the bunkhouse. "That leaves a room."

He shook his head. "Willy wants you in the house."

"But I'm just a hand."

"Not exactly."

"What about Lead?"

"He's yours to ride, barn-sour as he is."

Cal walked me to the house without speaking. I guess he was all talked out.

At breakfast Jiggers pulled up a chair. He said the others had gone into Dillon for the weekend and wouldn't be back until evening. He rolled a cigarette. "Enjoy breakfast. The new boys got mighty long arms. Hear you'll be bunking in the big house."

"Yeah." I asked if we were still partners.

"You'll be riding with Cal, from what I hear."

He smoked and watched me eat. I kept an eye on the house, all filled up with Willy's history. I thought about Sarge and Rita, then naturally about Betty. Something had changed between us, but that something was ambiguous, a wordless knowing. She was quieter around me now, and softer. She wouldn't look at me for long, but the looks she gave were sometimes dictionaries of words, and sometimes absolutely mute. I missed her already. But what were we to one another? We'd danced, laughed, drunk champagne, and had gone our own ways before dawn. That's all.

"It's changing, Pete," Jiggers said.

I looked back. He was dousing his cigarette butt on the saucer. "Don't let Conchita catch you," I said.

He took the saucer to the sink and rinsed it.

"What's changing?"

"Boys we hired are old men like me. Not many young fellas like you taking up wrangling. Then that war goes and kills a good one off. It's a shame. How's the gravy?"

"Good as ever. I thought Cal was going to talk my leg off," I said.

"Been like that for weeks. Come to my room three Sundays ago, shaving cream on half his face, holding his razor. He stood in the doorway looking dazed. I asked what the hell was going on in his empty mind. He said he was gonna marry Conchita and wanted to know did I mind."

"Guess she said yes."

"Been waiting on him to ask over twenty years. Guess it took Sarge and Pearl dying to snap him to. He was like Sarge . . . Well, I . . ." Jiggers stopped himself and said he was glad to see me. He wiped the saucer and excused himself, saying he had chores.

I took an apple with me and sat on the rail until Lead came over of his own accord. He watched me with his crazy blue eye and flared his nostrils until he got a solid whiff of the apple. He meandered over, stopping to nibble at the hay bin, and stood at a guarded distance. He smelled the air, walked closer, and pressed his muzzle into my hand. I talked until he got used to my voice. He took the bit and I slipped the bridle over his nose, then saddled him. I sat him for a while so we'd both get used to the idea, then rode him out.

As we neared a wash, something spooked him. He stopped at the cutbank, refused to go down. I told him it wasn't steep, that he was just barn-sour and stupid. He threw his head from side to side and tried to turn around. I reined him in. As I did, he reared up, cut the air with his hooves, and shifted suddenly, which sent me headfirst down the bank.

When I realized I was okay, I brushed myself off and cussed him. Above the thick scrub bluebottle flies filled the air, tens of thousands of them, big and bloated. The wash buzzed. I entered the bushes, swatting flies away with my hat. Near where the spring runoff had pooled lay the carcass of a freshly killed steer. It'd been butchered and skinned of its hide. I looked around. On the far bank were two more dead steers. I felt outrage and a sense of proprietorship. Whoever did this needed catching. I climbed up the bank, mounted, and rode around until I found tire tracks, a wide set that led away from the wash.

I reported what I'd seen to Cal, who told me to saddle horses for him and Jiggers, and a fresh one for myself. "Don't tell no one what you saw," he said and left to wake Jiggers from a Sunday nap. Jiggers caught up with us about halfway to the wash and asked what it was all about.

"More cows killed," Cal said. "Three this time."

Jiggers pulled the brim of his hat. "Willy won't be happy."

We sat our horses and watched the shrubs where the flies were thickest as Cal walked from carcass to carcass. He came out shooing away flies with his hat. "Killed with a axe," he said, "probably early last night. Two by the prints, though I couldn't make out particulars 'cause they brushed the ground up with sage. There's tire tracks aplenty, though, like Pete says."

We spent the afternoon tracing tire tracks east to the fence where the wire had been cut. Cal sat his horse and looked at Jiggers and me, then glanced at where the tracks crossed the sage and went up the shoulder of a back road.

That evening before the hands returned, Cal called Willy from the house.

I rode hay truck with Todd Darling, one of the new hands, a man of forty and a snuff dipper who habitually spat brown juice out the window and complained about most everything. When not spitting out of the side of his mouth, he told old jokes about sheep and lonely cowhands. I tried to like him, as I tried to like the other new hands, but I felt estranged from them, partly because I didn't sleep in the bunkhouse and partly because they called me Mr. Pete to my face. I could only guess what they called me behind my back. To prove my worth, I did my work and Todd's as well.

It'd been a dry winter and spring and was still dry and ninety degrees by noon. The clump grass grew too spare to sustain the cattle, especially cows that had calved that spring and needed fattening up. We bucked hay and dumped it near watering holes, hard work made harder because Todd would rather watch than do.

I listened as he bitched about the heat, the food, and the working conditions. But by week's end I decided he was just making conversation. He came from around the Missouri Breaks where the prairie was flat, the winters severe, and complaining kept a man sane. He said the 7-11 was the best spread he'd ever worked and the mountains made his blood circulate better, but apparently not well enough to inspire hard work.

I didn't often see John Laidy and Elmore Johnson, the other new hands, though I did get to watch John break a two-year-old paint Cal had picked up at auction. A short man of thirty-five and a Korean War vet, John was an intense rider who sensed what his mount was going to do before the animal knew. He rode the orneriness out of that paint in a matter of minutes. He shouted for Lon to open the corral gate and spurred the horse onto the road, where he rose up and leaned forward. He whipped up a trail of dust that floated up and hung in the still air until it slowly drifted to the backyard of the cottage where Conchita's fresh laundry hung drying. John caught hell when he returned, but he took it with bowed head and a good-natured smile. He handed flowers to Conchita, which he offered with a promise to help wash clothes. He reminded me of Pearl, and I especially hoped he had nothing to do with dead beeves.

Elmore, the eldest of the three, hailed from Alberta, Canada, and had worked ranches in the Dakotas and Wyoming before coming to Dillon. He used his false teeth when eating and the rest of the time went about with sunken cheeks and a puckered mouth. The pleasure he took from smoking seemed to verge on the sexual. His face would contort as he drew smoke deep into his lungs, and his eyes would narrow and glass over as he exhaled. So thin his muscles looked like wires tied to bone, he was a hard worker nonetheless and plenty strong.

When Friday came, Cal told the hands to go to town, that the cattle would be fine because he and I would keep the feed truck running, and anyone who wanted an advance could draw one. They talked boisterously as they showered and dressed. By six the ranch was quiet and empty except for Cal, Jiggers, Oso, and of course Conchita and me.

Cal armed the three of us with saddle guns, telling me to let Jiggers and Oso handle things, and if we spotted the thieves, I was to ride in and get him. Jiggers claimed Cal wasn't coming because he wanted to be alone with Conchita now that he'd figured out that a woman rode better than a horse. Oso laughed, but not nearly as loud as Jiggers. "Don't be taking advantage of my good nature," Cal warned. "Now, be careful out there, boys."

As we crossed the range, I felt I was playing a role in some Western melodrama. Soon I was caught in the motion of the horse and the sound of clopping hooves on hardpan. I daydreamed about Betty, thought of her as my girl, of the kiss I'd really wanted but didn't get, and her in my arms holding me as she cried over Rich. We tethered the horses in a draw and packed our bedrolls and rifles up to a promontory that overlooked the east. With three jars of Conchita's chili, ten sticks of jerky, and two loaves of sourdough apiece, we sat down to wait out the weekend if need be.

"Ain't much to worry about till dark," Jiggers said. "I'm grabbing some shut-eye."

He limped to his bedroll and lay down. Oso and I watched the valley go dim. At dusk a bull trumpeted. Oso said nothing sounded lonelier than a bull bellowing, except maybe a coyote howling. But, he clarified, the bull was brave and the coyote cowardly. He said bulls have a great heart and that is what gets them killed in the *corrida*.

"You're a romantic," I said.

"*Pues,* why else be on a 'ard rock weeth a dumb old cowboy and a more dumber kid?"

Early it was moonless and silent save for the crickets. Lights from ranch houses scored the black landscape. A breeze wafted up the draw. Now and then a horse would whinny. Oso remained concentrated and quiet. I asked if he thought one of the new men was involved. He claimed to have no thoughts on the matter, saying that time would decide something like that.

"We'll get the sheriff when we catch them," I said.

"Mebe, mebe no."

"Why not?"

He put a finger to his lips and said my name. After that, except to urinate once, he sat so still I began to doubt he was breathing. I kept my eyes open. Midnight passed. Oso scratched his chin, said he'd send Jiggers over, and tottered off. Jiggers plopped down beside me, rubbing the back of his neck and saying he'd ransom me for a cup of hot coffee, even though I wasn't worth one. He opened his pocketknife and whittled on a knob of pine.

"What can you carve in the dark?"

"Wood, maybe a finger," he said. "Seen anything?"

"A lot of black."

He stood, brushed off the rear of his jeans, and told me to get some sleep. I stomped the ground to get blood circulating in my bad ankle, and as I did, a flash of light caught my attention.

"You see that?" I asked.

"See what? You getting old, Pete."

"A flash." I pointed in the direction.

"Can't say I did."

Wings fluttered somewhere below, an owl most likely. The breeze rustled the pine branches. We strained our eyes to see for a time, but nothing appeared. I ascribed it to imagination, said good night, and headed for my bedroll. Then a blink of light from below sparked in the arroyo. It went on and off three times, obviously a flashlight.

Jiggers set his piece of pine aside and closed the jackknife. "Go wake Oso."

A touch on the shoulder told Oso all he needed to know. Jiggers pointed to where he'd last seen the light and said he had a good idea where they were. We gathered our bedrolls and hiked down to the horses. Oso held out the reins to his horse and asked for mine.

"You hurry on in. Tell Cal we'll light a fire," Jiggers said.

I sat Oso's horse. "What if they're armed?"

"Be damned fools if they weren't."

"*Ándale*, Pete," Oso said and reeled about.

I flicked the reins.

A Cadillac sat in front of the house. Willy was here. My sense of events altered decidedly as I swung off the saddle. What? Lynchings? I hitched Elmo to the post and hurried to the door. From the porch I heard Willy's muffled voice. I didn't knock, just threw the door open and walked into the dining room where Willy sat eating eggs and tortillas; beside him was Cal.

"Pete," Betty said. "You didn't say good-bye."

She reclined by the dead fireplace, leaning on an elbow.

"Hell, didn't say hello neither," Willy said, adding that I was too late to eat, but to have a seat anyhow. I did, beside Cal, and tried not to be obvious when I turned the chair so as to see her in the corner of my eye. "What brung on this rudeness, Pete?" Willy asked.

"We got them," I said.

"Happen to get any names?" Willy winked at Cal.

Betty smiled, whether at me or Willy's remark, I was unsure. "No, I figure Oso will soon enough." I said Oso would light the spot with a campfire.

Willy seemed pleased, but in no hurry. He casually dipped his tortilla in a broken yolk and asked Cal if he felt up to a night ride. Cal said it seemed a fine idea. Willy mopped up the last of the egg with his tortilla and told Betty and me to saddle two horses.

"Two? What about me?" Betty asked.

"Ride all you want tomorra," he said.

She and I didn't speak until we reached the stalls. I asked why she'd come along. She unhooked Willy's bridle, hung it over her shoulder, and dusted off his saddle. She flipped the cloth to me and hauled the saddle down. "Grab a blanket and toss it on Moe," she said. "Just didn't want to argue with Stella anymore."

I spread a blanket on Moe, then took the saddle from her and swung it on the animal's back.

She tightened the cinch. "There." She leaned against the rail and twirled a strand of hair.

"You okay?" I asked.

She didn't answer. I saddled Cal's horse. Finished, we tethered them at the hitching post next to Elmo. Betty sat down cross-legged on the ground and lit a cigarette. I caught a fleeting glimpse of her face in the flame and saw she'd been crying.

"Rich?"

"Mind your own business," she said and puffed on the cigarette. She snubbed out the cigarette before she spoke again. "Wonder what's keeping them? You going to go out and be a hero, Petey?" she asked, her voice acrid.

"I guess I'll go, all right."

"Stay here and play double solitaire with me instead."

"I don't like cards."

"Petey likes books and motorcycles and being perfect."

"Not me."

The door opened and slammed. Cal and Willy, speaking in whispers, checked the saddles before mounting. I untied Elmo and swung up into the saddle. They sat their horses looking at me, their expressions lost in the dim light. "Where you goin, Pete?" Willy asked.

"With you."

"Think we can't find a fire at night?"

"No. I mean, I know you can."

"Then no need you comin. Get on down off that dumb animal," Willy said. "He's been rode hard and needs lookin after."

No amount of arguing would change his mind. I slipped down off Elmo.

"You forget about what may or may not be," Willy said. Without another word, he and Cal reined their horses about. I held Elmo's reins behind my back and watched them ride off. Betty stood so close I could feel her breath. "What you're thinking, Petey, would be a mistake."

"What would be a mistake?"

"Following them. Or calling the cops."

I left her there and walked Elmo to the stalls.

I wandered about, listening to the night, occasionally looking in the direction they'd ridden. Barely visible, a campfire flickered near the foothills. I watched that for a bit, playing out scenarios in my mind, then went to the house and sat on the steps looking up. The northern constellations glowed and sparked memories of rides across the desert in the backseat of Mother's convertible. Too tired to stare at the sky any longer, I went inside. One of Willy's whiskey bottles propped between her legs, Betty sat smoking on the bottom stair. She uncapped the bottle, took a swallow, and handed it to me.

"Thought you were going to sit all night," she said.

I tasted it and handed it back. She patted the stair beside her, took another drink, and picked up her cigarette. "Glad you didn't go, Petey. Here." She drew off the cigarette and handed it to me.

We sat sharing the cigarette and looking at each other. There seemed to be nothing to talk about. I wanted to kiss her. But what did she want? She'd forgiven my imagined trespasses; that much I was sure of. She offered another shot of whiskey. "So, Petey, what're you thinking?"

I held the bottle to my lips and shook my head. My throat constricted as I swallowed. I felt very adult.

"I know what you're thinking. I owe you one." She tilted her head, inviting me to kiss her. What I knew about kissing came from watching movies. I touched my lips to hers cautiously. She wrapped her hand around the back of my neck and pried my lips apart with her tongue. She tasted of whiskey and cigarettes and lipstick, but her mouth was warm and her lips silken. This wasn't the movies.

She pulled away, looking me in the face as she did. "Bring the bottle," she said, took my hand, and led me up the stairs. When the door was shut, she turned to face me. I swallowed. She closed her eyes momentarily, then motioned for me to join her on the bed. I lingered by the door. She told me to come, that a man shouldn't hesitate. I walked over to her. She was framed in the pale light in the window. Her lips were moist. She removed the bow that held her hair in a ponytail and shook her hair loose. It hung freely over her shoulders and breasts. She cupped her hands behind my head and pulled my mouth to hers. We kissed gently and slowly, the way I had imagined our first kiss would be. She pulled away and told me not to move. Her fingers went to the top button on her blouse. She watched me looking at her as she unbuttoned it. She opened her shirt and let her arms fall to her side. She wore no bra.

"Go ahead, Petey," she said. "Touch me."

I reached out and brushed the back of my hand across an erect nipple.

"Yes, Petey. Easy."

She closed her eyes and tilted her head back, then told me to kiss her again as we had just done, slow and easy. I started to put my arms around her, but she took my hands and placed them on her breasts. My mouth closed over hers and we fell onto the bed. I felt as if I might climax at that instant, but she pulled away, sat up, and took a drink from the bottle. She offered it to me, but I shook my head. She set the bottle aside, took off her boots, and stood at the edge of the bed.

"Undress me," she said.

I sat facing her and slipped off her shirt, then unbuckled her belt. I fumbled with the buttons on her jeans. She helped me with the first one. The others unfastened easily. She moved her hips so that I could slide her jeans off. I knelt before her and held the jeans as she shimmied out of the legs. She wore a pair of pink cotton panties. I caressed her with my fingertips. She trembled. I moved my hand gradually up to the elastic and looked up at her.

"Go ahead. Take them off."

I did. She stepped out of the panties, looked down at me, and smiled as if she could read my thoughts. She was beautiful. I wanted the image of her from that angle to be the last thing I remembered before I died. She held my arms and helped me to my feet.

"Now you," she said and began unbuttoning my shirt.

I kissed her again, this time harder. I kissed her throat, her neck, her eyes, and her shoulders. She eased my shirt off and threw it across the room. Her hands went down to my belt, but didn't stop there. She rubbed my groin, then pressed her hips against me and swayed. Then she stepped back and unfastened my buckle. She unbuttoned my fly and reached in. Blood rushed to my ears as she took me in her hand. She let go and lay down on the bed.

"Take your boots off, cowboy."

I dropped my boots and slid out of my jeans. She lay with one knee crooked, her hands behind her head. For a moment I lay beside her, smelling her hair. I took a strand and kissed it. She looked at me. "Touch me, Petey, the way you've wanted to since the first day you saw me."

It was as if she could open my head and see every thought I'd ever had of her. I wanted to say I loved her, but knew that would be the wrong thing to say. I took a deep breath, licked my lips, and eased my hand between her thighs. She spread her legs. I covered her mouth with mine.

"Now, Petey, slowly. Very slowly," she whispered.

"Yes," I said, "slowly."

Later, after we'd made love the second time, she lay naked, phosphorus white in the gray dawn, the sheets damp from our sweat. She told me I had to leave before Willy came back. I kissed her and walked to the window to look west, where a fire still burned. I told her to come look. She leaned against me and held my hand. We watched for a moment as the sky lightened and a trail of fine smoke replaced the fire.

She said I was sweet and tugged at my hand. We walked arm in arm to her bed, where I laid her back and eased myself between her legs. She raised her hips. "Be good to me," she said, words that I didn't understand until years later when understanding came too late.

The door shut downstairs and awakened me. Someone mounted the stairs. I sat up, threw the covers off and slid out of the bed. I crawled about, gathering up clothes as calmly as a panicked heart allows. The footsteps came closer, heavy-heeled, the sound of boots. At the base of the door I saw a shadow. The knob turned, twice. I held my breath.

There was a knock and Conchita called through the door, "Señorita Betty, wake up."

"Let me sleep." The mattress shivered and Betty, her face extended over the edge of the bed, peered down, and crossed her eyes at me. "What're you afraid of?" she whispered.

"Jou sleep, but Pedrito bedder go before the *señor* come."

Betty stifled a laugh, but I was too scared to see any humor. She sat wrapped up in a sheet, watching, as I tried to dress without bumbling about. But I dropped my boots, clinked my belt buckle on the hardwood, and buttoned the shirt in the wrong buttonholes. Finally, I was dressed. She patted the bed.

"I gotta go," I said.

She stood, let go of the sheet, and came to me. Her arms around my neck, she kissed me softly and said, "I'm staying the summer."

29

Two days later at dawn Willy shook me awake and told me to fix some coffee. Betty and I had tried to act indifferent toward one another, casting only furtive glances across the table, but we'd spent time riding together. Up to then Willy had said nothing about the rustlers or about Betty. I did wonder what he knew and looked for a hint on his unshaven face, but all I got was that poker stare. I figured that Conchita had kept quiet.

I poured the coffee and waited at the table while he carried his bag to the car. He closed the door softly so as not to disturb Betty and walked quietly to the kitchen. He sat across from me. Elmore was noticeably gone, but no one had mentioned it, and Willy added exactly nothing to that as he swallowed coffee and ate a cold corn muffin with honey. I watched the eastern sky turn rouge as he poured the coffee into a thermos and twisted down the cap.

"Time to head on." He looked in the general direction of Betty's room. "She'd sleep through a damn war," he said. "Dead to the world the other mornin when I come in." He gazed at me for a time, then said, "Walk me out."

His legs gathered beneath the steering wheel, he started the engine. When I shut the door, he rolled down the window. "You're fillin out, Pete," he said. He could empty all expression from his eyes when he wanted to, and now they were as vacant as craters on the moon. "You ain't disappointed me too many times. Wish't I could say the same of my own flesh. But they's bidness you should keep out'a till you're a man."

"I didn't ask about the rustlers."

"I ain't talkin bout no rustlers," he said and rolled up the window. As I watched him back up and circle out of the yard, I was left to guess which he had in mind, Betty or Rita?

Thinking it best for everyone, I packed my gear, carried it to the bunk-house, and tossed it down in Elmore's quarters. His property, stuffed in a duffel bag and two cardboard boxes, sat in a corner. Atop the duffel bag was his hat. I hung my shirts on the rod by the door and stored the rest of my belongings. The floor joists creaked as Jiggers labored down the hallway. He stuck his head inside.

"See you're back," he said.

"Yeah."

"I never cared much for that Elmore," he said. "Just set his belongings in the hall. I'll store them later." He continued on his way, the floor creaking. I lay on the cot and tried to think of things other than Betty. She'd infected me in a terrible way. I imagined her exacting vengeance on Willy through me—the punk who'd stolen her purse, intruder in her life. Willy was gone. But who would be watching her for him? Caring for her wasn't going to be easy or safe.

We worked all day, then I ate with the hands, who were in good spirits. In a room full of boisterous talk, I sat as they lunged for buttermilk biscuits and corncobs, and I watched Conchita carry a food tray to the big house, where Betty would sit eating by herself. After dinner the hands brought out a deck as Lon and I washed and dried the dishes. The card game was soon in full swing and I slipped out. The sun hung just behind the cap of a mountain. I sat on the steps and stared at the big house. Just before dark Betty, wearing blue jeans and a red shirt tied at her midriff, stepped out on the porch. I stood. We didn't speak, but turned as if to a dance step and walked toward the stalls.

Above a pined ravine she stopped her horse and sat it. I pulled beside her, leaned over the saddle, and stroked Lead's neck. She swung down, removed her hat, and ran her fingers through her hair. "You going to spend the night on that ugly animal without talking?" she asked.

I swung my leg over the bow of the saddle and jumped down. Her fingers moved up to the knot that held her shirt together. I shook my head. She dropped her hands to her side, and with a smile, watched me untie the knot.

We worked the range days at a time, keeping the cattle in tight bunches, dumping hay from the tailgate of the pickup. Food was scarce. Cooper's and redtail hawks wheeled about in the blue waiting for a field mouse to dash into the open. On the steep slopes of the foothills the chaparral was brittle and dry. Bunchgrass and rice grass had all but withered, and what was left on the hard turf was yellow knots. Dust spooled up everywhere. The air burned the throat and chapped the lips.

We couldn't keep our eyes off the west. We searched the sky in hopes that every vagrant cloud was the scout for an army of them. We found calves killed and eaten by a mountain lion. Oso rode back to the ranch and borrowed hounds from a neighbor, who willingly volunteered his services. A big cat could kill a lot of calves. The dogs treed a lioness, and I watched her fight desperately for life. She hissed at the bothersome dogs, clawed them, and sent one sprawl-legged to the ground. In the end, a single round from Lon's .30-.30 saddle gun killed her. The loss of two calves to a puma was nothing compared to what was at stake if rain didn't come; killing her was akin to an act of redemption, for we were helpless to do anything about a prolonged drought.

Betty rode the chuck wagon with Conchita and helped feed us. We'd find a corner somewhere and eat. We talked about the silliest of things—what colors she liked, the smell of fried onions, things dentists say. The idea was to keep our ears used to hearing one another and our eyes used to seeing how we formed words and changed facial expressions. Though the men teased me about the boss's daughter and getting roasted over an open pit, it was clear that none of them begrudged us what we had. Talking in the shadows as the campfire flickered seemed as sacred and intimate as the time we spent wrapped in her sheets making love.

"Rain's comin, boys," Jiggers said on a Wednesday in late July. "Feel it in every joint of my broken body."

Friday came and the clouds we'd been watching for formed west of the mountains and brought smiles to everyone, especially Jiggers, who reminded us of his prophecy. Black and dull, they hung over the peaks for hours before rolling into the valley. The delay gave us time to find shelter. We were holed up in a line shack when the sky broke loose. Pellet-sized drops quickly filled every depression and hole. Jiggers stripped off his shirt, pants, and boots, and except for a hat, stood naked outside. He held out his hands palms up. Water poured from the brim of his hat. Oso and Lon told him to come in, that he was making a fool of himself. He laughed and dared them to do the same. I told Lon and Oso there was nothing for me to do for a while, then I pulled my poncho over my head and saddled Lead.

"Where ya goin, Pete?" Lon asked, never expecting an answer.

He got none.

Betty suggested we drive into Butte. It'd rained there as well and the streets were slick. The clerk at the Finnlander looked at us skeptically and demanded identification. Betty laid two hundred-dollar bills on the counter and said one was for the room and the other for him. He scratched his head, gave us a key, and said registration was unnecessary for one night.

As the storm spent itself outside, she and I spent ourselves in the bed. I spoke about Sarge dying here and how I'd held his hand and how his death seemed less real than the death of the lioness. I told her about the painting of her mother and how on the night of the prom she'd looked like her. This seemed to please her, though she remained absolutely silent for a long while. I reached up to stroke her arm, but she pushed my hand away. Instead, she pressed herself into my chest. "I know where she's buried on the ranch," I said.

She pulled away to see my face. "Take me."

I nodded.

The next morning the sky again threatened rain. I forced the window open and let in cool air. Coiled as one, we stayed in the room until an hour before checkout. More tenderness than passion, our lovemaking seemed to become a liturgy. Afterward Betty stared at the ceiling as she stroked my thigh. "Imagine. Willy and my mother may have made love in this very room."

It seemed a thoroughly romantic notion, but I didn't mention this, I just thought it.

Mornings were tempered by still air and low clouds that sealed the valley. Later it rained off and on, short violent blows marked by rising wind and sleet, followed by drizzle. The grass had died. With nothing to slow erosion, mud spilled down from the foothills. The flats turned into swamp.

We covered ourselves with slickers and sank into the clay. We tramped mud into the bunkhouse, and water dribbled off our hats. The arroyos turned into torrential creeks. Horses had trouble keeping their footing. Jiggers went down on his. The animal broke a leg and needed destroying. It had to be done, but he couldn't do it. He said he'd worked the horse for twenty years and someone else had to pull the trigger.

It was his mount and his responsibility. I waited for Lon or Oso to tell him just that. Instead, Oso levered his saddle rifle and climbed down. Saying he was sorry, he told Jiggers to walk away. The pelting rain muffled the shot. The animal trembled once, went stiff, then relaxed. Oso, grim-faced, uncinched Jiggers's saddle, freed the bridle, and slung them over his shoulder. I helped Jiggers up to ride behind me. He turned his face away, and muttering to himself, cried.

Oso, Lon, and I rode out later with shovels and buried the horse. We spent as much time dredging water out of the hole as we did digging it. Lon looked up at the sky and said, "I need a peek at the sun. Need it bad." But the rain didn't let up.

Nights being damp and cool, I would build a fire in the fireplace. Hands entwined, Betty and I would lie in front of it and watch the flames and listen to logs snap and to the rhythmic sound of our own breathing. She didn't seem much like the Betty Bobbins I'd known the month before. I told her that her transformation reminded me of Katherina, but she didn't know *The Taming of the Shrew* and said it was probably an insult.

We combed the house for the painting, which Willy hid away when not in the house by himself. After a two-hour search upstairs and down, we determined it had to be padlocked in the basement storage closet. As Betty held a flashlight, I removed the hinges and set the door aside. Draped over the portrait was a handmade quilt, old and moth-eaten. Besides the painting the only items stored in the closet were two boxes of ammunition and a hand-tooled silver bridle. Betty pulled the quilt away, handed me the flashlight, and told me to hold it steady. She knelt and ran her fingers over the painting until I carried the picture upstairs, where we hung it over the fireplace. She uncapped a whiskey bottle. We sat at the table and sipped out of shot glasses as she stared at the painting and I stared at her. I told her how I'd first seen it and how the woman had seemed familiar to me. "Familiar, Petey?"

"Yeah. I don't know why, but I felt it."

"That's crazy."

I downed my shot.

Betty poured another. "I look like her? Really like her?"

"She's just thinner."

"I feel cheated," she said.

I thought of Willy's warning. What did it encompass? I was taking a risk. I remembered something from *Heart of Darkness,* a passage in which Marlow speaks of not living from pulse beat to pulse beat. Chance, risk, to Conrad those were the things that suggested life. After making love, we returned the painting to its hiding place, just to be safe.

We made love everywhere in that house, even on the stairs and dining table, and we slept in her bed. Before dawn I slipped back into the bunkhouse, but no one was fooled. On a ranch live-and-let-live rules, and behavior is tolerated until someone is trespassed against. I felt sure no one would interfere. Then, near the end of the week of rain, Jiggers grabbed my arm.

"Pete, that's the boss's daughter," he said.

"I know."

"There's knowing and knowing. People talk, and some talk directly to Willy," he said.

30

The clouds lifted and Lon and I got a spectacular view of a fiery sun balanced like a gyrocompass on the craggy horizon. We rode out to assess damage. Our horses sank to their fetlocks. Ground puddles steamed; brush-covered slopes on the foothills turned emerald and red; water gushed down the arroyos from feeder streams that ran red like bleeding arteries. A dank smell clung to everything. Cattle bore mud on their legs and underbellies. Their forelegs sank out of sight as they tried to graze the flats.

We broke off in pairs. Cal rode beside me. From the way he fidgeted whenever we stopped and the way he looked at me from time to time, something was on his mind. I figured what it was. But I wasn't about to draw it out of him. At a turn in the stream we came upon a small herd in a cottonwood cove. Some were encased in mud and dead leaves. They struggled to their feet as we rode through. Cal said it looked like they'd dug in to weather the storm. He urged his horse up the bank, where the footing was solid, and dismounted. He dropped the reins, took out his fixings, and began rolling a cigarette. I rode Lead into the stream to let him drink. Cal hollered for me to hurry, that we were going to push the cattle back to the herd as soon as he finished his smoke. I rode over and stopped beside Cal's horse. "We got us a little problem, Pete," he said.

I watched the current rush against the rocks in the middle of the stream and said that the rain would fix most everything.

"Won't fix this."

I looked at him innocently. "No?"

"What I'm stuck with is what to do. See, if I don't tell Willy you been spending time with his daughter and someone else does . . . well, you can figure it out."

"Depends on what you mean by spending time."

He ran his tongue over his teeth, puffed on the cigarette and flipped the remains in the mud, where it died a fizzling death. "I mean spending time in her bed. With her. That accurate?"

"I guess."

"You see my problem."

I flicked the reins. As I passed on, I told him to do what he had to.

Two days later Betty and I rode over the soft ground to see the graves. Virgin grass sprouted most everywhere, reedy little slivers of deep green. As we neared the site, I pointed to the overlook and explained that the graves were below. The climb was steeper than I remembered, rocky and slick. In the narrow gorge our horses' hooves echoed off the granite walls. The ravine opened onto the deer trail. She asked to go on alone. I nodded and dismounted. Her braided hair swaying in rhythm with the horse, she disappeared in the shadows of the pine.

Betty came out of the trees at a slow walk. I said hello, but she didn't answer, just slid down and wrapped her arms around my neck. When she pulled away, she said, "You think you're one person and you're not."

"Who are you?" I asked.

"That woman's daughter," she said without hesitation.

We made love standing up, kissing each other desperately as if everything were on the line at that very moment and this was the last act in our lives. Afterward we sat on damp ground beneath the pines and ate tuna sandwiches. We shared the canteen. She brushed a strand away from her cheek, noticed me watching, and told me to eat. I wanted to say how lovely she was and that I loved her, but saying the words took more courage than I possessed. The words themselves scared me, and I was certain they would scare her as well. "Promise something, Petey," she said.

"What?"

"That you won't think bad of me," she said.

"Think badly," I said.

She slapped my arm. "Just promise."

So I did.

That evening when we returned, Conchita said Betty was to call Willy right away. My hands went cold as she handed over her reins and hurried to the door. Conchita looked at me with a grave expression, then urged me to hurry with the horses, as dinner was in the oven. Her expression switched to one of resignation when Betty shouted from the porch that two would be eating in the house.

Betty sat across from me as Conchita set the food before us. I used small talk—horses, new grass, weather—to hide my fears. I felt foolish, for Betty seemed half interested at best. This made me try harder, and the harder I tried, the more foolish I felt. She'd nod or shake her head, but didn't speak until Conchita closed the door. She asked for my hand. I reached across the table and took hers. She squeezed. "Dad's chartered a plane. I have to be in Butte tomorrow to catch it."

"Why?"

"Ruben Lee overdosed."

"Nothing else?"

"Jesus, Petey. He *is* my brother."

"I didn't mean it like that. I just thought . . . I wasn't expecting it, that's all."

"Drive me into Butte."

I nodded.

She asked if after dinner we could put up the portrait one last time and light a fire.

"Sure." It was too warm for a fire, but I would have agreed to anything she wanted. I expected the night to seem short, but instead it seemed long, because part of it became a puzzle we couldn't solve—what would happen after this? We talked in vague terms about a future that included me going to college and law school as if we were confirming Willy's plans. She added something unexpected into the equation, claimed Willy felt a particular obligation toward me. What it was, she had no idea, but an obligation in the sense of a debt.

"How do you know?"

"Because when I asked him to move you out last winter, he said he couldn't, because he was taking care of a marker."

"You asked him to move me out?"

"Yes. That was *then,* Petey."

"A marker. He said a marker?"

"That's what he said."

I couldn't imagine what debt Willy owed that would include me. And who would he owe it to? Mother?

Later, after we'd replaced the painting of Rita and walked to the corral and back, she said that I made her happy and she hoped she made me happy as well. She did, I said. We held each other anxiously and whispered each other's names reassuringly. After the lovemaking, we snuggled under the blankets. A breeze stirred the curtains. Moonlight slanted through the open window. Occasionally a bark or a whinny from the stalls broke the monotonous whir of the crickets. As I listened to her breathe, I felt a terrible dread of the next day. But it was long past midnight and tomorrow already.

In the early morning sometime we fell asleep in an embrace. We awoke to the shrewish screech of a mockingbird just before dawn. We left without eating. As I loaded luggage, she sat in the front seat, looking pale and tired. I recalled how she'd looked the week before she'd tried suicide, and it made my knees weak. She smiled as I climbed behind the steering wheel. She asked how I liked the Mustang—small talk made smaller by circumstances.

"When you come home, you can drive the 'Vette whenever you want. Pretend it's yours."

"I don't like Corvettes very much."

"Don't lie. I saw the look on your face Christmas Day."

The girl beside me was a puzzlement. She'd seemed so self-involved and all along she'd noticed more than I ever thought. Inexplicably, I wanted the old Betty back, the sassy one quick to answer, the high-strung Betty who drove recklessly. "You thought Willy bought it for you."

I turned the ignition. "I didn't either."

I held the steering wheel and turned my head to back out. She cupped her hand over mine and pecked my cheek with her lips. She thanked me, then pulled her hand away. The drive was made longer by words held back. She'd given me joy, the first I'd truly experienced, but I couldn't tell her that for fear I'd lose her or she'd make light of it. She rubbed my forearm as "Downtown" played on the radio. Mostly she looked deep in thought, troubled.

When we neared Butte, I asked if she wanted to eat, said that I was hungry. She said it might make her sick on the flight, so I drove up and down the streets trying to get the courage to say what I wanted to say. I chattered nervously about the roundup and coming home before the month was out. She listened, sometimes looking in my direction expectantly. Finally, she said, "Better get me to the airport."

At the terminal we drank coffee. I promised to call. We found the pilot waiting by the charter gate. He said the plane was warmed up and he'd give her a moment to say good-bye. I held her hand and said I hoped Ruben Lee would come out of it okay.

"Really?"

I shrugged. "I wish we could stay here forever."

She looked over her shoulder at the Cessna twin. The pilot waved and revved the prop.

"You're tall," she said. "I like that. I like your hands."

I gave hers a squeeze.

"I want to kiss you," she said.

"Go ahead."

But she didn't. She shook her head and said it had been fun, then swung about and dashed to the open door. Her hair blowing in the prop blast, she climbed aboard. The pilot reached across and closed the door. She waved. The engines whined as the craft skittered off toward the runway. When the plane was a shiny dot over the Great Divide, I gave up my watch and walked back through the terminal. I sat in the car for a long while feeling small and confused.

31

Stella threw open the garage door as I was bent over the trunk. She demanded to know what had taken me so long. "Made it in a little over a day," I said.

"Been expectin you a month now, Pete. What kept you?"

It sounded like an accusation. If anyone would suspect something had gone on at the ranch, she would. "Work," I said. "Cal was shorthanded after . . ." I didn't mention the rustlers.

"I do somethin to make you mad at me, Pete?"

"No, ma'am."

She looked inside the trunk. "Didn't pick up a present for me, did you?"

"Um, I . . ."

"Hell, I got ever'thing I'd ever need, but it wouldn'ta been the least unthoughtful to call."

I lowered my gaze and nodded. She watched as I lifted my duffel bag and box of books from the trunk. "Betty ain't around," she said. "If you was wonderin, I mean."

"I wasn't."

"I'll fix you somethin to eat. I could use a bite my ownself. Yep."

I slung the bag over my shoulder and left the box and followed her. She told me to drop the bag and give her a squeeze, that I was a damned unappreciative boy. I gave her a gentle hug. She pulled away. "She'll break your heart, Pete."

"Ma'am?"

"Don't play me for a fool. She come back diff'ernt. I know things, even when people think I don't," she said. "Go on, keep your mouth shut on it. That's the way we do it around here. Don't be no diff'ernt." She patted my cheek.

Betty came home too late to eat. She stood at the base of the steps and said she had to go out again right away. I tried not to react, waited for her to give me some kind of sign she was glad to see me or wanted to meet me somewhere, but she darted up the stairs without looking back. Stella asked my help clearing off the table. I could feel my heart beginning to crack.

I lowered the top before I turned onto Oakey. I drove unaware of the road, thinking of Betty's inexplicable conduct, which was constantly on my mind. She'd avoided me the entire week. I had to corner her and get answers, but she was constantly headed out the door to see one friend or another, friends who weren't really friends.

At Twelfth Street, near where Tennessee and I had committed the burglary, a gray terrier ran into my path and sat down. Barely missing it, I screeched to a halt under the elms, and the engine died. The dog sat in the middle of the road, cocked its head, and casually looked at the curb as if trying to make up its mind. Just as casually it turned back in the direction it'd come from.

The Corvette was in the driveway. I parked by the curb so the Mustang couldn't be seen from the house. I waited behind an Italian cypress under the eaves. She emerged and shut the door slowly. Her legs seemed leaden as she walked to her car. She unlocked it and tossed her purse on the seat. I stepped out of the shadows before she could get in her car. "Can we talk for a minute?" I asked, shutting her door and leaning against it.

"I'm in a hurry, Petey."

"You're always in a hurry," I said. I sounded pathetic, but couldn't help myself.

"So?" Her voice was hard and assured.

"So, I thought we . . . I figured we were . . ."

"Petey, don't be an asshole."

"I mean, look at what we . . . I don't know what to say. I never had a girlfriend before."

She looked into my eyes for the first time since the parting at the airport in Butte. "Why'd you start with me?"

I couldn't say for fear she'd laugh. Angry, I said, "I thought you'd have experience."

She crossed her arms and stared. "How about letting me leave. Lisa's expecting me."

I placed my hands on her waist and pulled her to me. She didn't resist, just stood lifeless, letting me hold her. I tried to kiss her, thinking that would help. She turned her face away.

"What?" I asked.

"I don't want to kiss you."

"Just a small one."

She looked away again.

"It's gone, isn't it?" I asked.

"I just don't want to," she said.

I let her go and stepped aside.

I'd worked hard on a speech for physics that had to be on the contribution of a major figure who advanced science. I gave mine on Galileo. I thought the presentation was thorough, but the teacher gave me an F. I told her that the grade was unfair, demanded to know why it was so low.

"You went beyond the assignment and undermined your purpose."

I called her a liar and was summoned to the principal's office from my afternoon class. After shaking my hand, he told me to sit. He was dressed in clerical garb, but for the collar that lay on top of the desk. He marked something in a logbook and glanced up at me over his reading glasses. He studied me as if examining graffiti on the rest-room wall. He dropped the pen and fingered the gold cross that hung at his sternum. "You know what this is about, Peter," he said.

I knew it wasn't a question but an accusation. "No, sir."

"Oh, I think you do. I've heard mostly good reports. You're an honor student."

"Thank you."

"I've had the unfortunate task put on me of having to call Mr. Bobbins about you."

"About me?"

"Yes. In your report to the physics class did you claim that Galileo was treated unjustly by the Church?"

"Sir?"

He picked up the pen and aimed the point at me. "You must understand that this is a Catholic school, and as such, supports the position of the Church in all matters."

"Okay."

"You must take what I say to heart. We can't allow a boy to challenge the policy of the Church. You addressed the idea of Church fallibility to the whole class." He seemed disappointed that I merely stared back. He frowned and continued. "I've talked to Mr. Bobbins at length, and we agree it is in everyone's interest that you apologize to your classmates for your stance."

"What I said was true."

"The option is that we must suspend and possibly expel you."

"For what?"

"I won't explain again."

I leaned back and folded my arms. "Galileo was a genius, and the Church should recognize it. Planets rotate around the sun. We put men in space and take it for granted."

He smiled benevolently. "True," he said, "but he challenged doctrine, as you're doing." He entwined his fingers and set his hands on the desk as a sign of patience. "Will you apologize?"

Stand up in front of Annette Sylvestri and her friends and apologize? "Nobody cares about doctrine," I said. "They care about what they wear and who they're seen with."

"Our students may stray, but they're God-fearing. You must be careful, Peter, not to compound your offenses. The Church, like God, can be forgiving or merciless."

"It's not my Church."

He looked at the ceiling and opened his hands palms up as he muttered under his breath—a prayer, I supposed—then looked at me. "I'm sending you home. You'll be allowed to return when you have a change of heart. Your teacher's failed you on the paper, and I concur with her." He paused to let this sink in. "Mr. Bobbins has a great interest in you. He'll be disappointed."

"I didn't do anything wrong," I said.

"Some matters transcend feelings. You'll be a man in a few years and will understand."

"I'm almost eighteen. I understand what's going on."

"Good day, Peter. I pray you come to your senses." He stood to shake my hand.

My hands at my side, I looked at his crotch. I couldn't resist the old trick I'd pulled on Julie. "Your fly's open," I said.

His cheeks reddened as he reached to zip his pants. He felt around, then looked down just to confirm what I already knew, that his fly was zipped. I wheeled about and left.

Unsure exactly of what senses I was to come to or how to come to them, I drove west. It was September and hot, and I was sweating. I wondered how Willy would react. Mad, certainly. And what if he ordered me to apologize? I didn't care about ideals for the most part, but the truth was just that. Betty would understand—a strange thought, considering she'd not spoken to me for three weeks.

A horn blared. I brought the Mustang to a skidding halt, its nose jutting into Main Street. A white Lincoln swerved past, the driver leaning on his horn and hollering. The car behind me wouldn't back up, so I sat in the intersection as a seemingly interminable string of cars went around, each driver taking his turn at the horn. When the light switched I drove on.

As I crossed the tracks at Industrial Road, a red 'Vette took a screeching turn south. Even if I wasn't sure it was Betty's car, I was sure she was driving it. With a wide, deliberate turn, I reversed direction. The Corvette had already chewed up half a mile.

Betty, slowed temporarily by the light on Sahara, didn't seem to notice me coming from a distance until I beat the amber light at Highland. She'd almost reached the Strip and, at the last instant, swerved into the right lane and turned south. Blocked in by cars on both sides, I watched her drive away until all I saw was a red glaze bobbing in the tide of traffic.

A log in a current, I drifted in twenty-mile-an-hour traffic past the Thunderbird, Riviera, El Morocco, and Algiers. I searched for her car. I talked to her, talked to Willy, talked to myself, and the more I talked and the slower the traffic got, the madder I became. The Desert Inn slipped in and out of the rearview mirror—the Castaways to the right, the Sands on the left; the Flamingo, Caesars Palace. A Corvette zipped by headed north, but the license plate was from California.

I drove in and out of lots, checked every red Corvette in every parking lot. I never imagined there could be so many red 'Vettes. I'd figured they were like rare butterflies. But, like cops when you didn't need one, they seemed to be everywhere, as if they procreated in Las Vegas parking lots. I pulled into the Denny's parking lot south of the Dunes and let the engine idle. Cars flowed by from the stoplight at Flamingo. Soaked with sweat, I gripped the wheel and stared vacantly as the afternoon heat siphoned off the last of my hope. Forget Betty. I needed to deal with school and with Willy.

At the Tally Ho I U-turned and fell in behind traffic. I had nowhere to go now. When I'd visited Mother on recent occasions, Leonardo had made it obvious he wanted every measure of her attention. Besides, it wasn't as if I'd ever confided in her. And Miriam, in her eighth month now, had her own worries. Floating along behind traffic, I somehow ended up in the old neighborhood on Boston Street.

I parked and walked to the apartment. The place needed paint on the trim, but otherwise remained unchanged. I sat on a lawn chair, watched the sun's reflection in the pool, and tried to gather my thoughts. I'd lost Betty. But why? That was the puzzle. If I could only understand. A couple entered the courtyard and crossed the pool deck. She was thin and waved a cigarette about as she talked. He was tall and broad-shouldered and seemed not to hear her. He keyed the door to our old apartment and they went in. He took a last look at me but said nothing. Then I thought of Ernie; in fact, I wondered why he wasn't at the pool. I looked at his apartment, pictured him in the doorway with his golf club and sardonic smile. I hurried up the stairs.

Footsteps from whoever was inside thudded over the carpeted floor. I remembered how the floors and walls carried sound—the lengthy episodes of lovemaking by the bartender and his girlfriend. A middle-aged man with a long, pale forehead and thick black horn-rims answered the bell. He said, "Solicitors aren't welcome."

"I'm looking for Ernie," I said, then in case my intentions were misunderstood, added that I used to live below and he'd become a friend of the family.

"Oh, I'm sorry."

"Did he move?"

The man hesitated. "You don't know?"

"Know?"

"He drowned. In the pool."

Everything was boxed out except for a single memory of him sitting by the pool, wineglass in hand, toasting me as I walked by. I leaned against the rail. The man asked if I was okay.

I stood tall and said, "I'm okay. When?"

"In July, I think. I took the apartment in August."

In August I'd been spending nights with Betty. I looked over the rail at the deep end, where he'd sat with his glass of wine and putter. "He was always alone," I said, not necessarily to the man.

He rested against the doorjamb. "Some people said it wasn't an accident."

I looked back. "Yes, it was," I snapped.

He seemed on verge of taking issue with me, but didn't. He had no stake in an opinion and obviously would just as soon see me leave. "Probably was."

"I'm sorry I bothered you," I said.

"From what I gather, everyone here liked him," the man said by way of an apology.

"Yes." I thanked him and left.

He'd probably thought about killing himself for years. He'd sat at the edge of the pool, enduring daily doses of intolerance and drinking wine, trying to build up the courage to dive in. I walked until I found myself in Circle Park, where Timmy Pendergast had introduced me to cigarettes and cynicism. I felt ghosts moving inside and seeds of new ghosts sprouting. I sat on a swing and swung, gently at first, toes scraping the ground, then more forcefully.

I wanted to silence my mind. I closed my eyes, leaned back and thrust my legs higher and higher. I saw Ernie toasting me, Betty undressed and sitting on the edge of her bed, Willy swinging a golf club in the middle of the high desert. I felt air on my cheeks and the soothing sun. I thought of Rich, the philosopher, the self-indulgent, sermonizing about chaos and decay. I weighed possibilities of godly intervention in this, but what God would let the Church condemn Galileo? let Ernie die? Pearl? What God would allow me to lose Betty?

"Hey, mister. My kid wants to swing."

A young mother stood holding her daughter's hand. "They're for kids," she said.

I scraped my feet to stop and got off.

"Not right you takin the swing like that," she said.

I didn't speak, just backed away. I had to face Willy, and I needed all my wits for that. I thought about going home and calling Miriam to tell her about Ernie, as she'd liked him. But at the moment she didn't need more drama in her life.

I drove just to keep moving. I was no longer looking for Betty's car. Perhaps that's why I stumbled on it under the sign in valet parking. I would make her listen, tell her about Ernie and Julie, about what it was like to live without money, sleep on a couch or in the backseat of a car, to have a mother who skipped out of rooms at night without paying. She had to understand what love meant to me. I would say the words, give her the power. I parked in the El Morocco lot and walked back to the Thunderbird Casino.

A wave of cool air hit me as I entered the casino and looked about. I'd find her and tell her first about Galileo, go soft, let her soak that up, let her understand how life can slide away from us, then I would enter cautiously into the bigger ideas, lay them out slowly so if she seemed to think it was silly, I could take a different approach. An obese burgundy-uniformed guard looking like a giant grape folded his arms across his chest and gave me the once-over to let me know he was watching. I moved away quickly to let him know I wasn't loitering, I had a purpose.

A few players, mesmerized by spinning reels, cranked the handles mechanically as if the roles of man and machine were reversed. Out of the corner of my eye I saw the guard closing in and wove through rows of chrome-legged stools to the entrance to Little Joe's Oyster Bar, where Mother used to feed Miriam and me when she felt bad about neglecting us. In the aquarium behind the bar seahorses gamboled about on bee-wing-like fins. She sat in the second booth, her back to the door, her glistening hair pulled into a ponytail. I started to step toward her, but a hostess stopped me and asked if she might help.

"No, I'm . . ."

Richie saw me at the same moment I saw him. Betty glanced over her shoulder. My thoughts drained from the center of my head to my chest. I looked down as if I might find something I'd lost, but there was nothing at my feet but brilliant red-and-pink-and-black-spotted carpet that spread in every direction. She called to me, but the blood pounded in my ears, and all I heard was that pounding and a voice that told me to leave.

I hurried out of the air-conditioning into the warm sun. The chill stayed with me as I sat in the Mustang, rerunning a picture of Betty as she turned to me. I put the key to the ignition, but it wouldn't go in. I threw the key ring on the floorboard and banged my hands on the steering wheel, banged them until I was sure I'd break them or the wheel, or both. I wanted to kill.

I was wiping my eyes when a gray-haired couple shuffled by holding hands. He unlocked the door for her and held her arm as she slid in. He glanced at me as he opened his own door. He asked if I was all right. I held my hand up and looked away.

In time I started the car and drove east on Desert Inn to the Stardust Golf Course, where the fairway was spotted with olive trees. I'd seen the course a hundred times, but it suddenly struck me as unnatural. Before I knew it, I somehow ended up west of the Strip passing warehouses on Procyon and Polaris, then I drove south to Tropicana and north again on the Strip. I saw the city anew—grass and trees, hulking masses of concrete and glass windows, air-conditioned to 72 ideal degrees, fifty-foot signs blinking at midday. Except for the honest, weed-scattered lots, it seemed so much tinfoil and sequins. Everything unnatural. And I knew I couldn't go back, couldn't return to the house or stay in the city where Betty lived.

At the First National Bank at Third Street and Bridger I handed the teller my ID and told her I wanted to withdraw my savings. She wrote the information down and told me to wait. When she returned, a man in a blue suit and striped tie accompanied her. He asked if I had parental permission to withdraw the money, some note with a signature on it.

"I didn't need a signature to open my account."

"It's a large sum for someone your age to be handling."

"It's my money."

"I'm not saying it's not yours, son. I'd like you to talk it over with your parents."

"My mother's in Hawaii with her new husband. I'm living with friends, and I want the money so I can move out."

"It's almost four thousand dollars. Why don't you take, say, five hundred and leave the rest where it's secure?"

I stared him in the eye. "I want it all."

"You're determined?"

"I worked for it."

He nodded to the cashier, then tried to pay me by check, but I refused. He shook his head and left. I walked out of the bank, the cash stuffed in my pockets.

A red-and-white Bonneville sat in the showroom window. I opened the door to a bell jingling. A salesman, ready to twist my arm, immediately cornered me. I pointed to the Triumph. Minutes later I rode it to the Department of Motor Vehicles, registered it, and from there rode back to the motorcycle shop. I drove the Mustang to the Lucky, parked it in the garage, and took a cab to pick up the motorcycle.

I phoned from the coffee shop in the Fremont. Stella answered the second ring and wanted to know where I was.

"They sent me home," I said.

They'd received a call from the school that said I'd been sent home for using heresy in a classroom. She asked if that was true. "An you said terrible things about religion?"

"No. I said that Galileo had been excommunicated by the Church and labeled a heretic."

"You made fun'a the principal."

"Yeah, I did."

"Well, all you gotta do is 'pologize."

"I can't do that."

"Yes, you can."

"I left the Mustang on the second floor in the garage at the Lucky. The keys are in the ashtray. I want to thank you for everything."

"Petey, what'n the hell you up to?"

"I don't know."

She was silent for a moment. When she spoke, it was to tell me that when I first came into her house, she was against the idea, that it was Willy's doing, but she was used to having me there and even kind of thought of me as her own. Whatever I had in mind, she claimed, was not a good idea. I told her I wasn't coming back.

"It's Betty, ain't it? Okay, you don't hafta 'pologize to them. I mean right's right, an heaven knows I'd never 'pologize if right was on my side. Ask Willy on that one."

"I'm sorry," I said.

"Petey, you get home right now," she said. "Never mind what Betty done."

Her voice broke. It was hard to imagine Stella crying. If I stayed on the telephone, I might lose my resolve. I knew what I'd be doing by nightfall. I said good-bye and hung up.

I swallowed down a cheeseburger, gulped two cups of coffee, and mounted the Triumph. I gassed up at the station across from the Tropicana. It remained hot, but the sun was plowing toward the Charleston Peaks. It would be dark and cooler in forty minutes, about the time I'd be crossing the border at Stateline.

32

I awoke and looked around the flat. Beside me on the mattress a girl of sixteen who called herself Moon Flower, but whose real name was Audrey

Pritchard, rolled over on her side and scratched the back of her neck. She was a runaway from Norman, Oklahoma. For weeks I'd been staying with her and others like her in an apartment leased by a twenty-eight-year-old named Sachs who was a poet by claim, a sign painter by profession, a radical by preference, a drug dealer by necessity, and a pervert by any means possible.

On a bare mattress across the room a guy named Rollie propped his head on the pillow and began to roll a joint. The primary reason I'd been invited to commune here was my bankroll, which was about down to nothing. Rollie, whose grass I had purchased, lit the joint and held the smoke in until his cheeks reddened. He let it go with a violent heave that shook the mattress. He squinted and said, "Mellow, man."

I slipped on my pants. He offered me a hit from the joint. I declined with a nod.

"What it is, Golden?" he asked.

Everybody here went by a nickname. Golden was the moniker Sachs had given me. I'd met Sachs through Moon Flower, and in one of his altered states, he'd proclaimed I was Golden, a descendant of a Viking lord, and recited some words that supported his theory. He called this poetry. He called everything he said poetry. Poetry, he'd declared on the night we'd met, was his guitar, and he asked what mine was. I'd flashed a hundred-dollar bill at him. He took it, held it up to the bare overhead light, and said, "Benjamin, the blessed bounty of the bourgeois, an eight-string guitar if I ever saw one," and asked how much I wanted, meaning weed.

"Where you going?" Rollie asked.

I shrugged. Moon Flower blinked her eyes and squinted at me. I touched her cheek. She was pretty in a heartbreaking way. She had a chipped front tooth that gave her smile more character than it deserved at her age. I alternately felt used and user when we were together. She made me think of Betty, and it was Betty I was making love to the whole while. I hoped for her sake Moon Flower was thinking of someone else as well.

"You mind if Moon Flower and I fuck?" Rollie asked.

"That's not up to me," I said. The house rule on such matters was clear. It was her call.

"Would you like that, Moon Flower?" Rollie asked. He grinned with his stained teeth.

Moon Flower sat up and leaned back against the wall. She seemed to consider his proposal quite seriously, then shook her head. "No. I feel like we should be brother and sister, Rollie. I can't fuck my brother. Could you fuck your sister?"

I needed air, not just the air outside, but the air of an open highway. This

San Francisco scene was for a different person. I stood to leave. Moon Flower looked up. She'd made the attachment and wanted to know where I was headed. I shrugged. Rollie took another hit.

"What was the question?" he asked.

"Never mind," Moon Flower said. "The answer is no."

I smiled at her. The apartment door opened. Crystal entered with a paper bag in her arms. She looked first at Moon Flower, then at me, and finally at Rollie.

"Didn't you lock the door when you left?" Rollie asked.

Crystal shrugged and dropped the bag on the table. It was filled with cans and landed with a harsh thud. She walked to the corner, where she picked up her guitar.

"Jesus, doesn't anyone answer questions around here?" Rollie said. "Man, the fucking feds could come in here and take me away. I burned my draft card."

Rollie talked interminably about running to Canada or Sweden, romanticizing it as some heroic stand, especially after smoking two or three joints. Sometimes he'd cry. In a sense I'd become a draft dodger by virtue of not having registered. He tried to convince me to go with him and if I was high enough, I'd agree to it, but later tell him it was just dope talk.

Pretty much what we did was smoke weed and babble about making an ideal world based on fuzzy ideas, but that didn't seem to bother anyone. I liked to stay straight and just listen. I once told them this idea of sharing everything would never go over. Sachs asked why not. I said Willy Bobbins simply wouldn't go for it. He thought Willy Bobbins was my nickname for the federal government. Crystal strummed the strings once. "A locked door wouldn't stop them."

"Do you want to fuck?" Rollie asked.

Crystal touched her fingers to the frets. "I want to play."

"Can I go?" Moon Flower asked me.

"No," I said.

"You're leaving?"

I nodded.

"See, Moon Flower, you should forget about that brother-sister stuff with me. He's going," Rollie said. "Going to Canada?"

She stared at the ceiling. "I think I'm about to be sad."

"Why can't I get anyone to fuck me?" Rollie asked.

"If you play it cool, maybe Sachs will," I said.

"I guess that's funny. Man, I'm a political fugitive. I should get a little consideration. Hey, this is a serious statement."

Crystal played a few chords and set the guitar aside. She went to the table and removed a can from the bag. "Want some soup, anyone?"

By then the joint was down to almost nothing. Moon Flower padded over to Rollie's mattress and took a hit. She sat beside him. "You can leave us, Golden. It's okay."

I had only sixty dollars left. I took a twenty out and dropped it on her lap. She stared at it.

"You should go back home, Audrey," I said.

"This is my home, Golden, unless you take me with you."

"I can't."

"Will you come back?"

A tear dribbled down her cheek and fell on the back of her wrist. She held the twenty to her breast in a tight fist.

"I'm going to join the army," I said.

She looked at the folds of her skirt and licked her lips. "Well, go, then," she said.

"Hey, man, that's crazy talk. Stay and share a hit or two," Rollie said. "Crystal, tell him it's crazy."

Though a year younger than Moon Flower, Crystal was hardened. She was Sachs's girl, though she was free to go with anyone else she chose and had done so from time to time. And there was ample opportunity, considering the number of gypsy youths who traipsed in and out of the flat. She'd never seemed interested in me, so I hadn't pursued her. She'd strayed up from Los Angeles, left a home where she was considered nothing more than a free baby-sitter for her stepbrothers and a concubine for her stepfather. She told me one night as we passed a joint back and forth that her stepfather had broken down the bathroom door when she was bathing, undressed, climbed in the tub, and made her masturbate him. She was thirteen then. From the front of the stove she looked back over her shoulder. She stirred the soup. "It's crazy, but he's free to be crazy. Anyone have a cigarette?"

I tossed a used pack on the counter by her. I'd decided on no more smoking, didn't like the taste anyhow. I told her to keep them. She thanked me and said, "Peace."

"Man, you're deserting a cause here," Rollie said. He licked another joint and handed it to Moon Flower.

I walked toward the door. "My name's Pete, and I don't see any cause around here."

Moon Flower looked up as I passed by. "Good-bye, Golden," she said.

"Good-bye."

She lit the joint and filled her lungs with smoke. I shut the door. As I came off the steps, I saw Sachs and another guy trying to kick over my Triumph. When he looked up, Sachs said he was going to need the bike. I shook my head and said, "I'll be needing it."

The other guy, Wallace, a new kid Sachs had brought into the fold, lifted his leg over the seat as if to take possession of it. Sachs said Wallace was going to Oakland to pick up some stuff from the brothers. "Guess he'll have to take the bus," I said.

"You don't understand, Golden. This is important business," Sachs said.

"Well, work it out."

"I'm saying we're using the bike. I made my pad your pad. That's how it works."

"No, I paid my way. And I bought that Triumph, and if Wallace doesn't get off it right now, I'm going to break your finger, Sachs."

"His name's no longer Wallace. He's Sun Boy. You like it?"

I grabbed Sachs's left hand, twisted it at the wrist, and drove him to his knees. I gripped his index finger. "Tell Sun Boy to get off my bike."

"Can't," he said.

"Suit yourself."

He screamed as I bent his finger back.

"Tell him to get off my machine, now," I said.

"Okay, okay."

Wallace climbed off and doubled his fists, as if he had a mind to help Sachs. I smiled and snapped Sachs's finger anyhow. He fell to the sidewalk screaming. "Don't even," I warned Wallace, who uncoiled his fists and stepped aside. "Take him to the free clinic," I said.

Sachs sat on his haunches and held his broken finger. "Why'd you do this?" he asked.

"Because you remind me of Rich. I told you it's my machine. Some things just belong to a person," I said.

"Who's Rich?" he asked.

I mounted the Triumph, pulled the choke, and kicked it to life on the second try.

33

Uncle Harve and Aunt Vivian had moved to a cramped three-bedroom house on Cornuta Street in Bellflower. I was five minutes away in Long Beach when I called from a pay phone to tell them I was coming. Before I cut off the ignition, the door slammed shut and Aunt Vivian rushed down the side steps. She stopped a few feet away and stared. I was a sight, dressed in black leather jacket and dirty jeans, my hair hanging over my collar, and a mat of eight-week fuzz and whisker on my chin.

She kept repeating, "Oh, Jesus, oh, Jesus," and flung her arms around my neck. Uncle Harve, a little lame from early arthritis, limped down the steps.

"I told you he was fine. I told you, and here he is."

He grabbed my right hand and pumped it up and down. When the initial astonishment wore off, they stepped back and looked me over. Uncle Harve said my hair was too long. Aunt Vivian said I needed a bath and clean clothes.

"Where have you been, Peter?" she asked.

"I just came from San Francisco. But I've been all over up there. Santa Cruz and Mendocino, Sacramento. Went to Truckee and up the Feather River."

"Doing what?" Uncle Harve asked.

I slipped out of my backpack. "Nothing. Thinking."

Uncle Harve took my backpack. Aunt Vivian looped her arm around my waist and urged me up the steps as if I were an invalid. Inside she helped me out of my leather jacket and motioned for me to sit at the table. Though newer and a bit smaller, this house, like the other before it had been, was filled with all kinds of clutter, shelves of knickknacks and souvenirs, yet it was tidy, the furniture functional.

Aunt Vivian smiled. "You like it?"

It was so unlike the Bobbinses' house, which was huge and open. There the only clutter was in the kitchen. I looked at the evening paper on the table where they'd been sitting.

"It's nice," I said.

"Not fancy like your mother's new house," she said.

"Or that Mr. Bobbins, I'll bet," Uncle Harve injected. "He drove down here looking for you. Nice man, worried about you, too, said if you show up, we should call him. He offered us money. Imagine that."

Aunt Vivian nodded. "You sit. I've got pork roast I can reheat. We told him you were like our own boy. No money was needed, thank you. We know our obligations. Isn't that right, Harve?"

"Exactly right."

"I'd appreciate it if you didn't call anyone," I said.

"Well, we promised your mother," he said.

"Can you wait on that promise?"

They looked at one another before agreeing.

After eating, Uncle Harve walked me to the bathroom. He laid out a towel, soap, and a razor on the counter. Aunt Vivian brought one of his robes for me. Nothing else he owned would fit.

"Harve, you bring his clothes straight to me," she said.

He watched her leave. "Always bossing. You had us all going, Pete. Your mother blames herself, says she should have left you with us, that you would have been better off. I didn't make it easy for her. She's right to blame herself. She's my little sister, and I love her, but she could have done better by her children. You're an uncle by the way, a baby girl. Esther. Is that Jewish?"

"Well, that's something, a niece," I said and began stripping. I handed my clothes over one piece at a time. Uncle Harve held his nose as I draped my shirt over his forearm. We laughed.

I showered until the hot water was gone. They were waiting in the den, furnished with a couch and two large recliners. We sat and watched television, talking during commercials only. They wanted to know my plans and said it was fine with them if I decided to stay and finish school. Willy had mentioned my being accused of being a heretic, which Aunt Vivian said was silly, that being Episcopalians didn't necessarily make us heretics.

"I am," I said.

"Nonsense," Aunt Vivian said. "You aren't one of those Hell's Angels, are you?"

"Aunt Vivian, I ride a Triumph."

She couldn't make sense of my answer. "I've read about them in the paper. I hate for that to happen to . . ."

"Let him be," Uncle Harve said. "We'll discuss it in the morning. It may be like I said. He'd probably make a good tax accountant. I could teach him while he goes to college."

"Never mind that, Harve. One tax accountant in the family's enough. He should be a dentist."

"Why a dentist?" Uncle Harve asked.

"What would you know?" she said as if that resolved the matter.

"I got a good practice and no one to turn it over to," he said.

I sat upright. "I'm eighteen." As I said it, the age took on a special significance.

"Oh, Jesus." Aunt Vivian looked at Uncle Harve. "Tell him."

"What?" He thought an instant and closed his eyes. "I almost forgot. Miriam's husband was shot down over North Vietnam," he said.

In the morning we ate in the kitchen. They were afraid of what I'd say about my plans. They were already making room for me in theirs. The tinkle of cups on saucers and silverware on plates seemed to exaggerate the silence. I found myself wondering what I'd done to deserve the love of these two. It seemed a shame, for they had so much love to give and gave it willingly but had no one but each other to give it to. It was too late. I couldn't enter their world and share that love. I had plans, and by the end of breakfast, though nothing was said, they knew it.

Before he drove off, Uncle Harve told me to come by his office for lunch. I hugged Aunt Vivian and thanked her for breakfast. She started to cry.

"Same old Aunt Vivian," I said and laughed.

She wiped her eyes and laughed. "I'm a silly goose. Always have been. I just remember how when you were a boy I'd watch you fall asleep on the couch and Harve would carry you into the bedroom. Now look. A man. What are you going to do?"

"I'll tell you later. What's my niece's name again?"

"Esther. Now, isn't that a strange name in this family?"

"*Bleak House*," I said.

"What?"

"From one of Miriam's favorite books," I explained.

"She read too much. I knew no good would come of it, and now she's . . . branded her baby for life with that name."

I kissed her on the forehead. She waved good-bye and watched me ride off on the motorcycle. I left carrying a sense of family in my guts. My life extended into the lives of others whether I was aware of it or not. I missed Miriam and even Mother. I couldn't help wondering what direction life might have taken us had Miriam and I stayed with my uncle and his good-hearted wife. Though I believed Willy and Stella were good-hearted, I'd begun to see myself as a sort of pet to them, a topic to use against one another, for they couldn't use their children in that way—secrets, and all that.

The recruiter opened a file drawer and found the appropriate forms. He slipped one in the typewriter and adjusted the top. "First off, are you a fugitive or do you have a felony conviction?"

"No?"

"Juvenile arrests?"

"Yes."

"Don't count unless they're for murder or something."

"No murders."

He typed the information from my driver's license, then asked the other questions on the form. Mother's name. Father's. There I balked. I didn't know who my real father was and was opposed to furthering the lie. "What's the name on the birth certificate?" he asked.

I told him and he typed it in. He asked my assignment preference.

"What's available?"

"Well, you can get fifty-five dollars a month if you jump out of a plane. Airborne units are always in need of soldiers. How 'bout I type that in?"

"I'd rather stay on the ground."

He handed me the form to sign, then administered a preliminary test. The process took twenty-five minutes. He told me not to worry about my draft status or registration, that he could handle that through my draft board. He shook my hand and welcomed me into the U.S. Army, though it wasn't official until I passed the physical and took the oath. He said he and another sergeant would be by at dawn to pick me up, that I was to be ready and waiting.

I called Miriam. She answered on the second ring. Her voice sounded hollow and weak. "This is your brother," I said.

"Petey!"

"Yes. I hear I'm an uncle."

"Yes. Where are you?"

"Promise not to tell?"

"Where are you?"

"In Alaska."

"How you'd get there?"

"A hot-air balloon. So, did you name your daughter Esther Summerson Holder?"

"You remember. No, in fact, it's Esther Leanne."

"Very pretty. Does Aunt Vivian remind you of Mrs. Jellyby?"

"Oh, my God, yes."

"Well, that's where I am, at Uncle Harve's."

"Maybe he can talk some sense into your head."

"Still in charge of the world?"

"No, just Esther, I'm afraid."

"I'm sorry about Alan."

She hesitated, then said that was why she'd answered so quickly. Sometimes they can get a pilot out, but it usually happens the first few hours or days. It'd been three days, she explained. After a pause, she said he was well trained and smart. If anyone could make it, he could. It was reassuring to know her spirits were up. She said once she got over the initial shock of hearing he'd gone down, other possibilities surfaced. There was an organization of pilots' wives for support and she'd received a dozen calls. She added that the Holders were very reassuring. "I think they've finally accepted me," she said.

"Good." The silence that ensued was an awkward one. I didn't know if I should volunteer the information that I'd enlisted or not, and she seemed distracted. It was she who spoke.

"Peter, where have you been?"

"Around. On a bike. I bought a new Triumph and took off."

"Willy's called three or four times a week to see if you showed up here. He's concerned. He told me to tell you he wouldn't make you apologize. He understands."

"I wish it was just that."

"You and Betty?"

"That and more. Yes."

"Oh, Jesus. I guessed as much."

"Miriam, I joined the army."

"Oh, no. Peter. No. Why do men do such stupid things? You're as dumb as Alan."

"You just said he was smart."

"I lied."

I said that Ernie had drowned. She said he was a sad man and she wished she'd known him better. I asked after my niece, and Miriam talked about the labor pains and changing diapers and having some completely unexpected feelings. After that there wasn't much to say. She mentioned Mother had been concerned and had called several times to talk things over. She asked if I intended to call her. I said no, and then we wished each other luck and love and hung up.

The next phone number was hard to dial. It rang four times before anyone answered, and then it was Betty who answered. I started to hang up. "Hello, hello," she said.

Memories sliced through me. "It's Pete."

"You shit. Where are you?"

"Is Willy there?"

"Petey?"

"What?" I closed my eyes, imagined her sitting in Little Joe's Oyster Bar, looking over her shoulder as if I were in the wrong. I needed anger to get me through the conversation from there.

"Willy's gone. Are you going to talk?"

"I'll call the Lucky," I said.

"He's in San Francisco . . . looking for you. Petey, come home. We'll talk."

"I can't. I joined the army."

She didn't want to believe it, but I insisted it was true and she believed me. "Maybe you'll get killed," she said. A lot of dead space followed. I asked how Stella was. Mad and hurt, according to Betty. I didn't mention Rich. That seemed unnecessary. I asked Betty to say something kind. She didn't. I said good-bye, but didn't hang up right away. The line clicked dead.

The evening was chilly. Uncle Harve and I wrapped blankets over our shoulders like two Indians contemplating a sunset, and he lit his pipe and puffed on it leisurely. He talked about his boyhood in Palouse during the Depression. He said it wasn't as bad as people thought—the being hungry and going without and all the hard work to put a meal on the table—it just wasn't good. I half listened, for I was replaying the calls to Miriam and Betty.

"No work to take pride in. That's what drove the old man off. Then the war changed everything overnight. There were jobs, but too late for us. The war scattered us around. Me, your mom." He puffed on his pipe. Deep in thought as he was, he just stared downward and sucked on the pipe until the thought ended. "Never understood men like Willy Bobbins who thrived in all that despair. Lucky, I guess," he said. He dismissed it with a shake of his head.

The pipe died, and he slapped the bowl on his palm. A glowing cinder dropped to the patio. He asked if Willy was a happy man. I couldn't come up with a suitable answer. I didn't know if Willy ever thought in terms of happiness.

I figured Rita had made him happy, and occasionally Betty. He liked poker. Happy? A word, like sad's a word. "I don't know."

"What I'm asking is, does all that money make him happy?"

That I could answer. "No. No, it doesn't make those around him happy either."

Hearing this pleased him. He puffed on his pipe and watched Aunt Vivian in the kitchen window.

"She's fixing something to take in the morning," he said. "The thing we missed in our lives was children. We came up just short of happiness. Guess that's why we keep trying at life." His eyes glistened in the light of the porch as he looked at her. In them I saw unconditional acceptance of his need for her.

"Don't get yourself killed over there. Come back to us," he said.

In the morning we were up by 4:30. Aunt Vivian fixed breakfast for the three of us and talked for the three of us and ate for the three of us, and as I helped clear the table, she cried for the three of us. Uncle Harve tried to soothe her with words, but when that didn't work, he hugged her and asked me to do the same. She said she was just a silly goose and nothing more, except a fussbudget and a fool. I laughed at her and called her Mrs. Jellyby. She stopped crying and told me it wasn't meant to be funny.

She handed me a paper bag with a peanut-butter-and-jelly sandwich inside. We sat in the den with lamplight to keep us company. When the recruiter honked the horn, I thanked them both, kissed them, and said I'd be back.

34

The last week of the cycle I was called out of the field where we were being tested. A Jeep driver awaited, his engine idling. I asked what was up. He shrugged and told me to climb in and hold on. He drove off as if pursued, gears grinding as he shifted up and down. The sky was overcast. It was too cold to hold on to anything metal, so I stuffed my hands in my pockets and hoped I didn't fall off.

I jumped down and double-timed to headquarters. The first sergeant looked up from his papers, gave me a scowl, and thumbed in the direction of the captain's office. I knocked tentatively. The captain hollered, "Must be some girl with a bouquet!"

I banged my knuckles on the door and was ordered in. I saluted. "Sir, Private Elkins reporting as ordered." I stood at attention while he read a memo.

He set the note aside. "Elkins, I don't like letters or calls from senators. You know that?"

"No, sir."

"Do you know what I'm talking about?"

"No, sir."

"Do you know that you are not to receive visitors?"

"Yes, sir."

"Then why am I talking to you, Elkins? Why do I feel like I'm running a day nursery?"

"I don't know, sir."

"It's because I've received calls and you have a visitor. I don't approve, Elkins. It's a good thing your time with us is over. You best get your head out of your ass before you get to 'Nam. Now get out of my face and go to the day room."

"Yes, sir," I said, saluted, and left.

In twenty minutes a staff car, red flags with a single silver star mounted on the fenders, rolled to a stop in front of the company pylon. A private first class stepped out and opened the back door. I knew it was Willy getting out before his boots touched the gravel. Looking stooped and tired, he stood beside the car surveying the grounds. The door to headquarters opened, and the captain saluted and gave a friendly smile as he descended the wooden steps. He shook Willy's hand and led him to the day room. After telling Willy what a promising recruit I was, he left.

Willy, unshaven and smelling slightly of whiskey, stood in the blaze of a bare window. He took his hat off. Obviously disapproving, he nodded as he looked me over. "Well, you put on some weight. You was always too skinny."

"Yes, sir."

He offered me his hand. "Forget my name?"

"No."

He shook hands and let go. "Say it, then."

"Willy."

"'At's right. What'd Willy ever do for you to treat him the way you done?"

I licked my lips and looked out the window, wishing this wasn't happening, and at the same time I was happy to see he cared. I said, "Nothing, Willy. You were always good to me."

"You think I would'a made you 'pologize in front of a schoolroom if you didn't want to?"

I hesitated, but answered, "No."

"Damn right, no. Now, I been workin on gettin you out. That boy in California, the one with the broken finger. The finger you broke?"

I'd almost forgotten Sachs. I nodded.

"He went to the po-lice. They's a report. I went up there 'cause a detective called to the sheriff's office in Vegas. So ain't no charges filed, but if you say do it. . . . You followin me? Army got no need for you, 'specially if you got a warrant on you. We can get that fixed later. Hell, got a gar-antee you get a general discharge. No record. You can finish school, go to college. Maybe a delay, but it'd come."

"I'm in the army now," I said.

"Really?" He let me think as he lit his cigar. Whatever he said was as good as done.

I thought about the golfing in the desert. It was easy to get caught up in Willy, his ways, and his family. I'd lost sight of me. I had no friends. He pointed his cigar at me. "Don't play no poker with me, boy. It's my game." He held the cigar away and looked at me, one eye squinted. "You a'ways kept a tight tongue, Pete. Never told on that boy what stole the purse, never said a word about Ruben Lee and them drugs. It's a good thing for a man to know, but you got somethin to learn about poker and such."

"I told you about Tennessee," I said.

He seemed puzzled. "Tennessee?"

"You know who I mean."

He shook his head. He looked so confounded, I was tempted to blurt out what I knew.

"You broke Stella's heart takin off. She says it was somethin I did. She wants you home. Take my offer, Pete. Betty wants you home, too, though she says the opposite's so."

My ears were burning. "Enlisting is the only thing I ever did on my own."

"And buy a motor-sickle. You got no appreciation," he said. He took a draw on the cigar. The smoke hung in the light of the bare window. "You're 'bout like a son to me, an in time I'll forgive you. Stella told me to bring you home if I had to carry you over a shoulder kickin. What should I tell her, Pete? That you don't care nothin for her an me an the things we done?"

"That's not true," I said.

He looked out the window. "This is 'bout as godforsaken a place as I ever seen."

We stared at each other. Before I took time to think about it, I hugged him. He patted my back, then withdrew. When he looked at me, he knew there was nothing more to say. "You come home when it's done. I'll tell Stella you love her just fine, you got some crazy notion 'bout being a hero. But don't go be no hero. Promise?"

"I promise."

We hugged once more, and he left.

35

As the tail opened, a stream of dust funneled in and brought a terrible stench. Every face in the plane reacted. One man gagged. The replacement next to him told him to breathe through his mouth. This was Vietnam, and whatever waited outside was home for however long we were here, a fact I figured I'd best resign myself to. Standing at the tailgate, the load master motioned for us to deplane. We stood, hefted our duffel bags, and started toward the rear with a fatalistic sense of resolve. The big turboprops of the C-130 screamed as the plane readied for a quick turnaround back to Tan Son Nhut.

I was first off. I stared at the fallow fields surrounding the strip. Shielding my eyes from the dust, I gripped my bag and hurried through the prop blast. The others followed. A bored-looking staff sergeant met us at the edge of the strip and formed us into a line. An artillery piece went off. Then the throttling plane lunged down the runway and launched itself into the cobalt sky.

"Welcome to goddamn Cu Chi," he said. "Grab your gear and follow." His skin looked like compressed redwood bark.

The guy beside me asked where the hell we really were. I shrugged. Again the artillery piece went off. We fell into step, bound for Twenty-fifth Division Headquarters, an olive-drab village of tents and Quonset huts that appeared much like a ghetto constructed by a sailmaker.

"What's that smell, Sarge?" the man behind me asked.

"What smell?"

"Smells like shit," the replacement said.

"You'll get used to it." As we marched, he meted out congenial in-country wisdom. The village was VC, he warned, "Men, women, boys, girls, goddamn pigs, goddamn goats, and even goddamn dogs. You can get anything there, dope, pussy, French cigarettes, a goddamn black-market stereo, and things you don't want, tuberculosis, clap, and goddamn dead."

The 155 mm sent another round beyond the perimeter. Cu Chi, he explained, was built on a rice field fertilized for centuries by human shit, which accounted in part for the smell—but just in part. It sat in the middle of a plain near Highway 1 and atop a catacomb, built over a period of twenty years by guerrillas. "Goddamn vulnerable to sapper attacks." He elucidated how occasionally a new tunnel would be discovered and engineers would blow the opening and declare it harmless. "Once a hole's harmless, it remains harmless no matter how many sappers crawl out of it," he said. An artillery round punctuated his every ninth or tenth sentence as if timed to emphasize his point. "If you're pullin guard near a hole that's harmless and you see a fuckin slope crawl out with twenty pounds'a C-four and a goddamn detonator, it's an illusion. The whole country's an illusion."

The guy behind me whistled under his breath.

The report of an outgoing artillery round went through the soles of my feet.

He marched us to a Quonset hut with a sign that read REPO DEPOT, where he turned us over to three spec fours who casually thumbed through files. When my name was called, my interviewer motioned me onto a foldout chair. His name tag read Hoffman. An unlit cigarette dangled from his lips as he opened my file to the test scores.

He studied the numbers. "These aren't infantryman scores. Elkins, can you type?"

"No."

"How'd you end up in the infantry?"

"Lucky, I guess."

"You're going to find this hard to believe, Elkins," he said, "but I'm like God, life and death right here." He held up a ballpoint pen.

"I don't find anything hard to believe," I said.

He lit his cigarette and exhaled. "Rifleman," he said and looked away. He ran his finger over a list on a clipboard. "After charm school, you'll be going to the Wolfhounds. You're lucky."

"How's that?" I asked.

"You'll get to meet new people on a regular basis if you live long enough." He stamped a series of forms, initialed them, and shut the folder. "They've got about the highest casualty rate in 'Nam."

We fed at a nearby chow tent, after which we returned to the repo depot and, with files in hand, waited for rides. A deuce and a half crunched to a halt on the dry clay and spewed a knee-high cloud of orange dust. The driver of the truck said three of us belonged to "Thirty-fourth Armor." Two PFCS and a spec four tossed their gear in the bed. Others were cooks or quartermaster clerks or medics who, like the men in the armor unit, went straight to their assignments. Hoffman stepped outside and lit a cigarette. "You'll remember me in a week, Elkins," he said.

"Why's that?"

He walked away without answering. A moment later a sergeant stopped in a Jeep and got my attention. "You the one for charm school?"

All day and all night at twenty-second intervals a 155 mm artillery piece fired outgoing toward some nebulous point on the map—the Twenty-fifth's version of Western Union, thousands of dollars' worth daily. *Thaboo!* You could set your watch by the report. *Thaboo!* Sixteen paces while marching. *Thaboo!* Twenty-two normal heartbeats. *Thaboo!* Thirty-four heartbeats if exercising. A monotonous, maddening ritual, it soon became a comforting sound, a lullaby of sorts.

By the third day everything, including the sound of artillery, made me homesick. I thought of Betty, couldn't get her out of my mind. I pictured Willy scolding her, telling her she should be thankful to have a boyfriend like me—a fantasy doubled. Yet homesickness was the last thing I'd anticipated suffering. The in-countries were the first. They came on the fourth day, and when they hit, I tripped to the latrine every other hour to relieve my bowels.

We couldn't step outside and take in fresh air. There was no fresh air, only smells I never quite got used to. Each and every day somewhere someone was burning shit with gasoline. Black smoke billowed up and drifted over the compound and brought with it more stink. I got somewhat acclimated to the heat and learned different ways Charlie could kill a grunt, got used to the sounds of artillery rounds and bombs and bullets at night, but I didn't ever adjust to the smell of urine and feces, of dust and mildew, and eventually of death. At night I thought of Betty.

After charm school, where I was shown a few booby traps and land mines and informed of the 307 painful ways to die in 'Nam, I was officially ready to join my unit. I'd learned a whole new vocabulary—AO, dust-off, *di di mao,* boom-boom, *xin fuckin loi.* Though not a bit wiser than on my first day, I was measurably more scared. And Hoffman proved right; I remembered in less than the week predicted. Hoffman was already hated—a Rear Echelon Motherfucker who swilled beer or smoked grass and watched movies and when not, sneaked into the cardboard-shack village with a fistful of piastres to court a boom-boom girl. To forget him, I thought of Betty.

One night I met a door gunner at the E.M. Club. Over his fifth or sixth beer he told a story about his crew landing Vietnamese regulars into a hot LZ near Dak To. One froze in the seat and refused to stand. The gunner claimed he shot the man and tossed him out as the chopper gained altitude, said it was him or them, meaning the crew, and he didn't intend to wait until the Vietnamese got in touch with his manhood. The pilot, he alleged, gave him thumbs-up as he pushed the dead Vietnamese out. The next night I bumped into the same gunner at the same club. He told me not to believe anything he'd said the night before, that it was all bullshit. I told him I had a girlfriend named Betty who was the best-looking gal in Las Vegas. The door gunner nodded and turned to his beer as if to say he detected some more bullshit.

At dusk a rangy buck sergeant named Belcher approached me outside the temporary billets. He was as tall as I, but blade thin with gray eyes. "You Elkins?"

"Yes, Sergeant," I said.

He looked me over and said, "Belcher, just Belcher."

"Okay."

He told me to grab my duffel bag and follow.

The unit, he explained, was out in the boonies most of the time. At present the company was on a stand-down, but this was its last night. They were heading out to a new area of operations, which he called an AO. As we neared the squad tent, Belcher said, "We lost Humby and Naider. Guys won't talk much for a while. Don't push. They're okay."

An NCO in charm school had warned how FNGs were treated at first, how grunts often felt like a new guy was in some way connected to the death of a buddy or just plain bad luck. No logic—but this was 'Nam.

Belcher spread the tent flap. A naked bulb dangled from a tent post. Three bare-chested men played cards on a cot. They glanced up, then re-turned to the game. They were all frame and wire, no casing—field-hard-ened—and they glistened with sweat.

"This is Elkins," Belcher said.

They were unimpressed. I got a nod or grunt as Belcher named off the squad. The fire team leader was Rains, a reedy spec four whose smooth black skin seemed to have a gloss on it. There was Leonards, another black, called "C's"; Apple, the M-79 man, a white kid from West Virginia who'd been drafted by the Cleveland Indians his senior year in high school and drafted by the army after his first season in the minors; Johnson, a kid from Montana who'd never been out of the state until the army claimed him; and Orlándo Ésteban Rodríguez-Paéz, a draftee from El Paso. We were supposed to number eleven, but there were just six, and I was the seventh.

Paéz swung his feet down on the pallet. "Well, welcome to Three Corps, vacation spot of the tropics. Free tan, free food, free lodgings, and all the exercise a man could hope for."

C's reached under his cot without sitting up, pulled out an M-60, and rested its stock against the edge of the cot. "Big sonofabitch like him aughta carry the pig," he said to Belcher. "You said next man comes gets it."

Belcher handed the weapon to me. "You're our man. Get a crib. We're goin out tomorrow."

Paéz smiled, and I did the same only because Paéz had. I spread my poncho liner, lay down on top of the cot next to him, and pulled the mosquito net closed. He lay on his side, his head resting in his hand. "Where you from?"

"Las Vegas," I said.

"New Mexico?"

"No, the real one."

"Ah." He turned his back to me and muttered, "He's too damn big to go into tunnels."

"Paéz," Rains said, "it's in your blood."

"Time to dream," Paéz said.

The card game folded and the men fell silent as they packed and loaded rounds into magazines in preparation for the coming day. I looked about furtively, snatching peeks of them cleaning rifles or reading letters in the glow of the bare bulb. Guys away from home, like me.

Once the light was snapped off, they drifted to sleep, a sleep best likened to anesthesia. The 155s fired at normal intervals. I lay awake listening to them and thinking of Betty. I remembered her with her shirt opened, her arms leaned back supporting her as she looked up at the sky, her breasts firm, nipples erect. I wanted badly to masturbate, but didn't dare.

I awoke scared and looked around in the dark. The tent walls rippled in a slight breeze, but inside, the atmosphere was thick. Snoring flooded the room and sweaty animal smells filled the air. I lay, eyes open, staring at a crease in the tent. I tossed about, wondering if I would ever sleep well again.

36

We bent under the swirling props of a Huey. Belcher, face painted black and green, told me to clear the chopper as soon as we hit the landing zone, especially if it was a hot LZ, no dogging it. The M-60 was our lifeline, and I carried it. Belcher patted my helmet and swung into the seat to my right. Then we were hanging in a cloudless sky above a kelly-green quilt of rice paddies and berms, a work of cubism, streams, and hedgerows, and red-clay roads that crisscrossed.

Paéz, loaded down with bandoleers of 7.62 mm rounds, plus ammo for his own weapon, sat to my left. He smiled. I smiled back. "What you smiling at, meat?" he shouted.

The noise of the whirling blades sucked up words.

"Nothing!"

He removed his helmet and took a picture out of the liner, one of a girl with long black hair and big dark eyes. She was holding a cat and waving. "My girl!" he shouted.

I said my girl was named Betty. It seemed important to have one. He motioned to say he couldn't hear. I hollered that his girl was pretty. He put the picture away. Below, the most perilous stretch of road in the world, Highway 1, spanned north and south, flanked by towns and villages with names like Trang Bang and Chau Thanh and Ben Cua. To the west and south flowed the Vam Co Dong River . . . and to the north and east the Saigon snaked to the fertile Mekong Delta. To the east lay the Ia Drang Valley. I saw for the first time Nui Ba Dan, Black Virgin Mountain, at the verge of the Cambodian border, its peak encircled by clouds. It seemed something concocted to fit a fairy tale.

The squad was too preoccupied to take notice. They'd seén too much of it up close to show interest. The door gunner locked his fist on his own M-60 and leveled the barrel during the descent. As the ground rushed up, minute details grew to exaggerated proportions, like a slide brought into focus on a microscope. Before I expected it, the chopper rotated right and hovered about two feet off the ground.

Like crabs at low tide, we scrambled out. It was a chaotic drill. I followed Belcher through ankle-deep muck. I half hoped to take fire, just to get it over with, a desire that passed soon enough. I caught my toe on a rock, tripped, but kept my footing with Paéz's help. "Do that often?" he asked.

We set up on a berm, where I locked the butt of the pig into my shoulder. Except for scattered tufts of grass and mud pools, the field was sun-hardened clay. Flies swarmed everywhere. I sweated from places I'd never before sweated, sweated until I couldn't see. My ears were wet. I began to wonder just what the hell I'd gotten myself into. Sergeants ordered us to dig in and establish fire lanes. We took our chunk of earth like claim jumpers, elbowing our way into position, claiming the plot as if snatching lakefront property. Paéz stripped to the waist, grinned, then jabbed his entrenching tool into the clay. When I slipped off my shirt, he said I was too white for the sun. I muttered, tossed the shirt aside, and picked up my tool to dig. We worked silently, shoveling dirt into sandbags, which we stacked around the edge of the hole as it grew.

Breaking the silence, I asked, "Why'd you end up with me?"

Paéz smiled and looked up at the sun. "Gloria."

"Your girl?"

"My charm. I figure Charlie's gonna kill someone, and it'll be you and not me."

"That makes no sense."

"Look around, meat. Nothing here makes sense."

A platoon of engineers came in with the next wave of choppers and encircled the camp with concertina. The air was still and hot, but we kept at our tasks. There was no respite from the sun until the holes were deep enough. Before the engineers finished stringing the last of three aprons of wire, the company had dug in, and one at a time tent halves and ponchos blossomed above the foxholes. The camp looked like a landfill covered with olive-green flags.

Paéz and I sat on the brim of the pit, our legs dangling over. "You got a girl, Elkins?"

I started to say yes, but changed my mind. I decided to let that lie go. "No."

He considered this as he looked at me. "You look like the kind who gets dumped."

I answered, "Hole looks pretty small."

"Fits me," Paéz said. "I've been in tunnels a quarter that size. Looks like you've got some digging left before it'll fit you." He explained that before the draft, he'd studied mining engineering at the University of Texas, El Paso, and this, in part, accounted for his interest in tunnels.

Choppers from Cu Chi landed with hot food and iced beer. We carried mess kits to the chow line. Ignoring me, Paéz kidded with the others. Later, we sat on our helmets and ate beef stew, creamed spinach, and cobbler cooked with canned peaches. I asked about his girl to make conversation. Paéz swallowed and aimed his fork. "I'll marry her and raise a dozen kids." He glanced about. "When I get out of this fucking place."

I took a bite and stared off.

"I know what you're thinking. Does Paéz always talk like this? I get on people's nerves."

Cox, the platoon sergeant, brought a second ration of beer. "Get your smoking done now," he ordered.

"Sarge, the *Stars and Stripes*. The army expect us to live without scores?" Paéz asked.

"Paéz, does the army ever forget the *Stars and Stripes*?"

"Could be. The mail's sometimes a little lost."

Cox asked if I was getting along okay. Paéz answered for me, saying I was fine.

"What next?" I asked when Cox had left.

"Nothing, and a lot of it. Get used to it, meat."

"Name's Pete. Rhymes, anyway."

Paéz shrugged me off and looked west where the sun bled into the horizon and a halo of red capped the tip of Nui Ba Dan. He nodded, something wild gamboling in his eyes. He swallowed his beer, crushed the can on his helmet, and said in a near whisper, "Civilization underground, hospitals, fueling stations, whorehouses. I am not a little crazy."

That night I slept fitfully, partly from fear, mostly from sunburn and visions of Betty. I thought to write her, saying she'd ruined three lives. In the morning I reconsidered that idea.

The fire base was in Tay Ninh Province east of War Zone C fourteen kilometers from the Cambodian border. It was the dry season and hot. A shovelful at a time, holes expanded into bunkers connected by intricate trenches linked like lacework. Dust abounded, a fine, choking dust that hung over the camp. It infiltrated our pores, our noses, and lungs; it pursued us into our sleep and greeted us at dawn.

Boom-boom girls from nearby villages posed around the perimeter, ready to trade themselves for money or cigarettes, all charting our defenses. Dressed in colorful silk, they looked delicate at a distance, but up close were sun-darkened country girls with brown teeth that showed when they giggled. It would have been okay if they'd carried spiked clubs and looked like Russian potato farmers. Johnson expressed the prevailing opinion when he said, "It's hard to find red-blooded American gals willing to do the same." Lonely and young and scared, we sought comfort and sex. If one of us wanted a girl, he went over the berm with a boom-boom girl, but took rifle and buddies along to stand guard, for in Tay Ninh everyone not American was VC.

Idle moments led to talk about home, shared experience, growing up, girlfriends, words that made me long for Las Vegas, long for Betty. When I got lonely enough, I went to the berm, where I fantasized that the woman under me was her. When I finished, I felt a terrible sense of shame. I didn't want to feel that way, but did. I promised, no more. But what else was there? I tried writing letters, but knowing some REMF clerk would be reading my words inhibited me. So everything I wrote sounded plastic. I would write a letter and tear it up. I decided on a log and passed the time jotting down observations, thinking someday it would come in handy.

"Five shovelfuls of clay fill one sandbag. The tip of Nui Ba Dan is often circled by doughnut clouds. Belcher must masturbate at night or he can't sleep. Paéz wakes up whenever he starts snoring. The sound of bombs dumped by a B-52 on the far side of the mountain takes four seconds to reach us after the initial blast."

I stored the journal in my backpack, allowing no one to see it.

37

When we came out of the rubber plantation, we realized it was a bad spot. Open paddies spread before us and there was no cover. The platoon formed a column and headed out, Elsworth heading it some twenty-five paces out. Belcher advanced, then Paéz. Fifteen feet behind, I carried the M-60. Leonards spat on his hands for luck.

Elsworth's trousers were black from wading through the rice fields. His jaw had a three-day stubble and his eyes a nine-month hunger. He knew signs and could smell and hear like an animal. He motioned for us to stop and climbed the wall of a paddy to see the other side. Atop, he crouched, his head swiveling, nose turned up as if sniffing the wind.

Paéz said something to distract me. Elsworth motioned it was okay, and we stood. Then something invisible knocked him off the dike, hard and solid, like an unexpected right uppercut. An immeasurable instant later an unmistakable pop came from the far wood line. We bellied down onto the ground. Shaking, I jammed the butt of the pig into my shoulder. Paéz crawled over to say, "Welcome to the show, meat."

Willy's offer rang in the back of my head.

It was Pham Cua on some maps, Bui Cua on others, a village, nothing, seven huts, a dozen women and children, brown spotted chickens bobbing heads, the smell of Vietnam all over it. The squad had called on Pham Cua before, seen the inviolable expressions on the villagers' faces, stares that communicated scorn. We searched huts for caches, found nothing, and left, taking a well-worn trail to the west. At a clearing overlooking the rice paddies, Belcher raised a hand overhead. "Smoke 'em if you got 'em," he said, knelt, and clamped his own lips on a cigarette.

We scattered among the boulders, all but Paéz, who was taking in the sights. Happy to unload it, I lowered the M-60 and propped it against a boulder. I'd lugged it too long already. It was a sweat-maker, a ball-buster, a cross, and I had yet to fire it. Diaphanous thermals shimmered on the emerald paddies below. The glassy pools mirrored the blue sky and scattered clouds that floated overhead. To the west the verdant land spooled into a rocky escarpment where the vegetation congealed into a dark green curtain too intense for the intellect to grasp.

"Find a rock, Paéz," Belcher said.

Paéz turned ninety degrees and framed a picture with his hands, a cigarette dangling from his lips. "Wish I had a camera."

"Goddamn it, Paéz," Belcher said.

Apple stood to shrug out of the straps that held the radio. The round, sounding more like a ping than a shot, struck the PRC-25 and slammed Apple and the radio to the ground. Belcher shouted at Paéz to get down, but Paéz just held the cigarette to his lips and gazed nonchalantly at the woods.

A second shot whistled off a boulder, but Paéz didn't move, just kept smoking until a third sprayed dust near his feet. Then he pointed his finger where the jungle tapered to a crest. Taking a final draw, he flipped the cigarette aside and headed toward the woods, strolling like a sightseer.

"He on drugs, Elkins?" Rains asked.

"Just crazy," I said.

Belcher hollered for Apple to get a spotter plane up. Apple shouted that the sniper had killed the radio. "Tell the goddamn world," Belcher said.

Paéz pointed to his crotch. "Hit this, you slit-eyed motherfucker," he said, raised his middle finger to the sniper, and began singing "La Cucaracha."

"Get 'im, Paéz!" Leonards shouted.

Belcher ordered full rock and roll. We unloaded on the woods for thirty seconds, pulverized leaves and branches, chiseled stones and chewed roots and scattered nearby animal life all the way to Thailand, after which the quiet that came seemed holy. Paéz walked back, flopped down behind a rock, and lit another cigarette. Closing his eyes, he took a long, deep draw.

Belcher grabbed him by the collar and lifted him to his feet. "Can't a guy just enjoy a damned smoke?" Paéz asked. "I mean, without someone trying to shoot him or yanking him by the collar?"

The sniper fired another round just to let us know.

A Chicom 7.63 ripped a perfect round hole in Johnson's helmet, and until the medic removed it, no one could tell he'd been hit. Simpson, a new guy, walked two steps away and puked in a rice paddy. Later we swept a village where the indigies looked at us as if they knew all about Johnson, where he'd come from, the color of his mother's hair, every detail, including the name of the doctor who gave him his first swat.

Monks, a guy in the first squad who hung with Johnson, lifted up an old man's chin and said, "Nice day. How'd you like your old dick shot off?" His eyes puffed full of hate, he stuffed the sight blade down the front of the old *ong's* pajama bottoms and stared. But the old man didn't seem to care one way or the other.

Belcher sat on a log and propped up his leg, making himself comfortable. He lit a Winston and told Monks to make sure the M-16 wasn't on full auto because it would make a terrible mess, then he blew a stream of smoke up at the sky. He puffed on his cigarette and dreamed of fields of corn and pumpkins in October—or whatever, on such occasions, went through the mind of a Kansas farm boy.

Monks flicked the selector switch. He intended to emasculate the old man, and no one in the platoon moved to prevent it until a kid named Benjamin laid a hand on his shoulder and said, "Be easy, be sound, man. Ain't worth it. Come on, now, think about what your mama would think if you was to harm this ol' fella."

Benjamin was right—it wasn't worth it. We took body count, the Vietcong kept score.

As he drew away, Monks stared over his shoulder at the old man. "Got VC goddamned tattooed on his ass. I know," he said. "Hell, we all know." He ran a thumb up and down the barrel of his M-16, shouting that he'd remember that old man, that one day he'd see him again.

Belcher finished his smoke and ordered the squad to search. We'd dumped over baskets and were bayoneting piles of straw when the rest of the platoon appeared. The lieutenant ordered us out, claimed the indigies were friendly. I wondered how the hell he knew. Was it indexed on the map?

Half a klick from the village a group of boys, the eldest probably ten, greeted us. We craved anything American, the most mundane things—hamburgers, hot showers, ice cream, a girl in tight jeans, the smell of new-mown grass. Here we had kids vending oversweet soft drinks and tasteless rice cakes, but they bartered with irresistible, grinning faces. "Hey, Joe, numba one sweet, same, same, boom boom. You buy." Kids being a weakness of ours, we bought soft drinks and sweets.

I gazed at Nui Ba Dan, ringed in clouds. I thought of the clouded peaks of the Bitterroots and Betty and summer in Montana—a night when I heard the splash of urine in the bathroom and I reached over and ran my hand up and down the sheet where she'd lain. It was warm and smelled of her. Intimate, wonderful.

Rain puddled on the floor of the bunker. We sat cross-legged on cots as Apple passed the pipe to Paéz, who took a languorous hit and held the smoke deep in his lungs. He passed the pipe to me. I took a hit and passed it on, just as we were passing time while the monsoon drummed outside.

Everything was damp now, the whole camp a mound of mold. Mildew formed on T-shirts overnight. The fire base was a huge fungus. Some acrimonious grunt had named it Green Acres, which became its designation and was decidedly appropriate. We hung a sign that read, WELCOME TO GREEN ACRES, HOME OF THE JOLLY GREEN GIANT AND A FEW UGLY ELVES.

"How come you got no picture of Gloria, Paéz?" Apple asked.

Paéz, who'd lost the picture in a tunnel, exhaled and leaned back, letting the drug take him. "Got her up here," he said, pointing to his head.

"Probably the only place she's ever been."

Paéz gave Apple a glassy-eyed look. "Don't mess with her. Fuck with my food or water. Gloria's off-limits."

I took another hit and passed the pipe.

"Yeah, leave the man alone, Apple," Rains said. "It's sacred. Scripture say a man and woman be each other's temple."

Apple's face glowed like a white moon in the thin light of the gas lantern. "Here we go. The Bible. What's it say about the goddamn monsoon? Tell us a story."

Besides days rolling one into the next and the ever-present sight of Nui Ba Dan, continuity existed mostly in our stories. C's ordered a travel guide to the best inns in Europe and read the itinerary as if he were leaving the next week; Apple got drunk, fell into a foxhole, and slept through a mortar barrage; Belcher fished a stream with a hand grenade.

"Got no story."

The pipe went the circuit again. As Apple reloaded it from his stash, he asked what day of the week it was. No one seemed quite sure. It wasn't a Friday or Saturday and not a Sunday, which Rains kept track of. For no good reason, we settled on Tuesday. Apple puffed off the pipe and nudged Belcher's forearm. Apple coughed out the smoke. "Where were we? Days?"

"Elkins knows," Belcher said. "He's keeping track of every shit he takes. Puts it in his journal. Things thicker 'an a . . ." He gazed at me, his eyes dope-thick, and asked what it was thicker than.

"Thicker than the bullshit," I said.

We were operating above the plantation lands. The days had been mostly lucky after Johnson's death. Near Chau Thanh the company had lost three on an operation with an ARVN battalion when the Vietnamese didn't block the retreating VC, and the platoon lost two on a sweep through a village east of Nui Ba Dan. But our squad was charmed.

The pages in my journal had become frayed and fat. The cover warped. I recorded what I could, though every event seemed part of a continuum—the same villages, the same trails in a palling cycle—and wherever we went, if there were holes Paéz checked them out. Any progress in the war had little effect on us. At least we couldn't tell any difference. Body count didn't matter. A dozen, a hundred, two hundred dead didn't stop the war, didn't slow it, and the only territory we could rightfully claim was in front of our sight blades. We held what we held because of firepower. This was absolute. Our platoon could dispense as much havoc as one of Genghis Khan's entire armies, but all it did was keep some of us alive to the next day.

Paéz passed on the pipe, as did Rains. Leonards, who'd been silent, sat holding the pipe in his lap. He said he needed a new charm. His were wearing out. Water trickled down the sandbag wall behind his head. "Take Pete," Paéz said. "He dropped out of school, ran away and joined the army. Talks about a girl in his sleep, but won't talk about her to his best friend. Man's memories are sacred too."

The pipe went out as it came to Apple. He leaned near the lantern as he lit it, his face contoured with flickering shadows. "Thick as bullshit," he said.

"We shouldn't get high. It's un-military," Belcher said.

"What's that got to do with Gloria?" Apple asked.

Belcher shook his head. "Who's Gloria?"

"You ever saw her, you'd go crazy," Paéz said. A drip of water splattered his nose. He stared at the leak. "Are we sick of rain? Why're you so damn quiet?"

I shrugged. I was thinking about being dry, being in the dry heat of the Mojave, a mild autumn, red-rocked rims and sparse vegetation. I remembered a letter I'd written to Miriam, a short, cautious fabrication, telling her I was in a safe place, that I'd landed a job as a clerk and spent most of my time reading. I'd asked if there was news of Alan, told her to kiss Esther for me, and requested paperbacks and ointment for athlete's foot.

"I got books coming," I announced to Paéz.

"You hear 'bout Noah and the Ark. 'At's more rain 'an we'd ever see," Rains said.

"What's Noah got to do with anything?" Paéz asked.

"Man can't complain, is all. Bunch of sinners. An books don't make you no less'a one."

Paéz put on his helmet to block the drip. "You know, Rains, we said no religion. Who's hogging the pipe?"

"Know what I think?" Apple asked and passed the pipe.

Paéz sucked on the dead pipe. "Needs a reload, Belcher," he said, then to Apple, "What do you think?"

"This sounds like a bunch of fucked-up dope talk."

We bent over laughing. Belcher repacked the pipe with hash. As he leaned to pass it to Paéz, a mortar round exploded somewhere outside. Rains doused the lantern, and Paéz missed the handoff. As the pipe splashed into ankle-deep water, he shouted, "Shit! We'll never find it now."

"Charlie's got no respect for a man. I mean, what's sacred?" Apple said.

"Ah-fucking-men," Paéz said.

Another mortar round hit the camp.

"Let's get," Belcher said as a third exploded, this one closer.

"Shee-it," Apple said.

We headed into the rain-soaked trench. Stumbling and sliding in mud on the way, I asked why Paéz told the squad about me talking in my sleep. "Don't you just love the rain?" he answered. "It purifies the world, don't you think?"

The fire had come from an area infested with tunnels, so we rounded up the villagers. Noticeably absent were young men, as if some singular pestilence had descended on the country and claimed every living male between the ages of sixteen and fifty. Belcher radioed the fire base to say we had command of fifty indigenous personnel, whom we called "gooks" or "slopes" or "indigies," for it was easier to herd indigies out of their homes and torch huts than to make humans suffer.

The indigies gazed at us with patient expressions, the kind only long-suffering people possess. Compliantly, they moved into a clearing, took the offered cigarettes, and squatted down. Young women nursed their infants, old *Bas*, the grandmothers of the village, chewed betel nut, old men smoked. They'd seen conquerors—the Japanese, the French—and knew what was required.

Apple used his Zippo to light the skirt of a thatched roof. Division had a policy against torching huts, but there were no generals in the field. We dumped incendiaries inside the huts and the villagers squatted down and watched their homes being consumed in orange flame. In 'Nam fire just seemed hotter and smoke seemed blacker. As they stared into the flames, the villagers' eyes said they would return to rebuild. They wanted only for us to leave so they could pack up what little they had and carry it to a relocation center. Leonards said the squad was "pissin off the get-even god." Belcher shrugged. It was hard to figure the moral high ground.

The smell of charred straw and wood drifted from the village. Nearby we found a tunnel. After shedding backpack and bandoleers, Paéz pulled out his flashlight and took the lieutenant's .45. He tied himself to the running end of the rope, raised a hand to me, and squirmed into the opening. As we smoked, Rains fed out line. From time to time he tugged on it. Paéz had been down twenty minutes. Then Rains had no more rope to feed and found it had gone slack. Belcher removed his helmet and sat down by the hole. The lieutenant said to give the line a tug. Rains wrapped the rope around his wrist and reeled it in. The squad crowded around, peering down as he gathered in rope an arm's length at a time until the running end hung over the opening.

"Call him up," the lieutenant said.

Belcher squatted over the hole, cupped his hands to his mouth, and pausing in between, hollered Paéz's name three times. "Maybe he's lost." Still looking down the hole, Belcher stood.

The lieutenant said they could borrow Simmons from another platoon to go down and take a look-see. "He'll come out," Belcher said.

"I'll go down," C's said.

The lieutenant shook his head. "Ten minutes, then we get Simmons."

Belcher reluctantly agreed and gave another call.

"What's all the shouting?"

Paéz stood next to Apple, who hadn't taken notice.

"Where the hell'd you go?" the lieutenant demanded.

Paéz said he came up where a *papa-san* was staring him in the eye like he was expected. "I shook his hand and wished him a nice vc day," Paéz said.

The lieutenant said, "Blow the hole."

As we plodded through the entrance to Green Acres, Paéz said, "There's one that runs to Hanoi and back to Saigon. We just haven't found it."

38

The field was like something cooked to a lumpy paste and dumped on a plate to spoil, with flies everywhere. Paéz crossed himself and kissed his fingers. "I thought you didn't believe," I said.

"I don't," Paéz said.

Medics issued stretchers and body bags, handed out a balm to apply to our nostrils, and dispensed advice—wear bandannas and watch for unexploded rounds while digging for bodies. I stepped out and immediately sank to my ankles. Flies blitzed about so thick we could reach out and grab them by the handful. Some guys walked away to puke.

Paéz told me to grab a pair of legs. We turned the body over to lay him face up and zip him in a bag. It was like lifting a barrel of water. At the count of three we hoisted him onto the stretcher, then grabbed the handles and picked up the load. We heard a moan and unloaded the stretcher. The body rolled back into the hole, where it lay motionless, its blank face seemingly indignant but dead, very dead. Paéz noticed dirt shifting beside the body and dived down on hands and knees, digging at the earth furiously with both hands, pitching fountains of loose dirt into the air. "He's alive," he said. "Alive. Imagine!"

I shouted for a medic and joined him, digging until we unearthed a man as thin as a wheat stalk. His pulse weak, but a pulse nonetheless, he lay gasping for air. I sprinkled canteen water on him and gently wiped away dirt so he could see. Like Lazarus, he'd been to the other side and could tell the tale with his eyes. When they opened, he looked at us and tried to squirm away. This wasn't quite the Vietcong heaven he'd anticipated waking up in. Paéz told him to take it easy, as if he understood, and said a doctor was coming. Soon a medic was cutting away the uniform with surgical scissors and checking the wounds.

"How bad, Doc?" Paéz asked.

"Shrapnel," the medic said, "in the upper back." He probed the man's back. The vc was tough, showed no pain, though he had to be feeling plenty. "And a piece . . . near the spine." His hands sure and quick, the medic started an IV and cleaned our man—for by then he was ours. He bandaged the wounds and shot morphine into the feeder tube. He said he'd call a dust-off ASAP and told us to cart the man to the helipad.

Apple and C's peered down.

"You the luckiest fucker in 'Nam," C's said.

Word of the miracle spread. A modest crowd gathered to watch as we hoisted our man onto the stretcher. We toted him to the LZ, where we guarded him jealously as others came to have a look-see. Some reached down to shake his hand. Others touched him gently or stuck packs of cigarettes or chewing gum on the stretcher beside him. One scratched initials on a bullet and put it in the man's hand. Others simply looked and shook their heads. Awe on every face. The lieutenant hung around after his peek. "Don't you two think he'll be okay?"

"Sir?" Paéz asked.

"Do you have to . . . ? I mean . . ."

"Sir, we pulled him out," Paéz said. He held a lighted cigarette up to Lucky's mouth.

The lieutenant nodded. "So you did. Carry on."

We took turns keeping his lips moist with canteen water and holding cigarettes for him while he smoked. As we lifted him onto the helicopter, he looked up and said, *"Chet roi,"* meaning dead.

We settled down to nap, though it was nearly impossible. The heat was despotic, and the smell of dead bodies permeated everything. Paéz wrote Gloria telling her what a beautiful day it was and how he'd made a friend. He read the letter aloud. I asked how he could lie like that.

"It's what she wants to hear. If you had a girl, you'd know."

Two Chinooks landed. Out of their bellies came two bulldozers, followed by a unit of combat engineers, who donned masks and went to work. The company sat atop bunkers and watched the bulldozers scuttle back and forth, puffing spouts of diesel smoke and plowing with a tireless energy as if there wasn't enough dirt in all of Vietnam for them to move. Methodically, they rent a hole wide enough and deep enough to accommodate the dead.

The pit finished, the operators turned their machines to the bodies, after which three medics poured gas over the remains. A sergeant pulled the pin on an incendiary, looked away from the mass grave, lobbed in the grenade; the trench burst into a wall of flame and black smoke. Sitting a hundred yards away, we felt heat as the sky blackened. When the fire died, the bulldozers plowed again and the flies swarmed the camp. Paéz said Green Acres was a perfect name for a cemetery.

Battalion helicoptered in hot food, beer on ice, and a movie, *The Sound of Music,* along with a dispatch praising the company. The men filled their trays, but picked at the food. Rains stared at the mound and muttered— about what, we couldn't tell. Belcher lit a joint and passed it, and Rains, who'd never smoked dope in his life, took a draw.

"*The Sound of Music?*" Apple said. "Who the fuck's in charge of this war? I mean, really."

In my journal I wrote: "Today the captain said we killed seventy-two, but didn't mention the one we saved, whose name was probably Nguyen; they're all named Nguyen. He smoked too much. Paéz lied to Gloria. Rains lost God." I had so many stories. I thought, who would I want to hear them? Willy? Maybe. Betty? Then, soft in my head, Betty.

A kid named Newman came back from R&R. Somehow he'd ended up in Hawaii by mistake. He met a nurse, he said, and shacked up with her for four days. He walked around letting anyone who wanted to sniff his fingers, claimed it was the smell of round-eyed pussy, grade-A American. He said he was thinking about cutting off a finger and preserving it. When he told this to us, Apple said, "Why don't you cut your dick off and preserve it?"

"Soreheads. Just jealous. I'm probably the only grunt in the history of this fucking war who got to Hawaii."

"Cut your dick off anyhow," Belcher said.

Paéz set down Malory's *Tales of King Arthur*, which he'd picked up from some helicopter pilot in trade for a Montagnard crossbow. "Guy's full of it," he said.

I looked up from cleaning my M-60. "So."

"I been thinking," he said. "We're subterranean by nature. We long to be inside things. The womb is our first home. A cave. A blanket's a womb. What's the first thing you want to do with a woman? Get inside of her, see what's hidden beneath her clothes. Another cave."

"What's the point?"

"The point? There is no fucking point."

"Do you write Gloria about going into tunnels?"

He took a drag off his cigarette and stared off toward Nui Ba Dan. "That mountain's full of tunnels. Most dug by the Viet Minh. A regiment could hide in them. Hospitals. Barracks. Service clubs with beer on tap. Health spas. Hotels with maid service. Tile entries. Baths like Romans had. It's a big mountain. Think of the possibilities." He crushed the cigarette out on a sandbag and turned to me. "I write her about blue skies and dumb grunts like Newman." He looked at the mountain, its peak covered with wispy clouds. "Let's put in for R&R in Hawaii. You, me, on a beach. Gloria'll meet us. Bring one of her cousins, one of the less fat ones."

"Hawaii? You heard what Newman said." I touched some oil to the trigger housing.

"He's full of shit."

That afternoon we signed up at the headquarters tent for R&R. Marshall, the company clerk, a draftee from Mendocino, said, "That's where the officers go." He was a small man with unmilitary sideburns.

"That's where we want to go," Paéz said.

"Officers and high-ranking noncoms. Grunts like you could be an embarrassment."

"An embarrassment? Pete knows important people. He's got a cousin in Congress. MAC-V wouldn't want an inquiry over R&R, would it?"

"Who's Pete?"

"Elkins." Paéz aimed an index finger at me. "This guy, my buddy."

Marshall looked me over.

"Don't let his appearance fool you," Paéz said. "I've seen pictures of him in a tux at the governor's ball."

Marshall shook his head. "Not likely." He handed over the forms to fill out. "Look, I don't care, but get this straight—you're not going there. This is the fucking army, and the army doesn't send grunts to Hawaii for R&R."

We were summoned to headquarters to see Lieutenant Bredlau, the company executive officer, who tossed the requests down on the table. Marshall, sitting there for the occasion, poured himself a soft drink and downed it in two gulps. He was grinning at us. "It's not policy, exactly," the lieutenant said, "but enlisted men don't go to Hawaii. Not grunts."

"Sir, they let REMFs go, at least that's what I've heard, and they're nothing but butt licks," Paéz said.

Bredlau shook his head. "Bangkok. All the whores you'd ever want, Paéz."

"Hawaii, sir."

"And you, Elkins?"

"Hawaii."

"Paéz, you think being a tunnel rat gives you license around here?"

"Sir, just the privilege of going down."

"Well, it doesn't."

"How about you, Elkins? You think you're privileged?"

"Sir, it's privilege enough to serve in Green Acres, sir."

Marshall went into coughing spasms. Lieutenant Bredlau told him to go outside and get some water. He said to me, "I'm not laughing." He weighed matters thoughtfully and asked, "What's your cousin's name?"

"Cousin, sir?" I said.

"The one in Congress."

"He'd rather not say, sir," Paéz said.

Lieutenant Bredlau shuffled papers from one side of the table to the other. "I'd rather he say."

"Sir, if it's all the same, I promised I wouldn't," but it suddenly occurred that Hawaii might not be such a fantasy, for Willy knew senators and congressmen. He'd introduced me to more than one on occasions when they'd eaten lunch with him.

"It's not all the same." With a shrug, Lieutenant Bredlau signed the forms. "Not until March," he said. "And there's a good chance you'll go to Bangkok or Singapore."

On our way out Marshall grabbed my arm. "You really have a cousin in Congress?"

"Would Paéz lie?"

"How would I know?"

"You wouldn't," I said, then asked, "can you get me a call stateside?" I figured Willy would appreciate a ring. Besides, Betty had been in my thoughts. I'd even composed letters to her, which of course I never sent.

"Maybe," Marshall said. "I'm interested in Hawaii."

"Planning on deserting?" Paéz asked.

"Put in a request," I said.

"Same time as you guys?"

"Sure," Paéz said. "Tell the lieutenant you're in, but don't expect one of Gloria's cousins."

We left Marshall asking who Gloria was.

Though we could see barely twenty feet ahead, we scaled Black Virgin Mountain. The trails were steep and slippery. Division had sent handlers with three German shepherds to sniff out the enemy, but a third of the way up the animals began to cough. The mountain was too rough, a handler explained. One dog coughed up pink foam. Its handler stroked it and talked gently, but it died anyhow—pulmonary arrest, the medic said. The lieutenant sent the dogs back.

Not far from where the dogs gave out we came upon a tunnel, a deep one.

"We can just blow it," the lieutenant said, which was only a formality, as Paéz never refused.

Paéz looked up at the black sky, then at the lieutenant and nodded to indicate he'd go. We hadn't eaten, so the lieutenant called for a chow break first and the men opened their Cs and began to eat. Paéz took my Oreos and Rains's peaches and wolfed them down. Finished, he stripped off his poncho and gear. C's unhooked the tiger's claw from his neck and put it around Paéz's.

"Luck, man," he said.

"Don't untie," the lieutenant ordered.

Rope about his waist and flashlight and gun in hand, Paéz disappeared just as the clouds burst. Rain beat on the forest with a sound as deafening as a waterfall, and water channeled down trails transformed into rivers. The mountain seemed alive. We kept one eye on the trail and one on the tunnel, while wishing we had a third to watch the mountain.

We were startled when the rope went slack and Paéz popped out of the hole unexpectedly. He scrambled away, shivering, his lips chalk-white. He held the gun, but the flashlight was gone. He pointed at the opening, said, "Blow it," and stumbled to the side, where he sat down on a boulder and stared at his feet.

Rains and Apple tossed in concussion grenades. The hole, like a gaping mouth, spat out dirt and black smoke as the explosions went off. The lieutenant ordered us to head down. Only then did Paéz look up. "What'd you see down there?" Belcher asked.

Paéz shook his head. "Can't see in the dark."

He removed the tiger's claw necklace and tossed it to C's, then didn't move. I handed over his gear and helped him to his feet.

We stayed two more days at the base of Nui Ba Dan, and Paéz kept to himself and wouldn't talk. His smile was gone. Rains and Apple urged me to find out what had happened, but two attempts earned a mere shrug. As we loaded onto Hueys to return to Green Acres, Paéz told the lieutenant that he wasn't going down anymore but refused to say why.

39

In January we were helicoptered to Cu Chi for a stand-down. I was glad to leave behind Green Acres and the smell of death that never quite dissipated. But though the camp was behind, the reminders of death seemed stronger. C's claimed the field was haunted; few doubted that.

Division billeted C Company near the motor pool, home to the armored personnel carriers called "tracks." There, diesel oil and solvents mixed with the odors of Cu Chi and human sweat made breathing unpalatable. We strung up a net and played volleyball and smoked dope and drank beer as rumors circulated—operations north, supposedly in Binh Long or a search-and-destroy in the Delta or the Iron Triangle.

It was a sweltering day, too hot to do anything. The walls of the tent were raised to capture whatever gypsy air decided to slip through. Occasionally a breeze informed us that Cu Chi smelled no better than Green Acres. Paéz lay on his cot scanning the *Stars and Stripes* as I field-stripped the pig and cleaned it. He lit a Lucky Strike. His smile had returned, and though he refused to discuss Nui Ba Dan, he was talking again. He snapped the paper. "The Great Gringo says we're turning the war around."

"You don't say," I said absentmindedly.

"No, I don't. The Prez does. Trouble with gringos is they don't listen. It's straight from his lips. War's all but over. That all right?"

"Doesn't matter."

Paéz rolled his legs over the edge of the cot and sat up. "What does?"

"Jock itch," I said. "Athlete's foot, sore arches, rash, leech bites, and a dose if I could find a whore."

"I've been thinking about Lucky," Paéz said. "Let's pay a hospital visit and see what happened to him."

"How the hell would they remember one vc?"

Paéz drew on his cigarette and used the tip to burn a hole in the photo of Lyndon Johnson. He blew smoke at the ceiling and spread the paper. "An unmanned craft landed on the moon—over two weeks ago. The Great Gringo wants a ten percent surcharge on taxes to lower the budget deficit. He means, of course, to finance the war."

Paéz lowered the paper. "We'd win this if they hired the Mexican Army. Trouble is Americans feel too underpaid to get themselves killed. Take a Mexican, he'd gladly go out and get himself killed for this kind of money." He turned to the sports page. "Green Bay Beats Oakland. Oakland, where all those antiwar punks smoke dope and get laid." Paéz looked over the top of the paper. "You may as well be my wife."

"You don't have one."

"But I will. And you, pathetic gringo, will die old with shriveled balls."

Sergeant Cox, his fatigues black with sweat from his hefting the mailbag, threw open the flap, looked around, and sniffed. "What's that smell?" he asked and dropped the bag on a cot.

I said, "The rose of Southeast Asia."

"Elkins, you're starting to sound like Paéz."

Paéz tossed the paper aside and asked if he had mail—though there always was—his mother, his sisters, or Gloria. Cox said, "Do I bother to look, Paéz?" which was what he said to anyone who asked before the mail was handed out.

"Ah, Sarge, you look for sexy stuff so you can pound your pud. Everyone knows."

"You're a draftee, aren't you, Paéz?" Cox asked.

"Guilty," Paéz answered.

Cox shook his head and tossed two letters to Paéz. "Be thankful for the war. Peacetime army wouldn't put up with your shit."

"I'm very thankful, Sarge."

"Elkins, you got a letter." Cox, who'd not yet been promoted to sergeant first class, blamed our squad, which he claimed was full of mutinous dope fiends. He flipped an envelope to me, turned the remaining mail over to Paéz, and said, "Tell Belcher to get the tent cleaned up."

The envelope, addressed in a flowing cursive, had been taped closed by the censors. I broke the seal. Embossed in bold lettering on white linen paper was an invitation to join in celebration as Betty A. Bobbins and James A. Norber take vows before God and man, the wedding to take place February 2, 1968, at 7:30 P.M. Enclosed was an RSVP envelope. Not even Rich! A bead of sweat trickled from my nose and splattered on the splendid white paper. Folding it in two, I stuffed it in my shirt pocket.

Shouting came from near the motor pool. I walked to the tent flap to see what it was about. Some REMFs were getting up a game of softball. They tossed the ball around to warm up, which seemed ludicrous since every muscle needed to play would be overheated by the time they got around to playing. I asked Paéz if he wanted to go watch. He looked up from his letter. "Gloria says she'll meet us. No cousins, but you, her, me in Hawaii, on the beach."

I wondered how he'd feel if he got a wedding invitation from Gloria. I said grunts didn't go to Hawaii and he could get all the tan he wanted in 'Nam.

"Very cynical. What came in the mail?"

"Nothing. A card." I said I was going to watch the game.

He lay back to reread his letter. I stuffed my hands in my pockets and aimed toward the makeshift diamond. The pop of the leather ball in their gloves was a piece of home. A player hollered that they were short a man. I shook my head, ambled to the center of the compound, and loitered by the mess hall until I spotted a latrine that wasn't burning. I took out the invitation, read it several times, brushed my fingers over the splendid embossed lettering. I held it to my nose and took in the orchid smell, reminiscent of an altar. Then I wadded it into a ball, dumped it in the cavity, and unbuttoned my fly.

In the early morning of January 31, Cu Chi came under a mortar attack. Division was near full strength, as most field units had been lifted out of the plateau. Sappers tried to breach the perimeter, but failed; this was followed by more incoming. In the distance to the south the battle for Tan Son Nhut erupted and in the predawn mechanized units were sent out to break the assault on the air base, whose outer defenses had been breached.

The next day C Company camped by the helipad ready to go out. Paéz and I sat in harness back to back, napping under ponchos. Belcher told the squad the whole AO was on fire, which seemed pretty self-evident as Division artillery fired outgoing every two or three seconds and from dawn to dusk naval guns were pelting the corridor between Cu Chi and Tay Ninh.

At nightfall a strict blackout was enforced and the company was posted on the perimeter, where I caught random flashes of the distant battles. Just before dawn the camp filled with a sense of urgency as the tracks warmed up and helicopters throttled to life. Almost immediately the first of the Hueys lifted off like bees abandoning a hive.

Tracks soon departed the gate, a harsh grinding of diesel engines marking their passage. Artillery continued to blast away relentlessly at positions to the south. As the last of the APCs rolled out, C Company was ordered back out to the tarmac.

Belcher asked where Paéz was, but no one knew. As we lined up behind the third squad, he came running with his web gear in tow, shouting he had to stop to take a piss. It was too dark to see clearly, but he was smiling, though not his normal smile. As I helped him with his strap, he winked and said, "Fuck the army."

Low clouds hung over the camp. The deep growl of words flowed among us, mixed tones of macho-ness and anxiety. A round-faced major called us to attention and said, "Light 'em if you have 'em." A spec four from the third squad with "Sweet Death" printed on the back of his flak jacket lit up a reefer. Seeing this, Apple lit up one. Paéz handed me the joint. I passed it on without taking a hit, as did C's. Belcher took a draw and held it in his lungs, then passed it to Rains, who shook his head. More Hueys were landing on the strip. Sergeants looked the other way as the weed circulated, even Cox, who walked up and down telling us for the umpteenth time to check our weapons.

The company lined up to board, each sound taking on a strange exactness—helicopter blades feathering, metal clattering, boots clopping. I bent my thoughts toward something other than what was ahead, and what came to mind was Betty's wedding. A great day for a wedding. I smiled. As we strapped in, Paéz asked what was so damned funny. I pointed to my ears and shook my head. The Huey shuddered and lurched, then hesitated an instant as if unaware of having breached gravity. It lifted itself smoothly through the light mist—cool, moist air spilling in its open doors. I'd forgotten my journal, and realizing this, I panicked. I had things to say.

I asked the door gunner if we could go back for my journal. He pointed to his ears and then the rotating blades and shouted, "Won't be long!" It seemed important to respond, so I nodded and said something about Wilt Chamberlain being the best.

At two thousand feet the sky cleared. Stars wrapped over the edge of the earth. It was wonderfully silent save for the sound of the engine and the whirling blades. The door gunner stared out, face tense, as he aimed his M-60 downward and swung its barrel back and forth.

Over Saigon rocket fire crossed the sky. Passing Hoc Mon we took ground fire, green tracers arching upward gracefully and fading away. A round dinged the side panel and ricocheted off the door gunner's helmet. He looked at me as if to say what luck. Won't be long, I thought.

Crossing Hoc Mon, the craft dipped and circled. Paéz was smiling. I shouted for him to give up the goddamn smile. He pointed to his ears. I glanced at Rains, his head bowed over the barrel of his M-16. The escort ships angled down over a stretch of rice paddies and let go with rockets and machine guns. C's licked his lips and clutched his tiger's claw, mumbling something. What exactly, I was unsure, but it had to do with him dying. The crew chief signaled and we crouched at the edge of the door.

The craft leveled over a paddy where the air abruptly erupted with incoming from AK-47s and Chicom machine guns. C's hesitated. Belcher hollered for him to move, lifted him up, and pulled him out. Apple landed first, followed by Paéz and me, then Rains and C's and Belcher. The mud slowed us. It was like taking fifty pounds of added gear.

While a second chopper landed, the first rose, hung suspended as if in doubt of its condition, then burst into flames, disintegrating as it fell. I sank up to my waist in a hole. A bullet snapped overhead and inspired me to hurry. C's dropped to his knees, his hands cupping his throat. Rains turned back to help. Paéz wheeled about, but Rains shouted for him to go, shoved C's to the ground, and covered him with his own body.

A bullet slapped the dike and spat mud in my face. I notched my finger on the trigger and squeezed. The feel of the stock hammering against my shoulder, the steam and smoke off the barrel got the blood pumping to my ears. I fired until Paéz tapped me on the helmet and told me to stop.

I laid my head on the damp grass and felt the rise and fall of my chest. I thought of Montana nights, Betty splayed out beside me, her hair covering the pillow, my hands exploring her, everything new and wonderful. I wanted it to last forever. I could feel her breath as I cupped her cheeks. A warmth filled my belly. Those moments had been God to me. They swallowed my soul. I blinked once and was back on the dike. There was only this, the cool grass, the smell of nitrates, and the cries of wounded screaming for help.

We lay listening to helicopters circle, ferrying in the rest of the company. Apple said, "They got C's bad." He shouldered his M-79 and pumped a grenade into the brush just to do something with his anger.

Paéz leaned toward me. "Don't forget Hawaii," he said.

I noticed he had no helmet. Belcher threw himself down next to us and asked Paéz where his helmet was. Paéz touched his head. "Back there."

Cox crawled over to say he was calling in artillery.

"Where's the lieutenant?" Belcher asked.

"*Chet roi.* Him and a bunch, even the company clerk."

Rains dragged C's to the foot of the berm. He was drowning in his own blood. A medic ran over and applied a compress to the wound, shook his head, said he was sorry. He swooped up his medical kit. Rains aimed his rifle at the medic, told to him to come back, that he'd shoot if he didn't. But Rains didn't shoot and there was no reason for the medic to return.

Rains slowly crawled up the slope, where he sat with his back to us, his arms folded over his knees. "Couldn't say good-bye," he said. "Took his voice box. Is 'at right? I mean, is it?"

The artillery came.

Apple and I tried to pull him down, but Rains pushed us away. His arms folded, he sat occasionally illuminated by flashes, but remained unharmed, as if C's charms had consigned their power to him. Dust-offs landed to evacuate casualties. Rains refused to notice Apple and Belcher carrying C's body across the field.

Belcher found a helmet, handed it to Paéz, and asked Rains what the hell was going on. Rains said he quit. "You can't quit," Belcher said.

But Rains said that was the case. He'd stopped, gone on strike, quit the army. Belcher looked at us. "You didn't hear this," he said and reached inside an ammo pouch. He pulled out a shot of morphine, which he clenched in his teeth.

Rains asked, "What you doin, man?" and tried to get away, but Belcher tackled him and jabbed the needle into a thigh. He called for another. We shot Rains up with two more and held him until he quit struggling. Belcher took a long breath and said, "Keep him close."

At dawn we found ourselves in a field of smoldering holes surrounded by heaps of fractured earth and splintered trees. The sun rose over the roofs of Hoc Mon and outlined the palm trees, an exotic postcard-like rendering of paradise, except for the smoke. We heard diesel engines. Between the company and the shimmering sun a column of APCs churned slowly over the charred earth. The nearest ran over a body, which sank into the mud, except for one stiff arm.

"Wolfhounds, come on!" a track commander called out.

We followed the APCs through deserted streets of skeletal dwellings, paths littered with men, cats, dogs, rats, and pigs, all dead. I wrapped a bandanna over my face. Paéz asked what day it was. I had no idea. Neither did Belcher or Apple. Rains said he didn't even know how many days we'd been fighting this damned thing. Paéz said that's because he was stoned most of the time. I vaguely remembered a variation of this very conversation.

"It's Tuesday or Wednesday," I said. "Or Thursday."

As we advanced on an undefended bridge, the chime of a bell came from behind. It repeated itself. I looked over my shoulder. A girl, perhaps fifteen, dressed in white silk, balanced her bicycle and tried to pass the file. Not far behind, another followed, and from the same direction a Vespa rode out of the smoldering ruins, its engine hacking like an early-morning cough.

The girls carried schoolbooks strapped to their backs. They acknowledged us no more than the randomly strewn bodies or clouds of black flies or smoldering craters. We stepped to the side. They passed with phantom aloofness, seemingly untouched, the sheer white tails of their silk *áo diàs* lifting up like gossamer pennants as they rode on calmly and purposefully.

40

His name tag read "Digbus." He was a lieutenant in charge of morale—which meant R&R as well. He'd not yet seen a tracer round and had a *mama-san* who cleaned his room and another who polished his boots. He sat behind his desk, shook his head, and told Paéz and me to take Bangkok—the best he could do. When I said we'd requested Hawaii months before, he said Bangkok, Kuala Lumpur, and Hong Kong were great, tried to sell the price of whores and booze.

"Sir," Paéz said, "we survived Tet. Grunts. See?"

"Whoop-dee-do, Paéz."

"No offense, sir, but I just don't want to go where there's a bunch of dinks, even if the prices are next to free. You understand, don't you?"

"No." The officer stamped our travel orders "Bangkok" and handed them over. As he was also in charge of emergency phone calls, I told him my adopted sister had gotten married and I wanted to congratulate her. He made arrangements for me at the Red Cross. It took ten minutes to get Willy on the line.

"Pete, you *here*. You home, boy?" He sounded amazed to hear from me. Empty silence followed.

"Willy, you have to say 'over' when you're finished. I'm still in 'Nam, over."

"Hell, boy. We been 'spectin somethin terrible."

Again I explained he had to say "over" at the end of a sentence. On a static-filled line we traded small talk for a minute until he got used to the idea of saying "over," then I asked for a big favor, fast. "What you want, Pete? Over!"

"I've got R&R coming, and this lieutenant wants to send us to Thailand. Paéz, that's my buddy, and I want to go to Hawaii. We asked for Hawaii months ago, over."

"What's this lieutenant's name? Over!"

I told him. The Red Cross lady pointed at her watch and toward the waiting line of soldiers and Marines. I said, "I've got to go, Willy."

"I got a job waiting, and you forgot to say over."

"Over, Willy."

"Over, Pete. I'll call them, right now, over."

"'Bye, over."

"Don't you . . . Hell, Pete. Good-bye, over."

Pale clouds floated above, the ocean shimmered below. The only enlisted men on the flight, we sat in the last two seats behind NCOs and officers, many noncombatants, who lifted ballpoints and courageously initialed documents. Flight attendants with frosted-pink lips served up cheerful smiles, in-flight meals, and drinks. They placed pillows behind our heads and said it was nice to have us aboard. They bent close so the smell of their perfume and the graze of their mint breath would remind us of all we missed.

Their smiles were something vaguely remembered and made me wish I was meeting Betty in Honolulu. I'd settle for less, but in truth, I expected nothing. A rosy-cheeked redhead with a ponytail, named Terry, made several out-of-the-way trips to our seat. She hung around to ask questions about our comfort—did we want a magazine? Another soft drink? She looked at me affably, but Paéz had her attention. When he looked up with his wet brown eyes and said he'd like a copy of the *Los Angeles Times* editorial page, she shot away. She returned smiling, handed him an editorial page from the *San Francisco Herald-Examiner,* and said, "I like bright men."

Snapping the paper open, he said, "This is more like it," and began reading about Bobby Kennedy announcing his run for the presidency. I looked out the window and watched a ship plow over the ocean; it reminded me of a Monopoly board piece. Terry reappeared to ask if Paéz was enjoying the paper. She asked where he was from. He answered Texas, and she said, "My favorite state after Hawaii."

"I don't want to go back," he said and added, "except for my girl." He said he was supposed to meet Gloria in Hawaii. Terry said sometimes girls don't show up. He smiled as if remembering a joke and said it was nice of her to pay us so much attention. I said, "Us?"

To be cordial, she asked my hometown. When I said Las Vegas, she smiled politely and said she was from Vermont, which she described as unlike Las Vegas, beautiful but provincial. As the plane descended for the approach, she checked our seat belts, then leaned over and handed Paéz a note upon which she'd written her name and the hotel where she would be staying for several days.

We taxied onto American soil and deplaned to face scenery that looked all too familiar—palm trees, tropical vegetation. No protesters, no signs, just a man with an electronic megaphone shouting instructions and a dozen Hawaiian women in grass skirts waving tiny American flags. Terry whispered in Paéz's ear as we stepped onto the ramp. I got a cordial handshake.

As two women flung leis over our necks, three musicians, two playing ukuleles and one a string guitar, accompanied other women who sang and danced a hula. Then we were hustled onto buses by the man with the megaphone, who handed us an itinerary. Paéz and I were booked into the Hilton Hawaiian Village.

Paéz asked the desk clerk for messages. "Nothing for a Mr. Paéz," he said and asked about baggage. Paéz showed him a carry-on. As he handed over our keys, he told us if we needed anything to go visit the shops and charge everything to the room, as Willy Bobbins was picking up the tab. "Willy?" Paéz asked.

I'd never talked about Willy or my relationship with him. I decided not to start now and settled on saying, "Willy has a little money."

Paéz stepped inside the suite and whistled. "This is living," he said. "How much money?" We wandered about, touching fabrics and furniture. Paéz flipped on the TV, turned down the volume, and picked up the telephone. I left him to his conversation and went to the shower, where I lathered up for half an hour under a hot spray and rinsed until my skin wrinkled.

Paéz was slumped on the couch watching television with the volume off. "What's up?" I asked.

He said Gloria was out with friends. He'd talked to her mother. "She didn't call me Paco," he said. "She always calls me Paco." He shrugged. "I'm too old for pet names. I need a shower."

After shopping, we dressed in sandals, flower-print shirts, and matching shorts that underscored the whiteness of our legs, though his were a shade darker. We strolled the beach. We purchased hot dogs and Cokes and sat under a cabana. A breeze blew in. Children dug in the sand and men in dark sunglasses sat and stared at bikini-clad women as surfers paddled out looking for waves. Three teenage boys tossed a football and made diving catches into the gentle breakers. Their mother pulling them along, telling them not to bother people, two small girls stopped passersby to say hello.

Paéz raised his paper cup. "To Hawaii."

I tapped my cup to his. "Hawaii." I started to toast again, to America this time, but a sudden pain hit the back of my skull.

"You okay?" Paéz asked and checked my eyes.

I shook it off. "Fine. Let's walk."

Though I felt dizzy getting up, I was better once I stood. We stepped out of our sandals and carried them as we walked. We strained our eyes trying to take in every sight—women, ocean, hotels, surfers staying with fruitless waves. We found a less crowded spot and sat down near four young women sunning in string bikinis. We sat with our backs to them so as not to perturb them. I just wanted to hear them laugh.

Paéz leaned back on his elbows as we stared at the waves. I thought about Betty, which made me feel small and lonely. As sweat beaded down my forehead, I began to shiver and a transitory pain crept up the back of my skull. Then my skin broke out in goose bumps and my ears began to ring. Paéz told me my lips were white.

"As white as my legs?"

"I'm serious."

Figuring that whatever it was would pass, I told Paéz I was fine, and the shivering did pass—momentarily. Then it returned uncontrollably. Paéz became a blur. The beach swirled. I rolled forward and threw up. Paéz grabbed me and patted my back, encouraged me to stand, but I was too weak to do so. The young women gathered up their belongings. One said, "Disgusting," as they shook sand from their blanket. "Animals," another said. They narrowed their eyes and looked at me accusingly. One asked why soldiers didn't show more respect for people.

"My friend's sick," Paéz said. "You ever been sick?"

"Soldiers!" the one carrying the blanket said.

They replanted themselves down the beach, complaining to people nearby. It didn't matter; I couldn't hear anything clearly by then.

Paéz laid my arm over his shoulder and hoisted me up. As we walked by the women, Paéz said, "Ever been sick?"

"Drunks!" one hollered.

"Bitches," he muttered as he guided me off the beach.

He explained to the house doctor how we were on leave and had only a few days to enjoy, that I was army property and truly only army doctors were permitted to malpractice on me, which made the doctor smile. After listening to my chest and looking down my throat, he wrote a prescription.

"Probably a stomach virus," he said, "I can't be sure without tests. Symptoms match a dozen illnesses and food poisoning."

"No tests," I said.

The doctor shook his head and stood. "I should report this to the health department. You may have something that could infect many people."

Paéz smiled. "He hasn't got the clap, if that's what you're thinking."

The doctor nodded. "No tests. I hope you feel good enough to enjoy your stay." He looked at Paéz. "Keep the room dark and let him sleep. If the fever gets out of control, put him in a tub with ice and run cold water. Call here if you need me." He handed over his card and left.

By then the chills were severe. The ceiling whirled as if it was going to fall. A vague outline by the bedside, Paéz propped my head up so I could drink and later bought hot oxtail soup—a Hawaiian version of the Jewish mother's chicken broth—to restore me. I awoke from my fog to see him dial the phone, only to hang up. Another time, though I couldn't tell whether it was in a dream or not, he was in a heated conversation and slammed down the receiver. Later still, I felt a damp cloth on my forehead and he was beside me, assuring me I was doing fine.

I awoke the third day rejuvenated but parched. Whatever had hit me was over and had left me with a strange new awareness. Sounds from below and colors in the room, even the ceiling, took on an intensity that overwhelmed my senses. I called to Paéz, who didn't answer. After showering, I went to the living room and sat on the couch, feet propped on the coffee table as *Rhapsody in Blue* played on the radio. I ordered lunch with a bottle of Beaujolais, as it sounded good, then opened the curtain and watched sailboats atilt on the bay.

Paéz returned at dusk. I was on a second bottle of wine. Paéz tossed himself down on the couch and said, "You're better." I asked where he'd been.

He held out a clean glass. "Got tired of watching you sleep," he said.

I had to ask. "Gloria?" I poured him wine.

"No Gloria," Paéz said and pensively looked at the glass of wine. "Terry."

That said everything. "Oh."

Paéz shrugged and stood to turn on the TV. "She helped with you, so I felt obligated to go to the airport."

We downed the bottle and ordered another along with two porterhouses, salads, baked potatoes, and cherries jubilee. "You asked for Betty," Paéz said.

"Willy's daughter. You were right all along. I'm the kind women dump."

"I'm sorry about that. Well, here's to her and Gloria," Paéz said and raised his glass.

"To them," I said.

"We'll be needing wine," Paéz said.

We ordered two more bottles and I tipped the room waiter fifty dollars on Willy's credit. We drank the first bottle, praising the wine's splendid attributes, though we had no idea what the qualities were other than alcohol. "The aftertaste of a Julie Andrews kiss," Paéz said.

I grimaced. "The texture of Cornish raspberries."

"Winsome on the palate," Paéz said, and we toasted.

We were watching a rerun of a *Beverly Hillbillies* episode when Paéz began to wipe his eyes with the back of his hand. With his other, he held his glass for me to fill and stared as if watching the screen. He drank and talked about everything but Gloria. He wiped his damp eyes with the back of his wrist and held the wineglass out.

"I didn't go to the airport because of Terry," he said. "I was going to desert, go home and find Gloria."

"Why didn't you?" I asked.

Paéz just looked at me as if I should know, should understand this one thing. I did and told him so. He'd come back because of me. His eyes seemed as hollow as the hole on Black Virgin Mountain. "You want to know about Nui Ba Dan?" he asked.

I poured more wine, and he explained how he'd crawled around a curve, and suddenly he wasn't alone. He could hear them breathing. One touched him. Then a hand snatched the flashlight from him and shone it in his eyes. It was, he claimed, like confronting evil. "I thought I was charmed, but I wasn't, was I? I lost it that day, and then . . . her."

I said I was sure he was charmed. It was clear he didn't believe it. He said, "No. On Black Virgin Mountain she took the charm from my life."

I suggested we sit on the beach and listen to the surf, but he shook his head and went to the balcony, where he stared at the stars. Even when I brought the wine and joined him, he kept staring. I gave him his glass. "We've got to salute Willy Bobbins," I said. "Besides you, my only friend."

"To Willy, who I don't know, but who got me to Hawaii."

We stayed drunk three days, then flew back to 'Nam. The day we returned we were promoted to spec four, then separated, Paéz going to a new squad. We stayed in the same platoon under a new platoon sergeant, Row Tailor, a large, muscular black from Arkansas, and a new platoon leader, James Bull, an ocs second lieutenant from Alabama. The company was operating in Boi Loi Woods.

41

I had seven months in the boonies; Paéz was working on ten—no scratches. It was time to consider mortality, time to think about Cu Chi, burning shit, and watching movies. I requested a transfer; Paéz volunteered to be a tunnel rat.

I told him he was nuts.

Paéz wiped sweat from his cheek. "It's cool. Winemakers could store barrels, let them age forever. Bring a whole new industry to this shit hole when the war's over."

The jungles of Boi Loi and Ho Bo Woods, located between the Michelin and Filhol plantations northeast of Cu Chi, were infested with underground networks. Trails were booby-trapped. Charlie hid in thickets too dense to penetrate with human eyes. Sometimes we'd walk down a trail and know Charlie was watching; sometimes we'd clear a village and have the sense that Charlie had been laughing at our backs.

Paéz no longer dawdled over the *Stars and Stripes*; he rid himself of Gloria's letters; he avoided conversation that went beyond hello; he smoked pot daily; his smile became introspective, a self-knowing smirk, a turn of the upper lip.

One day we found a *papa-san* on a trail. He'd been shot through the neck and left dead. As we passed by, each of us ritualistically shook the old man's hand and wished him a good day. When Paéz's turn came, he lit a cigarette and stuck it between the dead man's lips, then sat and chatted. He said that he felt certain the *papa-san* was Lucky's father.

Belcher asked what had happened to make Paéz so weird.

"His girl never showed in Hawaii," I said.

"Kind 'a shit happens," Belcher said. "Nothin to get weird about. Probably found some Jody."

It was a clear morning, dry and tolerable. "A day for picking daisies," Belcher announced as we spread out to enter a village north of Ben Cat, ten huts that didn't show on our map. A transfer to the squad named Sleeper looked over, claimed this could be his last ville, and said, "I'm so short I have to look up to see my knees."

A handful of women and children and one old toothless *ong* were on hand to greet us, if looking at the ground with cool stares can be called a greeting. We herded them into the open and searched huts, found nothing but some rice stored in baskets, hardly enough to supply a VC squad. These were some destitute villagers. The scout screamed and ranted at the old man, who sat mute. James Bull shrugged and said we were wasting time and ordered us out.

Paéz's replacement, an FNG named Henderson, walked to the left of Sleeper as they stepped over a hedgerow. There was a popping sound, and then a Bouncing Betty hung at eye level ready to do mayhem. Henderson hollered, "Holy shit," just before it exploded. Sleeper, two feet away, was thrust aside as if hit by a car. The blast knocked me down, but Sleeper had saved me from shrapnel.

A pillar of smoke hung where the mine went off. Henderson and Sleeper bleeding on the red clay and our clogged ears told the story. Each of us inventoried body parts before standing. Henderson was dead. Sleeper was trying to get up, but couldn't with just one arm. With his one remaining eye he saw the shredded limb that used to be his left arm. He tried to crawl to it, but that was as futile as trying to stand.

"Someone really messed up," he said and lay on his belly.

We zipped Henderson in a body bag and called in a dust-off. As he lay on a stretcher watching, Sleeper said, "So short I had to look up to see my knees and some FNG . . . Ain't it a bitch."

Belcher held his hand and said, "It's a bitch."

James Bull assembled the platoon. These were his second casualties, and he took it harder than a platoon leader in Vietnam should. We watched as he shed tears. He said losing a man was like losing one of his own. He said we weren't alert and that's why soldiers die. From now on our mission was to kill ten Charlies for every guy we lost. Paéz asked, "Who's keeping the ledger?"

But we'd been hardened by Tet and took our lot with a sense of fatalism— guys got wounded, buddies died, the war went on. Body count meant little if you weren't alive to do the counting, and survival amounted to spitting in the right direction.

Lieutenant Bull turned to Row Tailor and said, "Shake these men down for drugs. I know some of them are using."

As the lieutenant stood at the front of the platoon, Row Tailor inspected us in a haphazard, apologetic manner, overlooking the occasional stash he found while digging in a man's pack. He'd turn the troop around, take off the backpack, and run his hand around inside. We could see in his eyes when he found something suspicious, but he didn't report it. He was caught in a hard spot, as he had no desire to see his men humiliated or to roll over on a grenade in his sleep.

"Nothin here, sir!" he'd shout, then whisper in the soldier's ear, "Be cool, be cool."

Paéz placed his stash atop his backpack and stood with a vacant expression. As he looked over the pack, Row Tailor swallowed and looked up at the heavens. He picked up the baggie and asked, "What's this?"

"Oregano, Sarge," Paéz said, absolutely deadpan.

Sergeant Tailor grimaced as James Bull threw his shoulders back and charged over to Paéz. He told Tailor to hand over the baggie. After smelling it, he walked back and forth. Paéz's face never changed expression. Bull stopped pacing and propped his fists on his hips. He told us to have a smoke, but no one lit up. Bull towered over Paéz, who gazed about with absolute lack of interest. "Paéz, this is marijuana," the lieutenant said.

"Sir, it is? The local said it was oregano."

"Paéz, do you think I'm stupid?"

"Sir, it's great with spaghetti. I recommend it."

We thrived on the ludicrous, and so we smiled as Paéz delivered it onstage, a fact not lost on James Bull. "And you cook a lot of spaghetti here?" he asked.

"Never enough, sir. Not . . . enough."

The lieutenant said he'd give him a chance to change his story, but Paéz didn't crack, even when threatened with a court-martial and being busted to private, even when Row Tailor said he'd put him on point for the rest of his goddamn tour. Row Tailor motioned the lieutenant to a tree, where they conferred out of earshot. Other than Willy and Miriam, Paéz was the only person in the world I could truly call friend. I hoped the moment would resolve itself and he'd come out of it the same smiling guy I'd met in Cu Chi months before. James Bull walked back, dumped the contents of the baggie on the ground, and crushed it under his boot. "I'm going to overlook this, but I'll be watching," he warned. "Sergeant, get these men harnessed up and ready to go."

That afternoon we found a hole at the edge of a rubber plantation and secured a perimeter. James Bull called Paéz over and ordered him down. He must have envisioned refusal, certainly reluctance, but Paéz quickly shed his gear and accepted the flashlight and pistol from Tailor. He looked at me, mouthed the name Gloria, and descended.

We waited for an interminable period in the heat, minutes measured in sweat that beaded on our heads and drenched our fatigues. I pictured an ever-choking tunnel, one so narrow it seemed to grab Paéz's hips so that he could neither advance nor withdraw, a monkey hole that got dimmer and dimmer as the batteries drained off while Paéz slowly choked.

From time to time the lieutenant would ask Row Tailor just what the hell Paéz was doing down there. "Does he think we have forever to hang around here? We're goddamn targets. I mean, what the hell does he think he's doing?" Row Tailor had no answer. It was true the platoon was in a bad spot. We all knew it.

James Bull kept one eye on the hands of his watch and one on the hole and paced back and forth. When an hour had passed, he bent over the hole on all fours and called down. "Paéz, get your ass up here! Do you hear me, Paéz? That's a goddamn order!" There was no answer. Belcher smiled sardonically at me. We suspected something, but what?

The lieutenant waited another hour, shouting red-faced orders down into the hole from time to time, before he summoned Loftin, a slight kid with acne, who didn't talk unless he was drinking, and then wouldn't shut up. Bull told him to go after Paéz and get him out of there or someone would face a court-martial. "Sir, he's got the forty-five and the flashlight," Loftin said. "'Sides, if he's comin out, we'd just meet heads."

"Are you afraid, soldier?"

"Sir, anyone who isn't is a fool or Paéz."

Nevertheless, Loftin went down. Twenty minutes later he came up another hole outside the perimeter and reported he'd followed a maze, tunnels that crisscrossed one another.

"No Paéz?" Bull asked.

"No, sir. Nothing but tunnels and a bomb shelter near as I could tell."

"But you couldn't see?"

"No, sir."

Twice more Loftin descended and twice more came out empty. The rest of the company proceeded on the operation, leaving our platoon bivouacked on the spot. That evening a chopper brought in food and a flashlight and another .45. After eating, Loftin went down and found two camouflaged openings and another bomb shelter, but no evidence of Paéz.

The anger had faded from James Bull's face. He was at a loss to understand what had happened. He asked Belcher and the other leaders what they thought, but no one else could come up with an explanation. I sat by the hole, transfixed. Even when it was apparent that Paéz wasn't coming out, even as James Bull said, "We've stopped the war long enough for this," and commanded the platoon to form a column and head out of the plantation, I sat and stared.

James Bull ordered me to my feet. I wanted to rise. My legs simply refused to budge. Belcher hoisted me up and braced me against his shoulder. "Him and Paéz, they were buddies," he explained. "Went through Tet together."

James Bull nodded and said, "Get him up and moving, Sergeant," and left to join the center of the column.

Belcher sought help from another soldier, and together they urged me away, Belcher assuring me Paéz had found another opening and was somewhere nearby laughing right then. "Remember how he joked, always the joker." I couldn't remember. Just that hole. And Belcher had used the past tense—all the evidence I needed.

42

In order to shorten my enlistment, I took a three-month extension in Vietnam. It didn't matter. The army was the same everywhere if you weren't in the boonies. I was delegated to an officers' club as a waiter, but by accident found an assignment in the Eighteenth Military History Detachment, because the lieutenant in charge of keeping records of the Wolfhounds wanted a well-read soldier who could "slip through the smoke screen and write an accurate readable battle summary."

I wore clean fatigues and drank cold beer, stood guard at night and listened to that relentless artillery piece chuck bulletins out to Charlie. I monitored casualty figures, tracked dispatches and names of MIAS and POWS and KIAS. I was interested in only one. The rest was boring—filing photographs and composing synopses of battle reports, mostly unnecessary work made to seem important.

I spent those months listening to the lieutenant, Horn, talk about going out in the boonies with his own platoon. He envisioned himself a leader, spoke of the glory of combat. I didn't bother to wise him up. No point. Division history was as close as he would ever come to war. Short and round, he wore glasses that could magnify a blade of grass to the size of a tree, and he talked alternately in clipped military jargon and blocked-up semi-academic speech. He made no demands of me and seemed to enjoy my company. "What was it like, Elkins?" he asked me many times.

Once I told him, "This time, sir, I'll tell you the truth. It's like having a nightmare as a kid and you wake up and it's still there and you're a part of it, but you don't think you are. You know what's going down and your body acts, but your mind keeps telling you it's a dream. I guess we just distance ourselves from it; even the guys who were dying acted as if they were watching it happen."

"Is that really how it is?"

"No, sir, that's all bullshit. In fact, it's one big unending orgasm, a pulsating sensation that swells and shrinks and swells again immediately. Imagine a two-foot hard-on in all that noise and confusion. The only trouble is it's a wet dream. And that's how it really is."

"Elkins, you're a philosopher."

"No, sir, just a nothing REMF."

"Don't be hard on yourself. Did I tell you about the second battle of the Cynocephalae?"

"Yes, sir."

"Put the Romans in charge of everything. We've been the Romans. Now we're holding on to a dying civilization that never had culture except for jazz and baseball."

I was reminded of Rich's theories of the meta-civilization. I'd not thought of him for months and wondered what had happened to him.

"Sir, may I go to the E.M. club for a beer?"

"Sure, but remember your toxic reaction."

"Yes, sir."

When the name Lieutenant James Bull showed up KIA, awarded the Purple Heart and recommended for a Silver Star, I felt no satisfaction or sorrow, perhaps because I held out hope that Paéz had found an opening and had walked away from the war or found that tunnel that led to Rome. James Bull couldn't be held accountable. He was dead, a name, a statistic along with many. Belcher caught an RPG while sitting on top of a track near Dau Tieng. Half the platoon was killed or wounded in action. I was lucky. All I had was malaria.

I figured out on my own that I'd contracted the disease. Malaria was what had hit me in Hawaii. Despite identifying the attacks for what they were, I avoided treatment. It was easy to take a day or two away from cataloging photographs and writing one-paragraph summaries. It wasn't as if there was any rush to record the history of a war that kept replicating itself.

I kept the seizures to myself, lied and said I was hung over when the fever hit. I told Lieutenant Horn I had a brain disorder very much like epilepsy but not epilepsy, and one idiosyncrasy of the condition was the occasional toxic reaction to alcohol. Horn pushed his glasses up and said he understood, that if he'd gone through what I had experienced, he would have turned to booze himself. When asked why I didn't report to sick bay, I answered that the army would discharge me. Being a graduate of the Citadel, Horn figured that I was simply being honorable. I wondered how he would feel about honor if he was in the boonies with thirty-five grunts who wanted to burn a village.

I also kept quiet about my symptoms because I'd heard the army postponed discharges for soldiers who came down with incurable diseases. There was a rumor of a secret island for soldiers with incurable VD. The army kept it like a leper colony, but there only penises rotted off.

Occasionally the muted racket of a distant encounter drifted into camp, a battle at some far-off dot on the province map, sounds that seemed almost benign and left me to wonder if I'd actually experienced something out there. Perhaps I'd just imagined everything, even Paéz. War seemed inconceivable, something that had happened once upon a time when I was stoned—or was I straight? I felt like a malingerer or a quitter and now and then a coward.

Once a week I would hitch a ride on an APC or flag a helicopter flight into Saigon, where I'd ring Uncle Harve in his office or Miriam, who was rarely home, or Willy, who was always full of questions, the main one being when I was going to get tired of playing soldier. I wanted to know about Betty, her marriage and all, half hoping it had failed, but she was one subject I never brought up. There wasn't much time for a lot of chatting, which didn't matter, for there was little to be said. Familiar voices were what I was after, connections with loved ones who didn't go down holes and never come out.

When they hung up, I would feel utterly severed, a reaction just the opposite of what I'd hoped for. It was always the same. Their world had spun smoothly on its usual axis, but mine wobbled. I would find myself staring at a blank space, projecting myself into the field where I watched Paéz go down that hole, again and again and again.

One day it was my turn to mount the stairs and climb aboard a freedom bird. I counted the steps. Stopped at the door, where a flight attendant welcomed me into the air-conditioned cabin. My seat was next to the window on the left side, just behind the wing. Attendants came around with their tidy clothes and sure smiles to remind us to buckle up and keep the seat backs upright.

The plane taxied down the runway, gaining speed for liftoff. There was a last tire skid and the heaviness of the earth slipped away as if a carpet had been yanked out from underneath the wheels. The cabin erupted in cheers. I didn't root—barely heard the racket, in fact.

I gazed northward to the quilted countryside, the rice paddies and rubber plantations, and beyond in the direction of Boi Loi Woods, which appeared soft and grainy, like a picture slightly out of focus. From that distance the canopy seemed to have the shaggy texture of a cotton bath mat, something soft that God could dry His feet on. Somewhere in that dense, harmless-appearing foliage was one hole, barely big enough for a small man to enter, and deep inside that hole Paéz was burrowing like a badger, digging his way to America while I was taking the easy route.

The plane tilted left and the sun's glare reflected up from the mirrored surface of a rice paddy and blinded me. When I saw clearly again, Boi Loi and the Black Virgin Mountain and all of Tay Ninh Province and War Zone C had evaporated on the horizon. A terrifying sensation, a dark panic engulfed me. I felt as if I'd forgotten something, as if in my haste to go I'd left something behind, something I couldn't remember. Then I felt a tug on my sleeve. "What will you have, sir?" the attendant asked.

She must have repeated the question without me hearing. I looked as if at an apparition, which she was anyhow. Didn't she know she was an illusion, an image of what we were supposed to believe war was about? "Do you have mai tais?" I asked.

"Sorry, just miniatures."

She held her smile as an outfielder holds a ball barely caught on the fingertips of his glove—hesitant, hopeful. She knew about us. Anything might set us off. "I'll have a Jack Daniel's," I said. "On ice." Saying it sounded terribly civilized.

43

The traffic opened up. I zipped through the seams and soon found myself on the San Fernando Freeway with no idea how I'd ended up there or how to get off. I had to turn around and head south to get back to Uncle Harve and Aunt Viv's in time for dinner.

After I was processed out of the army at Oakland Army Terminal, I had flown to Los Angeles. I wanted to see Uncle Harve and Aunt Viv and pick up the motorcycle, and afterward, head out somewhere. Where, I had no idea, but someplace free of any past. For the moment it was just good being on the saddle of a fast bike and slipping in and out of traffic on the freeway.

I leaned right, crossed three lanes, and took the next exit. I failed to see the flashing light in my mirrors, so by the time I pulled over, the cop had been trying to stop me for half a mile. He removed his sunglasses and narrowed his eyes as I climbed off the Triumph. "License and registration," he said.

As Uncle Harve had kept the plates current, I wasn't worried, even though my driver's license had expired. I handed both to the cop. He studied them a moment, then excused himself. He was young, perhaps three years older than I was, and blond and tall. "Driver's license has expired," he shouted as he reached in for his car microphone.

"I was just discharged from the army," I said.

"Yeah, where?"

"Oakland Army Terminal."

"Vietnam?"

"Yeah."

"What outfit?"

"Twenty-fifth Division in Three Corps."

He held his hand up for me to wait as he spoke into the microphone. He gave them my name and date of birth. A moment later he returned and stood looking over the Triumph. "You made two illegal lane changes," he said.

"I had to turn around to get to Bellflower," I explained.

"Grunt?"

"Carried a pig."

He nodded to show his understanding. "A Marine myself. Got discharged over a year ago. Missed Tet by six months. Had some buddies buy it at Hue, or so I heard."

326 ♦ *The Lucky*

"It was a mess."

"Yeah. What're you going to do now, jobwise?"

"I think my uncle's going to ask me to learn to prepare taxes and work with him."

"Yeah."

I shrugged. "His idea, not mine." I hadn't yet made up my mind what to do. College was one idea. In time I'd have to go back and face Willy, but I wanted to hold off on that, give myself time to have a plan. He would want me to work for him, something I wasn't ready to do.

The cop nodded and handed over my license and registration. "Tell you what . . . go on and be careful. Wouldn't want to scrape you off a freeway after you survived Tet."

I thanked him and cranked up the bike. Before he shut his car door, I was traveling down the off-ramp. After a turn at the overpass and a second turn onto the freeway, I headed south, the sun slanting deep from the southwest. I darted lane to lane, playing in the seams in the traffic, leaning, a tight envelope of wind surrounding me. Speed, motion—antidotes for memories. They always had been.

A few miles later another flashing red-and-blue light showed in my mirrors. I checked the speedometer. The bike was clipping along at seventy and in the flow of traffic. I pulled over to let the cop pass. He didn't. I pulled to the far right and stopped. As he approached, he unsnapped his holster and ordered me off the seat. He advised me of my constitutional rights as he walked behind me. A minute later I was spread out on the hood of the car, his gleaming handcuffs shiny in the corner of my eye as he pulled my wrists back one at a time.

I was booked into the Los Angeles County Jail on a fugitive warrant for felony assault. No one explained where the warrant was issued from and when I asked the booking officer, he told me to keep my mouth shut. I was ordered to strip and the jailer took my clothes and placed them in a paper bag upon which he penned my name. Another officer searched me, made me spread my buttocks, and sprayed me with a yellow powder—for lice, he said. He handed me a blue jumpsuit and told me I could wear my motorcycle boots. He led me to a room to be fingerprinted and photographed.

One of my right profile, one face-on. The lights were intense. After the portrait session, as he called it, he rolled my fingerprints onto a card. Another jailer, Deputy Marfa, escorted me down a series of corridors and up an elevator. I asked when I got a phone call, but he didn't answer, just kept walking, his heels striking the linoleum with a steady thud. He recited the institution's rules as if they were etched on his eyeballs—no fighting, no weapons, no drugs, no sex, no defacing jail property, don't argue with deputies, no unnecessary noise—any and all infractions may be punished by solitary confinement or additional charges. As the elevator swung open, he held me aside.

"Give you some advice," he said. "We got prisoners like Sirhan Sirhan to worry about and guys who'd slice your balls off if they got the chance. Bikers and mob thugs. In here someone like you isn't shit. Don't think you are. Don't try to prove nothin. Cruise until you're released. We have ways to deal with fuckups and hard cases. More than one punk has tripped and hit those metal bars with his head. Shame, but it happens."

An inmate let out a chilling scream that lasted five or six seconds. The deputy seemed unaffected. The corridor was ablaze with white lights. It seemed quite narrow, as the ceiling was so far overhead. Prisoners lined up behind the bars on both sides of the hall to size me up. The deputy paused at one cell. "That you screaming again, Laswell?"

"It was him," another prisoner answered. "He don't belong here, Officer Marfa. Ain't right puttin him with us."

The deputy smiled. "Wasn't me put him in there. Someone hanged himself there and that created a vacuum. Now didn't someone explain to you that nature abhors a vacuum?"

"Vacuum got nothin to do with nothin, Officer. Nothin. Crazy what he is. You know ol' Timmers is a good man. Why you wanna do him this way?"

"Out of my hands," Deputy Marfa said. "Hey, Laswell, behave yourself in there. Don't go choking Timmers when you get upset."

"Ain't right," the prisoner repeated.

The deputy motioned with his head for me to follow. As we stepped away, he said, "Timmers killed a cellmate. We can't prove it. Now he deals with a two-hundred-fifty-pound psycho. It's poetry, Elkins. You understand this kind of poetry?"

I nodded. The message was clear.

Deputy Marfa opened the door to an eight-man cell that already housed nine prisoners. He told me to find a bunk. I asked when I'd get my call. He merely smiled and closed the door. The report as the door clanged shut sounded more deadly and final than the artillery piece in Cu Chi.

The men watched as I moved to the far wall. No one spoke. I found a spot by myself, leaned my back to the wall, and slowly sank to the floor. One guy kept looking at my boots. Others played cards or carried on whispered conversations.

About an hour later the inmate who was so interested in my boots scooted over and sat down. He was a pale blond, with straight hair that hung down his throat and back. His teeth were black at the gum line. He swiped his nose with the back of his hand.

"You a biker?" he asked.

Now I looked down at my boots. "I ride," I said, "but I'm not . . . no, I guess not."

"I'm in for burglary," he said.

I nodded.

"Didn't do it," he said.

"No?"

"Absolutely not. It was a roust. They stopped me with a sixteen-year-old chick on my bitch pad. Took one look at her age and my scooter and came up with a burglar who looked like me. Here I am. Fuck it."

"How do I get a call?" I asked.

"You ain't asked my name and you want information?"

"What's your name?"

"Skinner. Yours?"

I told him mine and listened as he explained that he was part of an outlaw biker club, but was thinking about quitting to join a clan led by a man who claimed to be Jesus Christ. He'd met up with the leader just recently at an abandoned ranch in the hills near Los Angeles.

"All these chicks, young ones, ready and willing. And drugs, psychedelics, all you'd ever want. The leader's recruiting bikers. Tried to recruit me right off. Gave me one of his old ladies, said, 'Here, she'll make you happy.'" He thought about that a moment, then said, "Interested?"

"I told you I'm not a biker."

"Don't get excited, man. In here you need friends."

"I'm not excited. I want to make a call."

"Can't help you there, man. Fuck it. Make the most of this place. Look at jail like goin to a convention. Here you make contacts, see?"

I thanked him to placate him. At least the others paid me no attention now. Skinner hung around for a while making small talk, then moved on just before the lights flickered.

Four days later a deputy called my name off a roster to step into the hallway. I hadn't used a phone and had no attorney. The deputies shackled us. As one slipped the chain over my neck and clamped the manacles on my wrist, I asked where I was going.

"A court hearing. Cops are here from San Francisco for you, Elkins."

"San Francisco?" Sachs. The pervert. I wanted to laugh.

"That's right. Open up your Golden Gates." He adjusted the manacles on my ankles.

Prisoners in various stages of the legal process went before the judge, who handled each case as if reading from a menu that had nothing appealing on it. The court clerk called my name, and a deputy motioned for me to rise and step forward. The judge, a man of fifty or so with thick eyebrows and reading glasses that dangled near the tip of his nose, riffled through a set of documents before looking at the assistant district attorney handling the docket. "In the matter of the State of California versus Peter Elkins, a fugitive charge of fleeing to avoid prosecution and the charge of felonious assault, does the State have all the proper documentation?"

The assistant DA addressed the court, saying he had the same copies as were before the judge. The judge nodded and asked if officers from San Francisco County were present. Two men in the first row of benches stood. "Are you ready to receive and transport the prisoner?"

One in a gray business suit addressed the judge and said they were.

"I suppose you'll want to beat the late-afternoon freeway rush," the judge said. The spectators chortled and the judge smiled.

"Yes, Your Honor," the cop said.

"Good. Mr. Elkins, who represents you?"

"No one, Your Honor."

"No one?"

"No, sir."

"Why not?"

"I haven't been allowed a phone call, Your Honor."

"No phone calls?"

"No, sir."

He addressed the assistant DA. "Were you aware of this?"

"No, Your Honor, but as he was in custody being held for another jurisdiction, he was ineligible for bail. Mr. Elkins has been a fugitive for almost three years."

"I see. I remind you that he is still entitled to a phone call and representation."

"He merely got temporarily misplaced in the system."

"Mr. Elkins, do you understand the charge against you?"

"Not fully, Your Honor."

"You've been hiding from this charge for almost three years. That indicates some understanding at least as to the nature of the crime."

"Sir, I had no idea. I was in the army for almost three years, the last fifteen months in Vietnam."

The judge looked at the assistant DA. "I'd like to see you at the bench."

After they conferred for several minutes the attorney returned to his table and said, "The State moves to delay this matter twenty-four hours until Mr.

Elkins has had a chance to talk to the public defender's office and make a phone call."

The judge looked me over. "How old are you, Mr. Elkins?"

"Twenty-one, sir."

"Honorable discharge?"

"Yes, sir."

"Does your family know where you are?"

"No, sir. I've seen only my uncle and aunt."

He nodded. "Mr. Elkins, the court is going to have a deputy and a bailiff escort you to my chambers. Feel free to call whomever you wish. What unit were you with?"

"The Twenty-fifth Infantry, sir."

"A grunt."

I nodded.

I called home, the only home I knew. When the receiver at the other end clicked, I felt my pulse race. Betty answered. "Betty?"

"Petey?"

"Yes."

"Oh, God. Everyone's going crazy. You disappeared. No one knew where. You okay?"

"I'm in jail in Los Angeles. I couldn't get to a phone until now."

"What did you do? Or can't you talk?"

"Not really. It's over something that was supposed to have happened three years ago in San Francisco."

"You're not hurt?"

"No. I need an attorney."

"Okay. I'll tell Willy. He figured you'd show up at the ranch or something crazy."

I heard Stella in the background asking what was going on. Betty tried to explain and talk to me at the same time, until in frustration she handed the receiver to Stella. "Pete, you get yourself home. What's the idea of gettin arrested?"

"Hello, Stella," I said.

"Hello. Don't you worry none. Willy'll get you home," she said. "You miss us?"

I had to look away from the deputy and the bailiff because my eyes were watering. "I'm ready to come home."

"Well, don't do nothin." She turned the phone over to Betty.

"Petey, hang tough. Where are you at this minute?"

"In the judge's chambers using his personal phone."

"Dad will love to hear that. What court?"

I relayed the information from the bailiff. "Where's your husband?" I asked.

"No husband, Petey. We got divorced last month." She said good-bye, as did Stella. When I hung up my eyes were dry again. The bailiff told me to relax—that the judge wanted to talk. "He has a son over there. A Marine lieutenant. He watches the news like an addict, talks to any soldier he meets just to keep up. He'll ask a lot of questions. Answer them so it'll make him feel good."

I said I would.

The judge made arrangements to hold me in court until a public defender showed up. He removed his robes and sat with me in his chambers. He sent the bailiff for soft drinks and cookies, said the one thing his son missed most was peanut-butter cookies. "You like them?"

"Yes, sir."

"This case, is there anything to it, son?"

"I shouldn't say, I guess."

"No. But if it's a cockamamie charge, I have influence with the district attorney's office in San Francisco. This isn't much of a homecoming, you being in jail. I'd like to help."

I smiled. "I broke a dope dealer's finger when he wouldn't get off my motorcycle."

"Dope dealer?"

"Yes, sir, in Haight-Ashbury."

"Because he wouldn't get off your motorcycle?"

I shrugged. "He wanted to use it or something, and I wouldn't let him. I stayed with him and some other hippies. He was this older guy who took in all these runaways and fed them drugs and . . . I don't know. It was a long time ago, and I forgot it mostly. Never thought a thing of it. It was the day I decided to join the army."

"Did you know there was a charge filed against you?"

"No, sir." ·

"Okay, son. Let me think on it a moment."

What he was doing stretched ethics. When I mentioned this he waved it off and called his law clerk into the office. They discussed my case until the bailiff returned with four soft drinks and a bag of peanut-butter cookies, at which time the judge asked the clerk if he knew what to do. The young man, a slight bookish type with darting eyes, said he did and left us.

For the next half hour, as we dipped our hands in the cookie bag, the judge grilled me on Vietnam, wanting to know the pitfalls of combat over there and the duties of a platoon leader. He asked about the terrain and the people and wanted to know most of all if it was indeed futile. To the last, I explained how we kept going over and over again into the same villages, that we controlled nothing and probably never would. He thanked me for my candor. For a moment I was jealous of that young lieutenant for having a father who cared so deeply. I said I hoped his son came back soon. "I thank you for that. I cross my fingers and pray. He won't like what he sees, though. He'll feel betrayed, as you must."

When finally I was returned to the jail, my lockup was a holding cell near the booking desk. Deputies who had once ignored my requests to make a phone call now took pains to assure me that it was only a matter of time until a public defender would be along. I was making small talk with a deputy when three lawyers arrived to see me at the same time. Two had flown from San Francisco to Los Angeles in a chartered plane. The other practiced law in Los Angeles and wore a three-piece navy-blue silk suit that was almost as glossy as his silver-gray hair.

When I was led into the conference room to meet with them, my first words were, "Willy sent you?"

They nodded simultaneously, then the silver-haired one told me to sit and tell my story. That was about the time the public defender showed up, holding in his hand a writ of habeas corpus granted by the judge who'd sent him. I was a free man.

44

Willy leaned against the back of the couch, his legs crossed at the ankles, a bottle of Jack Daniel's in the crook of his arm. He looked me over as if inspecting me for market. He'd changed, but I noticed that although he'd gained some weight, he seemed to be shrinking. There was a clouding in his eyes, and the backs of his hands were beginning to mottle. His skin bore deep wrinkles around his jowls. There was something else, too, a melancholy in his eyes. Perhaps it had been there all along and I'd never seen it. But now it was easy to discern. "Well, what you got to say?" he asked.

"Nothing."

"Nothin? Not a gawdamn thing?"

"I'd like to go to the ranch."

"In the summer. We'll go the summer an have a time."

I nodded.

"You're thinkin you don't hafta take nothin no more. Went off an fought yourself a war an come back a man, an independent."

"No, sir," I said, then muttered, "'I shall wear the bottoms of my trousers rolled.'"

"What's 'at?"

"Nothing. A line from a stupid poem, sir."

"We been through that before too. What's my name?"

"Willy."

"Don't be contrary. Enough 'a that from Betty, who's fixin to marry another gawdamn idiot. I ain't got time for play. Gettin older. Don't have things lined up. I want you to marry her."

"Betty?"

Willy gave me that old chilling stare that remained frightening despite his fading eyes. I apologized and explained that she wouldn't marry me. "Then you thought about it?"

"Willy!" Stella shouted as she entered the room.

"'Course he did," Willy said.

"Boy ain't home five hours, Willy, and you're fixin to run him off again," she said and took a seat next to me. "You let your own do as they damn please. Let Pete have a little rein."

"Let 'im keep that damned motorcycle, didn't I?" he said without looking away from me. "You thought about it, ain't you, Pete?"

"A long time ago."

"You ain't had no long time," he said.

"Don't answer none of his fool questions, Pete. He's been through enough, Willy. Hell, why should he leave a war to come home to somethin worse?"

I sat upright suddenly and startled Stella. She stared at him, but he was looking at me and pretending not to notice her. He shook his head.

"You promised, Willy," Stella said.

"Never mind. I ain't done nothin. Pete, forget whatever nonsense come from me. I'm just glad to have you home an a bit upset with Betty." He laughed and took a swig out of his bottle, which he handed to me. I thought about the judge and how he worried about his boy, about the possibilities of that kind of kinship and love. I felt as if I had ten fingerprints that all looked the same. I took a short nip and set the bottle on the coffee table in front of him.

As his fingers curled around the neck, I asked, "Willy, what now?"

He clutched the bottle and brought it to his mouth, his eyes never leaving mine. "Don't know, Pete, but I'll drink to it," he said and took a gulp.

Willy waved to the group from Texas and excused himself. I was left in his booth with Ruben Lee, who'd been sitting with a smirk on his face while Willy laid out his plans for me to come to work. George had said he'd be glad to have me back, that it was certainly good to have family on the floor. Ruben Lee had said that I wasn't family, but George had said I was close enough to family for him. He'd shaken my hand and gone his way.

"Hang around long enough you can meet my fiancée. Name's Belinda," Ruben Lee said.

"That'd be nice," I said. "Bet Willy's glad."

The casino thrummed in the background. He set his eye on me. "Well, Mr. War Hero? I heard dope's dynamite over there."

"Yeah, dynamite."

"Still have to be the hero?"

"Nice to be home, Ruben Lee. Can't tell you how nice."

"You probably sat on your ass in some office and got high."

"That's what I did."

"Now we've got something in common," he said. "I don't think . . ." He couldn't finish because Willy was walking our way.

Willy swung into the booth beside me and pushed his hat back. "You two start getting along. I ain't got the patience I once had. Hear that, Ruben Lee?"

"Sure."

"Pete?"

"Fine with me."

"It's all settled up, then. Far as I'm concerned you're home, Pete. For good now," he said. "Ruben Lee, you take him upstairs and work him out on the layout. Craps an then roulette. I want him to be the best damn dealer in here." He looked at me. "We'll talk 'bout schoolin later."

I followed Ruben Lee up to a small office adjacent to the eye in the sky. In the room was a flat board, hip high, a felt craps layout stapled atop it. Ruben Lee shut the door and walked to the cabinet, where he rummaged through one of the drawers. He held up a sealed baggie, grinned and said, "Thai stick. Can't learn if you're straight." After lighting up, he took a draw and passed it to me. "Good as anything you had over there, I'll bet."

I wanted to leave that behind. Vietnam and drugs blended together, flip sides of suspended sanity, something buddies did to find collective escape or others did to deal with fear or nightmare memories. This was the world. I'd made it. Home, where sanity reigned, where you could wake up and not wonder if it was your last day. I declined.

"Mr. Fucking War Hero. I was about to say downstairs I don't think you're going to find things the same." He held out the joint. "Go on. We're buddies now, aren't we?"

"I'm not . . ."

He smiled in a friendly way, inviting me to take it, offering it like a proposition. "Like a peace offering, Petey. Between, well, brothers, I guess." This time I took it. He watched me inhale and hold it in my lungs and smiled broadly. "What would the old man say now?"

45

Though I'd never planned on being a dealer, and resisted the idea passionately, I went to work for Willy doing what Julie had done. I stayed to myself and took night classes at Las Vegas High School to earn credits toward a diploma. I spent hours with Ruben Lee learning the craft and smoking marijuana or hash. I refused anything stronger, though I would watch him shoot up cocaine and heroin—a speedball, he called it.

On those evenings when I didn't go to school, I went to the Pussy Cat A Go Go to drink and sometimes dance, though I wasn't much of a dancer. I tried talking to women, but was worse at that than dancing. I was inexperienced with women. There had been Betty and a few prostitutes. But the women in the club weren't Betty or boom-boom girls who would giggle and pull down their pants.

I wanted someone to care, so I could learn to care again. I craved conversation that seemed impossible to find, the kind that pried words out. In terms of feelings, 'Nam meant something far beyond what I could understand. I'd found a friend, one who'd held a glass to my lips and fed me when I was feverish, one who'd stayed because of me, and I'd lost him and somehow myself. I expected to meet a girl interested in something more than slipping on hiphuggers and a tank top and dancing with a guy who puffed up his hair with a blow dryer. I wanted more than going out to a dark car for a quick feel and a snort of coke.

I would watch couples dance, look at the meat line by the bar or young women sitting by the dance floor, legs crossed, one swinging to the beat, a sign she was waiting. I didn't have the nerve to cross the room and ask for a dance. What would I say? There had been enough "nos" in my life. I would leave the club dejected, buy a fifth of tequila and ride to Calico Basin, where I'd park the motorcycle and sit staring at stars and contemplating a world that made no sense. Drinking, getting drunk, seemed appropriate. The world offered vice without condition.

The case in California came to an abrupt halt because Sachs died, an overdose of cocaine and amphetamines at a Rolling Stones concert at the Altamont Speedway—another emergency room statistic lost in the media shuffle, for that was the rockfest where Hell's Angels stomped an overzealous fan to death. With the case dismissed, the only legal problem remaining was to seal the record. Willy told me to sit as he called the attorneys and said the retainer he'd given them more than covered getting the record sealed. He told them I was a war hero and was going to be a lawyer someday and he wanted nothing on my record. When he hung up, I told him I wasn't a war hero. "Ain't how I see it, Pete. You was hero enough and it'll serve you someday."

"Serve me how?"

"We'll see. Finish your schoolin first."

At the casino our relationship took on an entirely different aspect. On my breaks I would walk by his booth, where he held court. He now enjoyed a kind of calm sovereignty; he reigned without the external worries that had once haunted him. The feds no longer pursued him. At last the almost-three-decade-old murder indictment in Dallas had been dropped. He'd outlived the witnesses. It was easy to imagine him in some Arthurian tale. A good knight or the villainous one, it didn't matter, for he'd survived the quests and aged pleas-antly, tough and not unscarred. His wounds were the same old ones—a son who used drugs, a daughter who wasted herself on worthless men and alcohol, another son distant and ambitious, and a love, perhaps his only love, buried but alive in his mind. If he noticed me walk by he'd call me over and introduce me as a boy he found in a basket outside the door of his office.

He kept tabs on me, but I no longer chatted with him, as George insisted I was to be treated no differently from any other dealer. George spoke only in passing, and pit bosses were under strict orders to show no favoritism. One did, Levi Ashberg. He remembered me as a busboy who used to pour his coffee and make sure he had a newspaper to read. His nephew was serving in Vietnam with the 101st Airborne, so Levi felt a personal connection with me.

From time to time I would notice Willy in the corner of my eye watching from the podium. He'd call the pit boss over and whisper something to him. Invariably the boss would come to my table and lean into my ear and whisper that I was holding my deck too low or that I was too slow in my shuffle or that I wasn't paying attention to the player in the last seat. If it was Levi, he would merely whisper, "The old man says you're too damned smart to waste your life in a casino dealing cards. Get to college."

I had good, if not gifted, hands, and of course Ruben Lee taught me well. But whether craps or blackjack or roulette, I came very quickly to hate each long hour behind the table, an hour spent on my feet, my hip leaned into the table's edge, my mind in a fog. I would daydream, often about the ranch or the Finnlander Hotel where Betty and I had made love, where I'd held Sarge's hand as he'd taken his last breath. I daydreamed about pleasant times. Vietnam, on the other hand, came to me in my sleep.

I saw Betty almost daily. She took only the occasional glance at me, and if our eyes met she would give me an enigmatic smile that reminded me of Paéz those days before he went down that final hole. She came to see her second husband, Neil Sumber, who worked in the cage. George had given him a position at Willy's insistence. But Willy didn't like Neil, called him the "dumbest turd never to fall out of a cow's ass." He considered him less than masculine, for Neil had been a fashion model before marrying Betty. Not the kind of work Willy thought of as manly. Betty had met him at a club in Los Angeles the weekend after her divorce. She picked him out of a meat line at the bar. He was the blondest of the pretty ones. Though she was seven years younger than he, she called him her pretty child.

Ruben Lee invited me upstairs into the peek, as we called it, where he lit up a joint. He immediately sat on his stool and watched the action on the casino floor, for whether high or not, he took his job seriously. He told me to slide closer. "Whatever happened over there made you more tolerable, Pete," he said. "You were too . . ."

"Straight?" I handed him the joint.

"Yeah. I want you to come on over tonight. We've got a couple of mutual friends you may want to see."

I didn't trust Ruben Lee. The memory of that night in the house at the ranch had never left me. It was in his face whenever I looked at him, a kind of knowing smirk. "Who?" I asked.

"Just come over after work. You'll see."

I parked the bike in the driveway at Ruben Lee's next to an old Dodge pickup. The light was on. The door opened and Ruben Lee stood barefoot before me, wearing jeans and a T-shirt. Inside, the only light came from the television set. He said he was glad I came and pulled me in. My eyes adjusting to the dim light, I followed him to the living room.

"There," he said.

The screen was on, but the sound was turned down. The TV cast a pale blue light on the room. On a chair in the corner sat Louie Skyles, his legs parted, pants rolled down to his ankles. A woman with long straight hair knelt between his knees. Her hair covered her profile so that I saw nothing but the back of her head as it bobbed up and down. Louie grinned. "Hey, shithead," he said. "Remember me?"

"Sure. I see your taste in sex partners has changed."

Ruben Lee poured a shot of tequila and held it in front of me. "Petey's quick."

Louie let the comment lie.

"Have a seat, Petey," Ruben Lee said. "Let's watch. You can have a turn after we take care of business."

He was on the fading side of a down, probably heroin, and seemed ready to crash. Glassy-eyed, he watched the woman perform and somehow managed to keep his eyes open.

"What business?" I asked.

He didn't seem to hear at first, and when I repeated myself, it took him a moment to make the connection. "Louie," he said. "Louie says you've got business."

Louie hollered, "Yeah! Okay!" And held the back of her head as he thrust his hips upward.

"I remember Louie," I said.

"Yeah," Louie said. "You're getting there." He leaned back, his eyes half shut.

"That's right," Ruben Lee said. "And if the three of us—four of us—are going to get along, you've got to take care of your obligation," Ruben Lee said to Louie. "And we've got to get it done before Belinda comes over."

"What obligation?" I didn't know what else to say. Good sense told me to leave right then, but I didn't. I decided to see this, whatever *this* was, through to the end.

The woman picked up a half-full wineglass. She spat Louie's semen into it, then looked over her shoulder at me. "Petey Elkins," she said.

"Annette Sylvestri," I said. "Never thought I'd see you like this."

"I'm home on break from school."

"She remembered you when I mentioned your name," Ruben Lee said.

"Yeah. What now?"

Louie buckled his pants and zipped the fly, but stayed seated. "Remember the club, Petey? You used it on me."

I nodded.

"Remember how we fucked you in the ass, Petey. In juvey?"

I looked at Annette. Except to shrug, she didn't react, just stood with her weight resting on one hip, her hands crossed beneath her breasts. She obviously wanted the confrontation, wanted blood. Mine, the way I saw it. I said that I remembered.

"Think you can kick my ass?"

As I matched his stare, I sized him up. He looked the same as the last time I'd seen him, except twenty pounds heavier, a considerable amount of it muscle. I was taller by perhaps an inch.

"Without a club, I mean?"

Ruben Lee smiled like a Roman lord about to turn the deciding thumb. "Louie spent the last two years in prison pumping weights. Looks pretty impressive."

"I'm no punk," Louie said. "Am I, Annette?"

She grinned. "You're disgusting." She grabbed his crotch then sat on his lap.

"Ruben Lee tells me you're a war hero, Petey. Is that right?" Louie said with a sneer.

I stood and walked over. Annette brushed her hair aside and smiled. "I'm going to Harvard, Petey. The men are all pukes," she said.

I said. "You must have changed to run with Louie. He used to steal change out of cars."

"Who hasn't?" she asked.

"Everybody has, I guess." I inched closer to the chair. Louie's eyes were glazed over. I was thankful Ruben Lee had been generous with drugs and even more grateful to Annette for sitting on Louie's lap. By the time Louie realized what I had in mind, it was too late. He shouted for her to get off and pushed her onto the floor. He came out of the chair in time to meet my foot with his face.

She shrieked, not out of terror but out of pleasure. I locked an arm around his throat and took him to the floor, where I smashed an elbow into his face. I struck and struck again until he went limp. She shrieked at each blow. Then I rolled off him. He was unconscious. My heart raced for a moment, then seemed to find itself. I looked up at Ruben Lee and Annette. Ruben Lee was dumbfounded. She was smiling. I shook my head and stood.

"Wasn't very friendly, was he?" I said.

Ruben Lee chuckled and offered me a joint. Annette said she'd like to go to the bedroom with me. I turned down both. Ruben Lee said he'd just lost a thousand-dollar bet. I asked to whom. Without answering, he demanded to know who was going to clean up the blood.

I shrugged. "Annette, maybe. She seems to like it."

She followed me to the door, where I asked if she had bet the thousand.

She shook her head. "I think it was with Betty." She said she would clean up the blood and gave me her phone number and asked me to call. I said I would, but I knew I wouldn't.

I bought a bottle of tequila and drove to Calico Basin. I climbed a rocky arroyo to the top, where I lay on my back and watched the stars as I drank.

The night chill had set in, and the sandstone was hard and painful. None of it mattered. Nothing mattered, nothing at all, except that I wasn't behind the table listening to some gambler asking me to go easy on him. I wondered if there was a hole from where I lay to the tunnels in Cu Chi or Ho Bo Woods. I toasted Paéz and took a deep swallow. I drank until I passed out.

46

Ruben Lee met me as I came off a game and handed me an envelope. He said it contained a couple of roaches and winked. I hurried up the steps to the room where the training tables were kept and shut the door. I wouldn't have time to smoke both joints. Save one for after work. I tore open the envelope and dumped the contents in my palm—two dead cockroaches. Ruben Lee was nowhere around, but I could hear him laughing all the same.

Ruben Lee opened the box. A scorpion crawled out. He dumped it on the floor and crushed it. "Nice try."

"Next time."

He took a hit off the joint and passed it. "Where'd you get it, Pete?"

"Under some rocks near Hoover Dam."

"Clever."

He looked at the cigarette lighter box. "Where's the cigarette lighter?"

"Don't know. Hey, don't Bogart the joint."

He handed it to me.

"I got the box at Leonardo's jewelry store."

"Might 'a worked."

I held the smoke deep in my lungs, let it perform its little miracle. "Well, guess the next time's on you."

"I'm a crazy fucker, aren't I, Pete? How would I have done in 'Nam?"

"Dead, Ruben Lee. Just dead. Crazy had nothing to do with anything. It was all whimsy."

"What if I put a rattler in your car?"

"I ride a motorcycle," I said and passed the joint back.

He took it and winked. "Fuck you, Petey."

"Yeah, fuck me, all right."

I opened the door. It was past two in the morning. Betty stood by herself, shivering, her arms wrapped over her breasts. She tried to steady herself. She smelled of whiskey. She stumbled in uninvited and looked my apartment over, a studio with a couch that made into a bed and a television. My clothes were strewn on the floor, on end tables, in the kitchenette, everywhere.

"You need a maid," she said and threw herself down on the couch.

I looked around at the floor, at the separate piles of dirty clothes. An empty tequila bottle sat atop the television. I picked it up along with a to-go bag of half-eaten fries and tossed them in the trash. I said, "I haven't had time to do laundry."

"This month?" she asked.

"These months," I said.

She looked much older than her twenty-three years. I remembered thinking how much older she'd looked when she drove into the car wash in Willy's Cadillac. Nearly ten years now. Even then I'd thought of her as a woman. But now she looked like a very old little girl.

"Sit, Pete." She patted the couch.

"Oh, I don't think so," I said. "Shouldn't you be home with your husband . . . or out getting drunk with him?"

"Ruben Lee says you're crazy."

"He'd know."

"Willy says you're sowing wild oats. I say you're just like this family—all fucked up. What happened? I mean, Petey, what the hell happened? You just couldn't stay? Come on, Petey, tell me, explain all this, 'cause you're so damned smart you just know every fucking thing."

"I don't know anything, Betty."

"But you're so goddamned smart."

I sat down on the biggest pile of clothing and crossed my legs. "I'm not smart, Betty."

"You loved me?"

"No one else."

"Yeah, you're not so smart. You have a drink?"

"Some beer. The tequila's gone."

"No whiskey?"

"No."

"Fuck you, then, Petey. I'm leaving." She started to stand but couldn't.

"I'll call your husband to come get you."

She laughed. "He won't. I kicked him out. Willy gave him a hundred thousand and told him to go back to California and to sign whatever divorce papers he gets."

"I'm sorry."

"He was pretty, wasn't he?"

"Very pretty."

"You're not pretty, Petey."

"No, not pretty. Un-pretty is what I am, Betty."

"Petey, will you sleep with me?"

"No, I can't do that anymore."

"Don't you love me?"

"I don't know what the hell love is, Betty."

"Come on." She stood and unbuttoned her jeans.

"I don't think so."

She shook her head and pulled the jeans to her knees. She pushed her panties down to her pubic hair and touched a scar. It was shiny and white against her pale pink flesh. She rubbed her finger over it. "I can still wear a bikini and no one will know. But I do, Pete. Know what it is?"

"No, Betty."

"They took it out. My uterus. No babies, Petey. None."

"I'm sorry."

"Yeah, me too." She tilted her head and stared at the fine, carefully cut adhesion. "That afternoon you found me with Rich?"

"Yeah, I remember."

"You were mad, jealous."

"Yeah. Not now."

"Not now. Do you think I give a shit about mad, now or then?"

"I don't want to fight."

She pulled up her jeans and buttoned them, which was no easy task. I asked if I could drive her home. "Home? Drive me? Petey, that afternoon Rich met me to take me to the doctor. I had no one to turn to. It was yours. I had no choice. Willy would have . . . I don't know. Do you know, Pete? You're so smart, do you know?"

"Mine?"

She pursed her lips. "I'll take a beer."

I went to the refrigerator, got a can of beer, and opened it.

"You've been back over a year and never tried to call, never tried to see me," she said.

I handed her the beer. "An abortion?"

"Yeah, happens all the time. Only I got infections. They took my . . . God, I hate cans. You got a clean glass?"

"You'll have to use the can," I said. "I messed up, didn't I?"

She gulped the beer down. "We've got so much in common." She laughed, then cried, then passed out.

I got a beer out of the refrigerator and sat on the floor listening to her snore.

47

I vaguely remembered what started it—a bump, an exchange of stares, then words followed by a second bump. I'd been dancing, looking for anything to make the night a little interesting. I didn't know my dance partner, just a young woman who'd left her daughter with a baby-sitter so she could party on a Friday night. Nor did I know the guy who bumped me or his friend and could barely describe what they looked like, just types—long hair, bell bottoms, deck shirts. After he bumped into me the second time, I hit him, the closest one, and knocked him to the dance floor. The other came out of my blind side and tackled me. People screamed all around us as we fell to the floor and grappled on the hardwood, rolling over twice. I came out on top.

Out of the corner of my eye I saw my dance partner press her hands to her ears and shout for me to stop. But I was beyond stopping, beyond reasoning. A man told us to take it outside, and I thought how ludicrous it all was, the whole scene, the spectacle of nightclubs and strangers shoving at one another, fighting over a spot of polished hardwood that belonged to neither of them. But its very ludicrousness took on some figurative meaning to me. I got a solid grip on my opponent's throat and began to squeeze. It was, to me, a simple question of what price he was willing to pay for coming to the aid of a friend who'd started the whole thing in the first place.

The first one got to his feet, came over, and tried to kick me in the head. I ducked the first kick as his foot grazed the back of my head. The next landed on my ribs. For an instant it felt as if my rib cage was going to split down the center, but I held my grip. The kicker shouted, "Motherfucker! Motherfucker!" and kicked at me again and again until I let loose of his friend. People were calling me an animal. I rolled away from his relentless foot, came up in a crouch, and charged him once I gained my footing. We went down in pile with two or three others, then I felt hands tugging at me.

The band hadn't missed a beat, as if we were just part of the performance. Two bouncers lifted me off the floor, pinned my arms back, and pulled me away. The kicker came up and took a free shot at my face. I brought a foot up into his groin. One of the bouncers landed a punch to my kidney, then they dragged me off in the direction of the entrance. Along the way the bouncers took a few shots with their fists at my face and ribs, and once I fell down and they kicked me. At the front steps a small group of nightclubbers congregated, smoking cigarettes and talking. They were indifferent spectators. The bouncers stood at the top of the steps. One holding each of my arms and legs, they counted to three and heaved me toward the paved parking lot. Gravity did the rest. That was when my nose cracked.

I stood outside in the parking lot, my nose bleeding, waiting for the other two, the longhairs, but they didn't suffer my fate. The group at the steps stared at me, but none of them spoke. One went inside the Pussy Cat to summon someone. A moment later the same bouncers came to the door and told me to get the hell gone. I told them I'd be back, flipped them off, and staggered to my bike.

All in all, it was a good thing I'd been at the Pussy Cat only long enough for one drink.

Somehow I managed to make it to my apartment. It wasn't the first time I'd come home a mess. I was out of control, both trouble and troubled, walking around much of the time with an anger that boiled up in my stomach just before I lost control. I didn't know why I was so angry, and worse, I wasn't looking for an explanation. I never offered alibis for what I did, the fighting and the drinking, felt no need to. I behaved however I wished as if immune to normal rules. I paid the tariff with my cuts and bruises.

I managed to get a wet towel for my nose and stumbled onto my bed. I ached, especially my ribs and jaw. I couldn't shut my mouth, which was probably best, since my nose was already plugged with dried blood. I passed out for a few minutes, then woke and sat upright. I'd been choking in my sleep, which caused me no end of panic as I fumbled through the pages of my address book. I couldn't bring the numbers into focus. That was when I realized I could see out of only one eye. The other had closed. From memory, I dialed Miriam's number. I could think of no one else to call. Certainly not Willy, who lately had been disgusted with me.

"Hello." Her voice was tired.

"I's me, 'Ete," I said. I couldn't bring my lips together to sound a "P."

"Who's this?" she asked. The words sounded as if they'd been pasted together.

"Your h'rother," I said.

"Petey?"

"'Es. 'Sme."

"Jesus, what's wrong?"

"'Eh h'eat me uph, uh."

"Oh, God. Are you at your apartment?"

"Uh, huh."

"Hang up, Pete."

I hung up. The room in my open eye swirled. The far wall seemed to be collapsing on me.

I remembered vaguely the telephone ringing and a tap at the door. But that was all.

A long day and a half later I found myself in the hospital, my head throbbing, conscious of my surroundings in a stuporous though strangely almost meditative way. The ceiling was white and seemed an endless backdrop for the shadow of a nurse who was staring me in the face. I kept blinking my one open eye to bring things into focus, but everything was blurry, lineless, and without borders. It was as if I were at the bottom of a rice paddy looking up at mist rolling over the surface. She must have noticed my eye blinking and asked if I could see her. "Yes," I said, but she was a two-dimensional shade. I touched my face. That's when I realized my hand had been bandaged. The skin had been torn from the palm when I landed on the parking lot.

She held a straw up to my lips and told me to take a sip. The water was icy cold and felt wonderful on my tongue. "I understand. You were pretty raw-looking when you came in." She smiled and said a doctor would be in to see me in a while.

The door opened. I heard footsteps, then a shadow crossed the room. I turned my head. It ached fiercely, but I was glad to see Stella. "You're a mess, Pete," she said.

"Stella?"

"That's right."

"When you gonna quit breakin other people's hearts? When?"

"Stella."

"Me an Croaker brung you in. Thought you was . . . Pete, I can't go through it. You gotta do something."

Do what? I knew that whatever was troubling me was more than I could handle. How many more scrapes like this one? How many broken noses or sprained wrists? How many predawn trips to the hospital? The last thing I wanted to be was a burden. The problem was, I didn't know who I was or the first thing whoever I was really wanted. Stella put a hand on my shoulder and told me I'd be okay.

"Did you know," I said, "that your name means star in Latin?"

"Someone told me that once, Pete. Yes." She squeezed my shoulder and began to cry.

She said she wasn't going to cry, that she'd cried enough for her own and I was just another ungrateful child. I told her everything would be all right, to not worry. She couldn't answer. I wanted to cry, but sadly couldn't, so kept saying everything would be fine, just fine.

Willy slammed the door and stared at me as if I were wearing women's panties. "Pete, sit down."

I sat.

"You been back over two years now, Pete. What 'a you done? Nothin."

"I finished high school."

"Hell, that ain't nothin. Betty finished high school. Never went half the time. Cheated wherever she could."

"I've worked for you. Isn't that enough?"

"No."

I looked around the office walls. His Charles Russell painting of the cowboys at the campfire was gone. "Where's the cowboy painting, Willy?"

"Where it belongs. At the ranch."

"That's where I belong, Willy."

"Drinkin and smokin dope two years, Pete. An fightin, though that I don't object too strongly to."

I couldn't look him in the eye.

"I expect fool stuff from Ruben Lee. Somethin never fit with him. He never got the kinda hold George got, though George ain't so damned perfect. An I wasn't much of a pa, especially with Ruben Lee. He wants to be like me, but it's hard to make a son be somethin the pa wasn't. I got hope in you still."

"Why, Willy?"

He walked to the window and looked down on Fremont Street. "I got all this one marker at a time from a man who couldn't play poker. That paintin you like an that ugly-as-sin armor over there came with it. I never cheated him, neither. He just was no good with cards. He sat right at that desk an put a thirty-eight to his mouth 'cause he lost ever'thing. That was in 'forty-eight. 'Course he didn't kill hisself, an for five years till he died, I told folks we was partners to save his face. When he died, his daughter, who never gave a lick 'bout him, threatened to sue me for stealin his share. I give 'er two hundred thousand, Pete. Money she didn't have comin. Know why?"

"Because you're basically good, Willy."

"I 'preciate you sayin that, though it ain't so." He walked back to the desk, and this time sat. "I give to her, 'cause I didn't want people thinkin I was an ungrateful sumbitch. Nothin nags me more 'an ungratefulness. You listenin?"

"Yes. Ingratitude."

"Don't be correctin my words." He opened the drawer and pulled out stacks of bills, all hundreds, which he laid before me one at a time. He counted the stacks—twenty-five. "Ten thousand in ever'one, Pete. A quarter of a million. Invested right, a man could live off it for life."

I stared at the money.

"Like the look of it, don't you?" He tossed me a stack.

I rolled the bundle over in my hand, riffled a corner, and tossed it back on the desk.

"Know why this money's here?"

"No."

"It's yours."

"Mine?"

"You can put it in that bag and carry it outta here." He pointed to a small soft-leather valise on the couch.

I stared at the stacks, recalling how much I'd dreamed of having money as a kid and the things it would buy—a Corvette. "I guess I should thank you."

"Whoa. Ain't that easy. You go to college an law school like I had planned so you can come back an help my boys run the Lucky. Though I intend to try, I ain't livin forever. It's nineteen an seventy-one, Pete. I'm sixty-nine years old. Someone gotta take care'a my baby girl."

I nodded.

"You'll marry her when you finish college. My boys're hard, like me, but different. Ruben Lee, he's got no control. George, he's all control like a calc'latin machine."

I gazed at the pattern in the Navajo rug. I realized Willy knew what had happened that summer on the ranch, probably orchestrated it. "The Navajo," I said, "weave flaws into their work so as not to insult the spirits of creation."

"Don't know what that means, but you're a damn smart boy, Pete. Knew soon as I set eyes on you. Got your face all healed up, but your nose been outta joint way too long."

"What's the deal, Willy?"

"You're goin away next time . . . You ain't no kind 'a drinker. Never will be. Betty's 'nough of a drinker for two."

"What if I don't take the money?"

He grinned. "Take your time."

"She was pregnant," I said, "with my kid."

He nodded, then stood, crossed over to the bar, and poured himself a shot of sour mash, which he downed. "You saved her when she tried to kill herself over that guitar player." He poured another shot and drank it. "I saw Hugh Stample put a gun barrel in his mouth at that very desk twenty-four year ago. Couldn't unnerstand, him bein so desperate an all. But later, I almost did the same. An you got the answer why.

"I never got over you readin *Gatsby*. Him ownin the damn world, but losin the woman. You asked 'nough questions to figure it out. Now, 'at's my baby girl from that love. Wasn't the Lucky kept me goin or Stella or them boys. Was her. I can't die an let them boys have at her."

"No. I guess not."

"We got a deal?"

I couldn't answer. I'd been disheartened so long I didn't know what it meant not to be. I wanted those feelings to go away, despair that I couldn't quite pinpoint, the losses—Paéz, being raped in juvey, Betty. A list. But the list was blurry. It wasn't the past or the future I grieved for, but the present, hours behind the table hearing the same themes, no one seeing me as a person, my humanity reduced. I folded my hands in my lap, stared at them, and started to cry, not deep sobs, just slow tears.

"Don't, Pete. Damn, boy. What's come 'a you?"

"I'm a drunk, Willy. I'm . . ."

He kneeled beside the chair. "I'll put you in a hospital. I know a good one. Been lookin at 'em for years for Ruben Lee."

"I'm not worth it," I said.

He patted my shoulder and whispered, "Don't worry, Pete. Don't worry."

48

Unlike the rest of the world, the ranch seemed unchanged, except for the addition of a second cottage. Cal had aged, and his years in the harsh weather showed in his leathery face, now permanently browned. He was still a handsome man, and Conchita beamed like a young girl when he wrapped an arm about her as I drove in. They'd been married a few years now, a marriage that seemed to have subdued them both. Cal opened my door. "Hear you're ready to work," he said.

I shook his hand. I was surprised to find I was taller than he was. Age was shrinking him—as it was Willy.

"What happened to the motorcycle?"

"Still have it. Just decided to drive up in one of the Cadillacs."

Conchita hugged me and gazed up at my face. She asked why I hadn't come sooner, since I'd been home from the war for three years.

"I was drunk most of the time."

She averted her gaze.

"Well, you'll have the house to yourself, Pete," Cal said.

"I'd like to sleep in the bunkhouse, Cal."

"Willy wants you to . . ."

I opened the trunk to get my bag out.

"Is Jiggers still here?"

"Near Billings, living in a cabin outside of town. Willy takes care of everything for him."

"I'd like to see him. How about Oso and . . ."

"Gone. All new hands, Pete."

I nodded. "I'll stay in the big house till they get used to me. It's no good being pushy."

"Yep. That's probably what Willy was thinking."

Cal grabbed a bag and helped me to the house. Conchita had decorated the table in the entry with flowers from her garden. The house smelled of . . . home. They stood with me a moment as I looked around from the base of the stairs. Was this where she lay dying in 1949?

"It's been haunted a long while," Cal said. "That's the problem with empty houses."

I looked at him as if seeing him anew. What a strange notion to cross his lips. Perhaps he'd always thought this way but didn't express it. I spread the curtain and looked through the pane at the purple valley, the sun slanting west, flowers in bloom. Spring. "I'll be here for the summer, Cal. I'm going to college in the fall."

"Good for you, Pete. Willy'll pay for the best education you could have, I'll bet."

"I'm not going to one of the best schools, and Willy's not paying."

"I'm sure that'll be just fine," he said.

"The place looks good, Conchita," I said.

"You eat with the boys?" she asked.

"Not yet. Can you fix me some *menudo* for lunch?"

"*Sí*, Pedro."

"May I have the key to Willy's liquor cabinet?"

Her eyes widened as she looked to Cal for the answer. He looked at me. I met his gaze. He told her it would be okay. She handed over the key, smiled, and took Cal's arm. They left me.

I unpacked and went to the dining room with *One Hundred Years of Solitude*. Someone in the clinic had recommended it, and it was the first book I'd bought when released. I set the book down and walked to the liquor cabinet, took out a bottle of sour mash, and set it before me. I turned to the first page of the book. My hand was steady. I felt good.

I'd spent months drying out and five more just talking to counselors, hard months examining, not just Vietnam but twenty-four years of life. I'd built wooden model ships and painted in oils, worked my hands in clay. I'd written thoughts and awakened in the night and paced. They'd given me language to personalize and internalize—survivor guilt, post stress, dependency. I'd craved drink, wanted to fight my counselors and fellow patients, considered escape, though I could have walked out, as I was free to do so. I'd had two malaria relapses and was treated for that as well. Gradually the process had led me to the place where the real search begins. I'd looked for the holes that I'd disappeared into and found that I had to crawl back out of them one at a time without someone pulling me up with a rope.

And now I was here.

I looked up at the bottle occasionally. Once, I picked it up and read the label, shook the contents, and watched the bubbles die almost at once. It was amber, darker than urine, attractive. I could smell the liquor in my mind. I could taste it the same way. My mouth went dry. My heart pounded. I set the bottle down and walked to a window. I knew that I must go through this, that every day would be a similar test. I returned the bottle to its place of rest. All of my life I'd been far from home. Home was just a thought. I hoped that would change. *Hope,* I thought. What a wonderful word to find.

I read and read, devouring a third of the book before Conchita arrived with lunch. I set the book aside and spooned up the *menudo.* To my mind it tasted better than I remembered. I ate and to feel useful toted the tray to the bunkhouse kitchen, where one hand sat braiding a hackamore. I introduced myself.

"Tom. Tom Bower from Yakima," he said and shook my hand.

He was my age and plain in most ways except for his oversized hands and feet. I washed the dishes and started to leave.

"Where were you over there?" he asked.

"Around Cu Chi, Tay Ninh Province."

"I-Corps," he said. "Hundred and First."

We nodded to one another and I left.

Cal gave me three days before he showed up at the door to tell me it was time to earn my keep. A thick-chested gelding was tied out front. Lead had broken a leg three years before and had been destroyed. I followed Cal down the path, mounted up, and rode beside him and Tom Bower.

Though stoop-shouldered and slow to mount, Cal went about his business with a calm smile on his face at all times. He lived in the new cottage with Conchita, but still slept on the ground during roundup. I was at once reminded of the rhythms of the range, sounds of cowboys and cattle and horses and wind in the sage; the chirping of crickets at night, the sudden explosion of an owl's wings overhead, the cry of a coyote. Strangely, it made me lonely for Vietnam.

Tom and I were chasing strays in a rocky arroyo when his horse threw a shoe and we dismounted. We'd not talked about Vietnam since that day in the kitchen. He slipped the reins over his animal's head and started walking. We didn't speak for a while, then he broke the silence.

"Ever feel like you left before it was finished?" he asked.

"All the time."

"Me too. You got a girl?"

I couldn't help but think of Betty, our summer on the ranch. She, too, had gone to a clinic, hers in Europe, to detoxify. She'd gone unwillingly, Willy having flown her by private jet at night. My guess was that she'd gone in kicking and screaming, but she was still there—a good sign.

"No."

"I heard you were supposed to marry the boss's daughter."

"Guess no one can stop rumors."

"Isn't it the truth," he said.

Tom and I rode often together. More and more I found myself sinking into a silence that I'd never before experienced. It was as if by not speaking I was saying everything I ever meant to say. He didn't talk much either. We'd sit our horses atop a rise and watch the steers raise dust. I learned gradually that he'd never ridden a horse until being discharged from the army. After his discharge, he'd tried living in Yakima, Washington, where he'd been reared, but that didn't work out. His old girlfriend, his job at a cannery, living at home all worked like acid on his soul. He couldn't readjust. When his girl-friend broke off with him, he drove his old Ford pickup to Montana and stopped in Dillon. Two months later Cal hired him.

Tom was clear-eyed and quick, a sometimes brooder, but that's the nature of cowboys. Like sailors looking at the endless sea, they are subject to wonder. Silent pondering of something so vast as the western horizon can pull a man into himself in a way that nothing else can. And he had weight on his soul. I knew from my own experience.

We threw our bedrolls down near each other at night and watched the stars. Days quickly spread behind as silent memories like a deck of cards skillfully fanned out and turned over. By midsummer, we were pals, and he had enough confidence in our friendship to ask questions. He asked about the Bobbins family.

We were working the fences and had just freed a calf that ran to his mother. Tom squatted by a snake hole. He took a stick and probed it. "Why're you doing that?" I asked.

"Just to see."

"Oh."

"So what're the sons like?"

"Why?"

"Just to know."

I stood by my horse, a thick-headed five-year-old roan that liked to run me into trees and scrub and fences. "The older one's not a bad guy. He runs the business side of the casino, the cash end of it. Smart, cordial, conversations to a minimum, never lets you know what's on his mind. Got Willy's poker mind that way."

Tom took this in, probed the hole again and stood. "The other one? I heard he's crazy."

"It's a word, isn't it?"

"Yeah," Tom said. "Is he?"

I told him how Ruben Lee and I now shared a strange camaraderie, one that was shaky at best. "Sometime back Ruben Lee brought me an envelope and told me it had a couple of roaches in it. I thought he meant a couple of joints."

"What was it?"

"Cockroaches."

"Crazy."

"I gave him a box of matches with a dead black widow in it. He handed me a deck of cards I thought was empty. It contained a live black widow. Scorpions were next. It was a game, a goddamn weird one."

"Do me a favor," Tom said.

"What's that?"

"Don't give me any envelopes."

Not then, but later, he asked about Betty. I had to think before I told him she was pretty and that she was trouble.

Willy arrived the second day in August. He brought news that Ruben Lee had eloped and was on his honeymoon in Hawaii with Belinda. Willy seemed pleased to announce it, said he wanted grandchildren, ones that would be a hell of a lot less trouble than his own had been and closer to him than George's were.

"Could be your turn real soon," he said jokingly, but there was an intention that couldn't be missed.

The matter of the money and Betty sat unresolved between us at dinner that night. Willy cut his steak slowly, watching me out of the corner of his eye. He talked around the issue, mostly asking how I was doing and if I'd had any problems with booze. I told him the truth. That, too, seemed to please him. "You ready for school, then, Pete?"

"Yeah."

"Good. Decided on one?"

"I think Northern Arizona or Arizona State."

He cut off a bite of steak and forked it. He held it in front of his face and examined it. "I kinda had somethin better in mind."

"Yeah, I figured you did."

"Why you wanna be contrary? Why does ever'body wanna be so gawdamn contrary?" He dumped the fork on his plate and walked to the liquor cabinet, where he gathered up two glasses and a bottle. He set the glasses upright between us on the table, poured two drinks, and sat down.

"You'll have a drink with me," he said. It wasn't a request.

"Can't, Willy. It's poison to me."

"Okay, you can get by with 'at."

He downed both glasses and picked up the fork. I didn't talk, just ate at the same pace as he. It was dark out and the crickets were chirping. Willy stopped eating to listen. "Best part of my life was here. Lasted two years. Hard to say now what it was like, but it was somethin. Used to sit here when this room was first built an listen to crickets. Didn't nothing else in the damn world matter. You ever feel that strong about a woman, you ain't never gonna be the same man."

"Willy, I've changed."

"You're talkin silly, boy."

"I'm trying to understand."

"Understand? Changed? Changed to a damned ingrate. Don't be troublin me with no newfangled crap."

"I don't want to go to Stanford or Duke. I don't want to be a lawyer."

"Don't matter, Pete." He gave me that look that could freeze words in the vocal cords. "You marry Betty. She ain't got a brain when it comes to men, a weakness I aim to rectify."

I looked past him at my reflection in the window. I saw a man, his face in shadows, a face barely discernible. Willy looked over his shoulder to see what had captured my attention. "What you lookin at?"

"I saw a man go down a hole in Vietnam, Willy. He knew he'd never come up. He quit the war, quit life."

"Quit? Ain't that too bad. I had to fight and kill to get what I got. You just have to be smart. I ain't askin more an that." He poured a shot and held the glass up to look at it. "On the mantel is a key, Pete. You'll need it to get a paintin outta the basement closet. Bring it on up an hang it on the fireplace, then pack your gear an find a bed in the bunkhouse."

I did as I was told. As I opened the door to leave, Willy shouted, "I'm offerin you the damned world, boy! Don't take it so light!"

49

Youthful again, hair glistening, Betty looked angelic as she climbed out of the car. Almost two years had passed since she'd come to my apartment drunk. She'd slept on the couch that night, and in the morning I'd left her there and gone to work. She'd lost fifteen pounds and her face, though etched with past suffering, was bright. Her eyes were as blue as Willy's had once been. She smiled as I picked up her luggage. "Petey, you're taller than me even when you bend down."

"Yeah. How are you?"

"Good as can be expected considering I've been jailed for months."

"Not jail, Betty."

"It was a jail."

"Well, you look great."

"Do I, Petey? Do I really?"

"Yeah."

Tom and Howie, a new wrangler from Colorado, came up the road on their horses. Betty cuffed her hand over her eyes and watched them. They rode on slowly. I set her bags down.

"Where's Willy?"

"Out. Can't say exactly where."

By then Tom and Howie were nearing us. Tom tipped his hat to her as he passed by. His eyes never left hers. "Hello, ma'am," he said. "Hello, Pete."

"Hello yourself," I said.

Howie waved and they rode on. Betty watched them pass. Tom took one last look, then looked ahead. "Name's Tom," I said.

She ran her fingers through her hair, then shook her head as if to answer her own unuttered question.

That night Tom was too quiet. He watched Howie and Arvis play cards, but paid no mind to the game. When it was time to turn in, I paused at his door and said, "Forget it."

"What?"

"Her. Just forget it."

Betty and I rode up to the graves. She talked most of the way, about Europe and two failed marriages that were both of her doing. She referred to her husbands as beautiful drones who wanted to choke the life out of her, but didn't have the strength or the will to do it. She asked nothing about me or my life, and I volunteered nothing. We reached the graves before noon.

It was a calm day full of life. My horse slapped its tail at a deer fly. A raven pecked at a dead squirrel lying beside the trail. He squawked as we approached and took wing reluctantly. The dead squirrel bothered Betty. She asked me to bury it. I told her the bird needed to eat.

I joined her at her mother's grave. She sat, her back pressed to a nearby tree. I squatted down by her. She lit a cigarette and blew the smoke skyward. "I want to be buried here," she said.

"Tell Willy."

"He expects me to marry you."

"Yeah. He's got it all worked out."

"Well?"

"Why didn't you tell me?"

She drew off the cigarette. "Tell what?"

"That you were pregnant?"

She shook her head. "It doesn't matter."

"It does."

She stood and walked to the grave. "We end up here. That's all that matters."

"Is it?"

"Don't test me on it, Petey."

"I want to know why."

"Okay. We were young. Willy might have killed you. I didn't want to ruin two lives. I was mixed up. Hell, I even thought I loved you."

"You did?"

"What difference does that make?"

"Not much now," I said.

"Pretty dramatic, going off to war."

Now I didn't want to continue the conversation. I watched her smoke the cigarette and crush it out, then suggested we take a slow ride back. She walked into the woods without answering, only to return a few minutes later, her eyes red. On the ride back she asked me about Tom, where he came from, whether he was single. I told her to forget it, that he was a nice guy. She grabbed a leaf off a tree and held it up to the light. "Pete," she said, "I feel like I have to hurry up and live, like time is running out. Do you ever feel that way?" I thought a moment and shook my head. She looked away. When we reached the foothills and the riding path, she spurred her horse and rode off churning up dust. I didn't bother to give chase.

The day following that ride Betty and I went our separate ways, speaking only when we were unable to avoid it. I worked as I always had—hard and long—perhaps more out of a sense of desperation than out of a desire to be a cowboy. Though the work was still rewarding, the ranch had lost some shine. The new men, except for Tom, weren't good company. They were silent, as Sarge had been silent, but lacked something. There was no sense of poetry about their work. The stillness of a starry night and a crackling campfire didn't prompt conversation. On occasion I would fall into a melancholy, especially when I thought of the old crew, but I sensed also that the melancholy was partly Betty's presence. This had been our place, our moment. Though the mourning of the loss was long over, I was reminded daily of that short summer in paradise.

Here and there, I caught glimpses of Betty and Tom talking across a fence or standing over the barrel of water, sharing a drink out of a tin cup. I wanted to warn him, but I'd done so once, and on a ranch a man's business is just that. It belongs to him as his saddle does. The only thing more private is his past should he choose not to reveal it. So I watched, expectant and pessimistic, thinking all the while that Tom, like Paéz, was insensible to the transient nature of life.

After a couple of weeks Willy arrived. That first night I could almost sense what he was thinking, coming as he had in the middle of the dark, his Cadillac grinding gravel. He looked up at the window to the upstairs bedroom and pushed his hat back. He expected to find me with Betty, hoped for it, I'm sure. But at dinner the next night he realized his hopes were for naught. Betty and I sat across from each other, she ignoring her steak, I engrossed in my food. Willy tried to spark a conversation among the three of us, but it was like trying to start a fire with wet matches.

Three days later Willy had figured out what was distracting Betty. He crossed the ground to the stables, his head aimed directly ahead, his step steady and purposeful. I took a deep breath and stepped off the porch. Cal saw me and shook his head to warn me off, but I kept following. Willy stopped and waited for me. "It's your bidness too," he said.

It was, but not in the sense he meant. I followed him past the corral to the stables, where he swung the door wide open. Sunlight bathed the building. They stood by the rail clutching each other in an embrace. Willy told him to let her go. "Dad, don't," she pleaded.

"Don't, hell, girl. I ain't puttin up with it, an neither is Pete."

Tom stood aside, doubt and fear condensed in his eyes. He looked to me for help.

"Who give you the right to touch my baby girl?" Willy asked.

Tom shrugged.

"I'm not a baby, Dad. I'm twenty-five. I've been married twice."

"Shut up," Willy said. He reached inside his coat and drew his pistol. He held it up for Tom to see. "Sumbitch, you think you can come along an do whatever you want with my family?"

"It was me, Dad. Me," Betty said.

"Don't, Willy," I said.

He stepped toward Tom, who didn't move, just watched and waited. I prayed for Tom to not say or do anything to add heat to this. Willy stood in his face and spat curses, demanded that he answer the question. Tom kept cool and silent as Willy stuck the barrel of the pistol to his throat. "Whose house is this?" Willy demanded.

"Yours, Mr. Bobbins."

"Damn right it is. I could shoot you, you sumbitch. I've shot men before."

Tom nodded. He didn't wither. Willy lifted the gun and brought it down on Tom's forehead. I grabbed Willy. He tried to throw me off, but I wrapped my arms around him and lifted him off the ground. "Lemme down, Pete!"

I held on. The gun went off. A horse let loose a terrible sound that came from its bowels. Willy kicked at me. I shook him hard until the gun dropped, then held him and told Tom to take off. Betty started to go too, but I told her to stay. Willy cursed me, but I couldn't let go, not yet, not until he'd cooled down. Gradually he did. Still, I held on. The horse turned about in panic and kicked at the stall. Blood dripped from its nostrils. Its mouth foamed pink bubbles. Then it leaned against the rail, offered a few heaving breaths, and collapsed.

I let go of Willy. Betty calmly walked over and told him he didn't have to do what he'd done, that she could make her own decisions. "I'm your pa," he said.

She slapped him in the face and walked out. He went after her, and for a second time I held him. He kicked and fought me even harder, shouted terrible threats at her and at me. He must have forgotten Tom by then. I let go of him and stepped back. He stared at me a moment, then bent down and picked up the gun. He aimed it at my head. "Don't ever touch me again like that," he said. He walked over to the horse and fired a round into its head.

As he passed through the door, he told me to get some help to bury the animal.

That evening I went to Tom's room. He was packing. He looked up momentarily and went about his business. "You warned me," he said. "Now I've got a headache and no job."

"I did."

"I guess I should thank you."

"No. What now?"

"Gave me five thousand in severance pay," he said. "Hush money. Guess that'll hold me a while." He tightened the last strap.

"I'm going to college in Arizona the end of the month. Why don't you come down and we could . . ."

"Thanks all the same." He tossed me a bag and gathered up two others. "Help me with these."

We loaded the bags in the bed of his truck.

"When Mr. Bobbins calms down, tell him I've killed men too. You were there. It's nothing special. It's a hard badge to wear for most men."

We shook hands.

Betty stayed on at the ranch. I drove to Billings to see Jiggers the week before school was to start. His cabin was a small one-bedroom log structure built on a stone foundation. It sat on the north side of a wooded rise that led to a box canyon. The place was surrounded by all manner of junk, including a rusted-out pickup, two stoves, a fire hydrant, and a few wooden crates filled with redeemable bottles. All the windows were raised.

I hollered to him.

"Who the hell's bothering me?" he asked as he threw open the door. "It's nappin time, and anyone with a bit of good sense would know so."

"It's Pete," I said.

He squinted. "So it is. That explains the lack of good sense. You woke me up."

"Sorry. I can leave."

He looked at me, the sky, the trees, nodding the whole while and grumbling under his breath. "May's well stay. You've already ruined my day, which I see now is a fine one. Probably look better through some glasses, though, as I'm damned near blind now."

I wove through the maze of junk to the porch. The cabin was surprisingly orderly and clean. In one corner was a desk with a typewriter and by it two sets of bookshelves stacked with books. I asked if he'd been reading. He said, "Every damned thing I can get my hands on."

"Why's that?"

"Don't have too long to live, way I figure it, so I've got to learn all I can now. I'm writing my memoirs."

"Am I in them?"

"One paragraph, I think, or is it just a footnote? I think you get roughly the same space as the infernal brown bear that comes banging about in the middle of the night."

He fixed us a lunch of salami on rye with lots of mustard and pepper and to chase it down, warm beer, which I declined without explanation. We talked about the ranch and Cal, and the war. He was curious about what it was like, said that he'd tried to get Sarge to talk about World War II, but Sarge wouldn't. "Damned obfuscator if there ever was one," Jiggers said.

"You liked him?"

"Worked with him seventeen years and never really knew him. Maybe that's why I liked him. Getting to know too much about a man makes enemies. You marrying Willy's girl?"

"What kind of question is that?"

"The obvious one. You were sweet on her. She was sweet on you. Willy wanted it."

"How'd you know?"

"Nothing ever happened there that Willy wouldn't approve of."

I finished my sandwich and watched him swallow down his warm beer.

"Got room if you want to stay over," he said, "but I'll caution you the bear'll wake you up for sure."

"Thanks, I've got to go."

"I don't get many visitors, which, if the truth were known, suits me. You being an exception, of course."

He walked me to the car and wished me well, said he was lying about the small part I took up in his memoirs, that I was at least two footnotes and a bad poem or two.

50

When the light changed, I twisted the throttle and rode the center of my lane up Oakey. A Dodge Charger swerved to my right, drove around leaving skid marks, and came close to forcing me into oncoming traffic. I swerved sharply and managed to keep the bike upright. I saw only the back of her head, the long black hair in a single neat braid. At Valley View the Dodge waited for the light to change, its windows rolled down. I pulled alongside. The woman shrank down in her seat and stared ahead.

"You could have forced me into a head-on," I said. "This isn't a car. It's got no protection."

She looked but didn't speak. She was perhaps twenty-one, dark-eyed, and lovely. I raised my voice. "Didn't you hear? It's got no protection."

"You should *get* a car," she said.

Of course. The obvious solution. Why hadn't I thought of it? I was about to raise hell with her when the light switched and she buried the accelerator. I caught up to her again at Decatur. This time as she looked at me, she arched an eyebrow. She had a slight overbite and full lips that turned up in a teasing smile. I felt a pocket open inside me, a small space in that part of me that had been closed to anyone since that summer with Betty. I smiled back. "What kind of car?"

"I'm sorry. I was embarrassed. It was the first thing that came to mind."

"You always run motorcycles off the road?"

She nodded. "Always." The smile never left her lips.

"Now you owe me a cup of coffee."

"I don't know you," she said, still smiling.

"I'm Peter Elkins. You?"

"Melody Cristobal."

"Coffee?"

The light changed and the car behind us honked. The driver shouted that if we were going to drive, drive, but if we were going to talk, pull off the road. She drove on. I followed her to Jones, where again I asked about coffee. The same man hollered for us to get a room. She pulled over when the light changed. She smiled again. I told her she had a smile that could raise the *Titanic*. She told me compliments like that might discourage her from running over motorcyclists. She'd be waiting tables that night at Paco's, a small Mexican restaurant on West Charleston, and if I came by, she would consider buying me a cup. "You *do* have a beautiful smile."

"Braces," she said.

She drove off—a wonder, no beauty-pageant, peaches-and-cream, sun-bunny type, just the garden-variety everyday miracle that every man hopes for. I watched her disappear over the rise a half mile west before I kicked the starter.

That night I went to Paco's. It was as she'd said. She hurried about waiting. In between, she stopped to visit. I told her I was home from college for Thanksgiving and had to ride back to Phoenix on Sunday, but would like to spend time with her. She said she'd think about it. The restaurant belonged to her parents, and she had to close it that night. I was welcome to stay until then, but not to get any ideas, a caution that was way too late already. I drank water and coffee, watched her work, and told myself not to feel what had already taken shape in my mind.

She set the alarm and locked the door. I walked her out. We stood by the bike, neither of us talking, just looking and not looking at one another. It was cool, past ten o'clock and dark, except for a streetlight up the block. She ran her fingers down the handlebars. I swung my leg over the seat and motioned for her to get on. She hesitated. "Seems we're at an impasse," I said.

"It's late."

"Or it's early."

"How do I know I can trust you?" Her dark eyes caught the glow of the streetlight and sparkled. I told her it would be nice to see the lights of the city with her from a distance. "How long?" she asked.

"No more than an hour."

"Promise?"

I promised. She rested her hand on my shoulder and climbed on. We rode west toward Red Rock and stopped by the wash. We talked about everything and nothing, and the lights were glittering, and I told her about Willy and how he'd gotten title to the Lucky because Hugh Stample owed him a fortune in markers from playing poker and Willy had threatened to sell them to the mob in Los Angeles. I asked if I could see her when I returned at Christmas. When she smiled this time, I was certain the *Titanic* was bubbling up from its watery grave.

"That would be okay, but what if I fall in love first?"

"Then I'll become a priest."

I was tempted to kiss her, but didn't. She would say later that was what swayed her.

Miriam arrived for the holiday, and she and Esther stayed at Mother's in a guest room. Despite Willy's offer of a suite at the Lucky, I stayed with Stella in my old room. She wanted company. She and Willy weren't talking, hadn't for almost a year, but he showed up Thanksgiving night. Miriam, Mother, and Esther came too. Leonardo declined, citing poor health. Ruben Lee brought his new wife; George was accompanied by Elaine and sons; Croaker showed up with Bee, his mysterious woman of twenty years. Notably absent was Betty, who'd flown to Acapulco for the weekend.

The table, set with Stella's best china and silver, had a twenty-five-pound tom as the centerpiece. Willy sat at one head and George at the other. Miriam and Esther, now six, sat beside Willy and opposite Stella. I sat between them and Mother, facing Ruben Lee, who was one step past the nods. Belinda, George's family, and Croaker occupied the other end of the table. Jamita had retired and Stella had taken on two new servants, Sommers, a thin, erect, elderly man who'd spent forty years as a waiter, and Penny, a broad-faced black woman with a large, ever-present smile and a good-natured laugh.

Sommers started to carve the turkey, but Willy stood, insisting it was his duty as head of the house. Sommers surrendered the tools much like a proud general capitulating to an overwhelming force, bowed his head, and backed away.

Willy looked at Miriam. "Well, I wisht we had more to be thankful for," he said. "It ain't a full table, but someday we hope it'll be." Then he directed his gaze at me. "An if Peter does right by Betty, it'll be a happier table."

"Willy, cut the turkey. Ever'one's hungry," Stella said.

Ruben Lee kicked my ankle under the table and motioned toward the backyard with his head as he mouthed the word "later."

"What does he mean by later?" Mother asked.

"Nothing," I said.

"Pass your plates on down. Young'uns first." Willy carved and set the meat aside for Sommers to serve on the plates as they were passed up.

"Pete, I want to talk to you," Miriam said. "Tomorrow? Foxy's?"

"Yes, you two should talk about how you've ignored your responsibilities," Mother said.

"'Lizabeth," Stella said, "I heard you're makin a trip to Borneo or some such place."

"Borneo and Sumatra, that's right. If Leonardo feels better."

"I'd settle for goin to Texas now 'at Willy's free to take a visit."

Ruben Lee laughed.

"What's so funny?" Stella asked.

"You've been wanting to go back ever since you dragged George and me to Montana. If we'd stayed in Texas, maybe . . ."

"Ruben Lee," George said as he stood.

Ruben Lee winked at us. "Guess George wants to see me outside. Imagine I'm in for it."

"Wouldn't hurt to bite your tongue," Stella said.

Ruben Lee stuck his tongue between his teeth and pressed down with his jaw. It looked painful, but he just smiled. Belinda winced and looked down at her plate. Willy looked out of the corner of his eye at Croaker. That was all the message needed. George and Croaker went behind Ruben Lee. He pretended to ignore them, even as Croaker placed a hand on the back of the chair and one on his shoulder. Ruben Lee pushed the hand away. "Excuse us, folks," Croaker said and lifted Ruben Lee up.

"Okay, all right," Ruben Lee said.

They whisked him outside. Willy handed the carving knife and fork over to Sommers and followed the others as Ruben Lee's bride watched nervously.

The men stood in view of the glass doors exchanging heated words until Willy shoved Ruben Lee toward the lawn and the four of them vanished into the shadows. Elaine said she didn't think her sons needed to witness this kind of scene. Stella told her to hush. "Show Miriam your ring, Belinda," Stella said.

Her hand shook as she extended her arm across the table. Miriam and Mother admired the ring and paid the appropriate compliments. Esther tapped her spoon on her glass and startled us. "Real crystal," she said. It broke the tension and we laughed.

Ruben Lee's high-pitched shouts drifted in. Stella said something about how hard it is to get the boys together.

"Well, let's dish up," she said.

As we handed down plates, she made small talk. Belinda sat shivering, her lip trembling. Miriam asked if someone would show her to the bathroom.

"You know your . . ." Stella started to say.

"Belinda, would you show me?"

Belinda said she'd be happy to. Miriam told me to keep an eye on Esther, who looked at her mother and said, "I can look after myself. Everyone knows Uncle Peter's irresponsible."

"Where'd she get that?" I asked.

Miriam took Belinda's hand and said she was in a hurry.

"I'm not irresponsible," I said.

"Mother said you'd lose your neck if it didn't have a collar around it."

"Ain't that the blessed truth," Stella said, smiling.

Elaine said she was going to find her own bathroom and disappeared. Sommers poured wine all around, but I covered my glass and told him water would do. When finally the men reappeared, Ruben Lee sported a lump on his cheek. Willy calmly asked if everyone had filled his plate. He took his place at the head of the table as the others seated themselves. We waited until Miriam, Belinda. and Elaine returned. Ruben Lee asked his wife where she'd been. Miriam said, "Putting on a new face for you."

Ruben Lee glared across the table. He didn't know Miriam very well. She smiled and asked if he'd hit himself, "or do you just limit your masochism to biting the tongue?"

"Just who're you?"

"A woman who doesn't wear a choke chain and leash."

Willy coughed and stopped Ruben Lee with a look. Then he stood and offered a toast. "Family and friends. We're damned lucky to have 'em."

"Family and friends," we repeated in unison.

Miriam clutched my arm. "I've missed you," she said.

"I know."

"But now?"

"We're here," I said.

"We're a family again," Mother said.

Miriam and I smiled. "Puh-leeze, Mother," Miriam said.

Esther dropped her spoon by accident at Sommers's feet as he was pouring more wine. He picked it up, excused himself, and said he'd get the young miss a new one to throw.

I went outside with Ruben Lee. I asked what he had in mind, though I'd already figured it out. He had some Colombian red in his car and asked if I wanted to try it. I declined. He said it was difficult to like me now. "You're a real pain in the ass when you're straight, Petey." I thanked him anyhow and went inside, where Willy was telling a story about cattle rustling in Mexico.

Miriam sipped on her milk shake and watched tourists walk by on the sidewalk. I stirred mine with a straw while watching her. Nearing thirty, she actually seemed to have lost some of her maturity, seemed more girl now. She glanced up. "I don't know who I am anymore, Pete."

"That doesn't sound like you."

"Nothing sounds like me." She looked over at her daughter, who was window-shopping the shelves of curios. "She was a good baby. She kept me sane."

"What's the matter, Miriam?"

"My husband's a prisoner of war and you ask that question."

"He's been one several years, and that didn't make you wonder who you were."

"Yes, it . . ." She shook her head and gripped the table. "Petey, I've been sleeping with another man."

"Sleeping?" I didn't know exactly how to respond.

"Not sleeping," she whispered. "Intimate. His name's Jim, a lawyer. I know what you're thinking, because I've thought it."

"What am I thinking?"

"Well, I know what you must feel. You were there. Didn't you know someone who was dumped for a guy who was here? You must have. I know the expressions. 'Jody stole his gal.' It's not true. He didn't steal me. I've been disloyal."

"Everybody seems to know what I feel. That somehow I'm . . . we're all disturbed. I want what you want, Miriam—a life."

She reached across the table and took my hand. She hadn't touched me that way since I was five or six. I squeezed her hand to tell her it was all right, that I wasn't her judge. She let go and folded her hands in her lap. "I had so much hope at first, then gradually none. The man I saw on the news a year ago isn't the man I married—I've seen it over and over until I know every movement and the time each one takes—and I'm not the woman he married. God forgive me, I almost wish the war would go on and on and he wouldn't have to come home to this. He looked terribly brave, didn't he?"

In the news release he and three other POWs had sat in front of the cameras, all emaciated, all wearing black pajamas too small for them. When his turn came, he stood and looked into the camera, his mouth drawn into a tight line as he announced he'd not been tortured, then he'd bowed to the cameras and sat down.

I pushed my milk shake aside. "It'll be settled in six months or less. He'll be coming back."

"I realize that." She turned away, her profile illuminated in the bright window. "I tried. I don't know what I'll do, Peter."

"Maybe you'll feel something you don't think you will. Don't make all your decisions right now."

She smiled bravely. "I hope you're right."

Esther came over with her inquisitive face and asked what we were whispering about.

"Nothing, Esther," Miriam said.

"Mother, you told me it's not polite to whisper in front of other people."

"You weren't around, Esther."

"Couldn't you see me?"

"Yes."

"Then I was around."

Miriam looked to me, a look of mild exasperation on her face. "What did I do?"

"You got yourself one just like you," I said.

She pulled Esther to her and gave her a hug. "So I did."

"Well, Miss Esther Summerson," I said, "how do you like Las Vegas?"

"I don't know. I'm a little girl. Mother, can we buy something for Daddy?"

"May we," Miriam corrected. "Sure, you pick it out."

This brought a smile to Esther, who stepped close and said, "Uncle Peter, my name is not Summerson, it's Holder, and my father's a pilot. He's a prisoner of war."

"I know. Being called Summerson is not such a bad thing," I said, "and someday you'll know why."

Temporarily placated, she scurried back to the shelves to pick a gift.

"We have a closet full of gifts waiting for him," Miriam said. "She'd be so disappointed."

I chose to change the subject. "You remember the cop who pulled me out of the old Ford convertible?" I asked.

"Yes. Andy. How could I forget?"

"He drank himself to death."

"How'd you find out?"

"He was in the inebriate ward when I was there, weighed a hundred pounds. They kept him going with ivs."

She lowered her eyes. "What happened to us?"

I took her hand again. "We became ourselves."

"How'd you end up so wise? You were so stupid."

"Miriam, I've met someone."

"You have?"

"Yes. She's not like anyone I've ever known. Will you and Esther go to dinner with me tonight and meet her?"

"Sure. What could make me happier?"

"Your new guy, what's he like?"

"Married."

"Oh, Jesus."

She grinned, then broke out in laughter. We laughed until she started to cry and then we ordered two more milk shakes. It was wonderful being with her.

51

That year I wrote Melody every other day and phoned her once or twice a week. Any long weekend, wind or rain, found me on the old widow-maker highway from Phoenix to Las Vegas. In town, I stayed with Stella, who became my fellow conspirator. She insisted one evening when I was on my way to Edwards Air Force Base that she go with me to Paco's. She and Mrs. Cristobal chatted as if they'd been friends for years, and Mr. Cristobal treated Stella like a queen.

Later Stella agreed, as I'd told her, that Melody was like no other young woman she'd met, and when I showed her one of Melody's paintings, of a woman sitting in front of a cactus garden in bloom, she bought it on the spot. "Pete, I'll be at this wedding."

Melody blushed. With what lay ahead and with me having no career and going to school on the G.I. Bill and working summers at the Lucky, we'd been practical and had avoided discussing marriage. Besides, she was close to her family, and her parents would never approve. I quickly changed the subject. After dinner, as I started the car, I explained the entire situation to Stella, who listened patiently, nodding where appropriate, but in the end shaking her head.

"Too damned practical. Me and Willy ain't had a marriage for years, but we had a good one at first. No money then. Those were the best years. Hell, the only years, but don't ask 'bout 'em. You love that girl an she loves you. Tell her ma and pa what's on your mind. They'll respect you. They just want her happy."

"You think so?"

"I may be a hard old woman, but I still got faith. Yep, Pete, I think so."

I shut off the car, excused myself, and returned to the restaurant. I cornered Mr. Cristobal in the kitchen. "Sir, you don't know me real well yet, but I'm not a bad . . . what I mean is I don't have a career yet and I can't . . ."

"I'm a very busy man, Pete. Would you say your piece and let me do my business."

"I want to marry your daughter."

"Of course you do. If you didn't, I'd run you off. What's your business?"

"That."

"Ask her. I can't answer for her."

"Do you approve?"

"Ask me in fifteen years when I have grandchildren to make me happy. Now, I have work to do. Don't tie Melody up very long."

I asked her and she turned me down. She said I should ask again in another year. All the while Stella sat in the car amused by what she'd initiated. When I slid in beside her, she asked what had happened, even though it was obvious from my expression. "It's that damned motorcycle, Pete. No lovin father in his right mind would tolerate his daughter on one 'a them."

She was a wise woman.

The plane taxied down the tarmac at Edwards Air Force Base. Miriam lifted her head as the band started playing. We stood on a red carpet surrounded by dignitaries and Air Force brass. Miriam gripped my arm and said, "I told Jim to go home to his wife." I patted her hand. We'd had no time to talk the night before, so I was pleased she'd given me that news.

It was May and warm in the Mojave, and I was behind in studying for finals because I'd taken a delay en route to meet Miriam. I'd not waited the year that Melody had requested, simply couldn't, and on the way to Lancaster,

California, I'd stopped in Las Vegas, pulled into the parking lot at Paco's, and proposed as she waited on a customer. She'd said she was very busy at the moment and asked if I'd settle for a simple yes. As he stuffed tortillas, her father gave me a five-minute lecture on my responsibilities to his daughter, then Mrs. Cristobal hugged me and called me *hijo*. She gave me a tray and told me to clean up a few tables. My eye on Melody the whole time, I wiped off the nearest table. She passed by and brushed her hand across the back of mine.

Mother stood on the other side of Miriam. "It's hot. You know, Leonardo and I are supposed to be in Saint Maarten."

The plane was nearing the ramp, its engines whining to a rest. Miriam licked her lips. She turned her face to Mother. "I don't care where you and he are supposed to be. I don't care if the two of you go to hell. Why isn't he here? I'd be there for you or him. So would Peter."

"I wouldn't either," I said.

"You would too," Miriam said.

"Wouldn't, absolutely not."

On the other side of Mother stood Alan's parents, his mother holding Esther's hand. In her other hand Esther held a single yellow rose that had withered in the heat. They'd been calm up to now, but it was obvious they were losing patience. Mr. Holder's eyes were watering. His Adam's apple bobbed up and down. On a cane now, which he'd needed since having a stroke, he leaned his weight on his wife.

The engines shut down.

"Oh, Jesus," Miriam said.

The band had gone silent. The ramp was in place and the door opened. It was dark inside and only a few furtive movements were visible from where we stood in the light. Then the band struck up "Stars and Stripes Forever." Miriam's hand tightened on my arm.

The first man down, a lieutenant colonel who'd been shot down in 1966, saluted, and the gallery erupted with cheers. The Secretary of the Air Force saluted and welcomed him to the United States of America. Second out was a major so weak that to negotiate the steps he held the rail all the way. He threw himself down and kissed the ground and had to be helped up from his knees. A third walked out and waved as he descended. None of them looked like returning heroes, just men who'd been through too much, men who'd never put the last sentence and period on that part of their lives.

Then came Alan, tall and gaunt, eyes like caverns, all arms and legs, and hands so big and well shaped they seemed separate beings unto themselves. After saluting, he skipped down the ramp, jumping the last two steps. He shaded his eyes and looked about, handsome and lost and helpless-looking, a little childlike. How could he feel otherwise? Five others quickly followed. Esther tore away from her grandmother's grip and rushed to her father. She stood before him, looking up at his tall, thin shape. She held up the rose, and said, "Daddy?"

He took the rose. "If your name is Esther, I think so." He lifted her up.

I felt Miriam start to move. "Don't tell him," I said. "I don't care if you leave him tomorrow, you make him think nothing ever happened."

She lowered her eyes and nodded.

"No matter how much guilt you feel, not even if you think your conscience will kill you," I said. "He deserves that."

Miriam pulled away, her first step a tentative one, but then she rushed off to join them. Mother grabbed my arm. "I'll be a better mother," she said. Astonished, I looked at her and shook my head. I loosened her fingers and walked to join Miriam.

She stood looking up at him. He swallowed and reached for her face with one hand. He held Esther in his other arm. Miriam searched his eyes. "They briefed us," he said. "I know you've had it tough and I don't expect much. I'm home."

She burst into tears, reached up, and squeezed his neck with both hands. He gathered her in his free arm. "Easy now," he said. "Easy. Oh, yes."

The rest of us gathered around, but she didn't let go and neither did he. It was their dance all over again, the waltz, this time to marching music and with Esther joining them. But they didn't move their feet, just stood locked in that embrace, listening to a tune inside that required no steps, that said to the world that something right was back in place, something good. I knew my sister would hold up.

A formation of jet fighters flew overhead and tipped their wings gently before hurling themselves up toward the billowing white clouds. The music stopped. Photographers snapped shots. Alan kept saying, "Easy, easy," but he didn't let go of her. His father and I patted him on the back. The Secretary of the Army was talking over the public address system, but no one seemed to listen. It was joy.

52

On July 12, Melody and I exchanged vows in a modest ceremony attended by some fifty people. I was approaching twenty-seven and she was twenty-two.

She insisted that her father not make it a big Mexican wedding, as this, after all, was not Mexico. In truth, she didn't want him to go into debt. She walked down an aisle in a flower-filled chapel that smelled of carnations and roses, where I waited with a priest who was about to talk us through traditional Catholic rites. We joined hands and repeated the priest's words, her dark eyes hidden behind the white veil. When we exchanged rings, I lifted the veil, saw those keen dark eyes, and fell in love all over again. All in all, a pretty ordinary wedding, except for all the extraordinary dashes of love and hope liberally sprinkled in.

We brushed off the rice and climbed into the back of a waiting limo, compliments of Willy. We'd agreed to delay the honeymoon until the end of summer so that we could enjoy it before I entered into graduate studies in history at Arizona. The trip to Hawaii was a reluctant gift from Willy, given at Stella's insistence, so George informed me. Like Stella and unlike Willy, he seemed pleased I wasn't marrying Betty and stood as my best man.

At the reception, held in a suite at Caesars Palace, Willy took me aside after the cake cutting and picture taking. Though he'd been distant since I'd finished my degree, he was generous, donating the reception and a four-piece band. He toasted me and wished me happiness. He lit a cigar and looked out at the Flamingo sign across the street. "I knew Bugsy, you know."

"Yeah, I know."

"Strange kind 'a guy. Big ideas, an look what. Got hisself kilt. Made a whole buncha people rich. He was like Gatsby maybe. What 'a you think, Pete?"

"Could be. Gatsby had a melancholy that made him . . . mysterious and . . ."

"It coulda been yours an hers, Pete. A third 'a ever'thing. You know that, don't you?"

"Yeah, Willy."

"You been a defeat in most ways, Pete, but you never took advantage 'a me. 'At's the thing."

"I guess I didn't want the debt, Willy," I said.

"'At's right. Debt's a bad thing. But we have 'em just the same." He tossed down the shot. "You ain't read nothin to me in years. You know how I like a good story. That one 'bout Gatsby's the best, though." He looked at Melody as she took a seat next to Miriam. "You done yourself proud."

For pleasure, I was taking a summer drama-lit course at the university. "I'll read you *Death of a Salesman*," I said, as we were to study it that coming week.

"Don't sound like my kind 'a story."

"It could be."

"You know how much I wisht this was Betty," he said.

Mother interrupted and said the groom was required to dance with his mother. I said the tradition was the father and the bride. She took my hand anyway and towed me to the floor. I eased my hand behind her back. She was changing. Her face and figure, both fuller now, showed telltale signs of age, but she remained striking. "Leonardo doesn't dance," she said.

"What *does* he do except make money?"

"You've never liked him," she said.

"I never disliked him either."

Melody, Mrs. Cristobal, and Miriam sat carrying on an animated conversation. Alan and Mr. Cristobal, as devoted Orioles fans, had hit it off and were talking baseball, while Leonardo and Stella stood by the punch bowl eating cake and gabbing. George and Elaine stood aloof. My bride's cousins and aunts and friends clustered together. Mother looked at them. "My grandchildren won't look like me," she said.

I pulled away and looked at her.

"I don't mean it that way. She's beautiful. I just wanted to see you and Miriam all over again—a fresh start."

"Any children we have will be just fine."

"She loves you."

"I hope so."

"Peter, was I so bad?"

"You weren't so bad." She said I couldn't keep step and hoped that my new wife would teach me how.

53

Though everything was packed and the moving van was coming the following morning, it seemed like just another Saturday as I slipped into my suit and kissed Melody. She'd found a job in Tucson, where I'd been accepted into graduate school, and we should have been more excited, but I'd spent the last year working for Willy to save money and had not yet gotten used to the idea that it was about over. Melody and I had a feverish three weeks ahead— one at the ranch before flying to Hawaii for the honeymoon, then back to settle into our new apartment in Tucson, where our belongings would be waiting.

"I'll see you at Paco's at eight," I said.

She shook her head. "I've changed my mind. I'm going straight to Hawaii. You can meet me there."

"Okay."

She kissed my chin, then licked her fingers and wiped off the lipstick. "Will you grow a beard for me?"

"Should I?"

"Good practice for a future professor."

I pulled her to me, held her for a moment, and said I'd see her soon. I walked backward down the apartment steps. "You know how lucky you are to have me?" she said.

"I know."

The casino seemed subdued. I deplored it as much as Willy loved it, and despite the suit I wore, I felt like a man serving time in jail. It was three o'clock. I had eight hours left. The man I relieved shook my hand and wished me luck, said it was a pleasure working with someone who showed up on time to relieve him. He offered a quick summary of all the table action and handed over a paper with the fills recorded on it. There was little of interest, three thousand-dollar-marker players betting a few reds and an occasional green. "Oh, and this." He handed me a sealed note from atop the podium and said good-bye.

I recognized the handwriting. I broke the seal. It read, "She's a lucky girl. I never was," and was signed with love from Betty. I remembered the invitation she'd sent to Vietnam with the words that had killed the last spark in me. I imagined her as I'd first seen her, a girl not yet fifteen, cocksure, getting out of a black Cadillac. I felt sad that that girl was gone. She'd dried out twice in two years, only to go back to the booze, and she'd taken a string of lovers, each one seedier than the last. I dropped the note in the wastebasket.

Willy strolled by and stood at the podium, looking around. He said Jay Gatsby died a sad man, but he hoped to do better. I asked what that meant. He pointed to the tables. "All of 'em like oil wells, Pete. We overcome anything. Even you."

"Even me?"

"Ain't nobody gonna miss you, Pete. You was a terrible busboy and a worse dealer."

"The worst, Willy."

"An 'at's the only reason I ever put you in a suit. Don't want you thinkin you earned nothin." He smiled and slipped his hand in mine and shook it, but something more. When he let go there was folded piece of paper in my palm. I opened it—a check for ten thousand dollars. No one could make his eyes go flat the way Willy could. He looked at me deadpan and stuffed his hands in his pockets. "Stella's idea," he said.

I smiled. "If it was her idea, it would be more and she'd have given it to me herself."

"I always said you'd make a hell of a lawyer. Well, make a hell of a professor."

"That's five years away, Willy."

"I'll be alive." He patted my shoulder and walked out of the pit.

I called Melody to tell her about our good fortune. The line was busy, so I slipped the check into my coat pocket and checked the dealers' racks before marking new fill slips. Levi came over to wish me good luck and say he was glad to see I'd come to my senses, even if it had taken years. His son was attending Loyola Marymount, and Levi mentioned his boy's grades and the stock market, the usual, then looked around. "Going to be slow, Pete."

"Hope so. I don't need aggravation on my last day."

"I'll eat with you later," he said. "I like your girl."

"Thanks."

By seven o'clock the casino was packed and so noisy I had to holler to talk to the players, and I was writing markers as fast as dealers were dealing hands. By the time my break came, I was on my second marker book, but figured it was best this way. Stay busy, let the shift fly by. I had a cup of coffee on my early break as there was no time to eat. Ray, Sylvie, and a new dealer named Ron were playing a hand of pitch. I watched for a while. Ron was out of his league with the others, who were blood players. Overrating his hand, he bid three and went set, slammed the cards down on the table hard, and muttered a succession of obscenities. The others chuckled and told him to pay up. The set cost him twelve dollars, which was about all he was worth, so he had to borrow money back to play the next hand.

"The best you've got going is you're a poor man and can't lose much," I said to Ron.

He rolled his eyes and nodded. Ray asked if it was my last night. "Yeah, last one," I said.

"I had twenty last ones," he said and smiled. His eyes had a sourness to them, but he had a wry wit and a friendly manner. He'd worked on the Strip, had aged two years for every year he'd put behind a table, and had been fired from most every job because of drinking or stealing. In the process, he'd lost houses and a couple of wives and even more children. His last stop was the Lucky, and he worked as if each shift was all that was between him and a flophouse or maybe jail. "Hope you have just this one."

"Thanks."

I was returning to the pit when one of Willy's friends, a cowboy named

Lyle from Oklahoma, asked if Willy was in. I hadn't finished answering when a ruckus broke out in the blackjack pit. I saw a man fall facedown in the aisle, but he sprang back up, doubled his fists, whirled about, and threw a roundhouse right at his antagonist that disturbed the air but nothing more. Customers stopped playing to watch. Most dealers didn't even bother to look up. A porter walked between the two men to sweep a torn coin wrapper into his dustpan.

Two guards charged in to separate the men. Their catches in hand, the guards hurried by me, rushing the men to the back steps. As I started toward the pit, Ruben Lee came running down the stairs to my right and nearly knocked me over. "Take that one downstairs," he said and reached over to grab the man's arm.

The man broke free and kicked. Ruben Lee's eyes widened as he clamped his hands over his groin. He folded at the waist and collapsed on the carpet, groaning. In that moment of confusion, the man hurdled Ruben Lee and shoved a bystander out of the way.

Even as I took off after him, I thought to myself it wasn't a good idea. He had a lead of four strides at the door. I pushed on the glass door. I saw him sprint up the side street, and gave chase. Gaining a step on him, I turned a corner. I felt certain from his labored breathing that if I just stayed with him, I could wear him down. I hollered for him to stop. As he looked over his shoulder, I got a look at his face and dark eyes.

His voice almost pleading, he shouted for me to leave him alone and struggled across Ogden Street. A car turned the intersection, screeching its tires, and barely missed him. The man slammed his hands down on the fender and caromed off the car, spinning like a billiard ball. We were back on the sidewalk again running west. I was closing on him by then. At the end of the Lucky's parking structure he swung left and probably sensed his mistake right away, but was going too fast to stop. Twenty yards into the alley he stopped and shrugged. It was useless to run any farther as the alley turned left and ended at the loading dock in back of the Lucky. He turned to face me.

There was no fight in his eyes. He placed his hands on his knees and bent over, gulping in air. With five feet of space between us, we both stood hunched over, catching our breath. He asked why I had chased him, what business was it of mine. I had no reason that I could put a pulse to, no investment in the outcome or any interest in this stranger who'd done me no harm. If he walked out of the alley right then it was of no difference to me. Still, I didn't move. I assured him he'd be unharmed if he came back voluntarily. "Leave me be," he said, more like a plea than a warning.

"Come back with me."

"No way. I'm walking outta here." It sounded like an apology and a question.

We'd recovered enough to start all over, and though my heart wasn't in it, I blocked his path. He was shorter and average in every way—not a tough guy. I could handle him if it came to that, but I didn't want to. "It's my last night at work," I said, as if that should carry some weight in this affair. "I don't want trouble."

"Look," he said, "I bumped him by mistake. I told him I was sorry. He hit me."

"You kicked Ruben Lee."

He eyes softened. He moved to his right. "I was scared. I'm nothing, just a guy."

"Don't," I warned, but I had no heart for it, none at all.

"I just want to go home," he said.

It came to me that I wanted to leave just as he did and go on with my life. I wanted to be beside my wife, to smell her hair and kiss her eyelids and pull my face away so I could see her eyes flutter to life. I stepped aside. He kept a cautious eye on me and as he passed, said, "Thanks." Then his eyes shifted to the entrance to the alley.

One guard hooked him in an armlock and bent him over until he cried out. The second pressed his weight into the man's backside. "Don't hurt him," I said. "Call the cops."

"Petey Boy." Ruben Lee stood beside me shaking his head.

He stepped up to the man and kicked him in the groin. The man grimaced and slumped forward, moaning. Ruben Lee lifted his head up by the hair and said to the guards, "Let him go."

Reluctantly, the guards released the man. Ruben Lee still held the man's hair in his fingers. "Gimme a gun," he said.

"Sir?"

"Gimme your gun." His voice bounded back off the brick walls.

"No," I said. "Don't."

Ruben Lee turned on me. "Stay out of it, Petey."

One guard unsnapped his holster and lifted his revolver. The slight pop of the snap and the sound of metal sliding out of leather seemed amplified in the hollow alley. It was a bluff. Sure. A tactic to scare the man, another sleight of hand, a trick. "I've got to get back," I said.

Ruben Lee said, "Petey Boy, hang around."

"Don't go," the man said.

I couldn't look him in the eye. I might have done something brave or insane, gone out in the street and hollered to draw attention to the alley, charged the guards, attacked Ruben Lee—anything that might somehow have stopped events from taking the course they were about to take. But I didn't. I left the darkened alley and walked toward the perpetual neon dawn that hovers over the downtown streets. I had a wife, a future, blessings that each step brought me closer to. I walked down the sidewalk toward the Lucky, a distance of less than a block to the side entrance. I was going to finish the shift, say good-bye to acquaintances I'd made, and go home to my bride.

With three steps to go, the shots rang out.

The funny thing about those shots, not them but the echo, is that if I hadn't known better, I would have sworn they'd come from elsewhere, from up the street in another direction or from a passing car. If I'd been alien to everything, an unsuspecting witness, I could have pretended I'd heard nothing, knew nothing, and gone on. But I knew where they'd come from and suspected that I might not leave with Melody in the morning. I took those last three steps and walked into the casino without looking back.

Dealers, coming off break, lined up by the podium awaiting table assignments. My heart pounded, my ears rang. I overheard a dealer say the man had done what a whole bunch of people would like to do, meaning kick Ruben Lee.

The relief floorman asked if I'd caught the guy.

I shook my head. "Too fast, I guess," I said.

He gave me a skeptical look and told me chasing the man had cost me ten minutes of my next break. If only that were all. I debated what to do next. Call the police? Melody? Willy? I decided to do nothing but wait.

Sirens blared and red lights flickered as squad cars converged from several directions, their sirens burping to a halt by the sidewalk outside. Security guards rushed outside to meet the cops. Curious patrons walked to the doors to glimpse the action and shook their heads in wonderment as several men in uniform pushed through the doors and shoved the crowd aside, then raced down the aisles heading in the direction of the back door.

Word rapidly spread of a shooting in the alley—from guards to cocktail waitresses and cocktail waitresses to bartenders and change girls—and traveled down the pit and back. The event was an escape from the tedium of their lives, no more than that. But each time fresh news was breathed in my presence, it was like another jab at my conscience. And each eye that caught mine seemed to inquire or accuse. They knew. I saw it in their faces, proof that another rumor was chasing this one, and it had to do with me chasing the victim. Willy, a guard on his heels, ambled through the casino on the way to the back door. He slowed long enough to look in my direction. How could he know already?

Detectives arrived and huddled in whispered conversation with officers in uniform. They left to exit the door to the alley. More detectives arrived. Ruben Lee came in, glanced toward me, and walked past with a police escort at his heels. Then came the two guards following the same path through the casino to the squad cars outside. The sounds of the casino died in my ears. I closed my eyes. I understood why Paéz had taken that hole, the silence he'd chosen.

Levi strolled down the middle of the pit and stood at the podium directly behind me. He leaned over my shoulder and whispered, "You can quit pretending to watch that game. The guy you chased is dead." His words put an exclamation mark on the truth.

The cops pulled me off the floor an hour later and advised me of my rights, then walked me outside to a detective unit where none other than Frank waited in the front seat. He was now a captain. A detective opened the back door and told me to watch my head as I got in. Frank said he wanted to be alone with me. Sealed off from the world outside, he reached back and shook my hand, congratulated me on getting married. He asked how I felt. "Am I under arrest?" I asked.

"No."

"Why read me my rights?"

"Scares witnesses." He smiled like a poker player about to force a hand.

"What am I a witness to?"

He leaned over the seat back. "You tell me."

"Do I need an attorney?"

"Pete, we go back. Now, listen to what I say."

Some people, he explained, had seen me chase a man out of the casino and that same man, William Schmilling, was dead, shot in the alley by a guard after a struggle over the gun. He paced himself, offering details one at a time like shells unloaded from the cylinder of a revolver until there was one left and nothing to do with it but play Russian roulette. He asked if I had chased a man and if that man was alive when I last saw him. It was all set up. Willy had smoothed the waters with his hand. I nodded slowly. "I chased a guy."

"Was he alive when you last saw him?"

"Yes."

"Was he belligerent?"

"Excuse me?"

"Did you fight with him?"

He pressed his face closer, so close his two eyes seemed as one and I could smell his cigarette breath and the faint odor of bourbon and mints. I wanted to know exactly where I stood, exactly how far the lie had gone and what my role was to be, so I said, "Ruben Lee killed him."

"Did you see it?"

"No."

"Ah. Pretty strong accusation, considering we have a guard who admits to the shooting."

I looked at him blankly. "Ruben Lee asked the guard for a gun."

Frank shook his head. "Between you and me, Ruben Lee was upstairs with sore balls when this Schmilling was shot."

I nodded to let him know I understood, but then said what I knew to be true. "Ruben Lee asked a guard for a gun and then I heard the shots."

Frank rubbed his palm over his beard and swallowed. "Willy told me you were a hero in Vietnam."

I shook my head. "I was there."

"I was in Korea. Inchon, the Yalu River. I remember the cold and just wanting a hot meal. I mean, a hot meal meant everything in the world to me. Told myself, When I go home I want the good things. You want the good things, don't you, Pete?"

"If I'd known how this would turn out, I never would have chased that guy."

"No, no, I guess you wouldn't have. Have you talked to anyone about this?"

I shook my head. "Just you."

He thought a moment, as much to give me time to consider my situation as to weigh his next move. He was going to ask me to lie; it was a question of how direct he dared be about suborning perjury and obstructing justice. "Papers are going to blast this story something fierce. We'll probably have to arrest the guard. He admits to it."

He gave this time to sink in. I recalled the wrecked Corvette, nose angled toward the sky, the next night hands holding me down, shame and anger. I wondered how much the guard was offered. Melody was waiting, asleep, her breath soft on the pillow. I bowed my head and felt in my pocket for the ten-thousand-dollar check.

"Look at me," Frank said, his eyes hard as billiard balls. "You're thinking about your future, aren't you? So am I. So's Willy. I'll forget what you told me. I'll have my men drive you to the station for a statement. A formality, you understand."

I nodded. Frank was a good messenger.

It was nine A.M. before I was allowed to leave the police station. It was bright and the sun stung my eyes. My mouth was dry. I'd waited hours wondering what to say when the detectives took my statement. They kept a mug of coffee in front of me and told me to be patient, but they never took me to the interview room. When they told me to go home, I was too tired to care. I walked the three blocks to the Lucky in a state of near-trance. It was morning, so the parking lot was deserted. As I unlocked my car, Croaker pulled up in one of Willy's Cadillacs. He opened the door, stepped out, and told me to get in. Ruben Lee sat in the back, a gun resting on his thigh. He said, "Petey Boy, glad to see you."

Croaker nudged me in and slammed the door, then got in behind the wheel.

"Just like a gangster movie," I said. "Is there a bag of cement in the trunk?"

Ruben Lee grinned. "Always got the wisecrack, huh, Petey Boy? But I'd keep my mouth shut if I was you." He placed the barrel of the gun against my ear.

54

Croaker drove out in no hurry at all, and in a few minutes we were rolling southbound on the interstate. Ruben smoked and looked out the window. Croaker kept his eyes on the road. We were nearly to Jean before I spoke. "My wife's expecting me."

"So's mine," Ruben Lee said, "but I don't care. You probably do, though."

The sun-sparkled sand dunes passed by. Somewhere before Zyzzyx Pass, Croaker turned left on a crossover, turned right, circled the car south, eventually leaving the paved highway to turn onto a washboard road that flowed into the distant alkaline flats. "Going to shoot me?" I asked.

"Now would I do that, Petey Boy?"

"Guess the guard's taking the beef for you."

"Shut up. I mean, who's got the fucking gun, you or me?"

I noticed the thin, dusty-looking gray hairs on Croaker's head, which was almost bald. He was Willy's age, perhaps, and this was a young man's game he was playing. "Croaker, what do you know about taking beefs for other people?"

Croaker swung a looping back fist and caught me just hard enough to snap my head, but not enough to hurt. "I warnt Willy a long time ago, said you was trouble."

I leaned back. He didn't want to be here any more than I did, but he'd done Willy's bidding so long he didn't know how to say no. I looked at Ruben Lee, who was smiling. "What's the deal?"

"Not yet, Petey Boy."

"I called Melody and told her what happened," I said and wished right away that I hadn't said that, as it might endanger her.

"You didn't call." He smiled, lit a cigarette, and blew the smoke in my face.

"No, you're right," I said. "How're your balls, Ruben Lee?"

"Good enough to do what I have to," he said. He acted calm, but his voice had an edge on it, and as he inhaled, his fingers twitched. He needed a fix.

"I saw guys with balls, Ruben Lee," I said, goading him. "Saw some die. Saw them face men who were intent on killing them. Saw one crawl down a hole and never come out. He knew when he went down he wouldn't be coming out. *He* had balls."

He held the cigarette in his lips and lifted the gun to my head. He cocked the hammer. His breathing filled the car as we bounded over ruts, the tires spitting gravel in the wheel wells. I closed my eyes, held my breath. It seemed a foolish thing to do. Might as well die breathing, I thought, and exhaled. "Road's bumpy, Petey. I could have an accident," he said.

"Let it go," Croaker told him. "This ain't no fun, Ruben Lee."

Ruben Lee pressed the gun to my temple, pressed until I turned away, then he lowered it and closed the hammer. I blinked. It wasn't twenty-four hours since he'd killed his first man for no good reason, except perhaps that he hadn't yet killed and wanted to experience taking a human life. Now he wanted to experience it again. Two in less than one day; that was what he was thinking. It was inscribed in his expression, in the wrinkles around his eyes and his smile. He wasn't Willy, never could be, but he'd killed, which he figured put him a step closer to his pa, a dangerous character.

I didn't consider pleading for my life or arguing that I'd found a special happiness. Why drip blood in a tank where you're swimming with sharks? How could they understand what it was like to reach across the table and touch her cheek, and for her hand to close on mine? I shut my eyes and wondered what she was thinking, if she was making calls. I'd never been late. I thought about how I went to sleep with my hand cupped to her belly, her warmth spreading up my arm.

Croaker slowed the car on a dry lake bed and swung to a stop facing north. They slammed the doors and left me inside. Ruben Lee paced and smoked while Croaker leaned against the front fender and gazed off at the highway. The sky was a clear, vast dome of blue. To the east a redtail hawk wheeled aloft on the currents. It was a fine, hot day, hotter still inside the car. I took off my suit jacket and undid the first two buttons on my shirt.

We stayed like that, the three of us, for about an hour, then Ruben Lee took his last cigarette from the pack, wadded the empty pack and heaved it in the air. He lit the cigarette, opened the door, and slid into the seat. He turned around and faced me. "Know who's buried out here, Petey Boy?"

"No."

"Guess." Saying this brought a smile to his face.

"Can't."

"Sam the Slav. Buried over there about two hundred yards." He pointed to the south. "Know why?"

"You shouldn't be telling me this," I said. It was a clever touch, revealing a secret that was big enough to be mentioned in a best-selling book.

He grinned. He was sweating and I was sweating, and I just wanted him to get to the point. But he sucked on his cigarette and watched a dust devil skate toward us. Finally he said, "He knew too much." He grinned again, this time with obvious delight, and took a draw on the cigarette. "You know what I mean?"

I tried not to react, as anything might provoke him. My hands were sweating. "It's too hot for this, Ruben Lee."

"Unexpected information, huh? I never heard of that Gatsby jerk, but I know things."

I unbuttoned my cuffs and rolled my sleeves up to the elbow. He watched, grinning and smoking. To avoid his gaze, I looked at my hands. He exhaled and looked up as the smoke rose, then grabbed my chin and made me look him in the eye. I stared at him now, contemptuously. What did it matter? I was dead either way in his eyes. "No going back, Petey Boy. Like Croaker says, you're just too smart," he said. "You know everything."

I had nothing to say. We stared at one another. He hated me, had for a long time, even when we shared a joint or a bottle. I told him I needed air and asked to open a window.

"Why ask?"

"Because you've got a gun."

He looked at the pistol. Now that he'd essentially pronounced my death sentence, the hate faded from his eyes, and all that was left was a kind of impish delight, the kind a salesman gets when he's bested a chump.

"Nothing to say, Petey Boy?"

"I've got to piss," I said and opened the door.

"Don't run," he said. "I'd have to shoot you."

After urinating, I paced beside the car. It wasn't cool, but it was better than inside the car. It was strange, waiting there, sharing silent time and space with the men who held my fate, one who would enjoy killing me and another who had always been an enigma. Ruben Lee became increasingly impatient. He needed a fix and had run out of cigarettes. Occasionally he threw a glance in my direction. The amusement he'd gotten from menacing me was wearing off. Soon he would want to do something more extreme. Until then, I held on to each second.

I wondered how I would behave in the end. It seemed peculiar to wonder about it. Isn't it how you behave the rest of your life that counts? Besides, who would say whether Peter Elkins was cowardly or brave? Not my executioner or the desert. The desert keeps its secrets. Melody would be left never to know. I imagined her calling the police, perhaps even Willy, who would tell her nothing. And the cops would ask about arguments, which she would deny. Frank would assure her that husbands do these things, and perhaps she'd believe it and grow to hate me. She would go on with life, bitter for a while.

The desert floor shimmered and a blur approached, followed by a plume of dancing dust. Croaker shielded his eyes with his hand to see. A moment later the glare off the windshield flashed, and the car came out of the dust and into sight. It seemed to move laterally like a crab. Ruben Lee was too preoccupied at first to see the dust that announced the approach. I had to tell him. He pointed the gun and told me to get into the car, then opened the trunk and took out two shovels, one of which he tossed down. The other he used as a staff to lean on.

The car skated over the salt lick. Its polished finish and chrome seemed to burn in the sun. Now that it was close, I saw it was a black Lincoln. It made a turn and stopped sideways in front of the Cadillac. Both front doors opened at once, George stepping out of the driver's side, Willy out of the other. Willy took off his hat, brushed his sleeves with it, and looked in my direction. George seemed all business. They ambled over to Croaker and Ruben Lee, where Willy grabbed the shovel and tossed it away. The four of them formed a circle at the front of the Cadillac.

From time to time as Ruben Lee spoke, Willy glanced over at me. George shook his head and aimed a finger at him. Ruben Lee pushed George's hand away. George nodded, raised his hands as if to surrender, and turned his back to Ruben Lee. Willy stared at the ground until Ruben Lee finished talking, then threw a single punch that set Ruben Lee on his haunches. George walked over, helped his brother up and handed him a pack of cigarettes. Sweating and thirsty, I sat in the closed car until Willy cracked the door. "How you doin, Pete?" He slid in beside me.

"Not so good, Willy."

"Guess not. We got a kinda sit'iation here, Pete."

"Yeah."

"What did he tell you?"

I shrugged.

Willy shook his head. "Hotter 'an hell in here. Sorry about that." He took a pint of Jack Daniel's from his coat pocket and unscrewed the top. "Nice day. 'Cept for heat, 'bout as nice as you could ask for."

"I was thinking that earlier."

"Too bad we can't just saddle up a coupla easy mounts and ride a while." He handed me the bottle.

I wanted nothing more than a drink but shook my head. "How do you stand that stuff?"

"Hell, if you had to drink what I did as a young'un, you'd think this was champagne."

"You going to kill me, Willy?"

His eyes narrowed as he looked at me. "Looks bad, Pete."

I nodded. "You do the shooting, then. Don't let Ruben Lee."

"Don't know as I can. I got awful fond of you, think of you as my own sometimes. 'Course I didn't make the same mistakes with you as I did with them." He took another drink as this settled like a layer of fine dust. "You sire a colt an hope it ends up bein a good stallion, an then you wonder why you didn't geld it in the first damn place when you knew it was a mean one." He handed the bottle over, and this time I took a swallow. "Maybe Croaker'll do it. Then again, he likes you a bit, so maybe he won't."

"Him, then, or George."

"Not George. No matter what he thought of you."

I took another drink and passed the bottle back. He held the bottle to his lips without drinking and looked out over the salt flats. He took a short nip and turned to me. "You seen the paintin. Your ma was her best friend. Come to the ranch more an once. I held you on one knee and Betty on the other when you was both in diapers."

I recalled the peculiar sense I had of the ranch, the men's faces, and experienced a sudden rush of incomplete memories spurred by Mother's treasure box of photos that accompanied her everywhere. I recalled Miriam sneaking them out and creating stories that fit the pictures. But at that moment I had only the vaguest of recollections and the revelation that I'd some ways sensed all along: the link between Willy and me had gone back beyond my memory.

"You're a long way from home, Gaddis Tellerman," I said.

Willy looked at me strangely. "That from some damned book you studied?"

I could have told him that I'd first come to know him from a black-and-white photo hidden in Mother's shoebox, and Miriam named him Gaddis Tellerman, but I didn't. "No."

"No time for nonsense. You got a lot to think about, Pete," Willy said. He slapped my thigh and stepped out. "Pete, thought I'd tell you that Sarge was your pa. Your ma was gonna . . . Well, you're alive an it's been a burden since, I guess."

"Sarge? Why didn't he? Why didn't they tell me?"

"He didn't know for a long while, and I told him not to say. And her . . . Well, you know her." He held the door.

Sarge. My father. "Willy?"

"What, Pete?"

"Do you have to . . . I mean? Does it have to be?"

"Ain't just my decision."

I was already a corpse dumped in a shallow grave, unable to hear, or see, or taste, even smell—just terrible darkness—language blanked from my mind, memory erased, landscapes wiped out—Melody, Mother, Miriam, Willy, Stella, Betty gone. It seemed strange to think of, but the living would be as dead to me and I would be dead to the living. I'd seen fields of death, smelled them, watched flies feed off the rot. I would smell no different. But I'd be free of the greatest worry of all—an uncertain future. Perhaps that's what Paéz envisioned as he slipped down into that tunnel.

"Melody?" I asked, for she was the only future I had left.

"I'll make sure she's taken care 'a."

He shut the door and didn't look back. He joined the others, who listened as he spoke—pleading for me, perhaps. At least that was my hope. Willy tossed his cigar away and looked at George, who got out a sentence or two before he was interrupted by Ruben Lee. George started again, this time addressing Croaker, who chewed on a toothpick and stared off. Ruben Lee shook his head at whatever Willy said. George stepped over to the door and opened it. He leaned in. Until that moment I never realized how much he resembled Stella. I'd always looked for signs of Willy in the boys. "Pete, mind if I ask something?"

"What're my choices, George?"

"None, I guess. Mom thinks the world of you. Went to church and prayed for you when you were overseas." He looked over his shoulder and took a deep breath.

Here was the man with the pencil, a bottom-line manager, cast in a role he seemingly didn't want. He licked his lips. "What would you say you saw last night? What I mean is, what would you testify to in court?"

"I don't know. I never had time to think. I wouldn't lie, so I'd probably not testify."

"They'd put you in jail."

"I suppose."

"You'd go to jail, then?"

"I've been in jail before."

"Would you take money? Twenty-five, fifty thousand? I mean, would that help make your decision?"

I was terribly thirsty. I didn't want to die thirsty. "It's not about money, George." I'd temporarily forgotten the ten-thousand-dollar check in my pocket.

He thought a moment, thanked me, and shut the door.

Ruben Lee flicked a cigarette in the sand and scuffed it out as George calmly spoke. As he did, I realized this was the final argument in a trial and George was my spokesman. Always, since first laying eyes on him, I'd thought he cared about nothing but calculations, profit and loss, yet he was my hope.

Ruben Lee lit another cigarette and shifted his weight from foot to foot like a kid waiting for the bathroom door to open. Finally he took a step back and aimed a finger at George as he shouted, "Hell, no!" his words splitting the calm air like the crack of a whip. They had a heated exchange, George arguing, Ruben Lee shaking his head and waving his arms.

Willy puffed on his cigar. Croaker stood to the side, arms folded across his chest, his dark skin glistening in the midday sun. A dust devil whipped up across the flats and sand began to shift. I was sopped in sweat and fear. Ruben Lee backed away, flinging his arms about, gesturing, shouting. George shook his head, showing his open palms as he appealed to Willy. Willy listened, his eye cast to the ground. In the end, Willy raised his hands and stepped away and George spoke to Croaker, whose face, as always, was impenetrable. He, I reasoned, was the odd vote and Willy had probably abstained. If that was what Willy had meant when he'd said the decision wasn't his. Hadn't Croaker told Willy I was trouble from the first?

Unnoticed by the others, Ruben Lee had gradually slipped closer to the door. But I watched, saw him draw his gun and aim it at me through the window. I rolled to the floorboard and reached for the door handle. The first round ripped through the seat. I seized the handle, but the door wouldn't open, and I couldn't budge it with one arm. A second shot tore a hole in the door panel. I yanked the latch down and drove my head into the door.

I came up running, heading toward the distant sand dunes, my only chance, slight though it seemed. He fired twice more. I ran, head high and chin back, eyes on the dunes that led to the shadows of the foothills and places to hide. I didn't look back. Better not to see. I ran with the conviction that one lost step meant my life. I charged across the hardpan for about two hundred yards without looking back, then glanced over my shoulder and realized that no one had pursued me. They stood gathered around Willy's car. By then I'd put some distance between me and them, enough not to be in any present danger unless one of them had a rifle, which I doubted since it was obvious that this had evolved without any thoughtful planning.

I faced the most foreboding and unforgiving part of the Mojave. Ominous sand dunes rose up as high as fifty feet and spread south and east for miles. They lay ahead perhaps a half mile, a distance that an Olympic runner could cover in less than two minutes, but though I ran regularly I was not in that kind of condition. Of course neither were my pursuers. No matter, I knew I would have to take my chances out there.

I was hungry and thirsty, which had already begun to take a toll. How long could I go and how far before my throat would swell shut? Already it was constricting. I decided to conserve energy, so I slowed to a trot, thinking that if I made the dunes I might be able to elude them. A minute or so later the ground began to soften. I was running on shallow sand and closing in on the edge of the dunes about three hundred yards away. There the sand was deep and no one dared take a car. Of course I would leave tracks, that much I knew. Still, I saw hope. I had learned from the history books I'd studied that prospectors had crossed this stretch on foot. I could do it too.

Then I heard the car.

No more than fifteen seconds elapsed before the Cadillac passed me. Twenty yards in front of me it swung around in what seemed a deliberately sluggish half-circle. Two were inside. I could make only the driver, Croaker. I picked up the pace and ran left. The car backed up and cut me off. Turned the other way and sprinted, but the car moved with me. My whole insides burned. It was futile to run. I covered my eyes with my hands and shook my head, then leaned over, place my hands on my knees and sucked in air as the car closed on me.

The car stopped. "Give up, Pete?"

It was George's voice, and George who got out and stood beside the car. For that I was half thankful. I didn't want Ruben Lee to have the satisfaction of killing me. I looked up at George and gulped in air. Filling my lungs would be the last pleasure of life. I couldn't even pass on a message to Melody through him. She'd have to spend the rest of her life guessing.

Save for the car's engine and the breeze that dried my sweat, it was silent. The desert, always silent, was an ideal place to spend eternity. I stood up and nodded to George. He walked toward me and aimed the revolver as he got closer.

"Get down on your knees, Pete."

I did as told.

"I'm going to pull the trigger. You fall forward. Don't nod or anything. Just do it."

He touched the barrel to the side of my neck. I closed my eyes. I felt hot powder sting the side of my neck, heard the deafening bark of the pistol. And reeled forward. "I'm going to fire two more. Jerk when you hear the sound."

The bullets split the sand near my head. I jerked each time. Then I rested.

"Don't move. Lie there until I come back."

I heard his footsteps mush in the sand, the car door close, and the car drive off. I didn't move. It was a long while before George returned. He wasn't alone.

"Well?" George asked.

Croaker calmly said, "I votes no."

"Don't get up just yet, Pete," George said.

I glanced up. There stood George and Croaker with shovels in hand. Croaker was smiling. They waited until they were certain Willy and Ruben Lee were gone, then George told me to get up, that I'd caused enough trouble for one day. I sat up and rubbed the powder burns on my neck.

"You can't come back. You understand," George said.

I understood that I would live and see Melody again. "Yes."

Croaker sat in the back of the Lincoln while I sat beside George.

"Look in the glove box," he said.

I opened it and saw a canvas deposit bag.

"Twenty-five thousand. I'll make sure your wife knows where to find you. Make up a story or just refuse to explain."

"Why, George? Why save me?"

He put the car in gear. "Do well at the university, Pete. Make Willy proud of you, but don't come back."

55

They dropped me off at a motel in Victorville where the sign blinked VA-CANCY. As I opened the door to get out, I told George he could keep the money, that I didn't want him thinking I'd been bought. He shook his head and laid the deposit bag on my lap. "Pete, the money's from Ma. She said I owed it to her to take it. She wishes you the best. Keep the money. I'll tell Melody where to find you. Let me know where you land. Leave a message at the Lucky."

"What about Willy?"

"He's fine with everything. Don't worry about Ruben Lee. He won't come after you. By the time he finds out you're alive, things will be settled in court and you'll be long gone. Stay away just the same, at least till I tell you otherwise. And don't ever talk about this or last night."

I nodded.

"We'll miss you. Call, Pete. If you ever need something, call."

I shut the door. Without looking back, George and Croaker drove away, shadows in the dark interior. I wondered what occupied George's mind as he drove off, what kind of sharp-edged teeth chewed at him. A decent husband, a good father, he was in a hard place and trying to keep matters sane. Perhaps that was his redemption. Who knows, the human conscience being what it is. I was alive and had a good deal to live for, but there was William Schmilling, shot because Ruben Lee wanted to kill a man, and the memory would follow me, as Paéz did, as Betty always would, just as Rita's memory would always follow Willy and Stella.

A buzzer went off as I opened the door. The elderly woman behind the counter folded her magazine. I asked for a room for one night. She looked toward the parking lot and asked, "Where's your car, sir?"

"Las Vegas. I lost it, along with everything else."

She laid a pen and a registration card in front of me and told me to sign by the "X." "Vegas? I've heard of people losing their shirts, but not their cars."

I smiled at her. "Now you've met one."

56

Melody and I settled into a happy life in the town of Thatcher, about two and a half hours southeast of Phoenix if you pay no attention to the speed limit. Over the nine intervening years George kept contact by phone or through an attorney. At Christmas every year a box arrived with presents and photographs of some of the Bobbins clan, though never any of Betty or Ruben Lee. When Laura, our first daughter, was born, George opened a trust fund for her and each year on her birthday added a thousand dollars to the account. It was the same for our second girl, Madeline, whom we call Maddy.

We lived in a modest but comfortable home and I taught history at Eastern Arizona College. Melody taught art in high school in adjacent Safford. We owned a car and a bass boat and barbecued in the backyard and grew wildflowers in the front. Once a week we went out for dinner, and once a month drove to Phoenix or Tucson to see an art movie and purchase books. We accumulated what could have been the largest private library in eastern Arizona. We took vacations twice a year, once with the girls and once without, and one holiday weekend each year, usually during spring break, Melody would fly to Vegas with our daughters to visit her parents. Unless you calculate the volume of love that filled our days, our life was largely uneventful, filled with day-to-day pleasure and minor pain, colorless when compared to the past, but full.

We enjoyed our daughters, delighted in watching them learn to read, or try their first dance steps, or attempt to play the piano, and we experienced the usual frictions. Melody often accused me of being unresponsive and not trying to mend old wounds with my mother, and I countered that she was too involved in our daughters' lives. But we truly loved one another and she became my most cherished friend.

On the morning of July 11th, 1985, George called. I was surprised to hear from him, as he'd called three days before. It was his habit to call about once every two months to check on us and update me on the Bobbins family. He seemed hesitant. I told him Melody had taken the girls into Tucson for a movie. Small talk.

"Pete, you've got to come home."

"What? I thought . . ."

"I've got bad news."

"Willy?"

"No."

"Stella."

"No, she's fine."

That left one. There was no need to, but I asked just the same. "Betty?"

"Yeah, the old man's broken up something terrible."

I closed my eyes and felt a spiraling chill in my spine. My hands went cold. "How?"

"They found an empty bottle of tequila beside the bathtub, and she'd used a carving knife on her arms. I'd told the old man we should put her away before the booze wiped her out."

"Not Betty, his Betty. He couldn't lock her up," I said.

I remembered her crashing on my couch, not once but several times. I remembered her asking for sex, not because she needed passion, but because she needed human warmth. But I could not rekindle those feelings for her. The Betty I'd once loved was in a sense long dead before this one took her life. I pictured the bathwater pink with blood and spilling over the rim, flooding the tiles. She could have taken an easier way. I felt numbness and pity, and a touch of guilt for the happiness I'd enjoyed in the ensuing years.

"Pete, I've made reservations for you. Tomorrow from Sky Harbor. Will you come?"

"Ruben Lee?"

"Stella and I think it's a good idea for you to come. We were never friends, but . . ." He sounded choked up. Cold, unemotional George, who'd kept me alive. How could he not feel some guilt?

"I'll be there."

I jotted down the flight number and time. George said he would pick me up at the airport. His voice sounded hesitant as he said good-bye. I sensed he was reluctant to hang up. He was the man he was, detached, unable to express feelings, perhaps unable to feel as others did. But he was responsible, terribly responsible and lonely—and his future seemed to offer up more of the same.

57

Croaker opened the door to Willy's suite. "They ain't nothin worse," he said softly. "Anyone come around, he just wanna fight."

The drapes were drawn and the only light came from a table lamp in the far corner. Willy sat on a ladderback chair in his undershirt and trousers, his back to the door. He was barefoot. Shoulders hunched forward, he stared at the wall as if it were talking to him. On a table beside him were an untouched meal and three bottles of whiskey: two empties, the other half gone.

I nodded to Croaker, who warned that Willy had punched Ruben Lee and George both. He shut the door. Willy paid no attention to the closing door or me as I crossed the room to sit on the edge of the bed. A clean suit lay on the stool at the foot of the bed. In one hand he held a shot glass. He didn't acknowledge me.

"Willy?"

He didn't answer. His jaw was covered with three days of gray stubble. He smelled of whiskey and sweat and urine. His fly was open, but he'd not bothered to walk to the bathroom.

"Willy. You've got to get dressed for the funeral," I said.

He gave me a fish stare out of the corner of his eye and poured himself a shot. He didn't drink it right away.

"It's in four hours," I said.

He held the glass to his lips. "Ain't goin."

"No?"

"You heard."

"Willy? George, Stella, they want you to come. You've been in here over three days."

He drank the whiskey and stood. He was wobbly, but managed to stay upright. "Stand up," he said.

I did. He took a swing that missed, then another. He lost his balance on the second, and I had to catch him. He told me to let go. He struggled to break free.

"Didn't I tell you once't to never touch me that way?"

I held on. "You did."

I marched him backward to the bathroom, him swinging and me trying to diffuse his punches, which, at best, were harmless. I held him in one arm and with the other turned on the shower.

"If you'da married her like you was 'spose to," he said.

I adjusted the hot water, ripped his shirt off, and pushed him in.

"Ever'thing okay, Pete?"

I looked back to find Croaker standing in the bathroom doorway.

"Yeah, fine. Willy, take those trousers off."

"I ain't," he said.

"Do it or I'll take them off for you," I said.

"Croaker, you take this boy on out an give 'im a lesson, one he got comin."

Croaker shut the shower door on Willy. "You just pass over them pants like he says," Croaker said. "No more foolery, Willy."

Willy didn't budge. I opened the door and turned off the hot water. The pants came over the shower door in a few seconds.

We shaved and dressed him, then using the service elevator half carried him down to the parking lot. Croaker said he could handle it without me from there, that it was best, in fact, for me to stay clear of Willy for a while.

Stella had asked me over the telephone to ride with her. She and her driver pulled up at the back entrance in her new Mercedes. She was almost blind now and depended on others to care for her basic needs. She'd not driven a car or ridden a horse in years, and I understood from George that she spent her days in the garden with a magnifying glass looking for aphids and other pests.

She took my hand as I settled into the seat and leaned close, squinting to see me. She smelled strongly of perfume and brandy. She'd been crying, but now had the tears under control. "I 'preciate you comin, Pete. How's the wife?"

"Fine. She and the girls are at her parents.'"

"We're ready, Lamont," she said to the driver.

He answered, "Yes, ma'am," and pulled the big car away from the curb.

"I'd like to see your family," she said to me.

"I'll arrange it."

"Hell's bells, I'd like to see 'bout anything right now." She squeezed my hand.

We sat holding hands in near silence until we came to the funeral home. She gripped my hand even tighter.

"Pete, stay with me."

I'd never forgotten her many kindnesses over the years. "I will. Don't worry."

"They blame me," she said.

"Who?"

"Willy. The boys."

"No."

"Oh, they do. Maybe not George so much, but I was the one who told her, though she prob'ly already figured. I said, 'Betty, I ain't your ma, but if I was I'd be ashamed of myself.' An I am. I tried to love her, but I couldn't. I kept her with us 'cause that's what kept Willy with us."

"You've got nothing to be ashamed of. You didn't ask for her to come along."

"You know ever'thing, don't you, Pete?"

"Yes, ma'am."

She let go of me and patted my forearm. "I told George any secret was good with you."

I felt the guilt that went back to an alley a decade before. Surely the guard had served his time and was now free. The legal mill had ground out its version of justice. One killed, one punished. And what had been his reward? My silence had been bought for my life and twenty-five thousand. I'd kept the money and one too many secrets. I was no saint.

We walked in together. She lifted her chin and held my arm. Willy sat between his sons in the first pew. I escorted Stella to the front and sat beside her. The casket, the walls, the floors were covered in bouquets—roses, lilies, chrysanthemums, orchids. The air was sweet with their smell. Willy and Ruben Lee cast an eye at me.

"He ain't welcome," Ruben Lee said.

Stella leaned across George. "Willy, you tell that boy to keep a tongue."

There *she* was in an open casket, a picture of her coming down the stairs on our prom night displayed on a stand in front of her body. When the time came, I helped Stella up for a last viewing. I found myself engrossed by the woman in the casket, thirty pounds heavier, wrinkled, hardened. She and I had fallen in love, had lost love. Now she was dead, her face waxy and pale, expressionless. I stared for a moment at her hands. Stella tugged at my arm, said it was time to leave. But I didn't budge. In the precisely folded hands were two snapshots: one of Rita, and one of me taken that summer on the ranch.

Stella tugged again. "Come on, Pete. We thought long enough on this. Take me to my car."

I opened the door to a knock. Willy, holding a dead cigar in his hand, nodded once to me and entered. He removed his hat and said hello first to Mr. and Mrs. Cristobal, then to Melody and my daughters. He asked if I would step outside.

I shut the door behind us. Croaker waited in the car. I waved to him. He raised a hand. After replacing his hat on his head, Willy lit the cigar and crushed the match out underfoot. He examined me as he might a poker opponent.

"I'll tell you now it ain't a good idea stayin, Pete. I need time on this one."

I'd seen him like this before—Willy obdurate and mean, Willy who could shoot a dog for no good reason. He was looking for a spot to aim his anger. But he was old and tired and neither patient nor cautious enough to do that kind of work, if work is what it can be called. His eyes were clouded, almost opaque.

"I guess you blame me?"

"You're guessin good. She left a letter. Cops read it to me. You was mentioned."

"I see."

"I ain't likely to look for you, but don't come back. Don't."

"I won't."

He drew off the cigar and blew smoke toward the porch light. "You coulda had it, Pete. Her, a share of ever'thing."

I closed my eyes and nodded. Those things hadn't mattered for a long while, if, in fact, they truly ever had. He puffed on the cigar several times, shook his head, and turned away. He carried himself as always, slowly and self-assuredly, but there was a falter in his step.

The door opened. Melody asked if everything was all right. I took her hand and pulled her outside. I kissed her under the porch light as I had wanted to the first night I met her. When we separated, she asked what that was all about. I held her close again and told her that I was the luckiest man on planet Earth.

58

Willy died two years later. I was tired of funerals by then, Betty's and Leonardo's having come back to back in one month. George called late in the afternoon to say Willy had passed on that morning.

"How?"

"Heart. Who knows for sure? It hurts, though."

"He was your father. Of course," I said.

"We weren't close."

"I'm sorry."

George asked me to deliver the eulogy.

"And say what?"

"He liked you, Pete. He asked about you all the time, always wanted me to send money to your family. Your mother was Rita's best friend. That, I guess, you know. You're his godson. That you never knew. He took the obligation seriously. A promise made at one time or other."

"You're right, George. I didn't know."

"Yeah. Ruben Lee doesn't want you to come, much less speak. He's claiming he'll keep you away. The drugs have him bad."

"I still don't know what to say."

"Don't think about the last time you saw Willy. Maybe that'll help."

"I'll give it some thought."

"There's something else, but I'll explain that in person. Bring your family. They can stay at the hotel. I took the liberty of buying tickets and booking you out of Phoenix tomorrow afternoon."

"Thanks, but I don't think we'll need the hotel room. We'll stay with Melody's family."

I offered my condolences, hung up, and went outside where my girls were kneeling on the ground playing with our new greyhound. Melody saw from my expression that something serious had happened. She stood, brushed off her knees, and came to my side.

"Willy's dead," I said.

"I'm sorry."

"He was old. In his eighties."

"You feel bad?"

"I feel a lot of things right now."

She put her arms around my waist. "We'll get someone to watch the dog and the house."

I pulled her close. "He was my godfather. I never knew."

She closed her eyes and squeezed. The sun was deep in the west now, rich and yellow, and the sky pristine. I felt a hardness in my throat, a knot that I couldn't swallow. My chest convulsed. The first tear rolled down my nose. It tickled as it dangled there on the tip waiting for the rest of the tears to follow. I told Melody I was going for a walk. She squeezed me once more and let loose.

59

The worst thing about the funeral service was leaving my daughters and wife behind at her parents' house. I had declined George's offer to stay at the hotel because the girls loved their grandparents to the point that Melody and I were almost jealous. We felt it best that the girls not deal with death until someone in their immediate family died. We felt death should be a fact obscured by distance. Melody wanted to attend, but I persuaded her to stay with the family. She argued until I told her what George wanted me to help him with and that I would have to drive to Montana the next day. It had been Willy's last request.

I wished Miriam and Mother could be there with me, but Miriam was in Europe with Alan, Esther, and new son, Peter Edward, and Mother no longer lived in Las Vegas, not since Leonardo had died. She'd sold his jewelry shops and had moved to Hawaii, which seemed somehow inevitable, as she had spent half of her time there for the past seven years. Lana's husband had died too. Now the two old ladies lived in comfortable elegance on Maui, taking tea on their verandas and watching waves break on the coral reef. My daughters knew my mother as a voice over the telephone and as a woman in pictures who sent birthday and Christmas packages to them. It saddened me that matters had come to this, but I was mostly responsible for the estrangement. Perhaps that was what saddened me most. So Mother wouldn't be there. Then, too, I truly had to face the funeral alone. Fact is, I had more than Willy's remains to deal with; there was Stella, who would need me, and Ruben Lee, who'd vowed to keep me from attending.

George picked me up at 10 A.M. I kissed Melody and the girls at the door. He came without a chauffeur. As I approached the black Mercedes, he reached across the seat and opened the door. He was dressed in black and wore a cowboy hat. I'd never seen him in one before. I raised my hand.

"Hello, Professor," he said.

"Hello, George. A hat?"

"In honor of the old man."

I slid into my seat, and we shook hands.

"I'll let you know that nothing's changed. Ruben Lee's dead set against you being there."

I nodded. "Couldn't expect anything different."

"No." He pulled away from the curb.

"It's what Willy wanted," I said.

"It's what he wanted," George said, and his words sounded like an oath. "If you want a nip, there's a bottle in the console."

I thanked him but declined.

"Sorry. I forgot," he said.

We drove to the house on Rancho Circle. The guard signaled us through. George said he and his wife lived in the house now. He said that Willy had moved entirely into the hotel the last nine months of his life and Stella had followed him there. Since Willy's death Stella had decided to remain in the hotel.

"But she always hated the casino," I said.

"Yeah. Just like her, isn't it? But she's had three cataract surgeries and needs a cane to get around. At least at the hotel I can watch over her."

"You had two ruggedly individualistic parents," I said.

"Are those college words for stubborn and eccentric?"

I chuckled.

He pulled into the horseshoe-shaped driveway. From the outside the place looked the same. How many years had it been? I stepped out. I'd promised myself not to feel nostalgic. This was a sad time but not a time for sentiment. Yet, as I stood in the entrance, for a fleeting instant I had the hope that when George opened the door Willy would be there ready to scold me for staying away so long and Betty would step up behind him and tell me it was about time I'd come back. Instead, George's sons, both grown men now and one studying to be an attorney, stood with their wives, one of whom held an infant.

We stepped inside. The house was dark, the shades drawn. Frank stood with a cup of coffee in his hand. He was retired now. He set the cup aside, shook hands with George, then extended his hand to me.

"It's good to see you, Pete. I hear nothing but good about you." He looked about the room. "It's a sad day."

George said Frank would be helping us later on. I had no hard feelings toward the ex-cop. Perhaps he'd been bought by Willy. Men can always be bought. That was one of the lessons Willy had taught me. But Frank was also a loyal friend and a reminder of the kind of loyalty Willy inspired. This was a day to remember such things and not a day to dwell on past griefs. I said that I was pleased he'd be going with us to Montana.

"Not that far," Frank said.

Stella sat on the couch nearest a portrait of Willy, her hands folded in her lap. She was old, her skin mottled, her eyes faded. I was introduced around, then took a seat beside Stella. Croaker sat in a chair across from her. He was nearly deaf. He looked at me as I took a seat.

"How's the professorin?" he asked.

I said it was fine. He pointed to his ear and said he'd just guess what I'd answered.

Stella reached over for my hand. "Glad you come, Pete. Where's the wife?"

"At her parents.' Not feeling well," I said. I hated lying to her, but it was a white lie, the whitest. Besides, one more lie didn't matter, since Willy's funeral was, in part, a lie. His ashes wouldn't be sealed in a family vault as she had planned. He'd chosen a different end for himself.

"Well, that's too bad." She leaned near and whispered to me. "Drank hisself to death. Locked hisself in a room."

I knew that wasn't true, as Willy's last days had been spent in the hospital fighting cancer, while waiting for some miracle cure. In the end he didn't want to die any more than any other man would. Nonetheless, his heart failed before the cancer could take him. "Yes, ma'am."

"Don't you be ma'amin me. An you stay close by my side, hear?"

"Yes, Stella."

We sat around drinking coffee and eating pastries served by a kitchen staff of three. For much of the time Stella talked about horses, especially Wrangler, one she'd owned in Texas, the first one Willy had brought her. She'd found out later that he'd stolen the horse and changed the brand. "He wanted me to have one. That was in the Depression when he was a hungry stockman in Dallas, running quarts of whiskey for Tex Henderson. We didn't have nothin then but happy times. Wisht we'd never left Texas, 'specially for . . ." She thought a moment, then squeezed my arm. "The will says you get part of the ranch, a share. He told me he wanted you to have that for you an your family." I said that was very considerate. She said Willy was a good man who'd done a few bad things and she'd forgiven him. She hoped I had too.

"He never did anything bad to me," I said.

"No. I wouldn't let 'im." I looked over at Croaker, who was nodding off.

The service wasn't to take place until two. At eleven the front door opened and Ruben Lee entered. He looked bloated, especially his throat, a middle-aged man with the map to hell on his face. He looked past everyone until he found me. It was obvious he was high. He tried to glare at me, but his eyes couldn't muster a genuine glare. He shook his head and came my way. Croaker chuckled, but George headed Ruben Lee off and pulled him by the arm outside to the patio. I stood and excused myself. Croaker stood.

"Don't you leave me alone," Stella said to him.

He pointed to his ear.

"Don't you pull that on me," she said.

He smiled and followed me. They were faced off in the shade arguing, Ruben Lee with his back to us, George's finger aimed at Ruben Lee's nose, Frank standing at arm's length. I knew what the argument was about. George shook his head at me, but I kept coming. I'd fled. I'd lied by virtue of never telling the truth. I wasn't about to run away again. Croaker pulled up and stepped aside. I wasn't sure what he anticipated happening, but I knew what I was going to do. I called Ruben Lee's name out. He wheeled about.

"Petey, we were just discussing you. I was saying how you just keep showing up where you aren't wanted."

"That's right, Ruben Lee. I do that."

"And now you're going to leave."

Croaker coughed. He grinned. "I been a-waitin some time for this. What'chu gonna do? Take out your little pricks and piss on the patio?"

I stepped closer. I knew he'd be armed, and if he was high enough or mad enough, he might try to use it. He took a swing at me, which I sidestepped. George started to grab for him, but I shook my head. I reached inside Ruben Lee's coat and pulled out a gun. It was one of Willy's .45s. I tossed it to George and held Ruben Lee by the collar of his coat. He tried to knee me in the groin. I shoved him against the wall.

"Give me your gun, Frank," Ruben Lee said.

"That ain't likely."

"It's your father's funeral," I said. "Doesn't that matter?"

He struggled to free himself, but was too stoned to break loose. "Fuck you, Petey. I'll get you killed."

I shoved him against the wall again. It was easier than I thought. He was weak. I looked in his eyes and saw that he was full of hate, but empty of fight. Frank came up behind me and said not to worry, no one was going to get involved. George patted my shoulder and said he needed some coffee and for me to do what I had to. Out of the corner of his eye Ruben Lee watched Frank go to the door and stand by with his arms folded so that no one could come out.

"You're not Willy," I said.

He didn't speak for a moment, just looked at George, who shook his head and told him it was over. Croaker asked if that was all there was, said he always figured there wasn't enough gumption between the two of us to make an interesting scuffle. He chuckled.

I held Ruben Lee by the collar at arm's length and shook my head. "Why?"

"Fuck you, Petey."

I understood why. I saw a man whose life was over and had been for a long while, a man who had failed himself and his father, a boy who wanted to be his father. Now his father, whom he'd failed and loved, had died. Ruben Lee had nothing left, no one to love, and it was easier to hate. Besides, for him hating was just another habit. He had his anger and his drugs; other than those he was dead. Several years would come and go before life would pass its final judgment on him and he would choke to death on his own vomit. I let go of his collar. "You'll never be your father," I said.

"Fuck you," he said.

"Yeah, fuck me."

I went back inside and took a seat beside Stella. She asked if it was out of our systems. I said that it was out of mine.

"Good."

Several minutes later Ruben Lee came inside. For a while he circulated around the room, shaking hands here and there until he saw fit to come over and say hello to his mother. He avoided eye contact with me.

At one the limousines arrived, three of them, and we packed ourselves inside and drove to Bunker Brothers Funeral Home on Las Vegas Boulevard North. I gave the eulogy as Willy had requested, talked eloquently of the man who'd taken me in and had given me the love of a father, praised his loyalty and his philanthropy, spoke of the sadness of his survivors. I stood with the family and shook hands as hundreds of mourners paraded by the casket—gamblers and governors, cheaters and priests. Everyone who knew Willy seemed to carry a piece of him away.

When at last the ceremony ended, George and I met the funeral director in the back. We switched Willy's body to another casket, then escorted the empty casket to the crematorium. I never learned what ashes, whose or what kind, went into the family crypt. That was George's business. I went to my wife and daughters and ate with them and laughed with them and enjoyed them as I never had before. It would be a long drive to the ranch the following morning, and I wanted to take them with me, but that was impossible. So I took them with me in my heart.

Jiggers sat in the cab of the truck, his dull eyes scanning the treetops. He was old now and bent and probably shouldn't have been with us, but he'd insisted, said it was more than an obligation, that he would be witness to the end of an era.

"You comin out, Jiggers?" Cal asked.

"Wouldn't do you no good, would I, an old man reduced to feeding chickens and ducks and keeping junk. No, I'll say my good-byes from here."

Cal shook his head and slammed the door. George climbed down from the rear end and pulled out the picks and shovels. He nodded to me. I slipped down from the saddle and took a pick handle from him. He handed me a pair of gloves, pulled his own on, and gathered up a shovel. "This is only my second time here, Pete," George said.

"It's beautiful, isn't it?"

He looked about. "Sure. Thirty-five years."

Shafts of sunlight converged between Rita's grave and Sarge's. "How about here, Cal? The sun will keep us warm." George said and sank the blade of his shovel into the ground.

Cal said, "Yep, that should make the ol man happy."

I lifted my pick and swung downward in a long arc. George and Cal planted their spades. We dug—two out-of-shape middle-aged men and one much older—a grave deep and wide enough to accommodate one casket. It took four hours of toil, and despite the gloves, the work blistered our hands. It was hard, necessary work. Repaying old debts often is.

Finished, the three of us lifted the casket from the bed of the truck and set it down beside the hole. It took a while to rig slings to lower it, but when we had them under it, Cal hooked them to the winch on the truck. That done, we lowered the casket, George and I using ropes slung about the handles to balance it. The box settled gently on the bottom.

I jumped down and set a bottle of Jack Daniel's on top of the casket. George handed down the saddle and the spurs. I placed them carefully beside the bottle. George gave me a hand up. Without ceremony we pulled the ropes free and shoveled dirt into the hole. It proved much easier work. After we tamped the dirt, we stood leaning on our shovels and looking at the mound.

"Suppose we forgot anything, George?" Cal asked.

George looked up. Beyond the trees the sun rested somewhere atop the western ridge. "Don't think so, but it doesn't much matter. This is pretty country, Cal," George said. "I wish there was some way for me to enjoy it, but that's not possible."

We lifted the marker, a simple granite stone that bore Willy's name and the years 1902 to 1987, off the truck, placed it at the top of the grave and covered the edges with dirt. Willy ended up with two graves, a corpseless casket inside a marble crypt in Las Vegas and this, the secret one Willy had insisted on. That said a lot about him. George was likely thinking that very thought, and so probably was Cal.

They climbed in the truck. George chose to ride in the cab beside Jiggers, who'd not said a word the entire afternoon.

"You following along, Pete?" George asked.

"In time."

"I hear you're writing stories, Pete," Jiggers said.

"Some."

"Oughta write this one."

George and I traded glances. "Couldn't do that, Jiggers."

He chuckled and slapped his thigh. "Guess you couldn't at that."

George called me over to the truck and handed me a manila envelope. "They won't do anyone else any good," he said.

I looked at him questioningly.

"Photos. He wanted you to have them. You and Betty, your mother, Rita at the ranch with him."

The truck rumbled down the arroyo to the flats. When the air was still, I opened the envelope. It contained snapshots, old ones, some duplicating those in my mother's shoe box. I thumbed through them. Willy was in most of them. I held one up. "Well, Gaddis Tellerman," I said, repeating a narrative my sister had invented, "your story's a strange one. You got shot in Mississippi defending the honor of a woman who had none and spent twenty years in prison. And now, you track down desperados."

I returned the photos to the envelope and put it in a saddlebag. I mounted the horse and sat it momentarily, just looking at the fresh dirt and recalling Willy and his golf game in the middle of the high desert. Some would say what I gazed on was a tragedy; others might say a romance. The Greeks understood human flaws and wrote plays about great men falling from great heights, for when a great man falls, it affirms our own fragile existence. But what signifies greatness? John D. Rockefeller, a great man, claimed he'd never broken a law, but that many were passed because of acts he'd committed. He'd made his own laws. Willy didn't cause any laws to be enacted. He merely defied and circumvented the existing ones to his benefit. He committed crimes, many. Who could argue that? He lived and died and left behind posterity. Animals and plants do the same, but Willy also loved and was loved; in that he was human.

I circled the resting places—Sarge, Pearl, Willy, the man who had taken me in, Rita, Betty too—all here where my family and I would also one day lie, as was Willy's wish. The world was filling its voids with darkness, which is itself a void. I watched shadows close over the range. It was a good thing to watch happen. Then I rode the trail home.